Third Time's A Charm

Book 4 Rule of Three

Ann Grech

Edited by: Hot Tree Editing
Cover design: CT Cover Creations

Blurb

My brother's best friend, Liam Masters—pro-footballer and temptation personified.

He's *so* off limits.

I've wanted him for years, but he still sees me as a kid.

Staying away is impossible. I can't get him out of my head, or my house. He's everywhere.

The spark Kingston ignites is a surprise. He's educating me on how to get over Liam. The hot teacher is quiet, caring, and an old soul. He takes me to heaven with his touch.

Doing Liam a favour, I introduce them so Kingston can be his tutor. But Liam's learning more than the maths Kingston is teaching. He's discovering a side of himself with my man, and now he wants Kingston too.

I tried to walk away from Liam and wanted Kingston to myself. Can the third time be the charm? Or am I destined to watch both men I love score together, leaving me on the sidelines once again?

Third Time's A Charm is a bi-awakening, opposites-attract MMF romance with NO cheating.

For Claire's grass, for getting me out of a tight spot...

ACKNOWLEDGEMENTS

You know how some authors will say that writing a story the words just fell on the page and it was such a pleasure to write. This book isn't it. I struggled with it. The words didn't flow. The scenes didn't come together. The characters kept changing their minds on what they wanted. But like good cats, I herded them (eventually) and here we are. I'm thrilled with the result. King is a teddy bear and Liam is so broken and beautiful. But my fave is Adelaide. She's strong and smart and I can't wait for you to meet her properly.

The biggest thank yous go to my beautiful friends who make up the MM DreaMMers authors (Viva Gold, LJ Harris, JJ Harper, Angelique Jurd, Tracy McKay and Megs Pritchard). Your advice, inspiration, daily pics, motivation and most of all, your friendship mean the world. I'm grateful every day for you being in my life. My friend, Kariss Stone, you talked me off the ledge more than once and for that I appreciate it.

To the team at Hot Tree Editing, thank you. Becky, my gorgeous editor and all-around story advisor, I have no doubt that this story wouldn't have even seen the light of day without your advice and input. I couldn't have done it without you. Your advice made this story into something I absolutely adore.

Clarise Tan from CT Cover Creations, thank you for the gorgeous cover to go with the rest of my Rule of Three series babies.

Linda Russell from Foreword PR, you are… how do I describe you?… phenomenal. That's it. Your advice, cheerleading, encouragement and friendship mean the world. Thank you for all the work you've done behind the scenes to get Third Time's A Charm released. It's truly appreciated.

To my hubby and kiddos, thank you for being you. You hand me the CC when I need it, or the wine when it gets really bad and I'm contemplating drinking straight from the bottle. You yell and scream at your Xboxes so I can't dictate—hubby, you were right, I should have put a door on the office. You (the kids) put clean clothes in the wash because you can't be bothered hanging them up again. Your fave word is "Mum" even when Dad is right there. But I wouldn't change a thing (except maybe the washing, it's a PITA)! I love you all to the moon and back.

Last and most certainly not least, thank you to my A-Team and to you, the readers and bloggers, for your unending love and support. Sharing, reviews, general shout outs and, importantly, reading our words means the world to every author. I never dreamed it would be pos-sible to be a fair dinkum author, but you've made that a reality for me. For that – the realization of a childhood dream – I'll forever be grateful.

Ann xx

GLOSSARY

This story is set in Queensland, Australia. It uses Australian English. There are some terms that you might not have heard before, so I have set out a few for you. If you come across more, please let me know and I'll explain the terms. You might also want to take a peek at my website too – I'll add more there as they come up.

Akubra – a broad brimmed hat.
Bloke – a man.
Brick shithouse – an outhouse made of bricks.
Brissy – Brisbane. Queensland's capital city.
Bundy Rum – Bundaberg Rum.
Car park – parking lot.
Cark it – die.
Dacks – underwear.
Footpath – sidewalk.
Fridge – refrigerator.
Hooker – in the context of this story, a rugby league position.
League – rugby league, a full contact sport played between two teams for two forty minute halves where the objective is to score more than the other team by carrying the ball over the 'try line' and, after making a try, kicking the ball between the posts to add an extra two points to the score (called a conversion).

Jumper – sweater.

Kitchen bench – kitchen countertop.

Kilos or kilograms – a unit of measurement (approximately 2.2lbs).

Metre – a unit of measurement (approximately 3 feet).

Mobile or mobile phone – cell phone.

Pram – stroller.

Premiership – the Australian rugby league's (NRL) equivalent of the Superbowl.

Prop – in the context of this story, a rugby league position.

Shopping centre – mall.

Tea – depending on the context, either a hot beverage or dinner.

Try line – the line a rugby player must cross on the football field to score.

Uni – university.

Vegemite – a savoury spread high in B Vitamins that has a strong, salty taste, aka the breakfast of champions (for everyone trying it for the first time, DO NOT eat it like peanut butter. Spread it thinly!).

   Winger – a rugby league position.

ONE

Adelaide

D odging pedestrians, Adelaide dashed along the footpath. As her heels clicked on the concrete, her skirt flowed behind her in a riot of colour. She'd worn the floaty skirt in a vain attempt at brightening her mood. It wasn't that she was angry or even sad, just fed up. Everything was just bleh. Grey and dull, instead of bright and exciting.

She was in a rut. One she couldn't seem to pull herself out of.

At twenty-three, the whole world should be at her feet, but she was bored and sick of being broke. Something needed to change. She could name at least one thing, but she'd been stuck on him for ten years, so why would that suddenly be any different?

Pushing it all aside, Adelaide skidded to a halt outside the open-air café where she was meeting her friends and eyed the time. She was late, but hopefully Katy, Emma, and Robyn hadn't been waiting long.

Adelaide adjusted the package under her arm and caught her breath, looking around to find her friends. They were already seated by the railing overlooking the tree-covered slope and rippling surface of the lake. Ducks paddled and a kite shaped like a dragon was aloft, drifting on the breeze coming in off the ocean only a couple of minutes' drive away. In the middle of winter, some might expect that the trees would be bare, with snow and ice covering the ground. But this was the Gold Coast. Most days—like today—it was warm enough for short sleeves.

There was a stark contrast between the peace and serenity in the gardens and the busy road the park was positioned on. She breathed in the fresh air, appreciating the scent of the potted flowers nearby before she headed over to her friends. Lunch, good company, and a few laughs was exactly what she needed.

As Adelaide approached, Katy turned. A smile brightened her face as she stood, reaching out for a hug. Adelaide closed the distance between them, squeezing her tight. "It's so good to see you," Adelaide greeted warmly. "It's been far too long."

"I know, right?" Katy shifted so Adelaide could greet Emma and Robyn the same way and motioned to the chair opposite. She slid into it and smiled in thanks when Robyn poured her a glass of water from the jug on the table. "Work has been insane and with Levi helping Mike out at the gym more often now, it's been a bit of an adjustment to all our schedules. We're still trying to make it work so that we have some time with the three of us together. We haven't ventured out to catch up with anybody in what feels like forever."

"With Connor working what—Friday and Saturday nights, and Sunday afternoons?—you being in the bakery early and Levi working afternoons, it's got to be a juggle," Emma commented and Katy nodded.

"Do you find the same, Robyn?"

"Yeah, Mike, Ez, and I are like ships in the night sometimes. Ez's hours at the hospital vary, I do business hours, and Mike works all over the place with the gym being open seven days. If nothing else, it's good for childcare—there's usually one of us around for the kids, but we can go days without actually spending any time together."

Adelaide lifted the package onto the table. "Hopefully this will help." Katy's lips curled into a cheeky grin, one of those we're-going-to-have-a-hell-of-a-lot-of-fun kind of smiles, as Adelaide passed her the package.

She'd wrapped it in thick brown paper, tied with a hot-pink ribbon. It was the signature look she'd developed for her brand. Adult's only toy parties were her speciality, where the toys her clients bought kept on giving back. It was why she wrapped her orders as gifts—after all, orgasms were pretty great presents to yourself and anyone else you might want to share them with. She was the Tupperware lady of sex toys. The Avon lady of orgasms.

"Thank you," Katy replied, still grinning and shuffling excitedly in her chair. She slipped the package—lube, anal beads, and a vibrating wand—under her cute little purse and opened her mouth to say something—

"Afternoon, ladies. Welcome to Lavender. I'll be your waiter today. Have you dined with us before?"

"No, but the menu looks divine," Emma remarked. Adelaide overheard Liam recommending the restaurant to Adelaide's brother, Elijah, and she'd wanted to try it out. "Who suggested we come here?" Katy asked.

"Liam." She willed the smile to stay fixed firmly in place, but even she could tell it had become strained. The waiter, oblivious to her distress, took their drink orders and promised to be back once they'd looked at the menu.

Katy waited until he was out of earshot to say, "I know that look. Still nothing? Really?" No one except the three ladies before her knew about her hopeless crush on Liam. It was embarrassing as hell to still be stuck on the same boy you were in love with when you were thirteen, and the closer she kept it to her chest, the better. There was less risk of Liam ever finding out.

She certainly couldn't tell her older brother that she'd been crushing on his best friend—the same best friend who still lived next door to them—for years. Her mum and pop were out too.

Liam Masters, professional rugby player, hair the colour of dark chocolate, hazel eyes that were more green than brown, which twinkled when he was happy, perfect smile and body to die for, Liam Masters.

Her brother's best friend.

The man who she was completely invisible to.

Yes, that Liam Masters.

Urgh.

She'd fallen for him on his first day at their school. He'd stepped in to stop some oversized twatwaffle picking on Eli. Her brother was three years older than her but hadn't had much of a growth spurt. He'd been short, skinny, wore oversized glasses and always had his head in a book. He struggled with his sexuality and was easy prey for the bored dumbarses at their school.

Then along came Liam, and he and Eli clicked. They'd become inseparable. He hadn't ever really had a best friend before, and even though Liam was new to the school, as the star recruit rugby player, he was instantly popular.

He was a good guy, had been even as a teenager. Liam accepted Eli without question, treating him like his brother from another mother. Within six months, the house next door was sold, and Liam's family moved in. If she thought they'd been inseparable before, it was nothing to what it was like after they'd moved in. Liam spent so much time at their place, he could very well have moved in.

Adelaide loved it at first, but it was torture too. Seeing him when he first woke up, sleep-mussed and wearing boxer shorts that always rode too low on his hips had her teenaged mind running in circles. Adelaide and Liam had become closer over the years, but back then, she was never welcome in Eli's room. So she had to settle with smiling and waving to Liam as he grunted a good morning to her. She was left longing from afar.

If being downstairs could count as afar.

Adelaide was low-key amazed that her brother hadn't confronted her with her hopeless crush on Liam. Either he was as blind as Liam, or he was ignoring it with every fibre of his being. She'd gushed over his best friend throughout high school, constantly telling her friends how perfect he was—he wasn't, but teenage love was blind. She'd memorized his stats, and soon went to every Saturday morning game he played too. Adelaide could laugh about it now, but back then, cutting out his photo from the yearbook and wearing it in her heart-shaped locket was the closest thing Adelaide ever got to a relationship with him.

Over the years, they'd developed more of a brother-sister vibe, which was even worse. She still cheered for him at his games and when he'd been drafted as a professional footy player, she was the one who organized the party to celebrate. But to him, she was still Eli's little sister.

Then he'd scored the contract of a lifetime. Playing in France had been his dream. He'd wanted to see Europe and do what he loved. Adelaide had been ecstatic for him. Finally, it had been her chance to move on. To forget her stupid crush by her stupid heart. Instead, Adelaide had pined over him. She'd missed him every day. Not even Eli had moped as much.

Liam hadn't stuck it out in France. He'd come home after a year, and had been back for nine months. Eli was working on an urgent manuscript edit the day he arrived, so she'd picked Liam up from the airport. She'd steeled herself, girded her loins or whatever the saying was, to try to maintain the distance she'd tried so hard—and failed—to get. But it was no use. The second she saw him, her heart tripped over itself so it could go rub all over him like a cheap hooker. It followed him around like a pathetic puppy dog and dragged Adelaide along for the ride.

She hated it. She hated having fallen in love with him.

Adelaide looked at Katy and let out a disgusted huff, replying, "Urgh. Where do I start?" She rolled her eyes and shook her head. "No, absolutely nothing has happened. Short of throwing myself at him naked, he's never going to figure out I exist. But knowing my luck, he'd just tell me I forgot to put clothes on. I'm sick of it, you know? I want someone to love me like your guys do you. Or... hell, I'd settle for good sex. Is that too much to ask?"

The young waiter chose that moment to interrupt them. His face flushed with embarrassment, he took their order and rushed away.

Katy bit back a laugh at the waiter and reached out to grasp her hand, her eyes softening in sympathy. "Are you putting yourself out there? Are you dating? You've been single the entire time I've known you."

Adelaide shrugged, her lips pursed. "I would if I could get past the creeps who just want a hook-up on every dating app I join. I've chatted to a few who seemed nice enough. Then I meet them and they're either totally different—one guy set off every known red flag within five minutes of me meeting him." Robyn winced and Emma groaned. Adelaide threw her hands up. "Exactly! I ducked into the bathroom, ordered a rideshare, and a waiter helped me sneak out through the kitchen." Thankfully he'd had no way of contacting her except through the app, so it was easy to block him. "The other dates have been okay until we get to the point of being intimate, and then it's like a switch flips, and they're in it for themselves. Not one has cared about me being comfortable or even enjoying myself."

"That sucks. Why is it so hard to get a decent guy?"

"Because you three are dating all of them! Five guys between the three of you is far too greedy." Adelaide grinned, letting her friends know without words that she was 100 percent supportive of all their relationships. Katie coughed out a laugh. Choking, she downed a sip of water and wiped her eyes.

"Haters are gonna hate." Robyn smirked and raised her glass to Emma.

"I only have one, but my horndog keeps me busy enough. Don't think I could handle two."

"You need to find a guy who Nick would be into. That way, they can go for it while you watch," Katy advised, mirth dancing in her eyes as her grin turned devilish.

Adelaide laughed and raised her glass in a toast. "Cheers to that. But seriously, I'm done with apps. So, start figuring out which of your friends are single because I'm gonna need an introduction."

"Yeah, friends are a no-go. The ones who are single, are single for a reason. You don't want to go there."

Katy dug around in her bag for her phone, tapping away before bringing up a website. She turned it around and showed Adelaide. "No friends, but this might interest you. The gallery is hosting an event next weekend. You should go." Adelaide wasn't an art buff by any stretch of the imagination, and her dubiousness must have shown in her expression. Katy scrolled down to the What's On calendar. "It's just been renovated and they're running a few show-case events to get people interacting in the gallery spaces. Next Saturday is Singles in the Sculptures Room. It's a speed dating night. I'm supplying cupcakes for each ticketholder, and Con is performing there."

"Something different, I suppose." Adelaide hesitated and scrunched up her nose. "It's not too desperate, is it?"

"No, don't be silly," Robyn encouraged. "Sounds like fun actually."

"I'd do it if I was single," Emma added, then narrowed her eyes at Katy and pointed at her. "Shut it. We don't need a third." Katy mimicked zipping her lips but instead of throwing away the key, she pretended to shove it down her bra.

When Katy turned to her, she added, "It's a chance to meet people outside of a club or an app. You only have like five minutes with each person, so if they all turn out to be douches, it's not a big deal," Katy encouraged. Adelaide bought a ticket—if she didn't do it there and then she wouldn't, and her friends were right. It was one night. Hopefully a fun one. But even if she didn't meet anyone to have a potential second date with, she would at least have had a night out.

* * * * *

Adelaide pushed at the pin in her hair that had come loose and hoped the messy updo she'd gone with didn't fall out halfway through the night. Her umbrella, being held in place with her shoulder while she fixed her hair, sheltered her from most of the unseasonal downpour as she skipped over the puddles. There was so much moisture in the air that she could already feel dampness setting into her clothes. The last thing she needed was to look like a drowned rat with a mop of pink frizz for a hairstyle. It was days like that she wished she kept her natural mousey-brown colour rather than dyeing it.

Dashing under the overflowing rain gutters to avoid the waterfall flowing from them, Adelaide ducked into the foyer and cursed the heavy rain. She shook out the umbrella on the mat and peeled off her coat, hooking it over her arm. As long as she held the dripping material away from the little black silk dress she wore, it wouldn't get ruined. It was probably stupid to wear the outfit, but nerves had got the better of her. Wearing something more casual would have been smarter, but in an environment like this, she knew that people would judge her based on her appearance even more than the words she spoke.

Putting her best foot forward, she showed her ticket to the usher, and was guided through the high-ceilinged lobby area into a grand hall about half the size of a basketball court.

It was filled with people chatting, sipping on glasses of wine and champagne, and eating canapés being passed around on silver platters. Sculptures positioned on pedestals protected by red velvet ropes hung off silver stands were the stars though, lights shining up to highlight the shadows or down to wash them in a white glow. In another room off to the side, much bigger than the one she and the other people were gathered in, were collections of chairs and tables, spaced equidistant, in a circuit. It wound between sculptures and took advantage of both the shadows and lights cast by the displays. What looked like gameshow buzzers were placed on each table, casting a warm glow, intimate like a candle.

Adelaide admired the pieces and smiled politely at a woman who looked her up and down, wishing they could get started. She hated events like this where she didn't know a soul. But she did. Swinging her gaze around, she searched for the small stage that Connor would perform on. There. Dressed in jeans, boots, and a button-down shirt with the sleeves rolled up, he was playing with his guitar. It didn't take long to spot Katy and Levi too, sitting to the side of the stage. She waved and started to head that way when an MC stepped up to the microphone. "Good evening, guests, and welcome to Singles in the Sculpture Room. Thank you for joining us tonight. Feel free to take a seat at any table with a vacancy. We will get started in a few minutes. Our performer tonight, Connor O'Reilly, will be playing for us and each of you will receive a gift bag with a cupcake from Delectable Cakes as you exit. Please head over to the reception desk on your way out. A light has been placed at each table which is set to a five-minute timer. Once the timer goes off, those of you sitting on the black chairs, please make your way to the next table." She would have to catch up with them later. In the meantime, she was on a mission to find a seat.

Her first three dates were a bust. Reid was a mad-keen fisherman, and his idea of a great time was camping out in the wilds. Camping, she could handle, but a toilet was a necessity. There was no way she was dropping her dacks where there could be snakes. The second man, Dean, reminded her far too much of her brother, and the third, a woman named Hayley, wasn't her type even though she was very sweet.

Adelaide slid into the seat across from a man who was a few years older than most of the other people in the room. She held out her hand and introduced herself. He slipped his roughened palm into hers, his hand cool to the touch, and shook. "I'm Kingston, but everyone calls me King. You look lovely tonight."

"Thank you, you look great too." Adelaide looked him over. Dark hair and dark-brown eyes, with a close-cropped beard, he was handsome in an understated way. His clothes matched her first impression that he was unpretentious perfectly—light-blue shirt and a brown suit jacket. He had the classic professor vibe about him. All he needed was suede patches on his arms and a set of wire-rimmed glasses. Adelaide licked her lips, eyeing him over and yet trying not to stare. He really was gorgeous. Lost for words, Adelaide had no clue how to start the conversation with him.

He laughed and scrubbed his hand over his beard. "My friend suggested I come here tonight. I'm not great at conversation starters, as you can see."

Adelaide grinned, relieved that he could laugh at himself. "How do you know your friend?"

"We've worked together for a few years now. We both teach maths at a high school here on the Coast." She grinned. She'd been spot on about the professor look he sported. "What about you? Are you based here or are you visiting?" The gallery was a two-minute drive from the centre of Surfers Paradise and was being spruiked as a must-see. She could understand why Kingston had asked the question.

"I'm local. I've lived here on the Coast nearly all my life. My parents separated when I was young, and we moved back from Brisbane to be closer to my nan and pop." She paused and regarded him, simply enjoying looking at him. A blush stole over his cheeks and he bit down on his pouty bottom lip. Damn, she loved that shy-guy look as much as she did the professor vibe. He really was incredibly handsome, in a nice-guy, boy-next-door type of way. "Why maths? Are you a number genius, or do you love torturing your students?" She laughed as his mouth curled up in a grin, his eyes sparkling. Adelaide reached for his hand before she could think better of it. Patting it gently, she added, "These things are important to know."

"I resent that you've described me to a T." The pout he gave her had Adelaide giggling and he continued, "I've always loved maths. The universality of it, the fact that it's the building blocks for everything. It's certain, yet there can be so many unknowns too. And now I sound like a complete nerd." He rolled his eyes and Adelaide's belly flip-flopped. This man was something special.

"It's okay, I like smarts, and I love that you're passionate about your job. Is it rewarding teaching kids?"

"It is. They can be moody brats sometimes, but seeing them work hard and get through the teaching materials is great. When they have those lightbulb moments where they suddenly get something they've been working on and struggling with, it's the best. I've always tried to be one of those teachers that twenty years after they finish school they'll look back fondly on my classes. But given what I teach, if I can get them to remember me as anything other than the ogre who taught them maths, I'll be happy. These kids often just need someone to listen to them, and help them figure things out for themselves, you know?"

Adelaide had no idea what to say. That kind of passion was inspirational. She loved that he adored what he did and was genuinely trying to make a difference in his students' lives. She hadn't minded school—it wasn't something she was ever overly excited about, but she hadn't hated it either. Maybe having a teacher like Kingston would have given her some sort of direction for her future.

"What do you do for a living?" he asked, seemingly unaware of how much he had moved her.

Adelaide swallowed. She hadn't told anyone she'd met so far that night the truth of what she did. But something told her to be honest with King. "I run parties like

Tupperware or Avon, but for adult toys. I also have a video series on Patreon where I talk about stuff related to that. It's not porn." She waited, watching his expression, but he had a hell of a poker face. He blinked, seemingly absorbing her words.

He opened his mouth, hesitated, and said, "I love that." He smiled, a genuine dawning of understanding in the curve of his lips. "It's great that people can choose things to make them feel good without having to go to an adult store, but when you're shopping online do you really know what you're getting? Having videos that give them more information is great—is that kind of what you do?" She nodded and he continued, "Yeah, being in the privacy of their own home with a real person in front of them, and then being able to watch a video related to the product they're looking at, would make heaps of people feel more comfortable with asking the difficult questions. I bet they would still have fun with it too. Inviting a group of friends over and laughing over the different size butt plugs would be a hoot. Do you love it?"

"I do, but I'm stuck in a bit of a rut too. I didn't see myself selling sex toys when I started this gig a few years ago." The light on their table flashed and Adelaide looked down at it, disappointment swirling in her belly. She liked Kingston, and would happily keep talking to him, but their conversation was about to get cut short. "Can I—"

"Ah, I'm not sure we can do this and totally cool with you saying no, but do you want to ditch this place and maybe see the rest of the gallery, or grab a coffee at the restaurant?" King's words came out as a rushed jumble, his hands clenched together until his knuckles turned white. He seemed nervous, and Adelaide found it adorable that a man who could happily talk about his work, and who literally stood up and spoke publicly for a living, could be so shy.

She stood and held her hand out. "That sounds brilliant." He looked up at her then down to her hand, a smile spreading slowly across his face. Genuine surprise mixed with a little relief too, lit up his eyes. He slid his hand into hers and stood, looking around them. A round of applause broke out and Adelaide froze, her eyes locked on the shy man in front of her. King blushed again, colour rising in his cheeks and spreading down his throat to the V in his open collared shirt. "Hands off, ladies and gents, this one's coming with me."

King's jaw dropped and he choked out a laugh before reaching to relieve her of her umbrella and jacket.

They wandered through the tables past the stage where Connor nodded to her, and Adelaide waved to Katy and Levi. "Friends of yours?"

"Yes, I've known Connor, the man who's performing, for years. He was a year level above my brother in school. When I started at the same school, people in his year level were buddied up with people in mine. He was my buddy, and we kept in contact via social media after he finished and joined the army. We reconnected when he got back. Levi and Katy are his life partners."

King nodded slowly and asked, "As in a poly relationship?"

"Yeah, the three of them are together. Connor and Levi have been best friends since they were kids. Levi met Katy just after they finished school. The two of them have been together since, and then with Connor after he came back from active service. Why's that?"

"I just wanted to make sure I didn't misunderstand their relationship." He squeezed her hand and added, "I'm bisexual, so it certainly wasn't to hate on them."

Adelaide was sure she wore a secretive grin, and the amazing thing was that she'd been lucky enough to snag him. There were only a handful of people in the room who'd gotten a glimpse of King. How was he still single? Smart, sweet, thoughtful and for tonight, at least, her company. She couldn't believe her luck. They wandered through the hall lit up to showcase the paintings hanging along its walls, pausing to admire local artists' talent, and pointing out pieces that they particularly liked. Each piece was complex and intricate—even the ones that looked deceptively simple—and the gallery left them in awe.

Their conversation flowed effortlessly the entire time, as did the laughter between them.

"Do you share your sexuality with the people you work with? Are there issues if you do?" Adelaide asked, wondering whether there were protocols around that at the school.

"I'm open about my sexuality, but it's a sensitive issue for the school. I'm a firm believer in the adage you can be what you see. If students see me living my life as an out bisexual man, then they know they can be comfortable with that too, but I work for a Christian school—albeit a progressive one—so I have to be careful about how I frame it, if that makes sense." He looked to her, a frustrated twist to his lips, and Adelaide nodded her understanding. He had to be age appropriate, and she guessed would have to frame it in more of a "I love the whole person like God would" kind of way.

She ran her thumb over his hand in silent support. Even after only having spoken to him for a few short hours, she already knew she wanted to see him again. In fact, she'd rather the night not end.

"Of course, I don't go telling the kids I have a girlfriend or boyfriend—we keep our private lives private so there's a bit of distance between us—but as the volunteer LGBTQIA staff member on the gay straight alliance, I talk to the kids about every aspect of sexuality, self-respect, coming out, dealing with violence. You name it, I've had the conversation. We've also had specialists come in to talk about sexual and mental health and a whole range of topics that both students and teachers benefit from."

"I really admire you. My brother would have killed to have had that kind of support in school—he's bi too," Adelaide explained as she wandered out of the paintings room into the wide corridor lined floor to ceiling with glass. Rain bucketed down outside, water streaming along the windows to blur the lights from the high-rise towers across the river. She leaned back against the stainless steel railing and added, "He was bullied in high school until he was sixteen. But he got lucky too. A new kid started at the school, and they hit it off. Liam, his best friend, was one of the popular jocks, so Eli suddenly had protection by association. The bullying might have stopped, but Eli still had trouble coming to terms with his sexuality. Even though we've always been open and honest about every element of sex with Mum—she's a nurse—it was years before he felt comfortable enough to tell Pop or myself. A decade at least before he actually felt proud of who he is. A teacher like you could have changed that for him."

"That's the aim—help people to be proud of who they are and take care of themselves and those around them." He paused as if he were thinking about how to phrase his words. "It's funny, you know. It's easy to talk to the students and give them advice and reassurance. But following that same advice isn't easy. It's one of the things I struggle with the most."

"In what context?" Adelaide asked.

"Well, for example, I'm naturally pretty shy. I tell students to hold their heads up high and own who they are, but walking in here tonight was one of the most intimidating things I've ever done."

"There's a big difference between being proud of who you are and extroverted. I think they're completely separate parts of ourselves. But in any event, at best, we're all works in progress. So even if you're a great advocate for pride in who you are and in being confident, you can still feel fear or need reassurance yourself."

Kingston stood just out of her reach. He nodded and cleared his throat. "Yeah, you're right. I'm definitely a work in progress, but like you said, we all are."

Adelaide reached out and tugged him forward until he stood bracketing her legs. She ran her hand down the lapel of his jacket and King groaned. Tilting her head to regard his wary expression, Adelaide asked, "Is this too much?"

"No… I…" He sucked in a breath and blew it out again slowly as if calming himself down. "It's been a long time since anyone's touched me and you… set me on fire."

Adelaide laced their fingers together, lifting them. "Is this okay?" He nodded. "When we're somewhere more private then, you can hug or kiss me. Or both, I won't mind." King dropped his gaze, his cheeks turning an adorable pink as he bit down on his lip.

"I'd like that a lot."

"I'd like to see you again," Adelaide added, hopeful he would agree.

He snapped his gaze back up to hers, wide-eyed. "You would?"

"Don't look so surprised," she chided with an affectionate smile. "You're charming and smart. Sweet. I like you. I'm still trying to figure out how you're still single."

"Yeah, well, that's where the work in progress comes in." King huffed out a laugh, but it didn't really hold any humour, and he shook his head. "Eve, my friend, pushed me to come here. Apps aren't for me, and I have no game whatsoever. Going basically anywhere to pick someone up is a lost cause. She suggested tonight so if I bombed completely, I'd only have to talk to the person for another couple of minutes before the buzzer went and they moved on." He ran his hand down his stubble and lifted his lip in a half shrug-smile and added, "I was supposed to be practicing breaking the ice with people."

"Oh, I'm sorry," Adelaide managed with a straight face. "Did you want to go back there and chat to other people?" She widened her eyes and blinked as innocently as she could, but the whole effect was lost when she couldn't hold back her laugh. King leaned in and rested his hand on her waist, hovering close enough that she could feel the brush of his jacket against her body, but also keeping her still-damp coat away from her. Adelaide licked her lips and gripped his lapels, tugging him closer. She needed to feel him against her. She wanted to know exactly what it was like to hold him.

King was all hard lines and thick bulges—and there was no mistaking the sheer size of the monster he was packing, even half hard. He leaned in close and ran his nose up her throat, rubbing his beard against her cheek. Adelaide's breath hitched and he hummed, nipping her lobe with those pouty lips that she really wanted to kiss. Her nipples pebbled, the cold coming off the glass against her back and the cool air circulating from the industrial-sized vent nearby, a contrast to the heat they were generating. She gasped when he growled, his gaze locked on her breasts. "I think I like it right here." Her clit pulsed and Adelaide arched into him, instinctively wanting to rub herself all over him like a cat.

"Yes," she breathed and tilted her chin up, straining until their lips were a hair's breadth apart. King nuzzled her nose with his, brushing his lips over the corner of her mouth. But he pulled back far too soon, putting some distance between them. Damn, she wanted to kiss him, more than anything, but she'd made it clear the ball was in his court.

"If I kiss you," he whisper-growled, "I won't want to stop."

"So don't," she challenged. He sucked in a breath, his nostrils flaring and eyes dark with lust, but he shook his head, stepping back again. She groaned and nodded reluctantly. "But that's probably the smart decision to make." He buttoned his jacket up, then tucked the piece of her hair that had come loose behind her ear, his fingers lingering near her jaw.

"Come and get a coffee and some supper with me. Maybe the restaurant here, or somewhere else. I don't mind much where we go." His offer had her heart beating triple time, the swell of hope that this could be more than just a single date hitting her square in the chest.

TWO

Adelaide

Yawning, Adelaide rubbed her eyes. Not sleeping a wink was the cause of her exhaustion, but she didn't begrudge her decision at all. She'd do it again in a heartbeat. Adelaide smiled a secretive, excited smile that bubbled through her veins like champagne, before gazing at the quiet space at the back of the house longingly. Swinging her hips and shoulders to a song only she could hear, she danced her way up the stairs, to her new makeshift bedroom.

Her meagre possessions resided in the open loft area at the top of the stairs now, just outside of Eli's room. He needed the quiet that came with being able to close his door—working from home most days meant that he was often deep in a manuscript or in video meetings. The volume that Pop kept the TV at was too disruptive when he was in the middle of talking to clients or in editing mode. The only reason Eli still lived there was to help their mum out, so she didn't have to work the same hours she'd once done when they were kids. Adelaide helped where she could, but she wasn't rolling in money either. Story of her life.

On the limited budget she had, Adelaide did the best she could with her new bedroom space. Rice paper screens separated the loft from the hallway, blocking the area off so she had some privacy, and the cupboards and shelving she'd picked up from the thrift store had given her plenty of storage space.

Moving into the loft was an easy decision given the alternative—Pop couldn't live on his own anymore and none of them wanted him in a care home. So, they'd changed up their bedrooms and made sure he had a place with them.

Adelaide slipped on comfortable clothes and tossed the ones she needed to launder into her cane washing basket before meandering downstairs again. Caffeine in the form of a hot tea, breakfast, and a rundown of her pop's plans were first in order.

Her date, the one that Adelaide had only just walked in from, was worth being tired over. After the gallery, they'd gone to the casino. The restaurants there were open late, and after their main course, they'd wandered through the cavernous space to find a quiet corner. The weather had done its part to keep people at home, leaving the after-midnight café almost empty. They snagged a booth against the wall of windows and talked until the rain slowed to a drizzle and eventually stopped. The breeze off the Pacific Ocean had blown the low-hanging clouds away, and the grey skies had turned to a pale blue as the sun crested the horizon. They'd talked the whole time, constantly touching too.

Holding hands and hooking their legs together left Adelaide's belly fluttering with excitement and the rest of her insides gooey.

She sighed happily. He was sweet, funny, charming, and thoughtful. The time had passed in a flash, their conversation ebbing and flowing like the waves crashing on the ocean only a stone's throw away. It swung effortlessly between flirty fun and more serious topics that left Adelaide wanting to know more.

She'd bought a ticket to the speed dating event in the hope that she'd stop pining over her brother's best friend. As much as she knew she would always love Liam, Adelaide couldn't have dreamed up meeting someone as wonderful as Kingston. A grin split her lips, giggly and effervescent like an excited kid at Christmas while she made her tea.

Moving around the kitchen with her pop was like a choreographed dance. They did this almost every morning. Her mum always worked the graveyard shift and wouldn't be home for a few hours, and aside from an early morning coffee, Eli always waited until mid-morning to venture down for food. She popped the milk back in the fridge and retrieved the margarine as her pop commented, "You were out late."

"Mhmm. I had a date." Her smug tone was loud in the quiet house, but she had to be when speaking with her hard-of-hearing grandfather. Now dressed in leggings, a jumper two sizes too big, and the thickest pair of socks she could find, Adelaide was toasty warm—a nice change from the chill in the frosty air-conditioning of the casino—and still high from the giddy excitement of meeting a man she'd clicked with. "We talked all night, Pop. He's so lovely."

"Is talking a euphemism?" Her grandfather eyed her with a raised eyebrow as Adelaide took a sip of her hot tea. He popped the lid off the plastic container with unsteady hands while Adelaide jiggled the teabag of Earl Grey in the delicate cup her nan had used when she was alive. Pop had been drinking from it since she passed, a testament to his love for her. He was a creature of habit, eating the same breakfast every day too—a slice of toast with barely a scrape of margarine and enough marmalade to keep an entire citrus grove in business. Adelaide cringed at the fragrance of the tea before her and carried the cup and saucer over to the table.

Looking over her shoulder, she feigned offence at Pop's question. "No! We only met last night." She knew he wasn't judging—no one in her family ever did. It was something Adelaide was so proud of. Her mum had raised her and Eli to say what they thought without beating around the bush. Mum had learned from the best. As he'd gotten older, Pop was even more forthright with his opinions. He was downright blunt now, not giving a fuck what was considered proper, and only now, at seventy-eight was starting to slow down. Progressive hearing loss had hit him hard, and the slight shake in his hands was a sign of how he was becoming frailer as the years went on.

"Where did you go?" Pop asked, and Adelaide's weary mind stalled, confused. She blinked, thinking back to their conversation when it clicked.

With a yawn, Adelaide said, "To the gallery of all places. They set up speed dating there and Kingston attended too." She watched, ready to jump in and help as Pop carried the plate of toast to his chair. When he was seated, she added, "You should go to the gallery. You'd love it."

"Don't try to change the subject, young miss." Her pop pointed the triangle of thickly topped toast at her and narrowed his eyes as Adelaide waited desperately for the caffeine to kick in. "I want details of this man who kept you out all night to know whether I need to kick his arse."

She laughed, wrapping her hands around the warm mug. Her pop's body may slowly be failing, but his mind was as sharp as ever. "There will be no arse-kicking." She raised her eyebrows, staring Pop down until he chuckled before she continued, "His name is Kingston. He's thirty... um, a high school maths teacher, and seems really sweet. He's super easy to talk to and he has his life put together, you know? He's got a nerdy professor vibe going on and it totally suits him."

Pop nodded slowly as he stirred a spoonful of honey into his tea. "Mhmm. And is he a good kisser?"

Adelaide's cheeks burned, and she hid the flush behind her mug as she raised it to her lips. The almost kiss they'd had at the gallery had electrified her, leaving her jonesing for more. Kingston had delivered in spades, despite keeping their goodbye kiss as chaste as it could be.

Pop chuckled. "That good, huh?"

"It was barely a brush of his lips, but oh my God, Pop. He had me spinning like a merry-go-round."

"When are you seeing him next?"

The high she'd been on dimmed a little. He'd said the three words that always spelled doom—I'll call you—then shut her door. He'd made the effort to walk her to the car and refused to leave until she had the doors locked. That had to count as a positive, but Kingston's words were almost at complete odds. Adelaide couldn't help her disappointment at the way it had ended their evening. "We didn't set anything in stone. I suppose he'll call me if he wants to see me again," she said quietly with a shrug that had failed miserably to hide her disappointment.

"Or you could call him. It's not the 1920s, love," he said pointedly.

"I know, but I'd really like him to call." She absently ran her finger around the rim of the mug. Looking up, Adelaide asked, "I don't want to feel like he only said yes because I called. Is that pathetic?"

"No." Pop shook his head and laid a warm hand on hers, squeezing it. "No, it's not. It's okay to want to be romanced, but remember that you aren't a shrinking violet. You're a capable young woman. You know how to speak up for what you want. If you like him..."

She nodded, mulling over Pop's words. He was right. Adelaide wanted him to call, but she wasn't going to sit around pining for him like she'd done with Liam. If he didn't call, she'd do it. The worst that could happen was a no. "You're right. I'll do it." Adelaide stood and kissed Pop on his temple before making Vegemite toast for herself.

She'd barely finished half her breakfast when her phone, charging on the kitchen bench, vibrated with a message. Jumping out of the chair, she saw the screen and her insides swooped like a magpie in spring. "It's him," she said excitedly.

I had a great time last night and this morning.

I'd love to see you again.

He was too sweet. Adelaide responded, resisting the urge to squeal. *I had a great time too. I have a few parties this week and the game on Fri, but I'm free next Sat if you are?*

Three dots appeared below the message then disappeared. Reappeared and disappeared again. What was he writing? Finally, a message came through. *There's a band playing at the night markets next Saturday. My students told me last week that they're great. Would you like to go?*

A moment later a rush of messages came through. *Oh. My. God. I sound old.*

My students?

I mean, they probably get out more than I do...

But taking recommendations from teenagers shouldn't be a thing when you're 30, right? Damn.

You're young though so I thought maybe you might like it too.

That sounded just as bad.

Going out on a limb here to say you're currently blocking my number.

Adelaide snorted out a laugh and dialled his number. He was too funny when he was nervous.

"Hi," he said tentatively.

"Hey, you," Adelaide said warmly, a smile in her voice. "I'm not blocking your number, don't worry." At Kingston's relieved huff, she added, "But I'm not going to touch the 'I'm closer in age to your students than I am to you,' comment. It doesn't matter, does it?"

"No, not to me. I just wanted to pick something that you might find fun."

"The night markets on Saturday sounds great. I'd love to go with you. But maybe we should do something on Saturday arvo that you're interested in. I'd love to learn more about you."

"Yeah?" The hope in his voice made her heart swell and shatter at the same time. She hoped his shyness wasn't because someone in his past had done a number on him.

"Yes, I would." Her answer was firm, leaving no room for misunderstanding. They sorted out the details and with a giddy fan-girl-at-a-boy-band-concert smile, she bade him goodbye.

She turned and almost walked straight into Eli, who smirked with a twinkle in his eye and stood his ground. It brought her up short and she readied for the playful interrogation. "Good date?"

"It was," she responded, keeping a lid on her gushing, but she couldn't help the grin splitting her lips.

"You're smitten already, aren't you?" It wasn't really a question. Adelaide winced and furrowed her brows, the smile falling off her face. Was she one of those people who fell hard and fast for anyone who showed her some attention? First Liam, and now Kingston? "What did I say?" he asked, tilting his head.

She opened her mouth, not even sure how to answer. "Am I being stupid?" When Eli frowned and raised an eyebrow, confusion written all over his face, she continued, "For liking him so quickly? I mean, I've just been gushing to Pop and now you come in here and call me smitten. Should I be playing hard to get, or... something? Do I fall for men too easily?"

He shook his head and angled her chin up. "In what universe is you being single for years because everyone you've met is meh, you falling too quickly? If you'd dived headfirst into relationships with anyone who got a first date, then maybe, but there's nothing wrong with wanting love. If you like him and want another date, it's good. I wasn't criticizing. I'm glad you're happy. If he treats you well, then it's great, in fact."

Even though he had no idea about Liam, she was grateful for Eli's reassurance.

* * * * *

"This is one of my favourites," she announced to the group of ten ladies gathered in a makeshift circle on her client's lounge room floor. They were the typical mix of ages for a first-time party—mums, daughters, friends, and a grandmother—and like usual, they were self-conscious, and a little flustered at the display of toys she had set up.

Most were verging on tipsy, and a few had passed that point into giggly, and all were casting furtive glances at the display table she'd covered with a hot-pink tablecloth before laying out her selection. Silly party games, like pin the penis on the celebrity and Never Have I Ever, had warmed the ladies up and encouraged them to eat a few snacks to soak up the alcohol they were downing. But the drinking always stepped up again when she moved into anal territory.

Adelaide held up the black silicone anal beads, which started a little larger than a pea and progressed to a golf ball size. "This is suitable for anyone's pleasure ranging from beginner"—she pointed to the smallest bead then moved her fingers along its nine-inch length to the largest—"to experts."

"Where do you use that?" a middle-aged lady asked in a murmur to another woman half her age.

"Up your bum, Mum," the younger woman answered with a laugh at her mother's horror.

"Why?" There was a measure of shock, disgust, and curiosity in her tone.

"Your sphincter has lots of nerve endings, so play can be pleasurable. However, there are a few rules." Adelaide launched into her explanation of lubrication requirements, the need to stick with toys that had a flared base, and the cleaning regime necessary after every use and between anal and vaginal use. "I don't usually recommend this toy for anal virgins, but if you've had some experience, this is a great option."

"Do guys really enjoy this stuff?" a woman in her twenties asked with a scrunched-up nose and a grimace. "It's... not a turn on."

Adelaide forced a smile and answered, "For anyone with a prostate, this toy and the vibrating plug are walking orgasms. The beads give you a sense of fullness, and when your G-spot is a couple of inches inside your rear, the pressure against it is incredible." She held up the smooth vibrating plug with a bulbous head and narrow base which flared to a flat handle. "The vibrations centred in your back passage from this toy create a different type of orgasm for those of us with vaginas, especially combined with another toy or appendage taken vaginally. But for people with a prostate, it's a G-spot massage."

She bit back any comments about whether it was a turn on or not. Adelaide saw a lot of perhaps unintentional homophobia and transphobia in this role, and she'd learned not to respond in the way she really wanted. Instead, she tried to educate.

"I tried it with a man back in the seventies," the grandmother interrupted. "I bent him over and he took my toy like a pro." A groan sounded from two of the women, horrified looks on their faces.

"Grammie!" the younger one—her host—cried, the horror in her voice loud and clear for the room to hear.

"Oh, hush. You think you youngins are the only ones who cut loose? The seventies were wild. I barely remember half of it, but that I couldn't forget."

"Yeah, no. It's gross," the same woman who'd commented negatively announced.

Adelaide held back a sigh. This was going nowhere. "The best part about sex is that it's personal to everyone. You can partake in it in whatever manner you enjoy the most and leave out the parts you don't like." She motioned to the lady who'd first spoken. "If you don't enjoy anal play, my suggestion is not to go there. For others who may enjoy it—" She swept her arm around the room and winked at Grammie. "—then I'd encourage them. A good rule of thumb is not to yuck another person's yum, so if we can keep comments positive, that would be great." She had fun at some parties, and this one was pretty good overall, but there were some people who were... urgh. Why did they always make themselves known when she got to these toys? The sooner she figured out a way to stop doing these parties, the better.

* * * * *

She watched as Liam ran onto the field to meet his team. It would likely be the last play of the night with only two minutes left in the game. They were two tries down, attacking hard to keep possession of the ball in their forward half so they could score. One, two, then three tackles and they'd moved it into the twenty-metre zone.

Adelaide held her breath as the ball was passed between the forward line on the fourth tackle, gaining another few metres. So close, yet too far away too. One more tackle, and they'd have to hand over possession and it would be game over. Defensively, Liam's team had struggled, letting through far too many tries, but they'd reduced some of the gap in the last ten minutes of the half.

The centre passed out wide to Liam's teammate. The ball missed its mark. It was too high to catch. He fumbled the ball.

The opposition shifted closer.

Liam was there in a flash. His powerful legs pumping hard as he threw himself bodily in front of the defending player.

They hit the ground hard, the tackle legal.

His teammate shored up his grip. Ran forward.

But the other defenders were already there.

"Nooo," Adelaide shouted, throwing her hands up in the air. "Bloody hell." The East Sydney team they were playing against were relentless, their attack flawless. Their defence—particularly the new guy, Bryce Flaharty—shut down too many attempts at scoring early on.

But they were on fire now, a fierce determination to avoid the loss.

The hooker went down under a pile of limbs directly before their front-row seats. She could hear the slam of bodies together, the *oomph* and grunts as wind was knocked out of their lungs. Three men on top of him. Pressing him into the manicured grass of the stadium.

Fifth tackle.

It was now or never.

The ball was still in play. It was still clutched firmly in the player's hands when he'd hit the ground.

The whistle blew. Defending players clambered up and off him. Standing, he shook off the tackle, straightened his uniform and placed the ball on the ground, rolling it back with his foot in a pass to the prop. Lobbing it out wide, the ball sailed at waist height like a bullet, shooting straight at the gap Liam was closing in on.

He sprinted up the sideline. Closing in on it with every step.

Thick legs pumping hard, arms outstretched as the ball sailed toward him.

Only metres from the try line. Only metres away from scoring.

Adelaide was on her feet. She screamed her encouragement. Eli was next to her yelling. Cheering.

Her heart was in her throat. Adelaide shouted, "Yes! Run, you've got it! Go, go, run! Yes!"

Liam launched himself through the air and closed his fingertips around the ball. He pulled it in close, tucking it into the crook of his arm.

He hit the ground.

Rolled.

Scrambled back to his feet. Punched out with a speed Adelaide had never witnessed before.

Sidestepped. Missed his opponent's charge. Jumped over another.

"Come on, come on," Eli urged desperately, his fists white knuckled as they slowly lifted into the air with every step closer to the line that Liam made.

Surrounded on two sides, the boundary line on his left, Liam sprinted.

Adelaide sucked in a breath as he neared the line, now less than a body length away.

A last-ditch attempt.

A low tackle.

Liam's feet were swept out from under him.

Adelaide watched in horror as he spun side on. Flew awkwardly through the air. Oh God, was he okay? Her heart double-timed in a rat-tat-rat-tat beat.

Liam landed. Hard. His body bounced like a rag doll, skidded to a stop. The other player was sprawled out next to him, clutching his elbow.

"Get up," she screamed, not caring any more about the score.

Liam crawled, reaching forward. Stretched out, reaching for the try line.

Two players to his right. They didn't slow. Big bodies. Thick muscle. They launched themselves, piling on top, tackling him hard. Adelaide screamed, tears springing to her eyes. *No. Don't get hurt.*

Eli reached for her, gripping her hand tightly as the whistle blew.

Too far away to see, panic boiled in her veins, the need to vault the barrier and check on him overwhelming. But

Elijah held her there. Stopped her from running across the field.

Vision blurry with tears, she looked to the screen. Waiting for news.

She prayed that he wasn't hurt.

Close-up footage flashed onto the screen, the players scrambling off him. Adelaide watched, squeezing Eli's hand. When Liam didn't move, her breath caught.

The screen flashed green. "Try" lit up in capital letters.

He'd done it. Somehow, against all the odds, he'd scored. But at what cost? Was he hurt? Where were the medics? What the hell was taking so long? Frantic, she looked around. Why weren't they with him? There, running to him, they held a backboard between them. Adelaide swallowed around the lump in her throat.

Video footage flashed to the live feed again. She watched with her heart beating like a hummingbird's wings. Liam gingerly lifted himself up, got to his feet, and tested his weight on his right ankle. Adelaide saw the grin he shot to his teammate. No pain.

Relief swamped her, making her dizzy.

Liam jogged the few metres to meet the medics and slapped one on the shoulder. Bowing their heads together, they talked for a moment before Liam turned to the stand. He looked directly to where she and Eli sat in the family allocation.

Her breath caught. He was so damn gorgeous. Larger than life too. Every one of the fans surrounding them screamed for him. But she knew he was looking for them.

His best friend and her, the tag-along younger sister. Liam shot them a double thumbs-up, and Adelaide choked out a teary laugh, reaching for Eli. Immediately, her brother let out his breath, his shoulders slumping in relief.

"Should have been a bloody penalty," Eli muttered.

THREE

Kingston

Adelaide. How in the heck had he managed to capture her attention? Him of all people. He was waiting for her to open her eyes, come to her senses, and leave him in her wake in a cloud of dust.

It certainly wouldn't be the first time he'd been dumped. Although, that implied going beyond asking someone out. On the odd occasion that the person said yes, it rarely went past that first date. He'd given up looking. His mum, bless her, was desperate for grandbabies and his dad could never understand why he was still single. He was a big, handsome boy. But that was half the problem wasn't it. Anything other than ripped and people stopped looking. He didn't blame them—he understood wanting to be with someone who looked after themselves. He was nothing special in the looks department either. He was just... him. But he did work hard to get where he was.

Hitting rock bottom had changed his life, and for that, King would always be grateful. He had a lot to offer a partner—he was smart enough, caring, had a decent job, felt like he made a difference to his students, and would treat his partner like a king or queen—but in today's world of perfect Instagram models, he never felt like he was enough.

He just hoped Adelaide liked what she saw enough for... anything more, really. The woman had him enraptured. Captivated. Ensnared.

He'd happily stay tangled up with her too.

She was intelligent and so full of life. Stunning as well. She'd been like a beacon to him the night of their speed date—in a sea of greys and blacks, she was colour. Bright tones and pastels all at once, shimmering and dancing together. A siren drawing him in and leaving him wanting more. Long fuchsia, soft-as-silk hair and rose-pink lips. King had watched her as she entered, struck dumb by her magnetism.

Without thinking, he'd rushed forward, taking a seat as close to her as possible so they'd get a chance to speak. He couldn't have dreamed up a better ending to the night than Adelaide wanting to spend more time with him. King couldn't believe his luck. He was still pinching himself trying to figure out if it was even real. Would he wake up only for it to have been a dream? Lord, he hoped not.

Eve—his friend—had pushed him to go, telling him that he needed to get out there and meet people. She raised it every time they talked. Like a dog with a bone, she hounded him, and King had given up, buying the ticket just to get Eve off his case. He hadn't planned on actually going. But when she'd shown up at his place a couple of hours before go time, ordered him to iron his clothes, threatening to shove

him out the door in his underwear if he didn't, he'd acquiesced. Now, he could kiss her for forcing his hand. Not only
had Adelaide wanted to spend more than the allocated five
minutes with him, they'd talked through the night and into
the next morning. It was by far the best first date he'd ever
been on. Adelaide had surprised him too, calling and texting
as much as he had with her. Every conversation of theirs
that week had lasted hours.

King was getting ready for their pre-date date, and he
was completely flustered. He couldn't believe that she'd
wanted to do something that he loved as well as dinner at
the night markets. So, there he was, lifting his bicycle off the
roof racks of his trusty Subaru. There was nothing better
than being outdoors.

Nerves churned in his belly, and he looked down at the
T-shirt and board shorts he was wearing. The dark colours
were flattering on him, and the shirt hugged his shoulders
and arms, highlighting the muscles he'd worked so hard to
build over the last couple of years. He was comfortable, and
that always boded well.

He lifted the second bike off his roof rack and wheeled
it over to the path they were cycling along. It was the first
thing he'd thought of when Adelaide said she wanted to
know him better. He loved cycling almost as much as surfing, two things that a few years ago he never would have
imagined doing. But a lot had changed in that time.

"Hey, you," Adelaide greeted him warmly as he looked
up, the smile in her voice matching the sweet tilt of her lips
upward. King swallowed, his eyes doing a slow lap down the

length of her body. Damn. She was fine. Dressed in a simple white singlet and purple knee-length yoga pants paired with beat-up sneakers, she was radiant. Leaning in, he hugged her and breathed in the vanilla scent of her shampoo. Her waist was tiny in his big hands. Need flared inside him. The desire to pull her close and press their bodies together, to take her lips in a kiss that would undoubtedly go from zero to scorching in a millisecond was tempered only by the fact that they were in far too public a setting.

"Hi, beautiful," he greeted her, Adelaide's eye-crinkling smile at his compliment warming his insides. He motioned to the bikes and said, "I thought we could go for a ride along the beachfront. The gym I go to is right on the beach just south of the mall and they serve great coffee there. I thought we could stop in there before moseying back. You up for it?"

"Absolutely." She stepped forward, hooked her arm around his, and pressed herself against him. He loved how she did that. There was no hesitation, no second-guessing herself. She went for whatever she wanted. As much as her beauty had drawn his attention, it was her vitality and confidence that had wound around him like a vine creeping up a tree, holding him tight.

She pressed her lips to his and his body came alive, nerve endings singing with the attraction ping-ponging between them. Soft and pillowy, her lips tasted of strawberry lip gloss, her breath minty fresh. He wanted more. But his far-too-sensible nature held him back. "This is perfect. I was excited when you said we would be doing something outdoors. The only thing I've done outside of late is mow the lawn. It's so overgrown."

He blinked and cleared his throat. "Do you mow the lawn often?"

"All the time," she groaned. "It's out of control. Wild at the moment. Hell, I'd do almost anything if I could find somebody to do it for me."

King bit back a laugh. He knew damn well the grass she was talking about, but he couldn't resist the urge to tease her. Either that, or his brain had taken a backseat to his traitorous dick—that bugger was more than happy to misinterpret her words. "I could come over sometime," burst out before he could bite his tongue, and then he kept digging that hole, adding, "Maybe I should do some push-ups or squats beforehand. You know, get the blood pumping." He unsuccessfully tried to stifle his smile again. A laugh bubbled in his chest, but he swallowed it down.

"No, save your energy. You'd need it to get through my patch." She stilled, her gaze shooting to his before her cheeks flushed a lovely pink. She opened her mouth to speak, but a laugh tore from her lips instead. "Oh. My. God. Did I just say that?"

King snorted, his chuckle breaking free until they were both breathless with laughter. He tucked an errant piece of hair behind her ear and nodded before wrapping his arm loosely around her waist. He kissed her forehead, his lips lingering against her soft skin.

She buried her face in her hands, protesting with a squeak, "I meant actual grass. The stuff that grows in my backyard." She groan-laughed again. "Green, overgrown, full of weeds. Grows on the ground. In dirt. That grass. Not that grass." She fanned her face, her cheeks flaming and her eyes watering with the tears of laughter rolling down her face. "Just kill me now."

"So that's no to push-ups?" he teased.

"I mean, hey, if you want to entertain me by doing push-ups, I'd gladly watch. As long as you're shirtless, and maybe not wearing pants either. But there won't be any mowing of my grass. My... grass... is perfectly maintained. No need for any trimming."

"That's... important." He hooked a finger under her chin and tilted her face up to his, pressing a soft kiss to her lips. Just a brush of his to the corner of her smile, tasting the salty tears that had tracked down her cheeks. He bit down his groan and resisted the urge to deepen the kiss. When her breath caught, King nuzzled her nose, their lips only a hair's breadth apart. God damn, he wanted her.

As if sensing his struggle, Adelaide pulled back. "Should we ride?" she asked, with a wiggle of her eyebrows. "Hop on and go hard."

"Oh, so now you're teasing me?" he growled playfully, nipping her lobe. "I can go all day, you know. Last the distance. Keep pushing until you're soaked and begging me to let up." His words, whispered against the smooth skin of her throat, left a trail of goosebumps in their wake. She shivered and rested her hand on his belly, her thumb teasing the waistline of his shorts. He froze. Every muscle in his body went rigid. Locked tight. His erection throbbed.

Man, if he didn't settle down, he was going to come in his pants like a randy teenager.

"Let's put a pin in this until we can get somewhere a little more private. But until then, I want you to know that I'm game." She pulled back, ran her gaze down the length of his body, her eyes snagging at the unmistakable bulge in his shorts and sucked in a breath. "Yeah, definitely game."

Just that thought, the knowledge that she wanted him, maybe as much as he did her, sent him rocketing to the edge of sanity. Instinctively, he reached down, clamping his fingers around the base of his cock, bringing him down from the precipice. He needed a distraction, or he'd embarrass himself spectacularly right there on the esplanade in the centre of Surfers Paradise.

Adelaide huffed out a laugh and added, "We should at least go on this date."

He nodded, mute, and still struggling with getting his body under control. She did things to him no other person had done before.

They clipped on helmets and started their ride, King almost going cross-eyed with the pressure of the seat between his legs. Long and narrow, it pushed against his sac and the base of his cock. His erection bent with the push and pull of his shorts from each rotation of the pedals, the material of his snug underwear feeling like a caress against his sensitive skin every time he moved. He set an easy pace along the flat path—one that wasn't too punishing on his trapped dick, and hoped that it got easier as they went along.

With wide beaches and sparkling white sand on his left and the famous high rises on his right, King emptied his mind. He concentrated on the wind on his face, sunshine on his arms, and the captivating woman next to him.

"I don't think us locals enjoy this place as much as we should," Adelaide remarked after a few minutes. "I rarely even come this way."

"I used to be the same, but I've been here a lot over the last couple of years. I usually surf just north of here and try to ride from my place to the gym and back a few times a week." It was a twenty-kilometre round trip—a decent effort that always left him pumped.

"You're super active. I'm impressed."

If he wasn't mistaken, the look she flashed was one of pain. More of a wince than anything. "I try to be. It helps keep me balanced," he replied hesitantly. "Is that an issue?"

"Only if you expect me to be able to keep up with you." She laughed with a distinct self-deprecating air. "I'm so not fit. I wish I was, but I fell out of sporty activities when I was like fifteen and didn't take anything else up. Suddenly, I'm in my twenties and I don't even know how to go about joining something other than a gym."

"Believe me, I didn't do it voluntarily. It's taken me a long time to enjoy exercising and what I do is mostly solitary, so it's hard to stay motivated sometimes." He didn't tell her that his motivation had been a panic so enveloping that he'd sometimes felt like he was drowning.

"Hmmm," she hummed. He wasn't sure if it was one of those I-know-you're-not-telling-me-something sounds or agreement, but he hesitated in offering more. Insecurity was a bitch.

They were quiet for a time when Adelaide asked, "So who were the students that recommended we see the band tonight?"

"A couple of my year twelves. I'm their homeroom teacher. They were talking about it in class, and I asked them about what music they listened to. Apparently the band playing tonight is a local one who's starting to get noticed."

"What year levels do you teach?" Adelaide asked over her shoulder when King dropped back to slip in behind her and make room for a couple pushing their kids in a double pram.

"This year I'm in the junior and middle school—years seven, eight, and ten—but last year I taught middle and senior. I'm experienced enough to be able to pick up whatever year level the school needs me in."

She smiled over her shoulder at him, her gaze warm. Pride filled him. His students meant the world to him, and he loved every minute of being their teacher.

"What inspired you to teach?"

Of the few good memories he had at school, Mr Anderson's classes were one of his favourites. "I had this history teacher. He'd walk in, toss his Akubra on the desk like some cowboy, and pull out a chair. He'd sit on the back of it with his feet on the seat and talk. No slides, no readings, nothing. It was amazing. Even as high schoolers, the discussions we had were deep. He'd raise events that happened thousands of years ago and paint pictures so vivid that we would sit there hanging off his every word. Even after the bell went, we'd be asking more questions and he'd have to herd us out of the class. I knew that was what I wanted to do within the first few weeks of starting his class."

"That's so cool."

Their conversation meandered, winding along as they pedalled. The sun dipped in the sky, dropping below the line of the high rises and casting long shadows along the beach. King shivered, resisting the temptation to pedal harder to warm himself up. Usually he rode in long sleeves, but the weather had been warm when they'd set out.

King pulled up beside Adelaide and motioned to the gym, which sat right on the sand. The café was a patch of AstroTurf with a window into the gym, but it was sheltered, had decent coffee, and expected everyone to be dressed in gym gear. "Should we stop for a coffee?"

A smile lit up Adelaide's flushed face, her eyes sparkling happily. "Yeah, I'd love to. My friend owns this place, but I've never been here before. I'm excited."

* * * * *

"You, ah, want to follow me back to my place to get changed for tonight? It's not far from here." King locked the second bike into place on his roof rack, checked that he'd tossed their helmets onto the seat, and closed the back door. He really wanted Adelaide to say yes, but at the same time didn't want her to think he was pushing for more than she was prepared to give. They hadn't progressed past teasing and tempting each other, a brush of their lips or a playful nip of her skin the most physical they'd been. He wanted more—a proper kiss, a proper hug. He would happily trade their date that night with making out on the couch, his body pressed against hers. But he was trying to be a gentleman too.

"I didn't drive. Caught a rideshare in. Can I, maybe, bum a lift with you?" Adelaide smiled, her eyes darkening as she gazed at him through lowered lashes. "Then you can drop me off. Tomorrow. Or whenever."

Oh, hell.

Reason and logic fled, fear dissipating as mist does on a sunny morning. His body lit up like a dash, warning lights flashing with every synapse of brain function shutting down until he could respond only to his body's base desires. Lust enveloped him. It was as if he was caught in an avalanche, the force picking him up and tossing him end over end, taking with it any rational thought.

He was drawn to Adelaide. She called to him, her pheromones capturing him and pulling him ever closer. But he wouldn't break free of her even if he could. He wanted her. Wanted to touch and caress. Worship her until she knew exactly how good he could make her feel.

He caged her in, her back against his car and held his breath as he pressed his body against hers. She shuddered, her eyes unfocussed. Adelaide's tongue swept out, licking her lip as her chest rose and she pressed her breasts against him, arching into his touch like a cat. A sigh escaped from those lips he wanted to kiss. Warm and soft, she was pliant in his arms. King ran his hands down her sides to her waist and it was King's turn to quake.

Taller than her by half a head, his hips at her waist, he tilted Adelaide's face to his. He could get lost in those expressive blue eyes, the invitation clear. She wanted him. Adelaide's stare was focussed on his lips. Her breaths were short and choppy, and faster than normal. He raised his hand to her throat, brushing his thumb over her pulse point. Her heartbeat thrummed, pulsing blood around her system so fast it would leave an F1 car looking like it was standing still. Her breath hitched and he shifted his hand, wrapping his fingers around her throat and holding her in place. Her eyes rolled back in her head at the possessive touch and King growled, desperation clawing at him to caress her. To push her over the edge.

Brushing his lips against hers, he kept his kiss light as he ground his lengthening semi against the softness of her belly. Telling her without words what she did to him. The pictures he painted in his mind's eye of them locked together were sensual as hell—shadows dancing over naked skin and moans like a symphony in the air as they writhed together.

Holding his mouth just out of her reach, he watched as Adelaide's eyes darkened. Her tongue snaked out and wet her lips, licking his too. He groaned, a rumble deep in his chest that vibrated against hers. Adelaide's pebbled nipples brushed against his ribs, pressing into him. She rubbed herself along his torso, her hands gripping his waist as she communicated exactly what she wanted. Any restraint, any hesitation fled, and the freedom it unleashed lifted a weight off his shoulders. Adelaide must have seen something in his gaze. Or maybe it was the punch of his hips forward, his shaft digging into her belly. Whatever it was, kicked her into action.

She reached up, hooking her hand around his nape, and dragged his mouth against hers. King squeezed her hip, pulling her closer. She licked into his mouth, their tongues touching. Her flavour burst on his tongue. Coffee, strawberries, and a something uniquely Adelaide filled his senses. Intoxicating him. Overwhelming him. Tangling her fingers in his hair, she tugged the strands until his scalp stung and he moaned. King was lost in her taste and touch. Drowning in her. His head spun and his body charged, amping up until he was electrified.

He gasped for breath and tried to pull back. Put some distance between them before he hitched her leg over his hip and ground against her until they were both shouting out their release. Adelaide growled and shook her head.

She wasn't finished with him.

She tugged him toward her, pulling him forward again. Teasing him with her lips like they were forbidden fruit until he fell into her arms.

He went willingly.

They stayed like that, making out and rutting together against the car until the air around them turned cold and King shivered. "Hey, you're freezing," Adelaide whispered, running her hands down his bare arms. "Let's get you warm."

"Burning up more like it." But the impact of his muttered response was lost when he shivered again, the southerly wind cold enough to have come straight off the Antarctic. Adelaide raised an eyebrow and smirked—one of those knowing smiles—as if to humour him. Her heat pressed against his front was the only thing keeping King from turning into a popsicle.

Opening the passenger door for her, he waited until she slipped in and closed it. He stilled for a moment, resisting the urge to pinch himself again.

FOUR

Adelaide

"So you went to the game last night?" Kingston asked.

"Yep, we go every time we play here or in Brissy." Adelaide looked up at him as they walked hand in hand through the narrow walkways of the night markets, dodging people carrying trays of food, pushing prams, and chasing after wayward children. Each food outlet had been set up in a recycled shipping container, slotted together in a simple grid system surrounding a large lawn and forecourt area with a stage at one end and chairs and tables dotted throughout. Large shade sails lined with twinkling fairy lights covered most of the space and protected the crowds of people from the weather. That night was so much more typical for Queensland winters than their previous date. The air held a certain crispness, the skies clear of even a single cloud.

The river bordered one side of the markets, a cold breeze blowing in from over the ocean. Balcony-style eating areas were set out along its length, overlooking the dark waters. The ferry and water taxis, as well as pleasure craft sailed the river, traversing between the towers of Surfers Paradise and Broadbeach to the south and the Broadwater and business and shopping district to the north.

Kingston juggled the tray of food and drinks in one hand while she led him away from the crowds and over to an empty table along the railing. It was the perfect place to have a more intimate dinner away from the crowded central space. The band, a grungy surfer-style rap, reminded her a bit of her mum's favourite, the Red Hot Chili Peppers. They'd even performed a few of their songs. While they were great and had the crowd dancing and singing with them, Adelaide wanted to steal away with Kingston and get back to a quiet conversation with the man that had enamoured her so much.

"I didn't realize you were such a big fan of the footy," Kingston remarked. With a cheeky smirk and a twinkle in his eye, he added, "I'm an East Sydney fan myself."

He slid the tray onto the table, and Adelaide playfully glared at him. She rubbed her hands together, as if wiping them clean. "That's it, we're done for. I can't look past an infraction like that. Why? Of all teams, why that one?" Adelaide added a roll of her eyes and muttered, "Typical, I find a nice guy and he turns out to be all wrong. He held so much hope."

Kingston laughed, a rich baritone filling the space between them, and slid his cool hand into hers. "Give me a good reason to change teams and I might consider it."

Adelaide's mouth popped open in mock horror, and she gasped, her free hand going to her chest. "No, you can't do that. You're supposed to be loyal to the end."

Kingston forked a green bean into his mouth and, after swallowing it, said, "Eh, I do have a favourite player, but you seem to be a rabid fan." He paused, furrowed his brows, and narrowed his eyes playfully. "Who should my favourite player be? I feel like I should listen to you."

Adelaide barked out a laugh, trying not to choke on the food she'd been chewing. He made her smile, her insides doing a happy dance when they bantered playfully. She pointed her chopsticks at him and said, "Well played." Swallowing, she added, "Honestly, I don't know much about the other teams, but East Sydney's new full back, Bryce Flaharty, is a friend of my brother's BFF. He's good, so... yeah..." The heat rose in her cheeks, and she looked away, pushing the noodles around her bowl. It felt like she'd revealed too much, that she was opening herself up to sharing the secret she'd never wanted to see the light of day. It had been a foolish, impossible, teenage dream that she'd let continue for far too long. It was time she got over Liam. But it was easier said than done. Liam held a special place in her heart. He'd rescued her brother, and he'd been a permanent fixture in her life and house for close to a decade. It just wasn't possible to do more than refocus her energy on being friends with him.

Could she fall out of love with him? Adelaide was going to damn well try, because although her stupid feelings by her stupid heart were all mixed up, she wanted this thing with Kingston to go further. She wanted to get to know him and give him the love and attention he deserved. He was restrained, quiet and shy, but when he shook free of it, he morphed into this hot-as-hell sex god. Mixed with his gentle caring nature and the way he seemed to focus in on exactly what she wanted and deliver it, she was itching to get him naked. It was more than chemistry though. She genuinely liked him. They had fun together. He was mature and knew himself. It was a refreshing change from the self-centred jerks she'd hooked up with in the past.

He was boyfriend material, and Adelaide hadn't realized how much she wanted that until she'd finally let herself look past Liam. She hadn't expected it to happen so quickly though. Kingston had been an unexpected surprise. Meeting him had thrown her into a tailspin. Two weeks ago, she was certain she was doomed to be on the wrong end of a one-sided love affair forever. A week ago, she'd met an incredible man who lit her up and whose attention set her on fire.

But last night's game had reminded Adelaide of how much she loved Liam, and she was still struggling with how to get past that fact.

"Is he the same boy who made friends with your brother?" Kingston asked quietly, squeezing her hand. She nodded and bit her lip, the reminder of that memory all too potent given the inner monologue playing on a loop. "In that case, I can see why he has your undying support."

"Yeah, he's a good guy." Adelaide cleared her throat, trying to dislodge the lump there, and giving herself a moment to gain some composure. Her emotions were like an overfull suitcase. She had to sit on that bastard and beat it into submission, shoving everything back inside before using all her strength and Twister-like abilities to zip that fucker up. Once she'd kicked it into the dark recesses, she added with what she hoped was a playful smirk, "S'pose your favourite player is just great at footy."

"Until you said he was good, I had no idea. I've never watched him play. It's more because of what he does off-field that I like him." Kingston eyed her, his smirk self-deprecating. "Bryce is active in high schools talking about cyber-bullying. We show a lot of the videos he made with the child e-safety organization he's partnered with. He seems like a good guy."

Adelaide agreed. How couldn't she? Doing that kind of volunteer work, using his fame for something important, was admirable. It was just like Kingston to respect that more than playing ability.

They spoke while they ate, Kingston asking her whether she watched any other sport. Adelaide struggled to keep a straight face, but she must have managed a blank expression just fine when she answered, "There's sport other than footy?" and Kingston snorted out a laugh.

With their bowls nearly empty, Adelaide motioned to Kingston's remaining small serving. "Saving room for dessert?" She was stuffed full, but his vegetable and lentil salad with a side of sizzling beef was half the size of her noodles and he still had some left.

"No, I don't really eat anything sweet. It's hard to keep my blood sugar in check when I do."

She tilted her head. His meal the week before had been similar—appallingly healthy—but it made sense if he had to watch out for his health. "You're diabetic?" she asked.

"Yes, type two." He pulled a small container out of his pocket and rattled the tablets inside. "I take medication to control it rather than having to inject insulin. I still test my blood sugar daily, but as long as I watch my diet and get plenty of exercise, it stays within a healthy range."

Adelaide admired him even more. That kind of self-discipline was incredible. "When were you diagnosed?" He shifted in his seat and stacked the now empty bowls, pushing them to the side. "If it's too personal, you don't have to answer."

"No, it's not that. I'm trying to figure out where to start." He ran his fingers down his stubble, pausing at his chin. He sighed and lifted his lips in a smile that looked forced, the strained lines around his eyes obvious in the dim lighting. "I was always overweight, the big kid in school, and the even bigger teenager. Uni wasn't a great place for me either. I tended to stress eat, and I wanted to do Mum and Dad proud. Anything less than straight As and they would have been worried I was failing." He rolled his eyes, but Adelaide got it. She knew he was close with his parents, and from what he'd told her on their late-night conversations since their first date, he was the first of his family to attend university.

"My parents are old school, so my topping the class was important to them. I suppose they ingrained it into me. They never expected to have kids. The doctors told them they couldn't. But then they fell pregnant with me, and I became their entire focus. Dad put off retiring to support me while I studied because they didn't want me juggling a part-time job. But that put a lot of pressure on me to succeed too." He winced and lowered his gaze. "It sounds like I'm complaining, but I'm not. I'm so lucky compared to so many other people. I have parents who love me, a university degree, and a steady job that I love that pays the bills. I'll never be rich, but I don't need to be." He shrugged. "The perk of having the summer off makes up for the long hours during the year."

"It doesn't sound like you're complaining. Every one of us has a different experience in life and with our parents. Yours put pressure on you, probably before you were ready for it." When Kingston was her age, he would have already graduated and be a couple of years into teaching. Adelaide still had no idea what she wanted to do with her life. Given the sacrifices his father had made—just like her mother's sacrifices—she could see exactly why Kingston had taken on those expectations as stress. It made her lack of direction even more pronounced.

"You're right, I wasn't ready for it. I stress ate, and my mum was glad to oblige. She shows you she loves you by feeding you and she's offended if you don't finish it. By the time I graduated, I was obese and gradually got heavier until a couple of years ago. Then I started to get these weird symptoms and I felt lousy. I eventually went to my doctor, and she tested my blood sugar. Unsurprisingly, she was horrified at the result." He sighed and squeezed the bridge of his nose.

Adelaide reached for him, interlinking their fingers, gripping his hand in encouragement. This was hard on him to talk about. The crease in his forehead was deep, his brows drawn together and his lips turned down in a frown. His shoulders were slouched, like he bore the weight of the world on them and Adelaide wanted to ease it. To comfort him. She wanted to lean in and kiss him, crawl onto his lap and hold him close.

"Dad has type one diabetes that was out of control for a long time. It was a miracle he didn't cark it years before he got it under control. It was why they had trouble conceiving—he was basically infertile and no one had picked it up because he refused to get help. He thought going to the doctors made him weak." Kingston shook his head and huffed out a sad breath. "My doctor told me some home truths when I got tested. If I didn't make some serious lifestyle changes, I was at high risk of more than just type one diabetes. Stroke, heart attack, and far too many other conditions that I didn't want to think about. It was the kick in the pants I needed to change up my life. I saw a dietician and learned what I should and shouldn't be eating and how to tell the difference, and I got a personal trainer too— Mike, the owner of the gym we went to. I sweated my butt off over that first year and dropped a third of my body weight."

Holy. Shit. A third of his weight? That was amazing. Absolutely inspirational. *He* was amazing and inspirational. "Has your diabetes stabilized? Is that the right question to ask?"

"Yes, it is and yeah, it's stable. I've been able to reduce the amount of medication I need to take, and my blood sugar levels are pretty much right where they need to be. As long as I take my medication." He popped the tablets into his mouth and swallowed them with a gulp of water.

"That's... incredible. I can't imagine the strength that it takes to do a complete U-turn and change your life so dramatically. I'm in awe."

He shrugged, clearly not as impressed with himself as she was. "I still have a way to go, and fending off Mum is a full-time job. She's constantly trying to feed me, but I'm getting better at it." He looked down and pulled his hand away from hers, wrapping his jacket around his body and shivered. A few things became clearer. She'd heard that people who lost a lot of weight felt the cold more. Apart from that afternoon, he'd never once taken off his jacket. Was that why?

She ran her hand down his arm to his elbow, and encouraged gently, "If you're cold, we can go..."

"I'm freezing, but it's nice out." He tightened his jacket around his midsection again and smiled. "I'm good."

Changing tack, she asked, "What's the biggest difference you've noticed?" She didn't know whether it was a good idea to keep talking about his weight loss, but she needed to know he was okay. Was he happier now? Did people treat him better? In and of itself that question made her ragey, but she had the insane urge to rip into anyone who made him feel lesser.

He huffed out a disbelieving laugh and shook his head. "Apart from not needing to pee every five minutes, it's that I'm always cold. I have to wear layers no matter what the time of year. The chill goes straight through me." He paused for a moment and looked at her through those long eyelashes, blinking as he seemed to mull over his next words. "I'll never be thin, but I feel like I'm healthy now. I'm gaining muscle too so I'm gradually getting the shape I want."

"If it means anything, I'm ridiculously attracted to you. Physically, you're sexy as hell." Adelaide laughed self-consciously, fanning her face from the heat crawling over her cheeks. Imagining stripping him out of all those layers of clothes and running her fingertips, then her tongue over the curves and valleys on his body was such a turn on. When they reached that stage—and she would see to it that they did—Adelaide would leave Kingston with no doubt about just how gorgeous he was. She reached out and linked their hands together, squeezing his fingers. "But there's so much more about you that draws me in than just your physical appearance. It's your personality, the whole package. Your honesty and sense of humour were what first attracted me to you. The way you could laugh off how awkward speed dating was..."

He nodded and sucked in a breath, squaring his shoulders. "Most people I was with when I was bigger had a thing for fat people. It was almost a fetish for them. They didn't see past the thing that I hated the most about myself, and I was miserable every second I was with them. I feel like I lived my life up to now stuck in a body suit that was a few sizes too big. I was trapped in it. Now, at least, I'm healthier."

Adelaide reached for his hand again and stroked her thumb on the back of it. Surprisingly soft, it was a contrast to the small calluses on his palm. His hands spoke of physical work. Exercise. Long, hard hours he'd dedicated to changing himself.

"I really like you for the man you are. You're gorgeous. So much so that I was left a little flustered when I met you. But it's your personality that has grabbed me and sucked me in. I wouldn't have spent hours on the phone with you every night or the day with you today if you were only a pretty face." She leaned in and whispered to him, a conspiratorial grin on her lips, "And you are pretty." She pursed her thumb and forefinger together, her nails only a few millimetres apart and winked playfully, letting out a laugh when he shook his head. "Just a little." Bringing his cool hand to her lips, she kissed his knuckles in a soft caress. "You wouldn't be the man you are today without having had those experiences, and I really like him. You're strong and resilient and smart, and that means so much more to me than whether you're a size twenty-eight or forty-seven waist. I admire you. Everything about you. I could see myself…" Adelaide clamped her mouth closed, shocked by what she was about to say. That stupid heart of hers had just gone and done it again and jumped headfirst into swirling floodwaters, consequences be damned.

"Yeah?" he asked, a small smile tilting his lips as a flush spread over his cheeks. It was adorably shy, but bashful had never looked so sexy. "You could see yourself getting naked with me?"

Her eyes snapped to his and the softness there stole her breath. Was she really that obvious that he could read her like an open book? He was letting her off the hook, changing the subject to give her a way out without admitting just how much he had shaken her foundations in the few hours they'd spent in each other's company.

She cleared her throat, trying to sound far more composed than she was. "I could."

"Thank you," he said quietly. "For saying the things you did, and for the record, I'd like to get naked with you too." He blew out a breath and laughed like he was surprised. "I really would. I mean seeing you naked is an obvious hell yeah."

He smiled one of those eye-crinkling smiles and his eyes darkened. It lit a warmth in Adelaide's belly that smouldered within her. She was tingling from head to toe. She licked her lips, anticipation spreading through her in the wake of the look that set her on fire.

"Enough about me. You told me you sell toys and do your videos, but never said how you ended up doing that."

She exhaled, the breath rushing out of her lungs. She was ready to leave right there and then, but he'd asked her something. What was it again? Oh, right. "I just wanted to try something different. A night playing with toys sounded more interesting than the date I had planned."

"O-kay," he said, dragging out the word. "Did you at least have a happy ending?" He wiggled his eyebrows and chuckled when Adelaide snorted out a laugh.

She rolled her eyes and grinned, but inside her feet were shuffling nervously and she was biting her lip hoping that he didn't think less of her for being so rudderless. "Mum's a nurse, right, and she's really open with us about our bodies and sex and what it could and should be like. But Mum has been single ever since she and my father separated. At first it was because she worked such long hours when we were in school that she was too exhausted to ever date. But then I think she got comfortable and the idea of going out and meeting someone scared her."

She sighed, hating that her mum had lived like a monk for fifteen years, hiding away from the world. Especially because at least initially she and Eli had been the reason for it in more ways than one. Now, with Eli working and helping her pay the bills, she'd dropped back some of the hours at the hospital, but she still worked the graveyard shift. She used Pop as an excuse, telling them that she preferred always having someone home with him, but even when she knew they were there, her mum didn't take advantage of it.

"I finished school and Eli was at uni studying literature. He had his whole life planned out like you, but I had no idea what I wanted to do. I just knew I didn't want to spend years studying something I wasn't passionate about. I figured there was no point starting anything until I was sure. I knew

I wanted to be around people, talk to them and help them somehow. I bounced around jobs for a bit." She shrugged. She'd only been seventeen or eighteen so it hadn't been a big deal, but the restlessness had set in again and she knew she needed to change things up and start something she was more than ambivalent about. That's what her Patreon was supposed to do, but so far it wasn't really gaining many subscribers.

"Then my friend's older sister invited us all for a toy party. She and her friends were giggling like it was scandalous that they were talking about sex. I was there and realized all my dates had been mediocre. The boys my age— and they were all boys—didn't know which way was up and didn't care either. They were all about getting off themselves. I figured having a toy or two would be more fulfilling."

King shook his head and huffed. "I feel you. I love teaching—the kids are all great—but the older I get, the more I realize how self-centred and clueless teenagers are. They just don't get that giving is even better than receiving."

Adelaide sucked in a breath at his inference, squeezing her legs together to halt the instantaneous throb. She shifted in her seat, his heavy gaze never leaving hers. There was a knowing glint in those dark eyes that put Adelaide under the microscope. Her pulse pounded and her breathing shallowed out. Sped up. Just a look, a comment, left her a needy, achy puddle of hormones. She closed her eyes, shivering at the memory of his lips on hers. His touches had been chaste since they'd left the beach. She wanted that to change. She wanted under him. Over him. Whatever and however he chose, she wanted it. She was all floaty. Words sounded like they were underwater, as her pulse pounded in her ears. Adelaide gasped, her pussy throbbing as she imagined a night with him. He squeezed her hand and Adelaide blinked open her eyes.

"Your Patreon?" he asked, his voice deeper, raspy like sandpaper.

It took a moment for the question to register, for her brain—which was off in a wonderland of lust and debauchery—to kick into action and get reacquainted with logical thought. "Patreon, yeah." She cleared her throat and brushed an imaginary piece of lint off her jeans. "It was like my eyes were opened. I couldn't believe what I was hearing. Sex isn't taboo; it's a natural part of life. I got thinking about it and wanted to get the word out. I'm restricted by most social media platforms' terms of service, so I have to be on one that allows me to post explicit content, even if it is just me sitting in front of a camera talking. I'm hoping to grow my audience more, but it's slow."

He blushed, a pretty pink spreading over his cheeks, and he ducked his head. "When you told me last week, I looked you up. I subscribed and I've been binge watching all of your videos. You're great in front of the camera, and your studio space is fantastic."

Adelaide's mouth popped open and she choked out a laugh. Heat whipped through her, her cheeks flushing. She pushed her hair back behind her ear, thinking about the things she'd revealed on her videos about herself. Now he knew. He knew what she'd liked and the experiments she'd tried. How she used some of the toys. The things she wanted to try; the question she'd asked more than once— why don't men give head as often as wanting to receive it? How had that translated in her feeling a mouth on her that way only a few times before? She pulled her hair free again, trying to hide her face. Oh, hell. He'd watched them? She didn't know whether to be mortified that he'd seen it or happy he knew she hadn't been lying when she said she didn't film porn. "Ah—"

"Have I made you uncomfortable? Because if I have, I'll stop watching them. I'll unsubscribe right now if you want me to."

"No," she said quickly, shooting her hand out to rest on his arm. "I'm kind of embarrassed?"

"Why? They're brilliant. I love how you're unashamedly telling women that what they want is important. Sex isn't all about men having Os."

He'd nailed the whole purpose of the series. It was the underlying theme and part of her motivation in talking about sex. "Right? Society looks at everything with a patri-archal lens, especially sex. We have to be pretty, but not too pretty to stand out. We need to speak up, but only if we don't make anyone uncomfortable. We need to open our bodies to men, but society wants us to be virgins and not sexually active. We have to wear knee-length dresses, but if we do, we're prudish and if we don't, we're sluts. It's bull-shit." She couldn't help the passion bleeding into her voice, the higher pitch and volume with which she spoke.

He nodded as she continued, encouraging her. He was leaning forward now, forearms braced on the table, fire in his eyes, as she scrunched up her paper napkin and tossed it in the bowls. Women had to walk a fine line, and when a toxic social media culture was added in, creating an impossible-to-achieve standard, it infuriated her.

She exhaled slowly, forcing herself to lower her voice once more, and added, "Removing the stigma around women talking about and having good sex—whether it's alone or with one or more people—is important to me. With all the shit happening around the world, we should be able to demand something as fundamental as an orgasm or five. You've seen some of what I talk about. I love being able to, I don't know, motivate women? Is that the right thing to say? Like, inspire them to stand up and ask for what they want while understanding that they aren't alone in what they're going through. I admitted this week that it's rare for a guy to get me over the line. There's nothing wrong with me—I can do it perfectly fine myself—but when I consider how much time I focus on them compared to theirs on me, it's not surprising. They aren't trying. Maybe it's because I haven't been vocal enough—"

"No, don't do that. Don't blame yourself for other people's shortcomings," he reassured her, linking their fingers together. He huffed and added, "God, if I had even a moment with you, I'd leave you in no doubt that my aim was to give you as many Os as I could."

Heat curled low in her belly, the tendrils of desire instantly rekindling and licking at her like flames. She shivered. Damn, this man was potent. Adelaide wanted him, and now.

She shifted in her seat again and his eyes darkened, his nostrils flaring at the motion. "Most guys don't think like you, at least not the ones I've been with," she clarified. "I was a means to an end, the way they got themselves off. I was using them too, but obviously wasn't as good at it as they were—"

"Again, that's not on you—"

"It is, though. They got what they needed, and I didn't. But I understand my body more now and can get myself off whenever I'm in the mood—multiple times when I want."

"And the record?" he asked, his tone like gravel and his eyes almost black.

"I'll let you know when you beat it." Kingston closed his eyes and slipped his free hand under the table. She saw him shift his weight, tugging at his jeans. He was hard. He was as turned on as she was; it was a hell of a rush.

"You ready to leave?" he growled, blinked, then seemed to shake himself out of the haze of lust. "Sorry, I promised you a date."

"Get up, Kingston. We're leaving."

* * * * *

He pulled up to the timber gate. If it wasn't for the break in the shrubbery, she wouldn't have known that a six-foot fence ran along the front of the property—a tall hedge grew to completely cover it. It and the tree that branched out above, creating a canopy over much of the front yard was all Adelaide could see in the dark. The giant eucalypt was beautiful.

"Wait here," he instructed before hopping out and opening the gate.

Adelaide couldn't help but admire the view. His jeans hugged thick thighs and the jacket showed off broad shoulders. Kingston was an enigma. Shy and retiring one moment, but in the next he'd drop his guard and say something that hinted at the lion he would be in bed. She couldn't wait to find out.

He slipped back into the car and eased it forward. Moving beyond the tree and along the narrow gravel drive, he parked next to a set of stairs leading up to the small high-set cottage. Adelaide had been enamoured when they'd arrived earlier. The house was old but well-loved and every corner showed Kingston's influence on it.

The light he'd switched on at the top of the stairs illuminated the thick reddish-timber steps guiding their way inside. The restored white iron railing was intricate in its design and matched the screen door. Behind the creaky screen was a timber door the same colour as the stairs outside and the polished timber flooring inside. The deep red contrasted beautifully against the olive-green exterior, white trim of the door and window frames and pale green-grey interior walls, all of it painted by Kingston and his dad. It was what they did—when something like the screen had seen better days, Kingston tried to restore it to its former glory. He said it wasn't because he wanted to avoid buying a new one; he had new things throughout the house, but he preferred to take a little time and give old and broken things a new life. He took such good care mending and rejuvenating his house and all the furniture inside it that each piece had a second chance to shine. It said a lot about how Adelaide thought he hoped people saw him—a renovated body with a second chance to really live.

Adelaide met Kingston at the back of the car as he closed the gate and held out his arm to help her over the pebbles. When they entered the house, he dropped his keys and wallet on the white distressed bookshelf sitting next to the door. That simple move—the shake of keys announcing their arrival—made the air between them crackle.

She couldn't wait any longer. Stepping around him, Adelaide grasped the lapels on his jacket and pushed Kingston back against the door. He didn't put up any resistance, instead letting her move him into position. She liked this part of him, the sexy, quiet-as-a-mouse teacher that she could control with a gentle shove.

His eyes darkened and his tongue swept out, licking along his bottom lip. Plump flesh that she wanted to bite. Pressing herself against him, Adelaide lifted onto her tiptoes and dragged his face to hers by the nape of his neck. She followed the path his tongue had taken with her own and slid her other hand to his hip, pulling him closer. His eyes rolled back in his head and he moaned softly. She nipped his bottom lip between hers, before sinking her teeth into the flesh there. Kingston inhaled sharply and his eyes snapped to hers. There was no mistaking the need there. The barely constrained desire.

She was right. He was like a pent-up lion, stalking across his cage, ready to roar and show her just what kind of king of the jungle he was. His nostrils flared and his pupils glazed over. Desire looked damn good on him. That look, the alpha predator waiting to be set free lit a fire inside her. His semi grew harder against her belly as he tugged her hips, grinding against her. It didn't matter that they had layers of material between them; Adelaide knew he would be a hell of a handful. There was no mistaking the generous bulge he sported even when he was soft.

With each slow grinding thrust, he rubbed himself on her, sending sparks of awareness to her clit. She was coming apart at the seams and if she didn't get her hand, lips, or her pussy around that gorgeous shaft, she was going to combust.

"Kiss me," he ordered, his voice a low rasp. Adelaide had never heard a sexier sound.

Cupping his face, she licked his bottom lip again before pulling back in a tease. She was on the edge, her restraint so close to snapping that she was going out of her mind. She wanted, no needed, to let that beast out to play. For all his talk of how he would care for her, Adelaide needed Kingston to step up, to look after her.

One hand slid down to her arse, gripping the cheek tightly, the other cupping the back of her head. He pulled her close and didn't give her a chance to hesitate. To overthink. His lips slammed against hers and he kissed her hard, his tongue forcing her mouth open as he hoisted her up. A squeak ripped past her lips, surprise shocking her into action. She wrapped her legs around his waist, and arms around his shoulders as he growled and shifted her, moving her up and down so she rubbed against his thick shaft. It was as if Adelaide weighed nothing, Kingston not even breaking a sweat as he held her weight in one hand, his other still holding her face to his.

She melted against him, wanting to keep holding on like a koala up a gum tree. Kingston growled and punched his hips forward as he pulled her weight down and Adelaide cried out at the quickening that sparked under her skin. "Oh fuck," she breathed, breaking away from his lips. He growled again, the vibration travelling through her chest and throat where Kingston had pressed his lips. Dragging her up the length of his cock, he thrust hard again, pulling her down once more and Adelaide shuddered.

Spinning her around, he shoved her up against the wall and rutted against her, long hard thrusts that rubbed the cotton of her underwear against her clit as he bit and licked the sensitive skin of her throat. Head thrown back, fingers in those thick, dark-chocolate locks, Adelaide moaned as Kingston cupped her other arse cheek in his hand and ground down harder.

"Can you come like this?" he murmured against her pulse point, scraping his teeth over the tendon there. The lick of pain thrust her to the edge, leaving her teetering there.

One more thrust and she'd be there

"Keep going," she begged as he retreated. The throb Kingston had ignited spread like wildfire through her with his next thrust. Her orgasm slammed into Adelaide. Its intensity took her by surprise, stealing her breath as she let out a silent scream as she shook in Kingston's hold. Her pussy clamped down, rhythmically contracting as waves of ecstasy crashed into her. But he kept going, kept up his hard grind as she cried out again, the sparks renewing themselves as he kept up the pressure against her clit.

Adelaide slumped against Kingston, her breaths choppy and bones turned to wet noodles. He hummed and effortlessly carried her across the room to the doorway off the lounge area.

With the lights still switched off, King laid her down on the pillowy bed, kissing his way along the V-shaped neckline of the cable knit sweater she wore as the sound of his boots hitting the floor echoed through the room. He slid his hands down, cupping her breasts before moving further, stealing up underneath the jumper and pushing it up. Her bare belly was exposed and Adelaide wished she'd thought to toss off her coat before she'd been whisked into the bedroom.

"Arms up," he mouthed against her belly button, before licking it and kissing a line up the centre of her body to her bra as he worked the material up. Kingston left a trail of fire in his wake, her clit throbbing again. With deft fingers, he ripped the clothes off her, her coat going flying at the same time as her jumper, leaving her only in a white T-shirt material bra. Kingston shrugged out of his jacket, leaving him in a long-sleeved shirt, fitted sweater, and those sexy-as-sin jeans. He hovered above her, his breath washing over her chest. Her nipples pebbled in the chill and she groaned, rubbing her pussy over her jeans.

Even in the dim light filtering in from the partially open blind, he was larger than life. His broad shoulders and the strength and heat radiating from him had her aching. Need pulsed through her. She needed more.

"Hands off my pussy," he growled, shifting to kneel back on his heels. Knees spread, he pushed Adelaide's legs apart, removing any way of gaining friction where she needed it most. Her hips arching up off the bed and her frustrated cry kicked Kingston into action. He slid her boots off without any flair, tossing them backward, her socks following quickly. The buttons on her fly were almost torn off when he tugged. She shifted, bending at the knees to bring her legs together when he curled his fingers around the waistband and tugged them down. Off they went, exposing her to him in her white panties. They weren't sexy—she didn't even own proper lacy or satin lingerie—but the way King's breath caught made her feel like a centrefold.

His gaze burned a path down her body emboldening her. She reached back under her and flicked open the clasp on her bra, sliding her arms out and tossing it aside. Hooking her thumbs under the waistband of her cotton panties, she bit her lip and stared up at him as he watched her every move like a hawk.

"You're exquisite," he breathed, his hands coming to her knees and pressing her legs open. "Mmm, you're right. Perfectly manicured," he purred, bending until his chin rubbed the tiny patch of hair she kept trimmed short. His whiskers rubbing her sensitive mound were like live wires, electrical currents lighting her up as he licked at her skin. She cried out, arching into him as he circled his thumbs on the inside of her thighs. Adelaide squirmed, desperate for him to get closer to where she needed him.

A puff of breath on her pussy had her shuddering. Desperate for touch. Then he was there, lowering his tongue to her clit, circling it before he sucked it between his lips. Adelaide's hips bowed off the bed and incoherent words fell from her mouth as Kingston used her motion to slide a hand under her arse. His thumb circled her hole and with the other, used two fingers to tease the opening of her pussy. He slid them up and down, pinching her labia gently as he ate her like a man starved. He was all writhing tongue at her opening, soft beard on her thighs, and his calloused fingertips rough against the walls of her pussy.

"Grip your knees," he ordered, and Adelaide complied, not even hesitating for a moment. "Knees against your chest. Open yourself up for me, gorgeous." She did, but heat washed over her, embarrassment mixing with a wash of vulnerability. "Oh yeah," he growled. "Such pretty holes."

"Oh God," she cried as Kingston shifted, lifting her hips even more. She was bent like a pretzel, her knees tight against her chest as he licked lower, his tongue circling her pucker. One flick, then two and Adelaide cried out on a shuddery breath, and he slid two fingers deep into her pussy. Her walls clamped down tight on him and he hummed, the motion sending another bolt of lightning through her.

"So tight. So perfect," he murmured before circling her hole again with his tongue. She'd tried anal with a toy once, the vibrating plug that she recommended to all her partygoers, but it hadn't been like this. It was as if every nerve ending was directed there, sending her higher with every move of his frisky tongue and deep delving fingers.

Kingston moved up again, licking at her clit and around his fingers, his thumb swiping her juices down to her pucker as he continued to soften the muscle there. Adelaide gripped her knees in a white-knuckled hold, the sensations ricocheting around her body overwhelming. He scraped his teeth over her clit as he stiffened his tongue and slid it into her pussy alongside his fingers. She tightened around him, his fingers perfectly curled to tag her G-spot with each movement. She was climbing, inching up the rollercoaster rung by rung, nearing the peak. She hovered there, ready to fly, and Kingston shifted again moving his tongue back to her clit.

She huffed out a breath, losing ground. He reacted immediately, doubling his efforts. Sucking her clit between his lips, he gave her that bite of pain she didn't even know she liked and curled his fingers more, plunging them deep. Without giving her a chance to tense up again, he slid his thumb into her arse and she shouted out, her climax taking her by storm. Lightning crashed and thunder rumbled long and loud as Adelaide was tossed around in the maelstrom like a dingy in a cyclone. He kept going, sucking, licking, and fingering her until she was too sensitive, too overwhelmed.

He pulled back then, twining their fingers together and kissing and licking his way up her belly until her hands were up by her shoulders. He sucked on her nipples, and Adelaide let out a shaky breath. "Mmm, you like that?" he asked, his stubble brushing against her sensitive skin.

"God, yes," she breathed on a moan.

She could feel his lips curl against her breast, a smile in his voice when he asked, "Can you come with me sucking on you?"

"Don't think so."

"Sounds like a challenge." He rested his weight against her, and Adelaide melted into the mattress. His solid weight, the soft cotton of his shirt against her mons and the swipe of his tongue and suction of his lips had her spiralling again, clawing her way to another orgasm. When he ripped it out of her, pinning her to the bed with one arm, and sucking a mark into the side of her breast as he pinched her nipple, she screamed, her legs squeezing his hips as she rubbed her pussy against his abs.

Adelaide didn't know whether she passed out or was carried away to another planet. She was floating in heaven as he shifted her, pulling the covers over her as he disappeared. Back a moment later, she jumped at the contact of the warm washcloth on her leg, but he manoeuvred her, gently wiping her clean. Her insides were like jelly, a buzz still traversing through her body. He slipped in behind her, taking her into his arms. Adelaide registered material between them, a soft cotton that she burrowed into. Sleep soon claimed her.

FIVE

Liam

"So what's been goin' on, man?" he asked Lij. He and Elijah had been friends for ever, but in the months since he'd returned from France, things had changed. They used to hang out together all the time, but now Lij was always busy. Liam couldn't begrudge him though; he was working and helping out his family.

"Nothing much. Working on a new client's manuscript. It needs a lot of corrections, so it's taking me a while to get through. Misplaced modifiers and long paragraphs every-where." He tossed the football back to Liam and laughed when Liam lurched forward to catch it and glared.

"Dude, you suck. Seriously, I'm standing right here and you still can't toss the ball accurately." He shook his head and pursed his lips, but it was all an act. This was what they did, Liam throwing the ball right into Lij's hands while he made Liam run for it. "What about your mum and sis? How are they going?"

"Mum's good. She's finally listened and dropped a shift at work. She doesn't want to rely on me, but I make enough that she doesn't need to work seven days. And I dunno about Addy. I didn't see her yesterday."

"How? She literally sleeps outside your room." Liam tossed Lij the ball and he fumbled the catch before finally grasping it.

"She's been dating this new bloke. Seems to be getting serious too, if her not coming home last night is any indication. Usually when she goes out on a date she comes home." He shrugged and passed the ball back like it was no big deal. But it was. She was… Liam didn't even know how to describe her. She was bright and bubbly, like a beacon lighting up all the dark spaces. He loved seeing that incandescent light inside her glow brightly.

Whoever the guy was, he must have been something special to capture her attention. An unfamiliar prickle washed over him, and Liam wasn't even sure how to label it. Frustration simmered in his veins. Maybe a little anger too. Addy was like a little sister to him, and the urge to put himself between her and this new bloke was overwhelming. "Hey, you gonna pass that back or you trying to burst it?" Lij pointed at the ball he was white-knuckling, and Liam shook off the frustration that had enveloped him.

"Yeah, ah, sorry." They tossed the ball back and forth until a silver Subaru pulled up at the curb. It was mid-morning, late enough that it wasn't a walk of shame but a weekend away. A burly guy, who had to be close to his height but much broader in the shoulders, got out and rushed around to get the door for Addy and Liam's pulse tripped. She stepped out and he reached in for her backpack. They stayed close, moving inside each other's personal space. There was a comfort between them too. Chemistry that was off the charts. Liam bit his tongue trying to calm his racing heart.

When the man slung her bag over his shoulder, Addy gripped his belt buckle, pulling him against her. The smile he shot her was filled with affection, warmth lighting up his eyes. He cupped her face, reverently touching her hair as he leaned down to kiss her. It was chaste, a soft brush of his lips against hers, and Liam's breath caught. Heat crawled through his veins, a tingling sensation in his fingers. What would it be like to caress Addy in the same way? To see if her skin was as soft as it looked, and her hair as silky. But that was ridiculous. He couldn't. They weren't like that. They never had been. So why did Liam suddenly want to know? Why did he want to find out what it was like to be a part of that magnificent picture?

Addy looked tiny wrapped up in the man. He couldn't turn away. The bloke's arms were like tree trunks. Thick and strong. Liam tried to shake off wanting to know what they felt like. When Addy slid her hands up, they didn't even come close to covering his bicep, and Liam shivered. The image of the two of them together was incendiary. He shouldn't—no couldn't—want her. She was Lij's little sister. It was a line he couldn't cross.

He watched as her guy stroked her cheek and dipped his chin once more to press another lingering kiss to her lips. Would they be strawberry flavoured like her favourite balm? What would the scent of her skin be? What would the scent of her and her guy be like mingled together?

No.

No, no, no. He definitely couldn't go there.

He had to back the fuck off now. But he couldn't tear his eyes away, watching as he held her and kissed her slowly, worshipping her. Liam's gut twisted. He sucked in a breath and erected, brick by brick, the wall of attitude he needed to process what the fuck these insane thoughts running around his stupid head were. It was as if there had been a seismic shift in the ground under his feet since they'd pulled up. Actually, since Lij had told him that Addy was seeing someone. Fuck. He cleared his throat and shot a look at Lij that he hoped looked more incredulous than pained. "This guy? Really?"

"Why not him?" Lij asked. "He's hot in a lumberjack kind of way, and they seem to have plenty to talk about—they've been on the phone every night this week."

"Yeah, 'cause it looks like they're doin' lots of talking," he muttered, forcing himself to look away. "He's gotta be twice her age, and who the hell drives a Subaru?"

Lij rolled his eyes and passed the ball back, but Liam was done.

Without even knowing what he intended to do, he stalked over to them. With every step closer, his view improved and he watched, riveted as the man's tongue dipped into her mouth, teasing her lip. She smiled into the kiss as he pressed a hand to her lower back and cradled her head with the other.

When they finally broke apart, Liam blinked, meeting the other man's eyes. Heat flared in them, his pupils lust drunk and blown wide. His kiss swollen lips glistened with the remnants of Addy's gloss and he was breathing hard, Addy's body pressed against his from shoulder to knee. Their gazes locked and Liam shifted, the low thrum of desire pooling in his belly and waking up his cock. God damn, the man had the most spectacular eyes. Dark and rich like melted chocolate. His pouty lips were framed by a few-days-old stubble that looked soft to the touch. He was gorgeous.

Wait, what? Gorgeous? Liam gave himself a mental slap across the back of the head. What was he thinking? He'd give it to Lij—the dude was good-looking—but Liam hadn't been checking him out, not really.

"He's not quite twice my age, only seven years older." Adelaide's words stopped him in his tracks. "The Subaru lets him carry his bike or surfboard, or whatever else he feels like taking somewhere—"

"What, like bodies?" Liam looked at her with a raised eyebrow, his attempt at humour falling flat. Addy's laugh in response was harsh. Derisive. She flashed him a look filled with contempt, and it was like a kick in the guts. She'd always been sweet and cute. Years ago, she'd been the annoying little sister who idolised her older brother. But then she'd grown up. He'd be blind not to see her beauty, but this craziness that had swept over him was... ridiculous. It had to be just a momentary lapse. His brain catching up something that he'd always known but never really seen.

She was beautiful and now she had a man who was… equally hot?

"Kingston, my dickhead of a next-door neighbour and— for reasons completely unbeknownst to me—my brother's best friend, Liam."

"Pleased to meet you, mate," Kingston replied with a half-grin, his voice washing over Liam like an expensive whiskey sliding down his throat.

Lij was wrong in his assessment of the lumberjack vibe. The guy was more refined than that. His cream knit sweater was far too sophisticated for that. His blue jeans were too clean, even though they were well-worn. They looked comfortable too, the denim soft where they hugged thighs that Liam was hella jealous of. He was built for speed, with smaller compact muscles. Kingston, on the other hand, was sheer bulk. The short beard gave him a ruggedness that bordered on smouldering, and he found himself wanting to run his fingers through it. Was it as soft as it looked?

It was insane how topsy-turvy his world suddenly was. Checking out Adelaide and her new guy? Liam didn't do that. What the hell was wrong with him? Scowling, he glanced at Kingston again. Reflected back was a zen-like calm. His smile, just a small tilt of his lips upward, was the same—relaxed and at ease. Kingston's voice too. It was deep and smooth. The kind you could listen to for hours and never get sick of hearing.

As much as Liam wanted to feign indifference toward the man, his first impression was the opposite. Without a word, Kingston was drawing him in, making Liam want to get to know him. The notion was ridiculous. How could someone let off tranquil vibes? How could they put out a calmness into the world that settled him without even saying a word? The idea of it set Liam on edge. Put him on high alert. Kingston held out his hand and without even thinking, Liam reciprocated. They closed the gap between them and electricity zinged up his arm from their connection. Kingston's hand was dry and cool. Calloused. Liam didn't want to let go, squeezing harder to keep their connection intact.

Liam ground his teeth together, his head and his body in a desperate battle to break the contact between him and Kingston or to keep it going. He wasn't sure which part of him would win. But Kingston didn't flinch. It was as if he was waiting for Liam to get over himself and decide what his body was doing. Liam looked for the fire he managed to provoke in so many people, but all he saw were deep still waters.

He exhaled slowly, loosening his grip and Kingston blinked, his stare seeming to communicate a million words to Liam, without his understanding any of them. When Kingston turned his attention to Lij, Liam wanted to object. To have those pools of liquid silk on him again. It had never bothered him before, but Liam had instantly hated the idea of Addy having a boyfriend when Lij had told him. He didn't think there was a single man who would be worthy of her—but Kingston was something else. Something that terrified and enthralled Liam simultaneously.

Addy moved to stand in front of Kingston, her arms crossed over her chest looking up at him with fire in her gaze. Her lips were pressed together, pursed in determination, her eyes narrowed a challenge in them. Liam's dick twitched again, loving her sass and the way she stood up to him. Addy wasn't scared to ride his arse if she thought he was being a dickhead. She never hesitated to call him out on his shit either. Was it completely fucked up that he loved provoking a reaction from her?

His stare locked with Kingston's once more. Heat suffused Liam, those umber eyes on him almost a caress. He shivered, unsure whether the perusal turned him on—a match to Addy's challenge—or was a dare to lash out against him. Liam didn't intimidate easily, despite being a lover, not a fighter. He pursed his lips, his ears flaming as they continued watching each other. There was a shift in King's expression. The heat had diffused, humour and light danced in his expression. There was a spark in his gaze that matched Addy's zest for life.

"Liam, pull your head outta your arse for five minutes and quit your stare-down." He blinked, shaking out of the spell that Kingston had weaved over him. "Kingston's a nice guy. You'd actually like him if you gave him a chance. Stop acting like some macho idiot that puffs up his chest when he's feeling threatened."

His mouth dropped open in shock. What was she talking about? Threatened? Not so much. Inexplicably turned on, definitely. He couldn't even begin to figure out what the hell was going on with him, but he needed to get out of there.

"Kingston, my brother Eli. Eli, Kingston."

"Good to meet you, bud. Ignore Liam. He gets hangry when he hasn't eaten a steak in a few hours." They shook hands with a smile, and a thick sludge slithered through him like oil, sitting heavily in his gut and coiling tight. An irrational anger pulsed in his veins, the desire to get Lij's hands off Kingston surprising Liam. It lifted, like the sun coming out from behind a cloud once Lij let go and stepped back. But Addy had seen something in him. With her eyes narrowed as if she was trying to solve a puzzle, she studied him. Her keen gaze assessed the freefall in his belly as he zoomed around the rollercoaster that had taken up residence since they'd arrived home.

Liam shifted his weight from side to side, understanding in that moment what it was like for an organism to be studied under a microscope. He was all muddled up inside, confusion reigning supreme as his gaze ping-ponged between the woman he seemed to be seeing for the first time, and the man who'd captured her attention. And his.

Instinct told him to hide. To get out from under Addy's watchful gaze before he revealed just how shaken up he was. Frustrated, he turned and walked away from them. Better that she think he was a rude prick than one who was... he didn't even know what.

Snatching up the ball, Liam jogged up the drive and let his back gate bang closed behind him as he walked out back. It would be less than five minutes of peace that he had before Adelaide barged in and ripped him a new one, but so be it. He rolled his eyes and went straight to the kitchen, putting together a protein shake for his mid-morning meal.

Lij was joking, but he actually hadn't been that far off the mark. He did get hangry.

Six

Kingston

King dashed up the stairs to the landing where he'd dropped his phone, answering it on the third ring as it was about to go to a message. "Hey, you, how are you?"

"I'm good," Eve answered. In a sing-song voice, she added, "Whatcha doing? I haven't interrupted anything have I?"

He barked out a laugh. "Only gardening."

She grumbled, unimpressed. "Disappointing. How did the date go?" Eve, god love her, was nosy but it was out of friendship, not a need for gossip. She was a vault and loyal to a fault. She'd seen him at his worst and was like a guard dog with him, complete with both bark and bite for anyone who hated on him.

"The date went brilliantly." He hesitated, not adding more. He was oddly protective about the time he'd spent with Adds. He wanted to shield their fledgling relationship from anything that might damage it. Like a tiny seedling, he wanted to let it take root and strengthen first before exposing it to hail and frost. It wasn't that he wanted to hide or tuck themselves away in a bubble. Instead, it was more that he wanted to enjoy their time together and ride the high of a new relationship without the pressure of other people's expectations. These last few days had been special to him. If it made him selfish to want that to continue for as long as possible without the world sticking its nose in, so be it.

"That's it? That's all you're going to give me?" she asked with an exasperated sigh.

He rolled his eyes at her antics. He trusted her. He knew Eve would always be in his corner. "I only just dropped Adds home. I didn't go inside or anything, but I met her brother and his best mate." He didn't elaborate. He wasn't even sure how to. Eli was a lot like Adelaide—he could see the familial resemblance—but Liam? The man had taken his breath away. He was gorgeous. Brown hair and green-hazel eyes that zeroed in on him and pinned him in place. It was as if Liam had looked straight into him, seeing inside him to his very core. He'd tried to stay calm, tried to slow his frantic heartbeat to something that wouldn't give away how strong his attraction had been.

Liam ticked every one of King's buttons. Tall and lithe, with compact muscles that whispered speed and power. Seeing the way he handled the ball, even just as he and Eli tossed it between them in the yard, was a study in restraint. King had flat out drooled. That natural talent, honed by years of dedication and hard work, was breathtaking. The first thing he'd done when he'd arrived home was look him up and watch reels of his plays. It had hit him then how tossing the ball to Eli in the yard wouldn't even use 1 percent of the talent the man had. He was literally a Master—both in name and in ability. And yeah, gorgeous.

King snapped back to the conversation when Eve asked, "Does she still live at home? How much younger than you is she?" The surprise in her voice lifted her tone to a higher pitch, but there was no judgement. Never judgement from her. He hadn't told her they were a few years apart—King hadn't mentioned anything other than she was beautiful and fun and had a second date planned.

"She's twenty-three and still lives at home because she helps care for her grandfather." He bit back the smile that threatened to rival the sun for size and added, "We had a great time, Eve. I really like her."

She squealed. "I'm so happy for you. You deserve someone who makes you sound all giddy."

King huffed out a laugh and was grateful to be alone where no one could see the heat crawling up his throat to his cheeks.

"Tell me a bit about her. I don't even know her name."

"Okay, um... Like I said, Adelaide's twenty-three—"

"Pretty name."

"Yeah, it is. She's an old soul but fun and passionate too. We can talk for hours. I told her I'd lost a lot of weight and she was incredible about it. Looked at me like I was some kind of superhero for changing my life." This time, his smile was one of those sappy I'm-already-falling-head-over-heels-for-this-woman smiles as he spoke.

"That's because you are, King. It took guts to follow the nutritionist's advice and that PT you had was insane—what was his name?"

"Mike. He's a good guy. Did what it took to get me where I needed to be so I could run. It was so far above and beyond when he taught me how to surf."

"But see that's it, King. You inspire people to do that because of who you are. The way you stuck with the plan and achieved your goals was inspiring." He waved off the compliment. She'd said it a thousand times and he'd never believed her. Odd that when Adds said it, he started to listen. *Huh.*

Leaning back against the wall, his elbow propped up on his bent knee and his eyes closed to the sun, he added, "She works in sales. Think Avon and Tupperware but adult toys, and she has this great Patreon—"

"Wait, what?" Eve asked. "Say that again." He did, getting as far as mentioning her Patreon for a second time before Eve interrupted him once more. "King, are you sure that it's a good idea dating her?"

"What? Why?" he asked, his indignance clear in the defensiveness of his tone.

"Bloody hell, I'm sorry. I didn't mean it like that." He growled and she hurried to continue. "I meant that don't you have a morality clause in your contract? If you're dating a woman who sells sex toys, then you might be risking your job." Her voice was gentle, but he could hear the concern in it. "I don't want you to get hurt because of what someone else thinks."

He scrubbed his hand over his face, rubbing his eyes. "There's nothing wrong with what she's doing. Her clients are adults and her Patreon isn't explicit or anything, and even if it was, it would still be fine. It's behind a paywall anyway."

"I agree. One hundred percent."

There was a pause, and King resisted the temptation to jump in and defend her. He knew Eve. He trusted her. If she said she agreed with him, then she did, but he could also tell she had more to say, and he desperately wanted the chance for her to explain before he tore her a new one.

"I don't know if I'm being paranoid—I don't exactly know what it's like to work at the school—but would they make assumptions that you're dating a sex worker—"

"Whose side are you on?" he demanded, his voice a sharp bark.

"King," she cautioned, "cut the crap. You know I'm on your side. I'm trying to protect you. I just said that I agreed with you. Even if she was doing explicit videos, it doesn't change my view that it's her choice. It doesn't make someone a pariah if they're a sex worker. There's nothing bad about it, and even if you or I didn't agree with her career, ultimately, it's her body and her choice."

Damn right it was, but it was an argument that he didn't need to have, especially not with his friend who seemed to be agreeing with him. It didn't make his frustration and the dogged need to defend Adelaide dissipate though.

"I'm not saying break up with Adelaide; I'd never say that, especially not if she makes you as happy as you seem to be. What I am saying is that maybe this is one of those times work doesn't need to find out about your private life."

"You're saying keep our relationship a secret?" Even he could hear the hurt and despair in his voice. He wanted to put her beautiful face on a billboard. To have one of those planes towing a banner behind it or a sky writer paint news of their relationship from horizon to horizon.

"Not secret per se, but maybe just on the down low. I've seen it far too many times where people lose opportunities because of what they put on social media. I'm worried what the school will do if they get a complaint, no matter how ridiculous it is."

He groaned. She was right. The school wouldn't care that Adelaide was a good person, or that she was trying to help people. They would likely conclude she was promoting immoral activities, especially with placing content behind a paywall. He would be guilty by association. The school had strict social media policies. His profile was locked down to private, but he was active in the school's groups, and he was friends with a number of the teachers and other staff members. He hated that there was even the remotest possibility that Adelaide could pose a risk to his career. But there was no doubt in his mind that the school would be in the wrong, not her. Hiding her like a dirty secret was out.

No, just no. There was no way he would do it. He'd change jobs before he hurt her like that.

"Talk to her about it. Be honest. Show her your contract if you have to. Just be upfront."

He nodded, then realized she wouldn't see him and mumbled his agreement. "I'll just have to change jobs."

"Woah, that's a big step. I'm... happy for you, I really am." Eve's voice brightened. "She's obviously special. You wouldn't even consider leaving if she wasn't important."

"I wouldn't. But I think she's worth it." There was no thinking though. He knew it down to his bones. Adelaide was special, and even in the short time they'd been together he knew he wanted her for the long haul. Changing jobs wouldn't even be a blip on his radar so far as sacrifices go if it meant being able to be with her.

"She sounds wonderful, King. I can't wait to meet her."

He could hear the smile in her voice, and the knowledge lifted him. But the reality of the conversation he had to have dawned on him, and his spirits dropped like an anvil.

He rubbed his forehead, massaging his temples with one hand while holding the phone to his ear with the other. "I can't believe I have to even have this conversation. It's screwed up."

"It is. I'm sorry, King."

"Don't be. It's okay." He groaned. "But I should go. I need to talk to Adds."

SEVEN

Liam

He lifted the bottle of Bundy Rum and took a long swig, wiping the back of his hand across his mouth after he'd swallowed. He cringed, shuddering as the strong-as-fuck liquor burned a path down his throat. He didn't even like it, but it was the only liquor his dad drank, and during the season, Liam didn't indulge, so he didn't have any of his own on hand. The rum was the only bottle in the cupboard, forgotten from his parents' last trip.

Addy hadn't gone to see him. He'd waited for her. Sat in his room like a stalker to see if he could get a glimpse of her through Lij's open blinds. That had been a bust, so he'd parked his butt in the guest bedroom by the front door to watch out for her in case she came up his drive.

But nothing. She'd just gone inside and gotten on with her day. Lij had done the same. There were no recriminations for his rude departure and no complaints because of the less than stellar reception he'd given King. No nothing. Except for silence. It was as if he simply ceased to exist to them once he'd crossed that threshold into his house.

He'd been rocked to his core. His feet were barely holding him up. He wasn't normally a dick, but he'd officially crossed the line that morning. Addy not going there to entertain his pathetic self shouldn't surprise him. She wouldn't have had any idea of the apparent identity crisis he was having. Not that she had any responsibility toward him either.

Logically he knew all that, but he was still hurt that he was alone when they were enjoying their family together. It stung that he was so clearly an outsider. It shouldn't bother him anymore. After all, it was what he experienced every day with his own family. But his mind ran in circles, tripping him with all the worst-case scenarios it could think up while he was drunk.

Was Addy getting a boyfriend the beginning of the end for his friendship with the McMahons? Had he brought it on himself when he'd let jealousy well up and explode in the form of a bad attitude? He'd acted like a caveman, staring down the new suitor as if challenging him to a battle for the fair maiden's honour. Except, that didn't ring true either. He'd admired Kingston just as much as Addy. Individually as much as together. He'd experienced something, but jealousy didn't seem like the right word. He'd watched them. He'd wanted… something. He couldn't put his finger on precisely what though. Couldn't identify what the desire was other than that he'd had his eyes opened. It was as if King was shining a spotlight on Addy, and he was seeing her in a new light. It wasn't as if it was reciprocated—she was dating King not him.

So why was he remembering the distinct feeling of jealousy? Why was he running through their interaction from start to finish, knowing that he'd been envious? It had slithered through him like a poison, stirring the waters until they were murky.

He closed his eyes and replayed the morning. Playing catch, the car pulling up, his feet carrying him to them, heat as he watched them kiss, a desire to touch, awareness of Adelaide—the realization that he'd been privileged enough to watch the most beautiful woman he'd ever seen grow up. Want. Shaking hands and the spark of energy that had ignited, staring at Kingston's eyes and getting lost in those deep tranquil pools of still waters. Adelaide's fire. Lij reaching out.

A growl erupted from his chest, a possessive, feral sound.

Oh, fuck. He had been jealous. Of Lij. When he touched Kingston. Liam wanted to do it. He'd never wanted to let go of the man's hand to begin with. He'd held on, squeezing and savouring the cool, rough palm in his.

Liam's eyes shot open. His world had tipped again. But this time, it righted itself. He was no longer teetering on a tight rope. It was as if his feet had returned to solid ground. He could see clearly, a veil having been lifted from his eyes. Kingston had shown him that he wanted Addy. He'd shone a light on her beauty in the way he kissed her, the gentle touch and reverent caress of her skin.

But then his eyes had been opened again. Lij had reached out and shaken Kingston's hand. He hadn't been jealous of Kingston with Adelaide. Not at all. The man had captured his attention and confused the fuck out of Liam, but he hadn't been jealous of him. No, the jealousy had been reserved for Lij. Even thinking back on the way their hands had clasped together innocently in a simple hand-shake had Liam's muscles tensing and his teeth grinding to-gether. He was readying to fight, to aggressively defend his territory. But defend it against whom? His laid-back, go-with-the-flow, introverted best mate? Adelaide's brother? The one man who'd never want the woman he'd apparently been blinded to before that morning, and the man she had on her arm?

And why was he even including Kingston in the equa-tion? It wasn't like he was attracted to men. But Liam couldn't deny that his possessiveness extended to the man. Was it a recognition that he and Addy were a package deal? Perhaps. But it still seemed outlandish, surreal even, be-cause that instinct to fight—to defend what was his, despite them not being his at all—was far more than a simple acknowledgement that Addy and Kingston were together. This was want and desire, although for what he didn't know. There wasn't enough alcohol in the world to figure out how far he dared let his imagination run, and drinking until his inhibitions fled certainly wasn't something he could do in the middle of the season.

The quiet of the evening settled over him like a heavy cloud. He was alone, the quiet a constant companion. It was a dangerous reminder of how disconnected he was to his family—something he never liked to dwell on—when he was already so precariously unbalanced. It wasn't like Lij to leave Liam to his own devices on his one day off that week. They'd spent his free day together for as long as he remembered. The niggling voice of his conscience asked why he hadn't gone to their house after he'd finished sulking. Liam couldn't give any form of satisfactory answer to that question. The most honest answer, though, was that he wasn't sure if he was ready. But silence reminded him of his parents and that always hit him hard. It played games with his mind and tended to attack him like a coward punch to the back of the head.

Liam knew his hatred of silences was fear manifesting—fear of losing the people who loved him. He loved how Lij could happily retreat to his room and be perfectly content by himself or with the small group of people he let into his inner circle. Liam was the opposite. He needed people around him and the sense of inclusion that gave him. Anyone who knew anything about him would label it as a fear of abandonment, and it totally was. But that was Liam.

He closed his eyes again, determined to enjoy the silence for once in his life. Shuffling down on the chair, he spread his legs and rested his head against the back, the tide of sleep slowly rising. Adelaide's smile against Kingston's lips flashed in his mind's eye. Yeah, that was more like it—thinking about a beautiful woman in his arms. He dropped his hands in his lap, adjusting the bulge of his semi. He could imagine them together too. Her delicate hands balancing her weight as she rode him, her breasts bouncing as she rocked her hips taking him deep.

Liam shifted and a symphony of ecstasy-filled moans filled the air. Kingston hit a sensitive spot inside her and Liam kissed her, their tongues tangling as he brushed his thumb over her nipple. Adelaide broke the kiss, panting, and Liam licked a path down her throat to her breast, latching onto her pert nipple. He shuddered, warm lips closing around his cock. The suction was enough to send him cross-eyed. He moaned, thrusting into the wet heat as he tasted Addy's dewy skin. In the dim light, he reached out, running his fingertips over the curve of her spine down to her waist and the swell of her arse. Sweat-slicked skin slid under his fingertips. Gooseflesh appeared as he chased the path with his tongue. His cock slipped free from the other man's mouth and—

Liam sucked in a breath and scrambled to sit up. He was awake. Very awake.

His heart pounded against his ribcage. Oh God. Oh fuck. What the hell? A threesome would be hot, especially with two people as gorgeous as the woman next door... and maybe her beau too. But what did it mean? Sure, he could see himself having a threesome with multiple women, but since when did another man factor into the equation. It hadn't ever before. But bloody hell, the visual was the hottest thing he'd ever conjured up.

He sighed. Nothing could ever happen between them, and the sooner he stopped fantasizing about it, the better off he'd be. Addy was dating Kingston. Liam was best mates with her brother and... and that was it. It had to be it. He couldn't afford to even risk thinking about more when he would lose everything as a result.

He rubbed his eyes, shock still pulsing around in his body. He pulled his sweats away from his erection, adjusting himself. The wet patch from the steady stream of pre-cum was a sticky mess against his leg. "You stupid thing. Now you're gonna get interested? When she has a boyfriend?" Unsurprisingly his dick didn't answer, but the sliver of want that passed through him when he thought about them together centred there. "Couldn't have been when we were teenagers, could it? I could have at least blamed being drunk and stupid then. And what the fuck? A dude?"

Kingston definitely weaved some kind of magic. Something that drew Liam in as if he was on a lead. The man had an inner spark that lit him up, and it had captured Liam's attention. And apparently that of his dick too.

He needed to keep reminding himself Addy was out of reach. Echoes of his parents' voices in his head made the rum slosh around in his belly. *You're not good enough. Do better. Be better. Try harder. More, more, more.*

Story of his life.

But even if he was good enough, it still wouldn't help.

He'd been one of the best a couple of years earlier—the winger with the most impressive stats for the season. People were watching him, praising him. It had been… nice. To be noticed and recognized as being good for once. But it was nothing more than being a big fish in a little pond. Australia's rugby league talent pool was deep. Lij had told him over and over that he should be proud of his efforts, but it never rang true for him. He put getting into the pro-league down to a fluke—he was in the right place at the right time to be seen by the scout. He'd worked hard to make the people he loved proud, but it was never enough. Not really.

Then he thought his life had changed. He thought he'd finally achieved something to really write home about.

Liam would never forget the night his agent called. He'd been lying on the couch at Lij's house as they watched a movie together. Addy was on the floor closest to him passing the popcorn between them, and Lij had the armchair. His phone rang and Lij paused the movie. He would have blown it off, but his agent only called when it was important. The news she'd delivered had floored him. An offer from one of the top French teams. Addy hadn't been impressed by him even then. She'd walked out in a huff, dumping the giant bowl of popcorn on the floor.

She'd been right not to be impressed. Moving was so much more of an adjustment than he'd expected. Deferring the degree he was already failing had come as a relief, but leaving his friends was tough. Maybe there was a part of him even then that had recognized walking away from Addy and Lij wasn't a good idea. Playing was... a challenge. One he hadn't lived up to.

He'd been scooped from the pond he was used to playing in and dumped into the ocean and Liam simply was not equipped to swim in it.

The season had only just started when it all turned to shit. It snowballed from there, like a dung beetle's giant ball of crap growing and gathering in speed until it crashed. The resulting fallout was reminiscent of a sewer exploding.

He'd blamed the language barrier. Calls were made in rapid-fire French, but there wasn't a whole lot of conversation on the field. Looking back, he could see that he hadn't trusted his instincts. His confidence had taken a battering and the voices in his head that he could usually silence grew louder and louder. He got stuck in there, overthinking everything rather than letting instinct rule his plays. He'd trained hard and played harder, but it was no use. The tragedy was that he'd psyched himself out of winning before he'd even walked onto the field.

The team was welcoming, but he couldn't settle. He couldn't let his walls down and trust them when he he'd been so alone. He knew it was a chicken and egg situation—he'd needed to trust them to be there to catch him to give them an opportunity to prove they were trustworthy. But he'd failed. He hadn't gelled with the team and their plays reflected that. The passes between them were stilted, and even after months of gruelling work, they'd never found their groove. As much as he'd wanted to ace his season abroad and extend it out to a few years, his stats had consistently dropped. In the end, the team was reluctant to renew his contract and Liam had been grateful for the out.

He'd been homesick. Desperate to come home and see the people that mattered to him more than anyone else—Lij and his family. He'd missed all of them and was constantly scrolling their feeds on social media for updates. Even just for photos. Liam hadn't expected to miss Addy as much as Lij, but he had. When he found her Patreon, he'd sat and watched far too many hours of her talking and joking around, teaching him something new every week. He had a new respect for her when he'd seen them. She was quirky and insightful, and her blunt honesty was refreshing. The way she viewed the world inspiring.

Going home and seeing her again was weird though. He'd wanted to tell her that he'd missed her too, but there was a mental block. He couldn't and had no idea why, other than he didn't want Lij to get the wrong idea. The whole debacle just served to highlight that he didn't really belong anywhere except on the outskirts.

The winter breeze held a crispness that shook off the last of his dream-filled nap. He swiped at his phone's screen, bringing up the email from the team's player liaison. Deej had come across from a Sydney team while Liam was in France and got along with everyone. Importantly, he knew how to manage a bunch of overgrown man-children like himself. He seemed like a good bloke, but at the moment, he was Liam's least favourite person.

The email had arrived earlier that afternoon. DJ had pointed out a term in Liam's contract, one he'd hoped would be ignored. No such luck. There was no room for argument in the man's email. Liam knew it was for his own good, but he wasn't happy about it. Liam had two options— re-enrol in his degree or find something else to pursue outside of football. If he didn't, he'd be benched.

He wanted his business degree, but actually reactivating his enrolment was like asking him to climb Mount Everest.

He knew that climbing a mountain began with a first step, but taking that leap—even the barest of shuffles forward—made his heart beat faster and his palms sweat. Liam hated failing at anything, and this degree seemed to be designed specifically to break him. He was good at words. Reading and writing were all good. He could spin a story like the best of their media people. But numbers? They were a foreign language swimming on the page and blurring together into something that was a senseless mess. He'd already flunked his introductory statistics class, so a repeat was necessary. Assuming he passed it the second time around, his reward would be the advanced statistics class.

It was times like this that he wished rugby was more like pro-football in the States—getting his degree out of the way while he played university level football sounded so much better than the path he and the other rugby players took. It was a grassroots community sport relying on volunteer coaches and fundraising. He was lucky—he'd been picked up by a feeder club early on. But like everyone on those teams, he needed something else besides football—something to pay the bills.

He'd still been in high school when he was playing for the feeder club, and then he'd been drafted to the pro-league after he'd graduated. Players were paid well as pros, but injuries, poor performance, bad media coverage, or anything similar could see a player get shunted back down to the reserve level. It happened all the time. Contracts were only renewed if the player was worth it. Caps on the maximum amount a team could spend on player salaries kept the competition between the least and most popular clubs as close to par as possible, but it also meant teams had to pull their limited purse strings tight to get the best outcomes. His and every other players' reality was that they needed a backup for after their playing career ended—a qualification, a business, whatever—because that career could be short. So for the younger players like him, the teams often wrote a condition into their contract requiring them to study or do an apprenticeship to give them a chance at a life once they were no longer playing.

Liam supposed he could get a security licence or maybe even do a personal training course to get them off his back, but he hadn't wanted to settle. He had dreams of what he wanted life after playing to look like, and those plans involved a business degree. He wanted to be a player agent, to negotiate deals, look after media engagement and strategy, PR, and marketing after he'd retired. But to get the degree, to get the career, he had to climb Mt Statistics.

"S'pose I just need to suck it up," he muttered, eyeing the university app that still taunted him every time he unlocked his phone. He was such a masochist.

Before he could rethink things, he opened it, reactivated his enrolment, and sent an email to his advisor. With any luck, he'd be starting classes in a few weeks.

EIGHT

Liam

THREE MONTHS LATER - SEPTEMBER

L iam grabbed a hold of the towel still around his neck and leaned his head against the wall of his cubbyhole in the locker room. He banged it, the sound a dull thud in the nearly empty room. The team had gone into the game with a string of wins, the longest streak in the club's history. But they'd choked when it counted.

He'd choked.

A hand clamped on Liam's shoulder and squeezed. "You did everything you could, mate. Don't beat yourself up. This shit happens," Daz, the team captain, said. He was a good bloke and an even better captain. He knew just what to say, but the truth was undeniable. It was right there in front of them, the final score the written proof.

if he hadn't hesitated, if he hadn't flicked his gaze sideways to see how much space he had to move, they would have won. He would have carried that football over the try line and they would have been five points up, rather than one down. He'd snatched defeat from the hands of victory. Letting the team down killed him. One metre—three feet— was all that separated them from their season ending, and then progressing into the final rounds. And he'd fucked it up.

Daz's footsteps faded, leaving the room silent. Nearly everyone would be on the bus already. If he hung around long enough, they'd leave him there and he could make his own way back to the hotel. It would be a relief not to have to face them, but it would only be delaying the inevitable. The team would eat together that night, a buffet of some sort in the function room; they always hired out when they went to Parramatta for their games. Liam didn't have an excuse for flaking on them, and even if he did, the thought of being alone was worse.

"Get a move on, Masters," Coach called out. "We're waiting on you."

"Go on without me. I'll find my way back to the hotel." His voice sounded thin, like the wall holding back the tide of emotions was about to crumble. He blew out a breath and blinked, willing away the tears that were ready to engulf him.

Footsteps came closer, Coach's rubber-soled shoes squeaking on the polished concrete. "I know it doesn't feel like it, Masters, but you did good out there. This loss is not on your shoulders. It was the fifth tackle, and the other team were just in the right place at the right time. The way you ran for that ball was inspiring. The whole stadium saw how much you wanted it. But no matter how close to the line you were, five guys landing on you is gonna stop you in your tracks."

He turned to face the man who he respected probably above any other. He'd been one of the football greats in his time, and was an even better coach. He deserved the truth. "I hesitated. I looked to see where they were instead of diving for the line. I lost us that game, and no matter which way you sugar-coat it, it'll always be on my shoulders."

"So, you're the only person on that field, hey?" He raised a brow and passed the ever-present football from hand to hand. Gripping the ball, he raised it and pointed his finger at Liam, staring him down. "Lock could have passed in the other direction. Hayes was open. More open than you. Fuimaono was just behind you and closer to Lock. If he'd run half as fast as you, he would have intercepted the ball and those defenders would have had to pivot and stop him. But he didn't. Neither did Lock."

Coach spread his arms and tilted his head as if waiting for Liam to acknowledge his words. But he couldn't. The fact was that his teammates had relied on him to get the ball over the line and he'd failed. Liam dropped his gaze and shook his head, and Coach passed the ball to his other hand again and nudged Liam with his foot.

"The decisions your teammates made have as great an impact on the outcome of the game as your decision to catch the ball and try to make the play. You just happened to be the unlucky bugger who had possession on the buzzer. From my vantage point, you got there first, you caught that ball, and you didn't slow down. I'm proud as hell of the effort that you've put in this season. Now come on, get dressed and let's go get a feed."

"Yeah. Yeah, okay." He pulled on the suit jacket their sponsors required them to wear to and from games, and trudged along the deserted hallways to the player entrance. The mood in the bus was subdued and as Liam slipped into the empty seat just behind Coach, Rogers ruffled his hair. He ducked out of the way and brushed him off, not in the mood to fuck around.

Rogers laughed and teased, "Aw, don't be like that, Masters." He was one of the team veterans and probably only had a year or two left before his retirement, but he was the biggest doofus out of all of them. How his wife managed to keep him and their seven children in line he would never know. "You did good, bud. I know it feels like it's your fault but not one of us think that."

His phone vibrated and the bottom fell out of his gut. He knew who it would be before he even saw the caller's name. It wasn't only the team he'd let down, but everyone else too. His father, no doubt, would be reminding him of that.

Liam slipped it out of his jacket pocket, tossing up whether to ignore it or deal now. They'd only keep calling if he didn't. But the relief that hit him almost knocked him sideways. It wasn't his father. He huffed out a shaky laugh and swiped to answer.

"Those bastards," Lij yelled through the phone before he'd even had a chance to speak. "It was pure-arsed luck that got them the win."

The beginnings of a tentative smile curled Liam's lip upward. "Hello to you too, Lij. I suppose that means you caught the game."

"When do I not catch the game? Dude, you were on fire."

He shook his head, the smile falling from his lips. "Wasn't quite good enough though, was it?" He sighed and Lij grumbled something unintelligible.

"That's bullshit and you know it—" The line crackled, a buzzing noise drowning out Lij's words before it went dead. Almost immediately it started ringing again and Liam answered.

"Yes, I know. It's a team sport, we all get the credit when we win, so we should share the burden when it's a loss," he quipped, repeating the advice he'd heard more than once already.

"That would be true, if the loss was something that wasn't so obviously your fault." His dad's words were like a sucker punch, stealing his breath and making Liam double over.

"D-Dad," he stuttered. "I... I was just talking to Lij." His explanation fell on deaf ears.

"You messed up tonight, son. I expected more. Your plays were sloppy and you weren't fast enough." His dad had thrown money his way to pay for the endless supply of equipment football players needed. He'd taxied him to and from practices and games, and even stayed to watch a few times. Liam hated that after everything his parents had done for him, he was a disappointment. He'd failed them. Again.

"I know, I let the team down," he admitted quietly. "There are some things I can work on during the off-season that'll put me in a better stead for next year." He trusted his dad to say it how it was, something Liam couldn't argue with, especially when it was true. He'd always been a disappointment to his family. Both his parents and sister had all wanted another girl—two princesses to take to dancing and gymnastics lessons. They thought they were getting one too, the scans all failing to show his tackle. But instead of their baby girl, they got stuck with a rough and tumble boy who lived for the game.

His dad added, "Good," but Liam was lost in thought. He didn't realize his father had hung up until he pulled the phone away from his ear a moment later. The cavern inside his chest expanded, swallowing him in the gaping void. The heavy weight pressed down on his shoulders and his stomach churned, bile threatening to come up.

When they arrived at the hotel, Liam begged off the team's dinner, heading straight back to his room. He'd already let them down once that night. What difference did it make if it happened a second time? The sooner room service arrived, the sooner he could go to sleep and forget that this day ever happened.

* * * * *

It was early when his phone vibrated with a notification. He checked the screen—an email to his student email address. Liam had been waiting for this one. His statistics midterm results were posted. He sat up, the sheet pooling at his waist as he scratched his chest and gathered the courage to open the university app. He didn't know if he could stomach two losses in less than twenty-four hours.

Nope, not right now.

Handling the phone like it was an unexploded ordinance, he gently placed it on the bedside table. He side-eyed it. The phone stared back at him, the black screen mocking him. Taunting him. It vibrated again and Liam jumped out of his skin. Another notification from the app.

"Dude, is that thing gonna keep going?" Taufa grumbled. His roommate had arrived sometime after Liam had crashed. He hadn't even heard him come in.

"Sorry, mate." More grumbling and the big back rower rolled over. Liam swiped the screen and bit his lip, praying to a god he didn't believe in that he'd somehow pulled off a miracle. He'd studied hard for the one-hour in-class quiz. The other students had walked out early but he'd stayed until pens down. The others all said they were pleasantly surprised by how easy it turned out to be. Liam had struggled. He had no idea whether he'd done enough to pass. If he hadn't, he had another repeat in his future.

He bit the bullet, opening the app and navigating to Introduction to Statistical Analysis. He held his breath. Shot out another pleading prayer. Clicked on the tab for his marks.

Seven out of forty-five.

It was dismal. He sighed and dropped the phone, scrubbing the grittiness from his eyes with the heel of his hands. What the hell was he going to do?

"Masters, seriously dude, shut the hell up," Taufa huffed.

He needed to get out of there. Liam stumbled out of bed, heading straight to the bathroom. He shut the door a little too hard, ignoring the curse from his roommate, and turned on the shower. Without even waiting for it to warm, he stripped off and climbed in, the freezing drops like needles on his skin. Liam slid his arse down the tiled wall until he was sitting in the stall, his head hanging under the stream. Wrapping his arms around his knees, he resisted the urge to lash out, kicking at the glass closing him in.

After the loss of the game yesterday, the test results were a kick in the teeth.

NINE

Adelaide

Adelaide was quiet as she watched her mum potter around the kitchen. She'd needed an afternoon like this—some time with her mum. King would be over soon to have dinner with them, but until then, they were the only ones at home.

She adjusted the flowers on the table, turning the orange gerbera toward her. They were a gift from King, one of many he'd given her. Whether they were thoughtful presents that showed he cared, cute and silly ones, or romantic ones like the love notes he posted her, Adelaide constantly had a smile on her face.

"Did you sort out what you were arguing with King about?" her mum asked, always blunt and to the point.

"We weren't arguing. He's going to look for another job, but I don't want him to do it."

Her mum snapped her head around, the look on her face almost comical. Adelaide choked on the water she was drinking. "Why not?" her mum asked, her tone aghast. "You know I love King. I think he's a wonderful man. He loves you in the way I dreamed you kids would experience love. But allowing this ridiculous notion that you're some dirty secret to go on is awful. Why are you encouraging it?"

"King's all in. I mean, I am too," she answered, before blowing out a breath. She didn't know what she was trying to say. She wanted to move her relationship with King forward, but she was holding herself back. It wasn't King. After their second date, Adelaide knew she could fall for him. It hadn't occurred to her that King's school might have an issue with their relationship. He'd dropped a bombshell on her when he'd told her, but he'd come prepared with a solution too. He was ready to quit immediately and move to another school. But how could she agree to that? Her mum laid down the knife in her hand and rested her palms on the kitchen bench. "You're going to need to explain the mental jump you need me to make there, Addy." "King was ready to resign on the spot. But it's too soon, isn't it? What if we don't work out? King said he'd be able to pick up a new position fairly easily, but why should he have to? If we split, it'll all be for nothing. He would have uprooted his whole life, settle into a new school—one that he can't guarantee he'll even like—and for what?"

"So, you don't want him to continue like this forever, you just want him to wait?"

"Yes." She nodded, affirming her answer.

"That's good to hear. When will he leave?"

"Changing jobs in the final term of the year also isn't fair to King or his students. Leaving would upset him. He's made such an incredible contribution to the community. I don't even want him to have to walk away from it."

"I get that, but if he doesn't leave, you'll remain a secret." It wasn't a question, but her mum raised her eyebrow, waiting for Adelaide's response. She shrugged. The choice sucked. "No, don't do that. You said that you're both all in, but you want him to wait because it's too soon. But given there's the summer holidays coming up, wouldn't he need to look for a job now?"

"Maybe," she conceded, not wanting to admit both her mum and King were right. Maybe it was fear talking. Maybe it was itchy feet. That was her sticking point.

She didn't want to change who she was for anyone, but at the same time she wanted more for herself. Keeping her relationship with King secret was only one part of it. Her restlessness wasn't going away even as her relationship blossomed—she needed more. She wanted to change things up, and a possible career path was unfurling itself before her. Would it make things easier with King? Absolutely not, especially in the short term. But did that mean she shouldn't pursue it at all? Or wait? She didn't have the answers, and they were what was holding her back.

Adelaide snapped back to the conversation when her mum nudged her, refilling their glasses with iced water. "There's something else bothering you. What is it?"

She looked at her mum and gratitude for their being so close swelled within. "Could I maybe get your advice on something else?"

"Of course."

"Okay, well, um… I'm thinking about going back to school. The thing is, it could make things worse between King and me, and I don't know whether that should stop me or not."

Mum placed her glass on the coaster, aligning it perfectly with the timber grain on the table and waited for Adelaide to continue. "I'm getting comments on my videos saying that I'm helping people, and a little while ago I spoke with some clients who I was selling toys to. Sitting in their lounge room, I was looking at the photos on their wall and listening to the two of them talk. The man was struggling with his sexuality. He'd fallen in love with his best friend, and it was killing him to keep denying it to himself."

"Oh no," Mum replied, wincing.

"No, it wasn't just him. The photos all around their house were of the three of them together—my two clients and their best friend—and the way his girlfriend looked at their best friend in the photos made it obvious she was in love with him too. I didn't do much except encourage them to have the conversation. But I walked out of there riding a high knowing that I might have brought them together."

"Or broken them all up," Mum mumbled.

"Hush," Adelaide scolded with a playful flick of her wrist.

"How did it turn out?"

"They've been together for a year or so now and they're ridiculously in love and happy. I want to do more of that, you know?" Adelaide turned in her seat, tucking her foot under her leg.

"Play cupid? Like dating agency stuff?" her mum asked with a tilt to her head. "Or more along the lines of counselling?"

"More like counselling, but sexuality and sexual education focussed rather than emotional or trauma stuff. But I guess both would play a big part when it comes to sex for lots of people." Mum nodded, agreeing with Adelaide's conclusion, and she hurried to continue, wanting to lay it all out. "I've found a course to become a somatic sex educator. It'll take me about a year to complete and what really attracted me to it was the supervised hands-on client work that's included as part of the course. It's not just classroom teaching."

"Okay, somatic as in the body rather than the mind. I suppose that pushes you out of the counselling only sphere and into a more hands-on role."

Her mum's nursing experience was exactly why she'd needed to speak with her first. Knowing that she understood it would be focussed on the body rather than the mind—and there would be an element of touching—was important. Adelaide needed her opinion and her advice on whether it would be a bad or good idea.

"I think that if you're moving into a role with that focus on touch, incorporating the client work into the course is essential. The sex education will allow you to take what you're trying to do with your toy business and Patreon up a few steps too." Mum nodded thoughtfully, and slowly smiled, her lips widening in a proud-as-punch grin. "I love the idea. I think it's the perfect progression for you. It's the most thoughtful and passionate I've seen you about a possible career move since you started up your Patreon too."

They spoke about the course specifics, her mum looking more impressed as they went on. "You've always had such a curiosity about the human body. When Eli had his eyes glued to fantasy and mystery books, you were reading up on the body. The course will give you an accreditation to practice, and there aren't any qualified practitioners here on the Coast, so there's at least a geographical market for you. I say go for it."

"But what about King?"

Her mum sighed, a mixture of sympathy and frustration in her tone. "My reaction as your mum is to say 'what about King?' You furthering your education and pursuing a possible career path shouldn't be impacted by him, but I understand what you're asking." She paused, adjusting her necklace to make sure the pendant sat perfectly centred. It was her mum's tell—she'd be a hopeless poker player—but Adelaide was stumped. She had no idea what her mum would say. "King said he'd find another job. Trust him to do it. You're the one insisting he keep your relationship secret, not him. You're the one telling him to wait. Let him look for a job. Once he's out of there, there's no problem."

Adelaide swallowed, voicing her fear for the first time. "What if he can't find another one?"

Her mum hummed and nodded slowly, as if by asking that one question she'd revealed her deepest darkest secret. Maybe Adelaide had. "The course could work in your favour. At the moment, you sell sex toys. While there is absolutely nothing wrong with having sex for enjoyment, the traditional churches preach otherwise."

"The videos you produce give your brand a bit more depth than simply being toys sold for enjoyment, but King's school would never see them. They would presume the worst. But say you do this course. You'll be qualified. You'll be recognized as a practitioner of an uncommon, but legitimate field. You'll be teaching people."

"Yeah, but teaching them what? They'd consider it to be immoral."

"You're teaching students to tap into an awareness of their body to actively receive experiences. Keep sex out of your descriptions—a stress reaction or a fight-or-flight reaction is just as valid as a reaction to sexual stimuli."

"I suppose. I'm worried that the school would say it's a fancy way of describing me watching people have sex."

"Instead of worrying the worst-case scenarios, why don't you focus on moving forward? Do nothing and you'll be stuck in this career no-man's land you're in. But act and you'll be completing a formal qualification with international recognition. Sure, you could wait and see what happens in your relationship with King, but if this is something that would make you happy, why would you wait? If you wait—just like you're asking King to do—are you assuming you'll break up? If that's the case, why are you together now?"

She raised an eyebrow and Adelaide bit down on her lip, wanting to challenge her mum, but she wasn't finished yet.

"Another option would be to change course altogether and move out of the industry. But it drew you in when you were eighteen and hasn't let go. Would you be happy working a nine-to-five job that doesn't inspire you? Isn't that spark you needed the reason why you've waited to enrol in anything?" Adelaide nodded, opening her mouth to say her piece, but her mum raised her hand in a stopping motion. "On the flip side, would changing career so that you can post pictures of you and King on social media be worth it? Big deal, you'd be able to attend one of his work functions in the next couple of months before he leaves, or longer if he stays there. How does that help you grow as a person?" Her mum looked at her, waiting for a response, but all of Adelaide's words had upped and left.

Everything her mum said was true. She'd struggled to decide on a career path for years. Lots of self-reflection and really looking at what she loved doing—helping people, talking to them, facilitating their discovery of something more about themselves that brought genuine pleasure and helped tear down outdated taboos for women and men alike—had prompted her Google search. What she'd found excited her more than anything in a long time.

"Or do you go for it and potentially discover a career that could be everything you've ever dreamed of?"

Adelaide huffed out a laugh. "You don't play fair, Mum."

"It's my job." She winked and grinned. "You should talk to King. If the course is something you're really interested in and could lead you to a rewarding career, King should be happy. If he isn't supportive, then perhaps you need to re-consider your relationship."

"There's no need," King's deep voice rumbled from the doorway behind them. He spoke quietly, but his words had a profound impact on Adelaide. She held her breath and waited. "Adds, I will support you in whatever you want to do. I don't care what the course is, if you want it, I'm behind you 100 percent."

She turned in her seat, a lump in her throat forming at the look of sincerity on his face. Eyes locked on her, he didn't blink as he stepped over and dropped to one knee. He reached up to finger the curl of her hair and brush his fingertips over her cheek, her lids fluttering closed at the soft touch.

"How much of that did you hear?"

"Only that what you're thinking of is a recognized qual-ification and internationally accredited." He shook his head and frowned, sadness radiating off him. "I didn't mean to eavesdrop, but I want to give you everything, and hiding you isn't good enough."

She reached for his hand, lacing their fingers together. "There's a risk that I'd be making things worse by doing this course. It's a qualification for a somatic sex educator."

"I don't know what that is." He laughed, his eyes filling with mirth—no, something deeper, something more like adoration—and cupped her face. "But if it's what you want to do, then do it. You deserve to have a career that makes your heart sing like teaching does for me."

Her heart expanded in her chest until fireworks deto-nated, choirs sang, and love hearts exploded. She was damn lucky to have this man.

"Where is the course?" he asked. He furrowed his brows and pursed his lips for a moment as if thinking something over, but then lifted his chin and smiled at her. It was filled with warmth and a little hesitation too. "I've been applying for new positions. I have three interviews in the next couple of weeks for jobs starting next year. But, if the course is in-terstate, that's okay. I can beg off the interviews and apply for something elsewhere. Whatever you need to do, do it. If you need to travel to do the course, to go interstate or whatever you need, we'll do it."

For him to be prepared to pack up and leave—to follow her—because she wanted to go back to school meant the world to her. He was… the love of her life. She loved him. More than she could ever have imagined would be possible.

"Who's going interstate?" Liam asked as he waltzed in and ruffled her hair.

Her heart swooped and breath caught. Adelaide had ab-solutely and utterly failed at falling out of love with the man. Instead, she'd gone and fallen for both of them. Hiding it hadn't been easy either. She'd resorted to treating Liam like an annoying older brother, ignoring him, and picking disagreements while internally wishing she could have both of them. Adelaide batted Liam's hand away, feigning annoy-ance, and rolled her eyes at King, getting a grin in response.

"Hi, Mum," Liam added, kissing her mother on the cheek.

"No one," Adelaide responded, glancing over her shoulder at him. He looked good today—grey sweats that moulded to his powerful legs, a white tee that could have been painted on, and a pair of white socks. His sneakers were no doubt toed off at the door, sitting in the spot on the rack her mum insisted they keep for him. "I'm thinking about going back to school," she added. She turned back to King and explained, "It'll take me a year to get through it. Part is online, then there's a three-week component in Sydney and after that, a few months of supervised practical training. The format is repeated in the second semester. There are a few practitioners based in Brisbane so I'll see if I can get in with them, but I might need to go away for a few months to do work experience."

"You should definitely go for it," he said with a goofy grin as he leaned up and kissed her with smiling lips.

"You don't know what a somatic sex educator is. Don't you want to know before you encourage me?" she asked, nerves tightening her belly. What if he hated the idea? What if he thought the same thing that she feared his school would say?

"I'd love for you to tell me, but don't think for a second that I should have any bearing on what you study. Like I said, you should have a career that makes you happy."

"And if it puts a strain on our relationship?" She raised an eyebrow and hurried on before he could assure her that he'd be fine. She knew he'd say it too, even if he hated the idea. Adelaide was worried that he'd just bury his concerns, whether valid or not, and support her. But she didn't want that. She didn't want jealousy or resentment to poison their relationship. "I'll be training people to understand their bodies, to discover then communicate what they enjoy and help them overcome any roadblocks that they might experience to that enjoyment. I'd be doing workshops and couples sessions, even some one-on-one sessions where we talk about sex and everything that goes with it. They'd likely be touching each other if they're couples or more, and I might even have to touch them if it's part of their treatment."

"Okay." He nodded slowly, stretching out the syllables of the word as if he were deep in thought. That was good—anything other than him walking out or telling her that it would bother him was a win in Adelaide's book. "Would they touch you?"

She shook her head, explaining that the touching would be one way and she would be wearing gloves at all times.

"So tell me then, if you were going to study gynaecology or become an andrologist, would you be worried about my opinion?"

"Well, no, but they're professionals—"

"You will be too, won't you?"

Adelaide looked at him and blinked as he gave her a small, encouraging smile that warmed her insides, making her feel invincible. She gave him a small nod and King's smile turned into an eye-crinkling grin.

He asked, "When do enrolments open?"

"They're open now. Classes start in a few weeks."

He passed her the phone sitting on the table. "What are you waiting for?"

This was it. The possibilities opened before her, scary and exciting at the same time. She could picture herself sitting down, reading, and listening to videos. Except... where the hell would she study? The space she'd made into her bedroom was too open and way too small to fit a desk, she'd already taken over the part of the garage that didn't have boxes and the furniture from Pop's old house piled up in it, and the kitchen table was just off the lounge room— the loudest room in the house. "I don't know where to study," she rushed out, cringing. "Shit. I'm going to have to go to the library every day."

"It's out of the way, but you can come to—" King started. He looked down and a pretty pink flush dotted his cheeks. He tried to bite back the shy smile, but Adelaide wasn't having it. She loved that smile—it was perhaps her favourite of his, one he didn't share often.

"Study at my house," Liam responded as if it were the most natural thing in the world to suggest. "I'm right next door and there's plenty of room. You can have a key. Come and go whenever you need."

"You wouldn't mind?" She looked between King and Liam. When they both shook their heads, Adelaide threw her arms around her boyfriend and gave his lips a smiley kiss. "Thank you!"

TEN

Adelaide

L ightning flashed across the sky, lighting it up. The crack of thunder shook the house, startling Adelaide even though she knew it was coming. They were curled up watching a movie together, listening to the howling wind outside, but Adelaide suspected she and King should be watching the night sky instead.

The light in the kitchen flickered, dimming before powering back up again. "One sec," King murmured against her hair before he slid out from behind her and fished out a box from the bottom of the cupboard, placing it gently on the coffee table he'd been resting his feet on. "Just in case the power goes out."

He'd barely finished speaking when another flash lit the sky. The TV went black, but the room wasn't plunged into darkness. The spiderweb of lightning across the sky took care of that. But as it faded, King pulled out old-fashioned hurricane lanterns. He lit them and Adelaide smiled serenely. She loved how he was a caretaker. So prepared for anything. It was the little things he did that meant the most to her. The way he'd looked in three different nurseries to find her favourite flowers so he could plant them in his garden and give her bunches whenever new flowers bloomed. He'd changed the milk he drank with his coffee because Adelaide commented she preferred the farmer co-op brand and had even placed an order through her online store for the condoms she stocked too, despite Adelaide being able to grab a box from her supplies.

The rain began its pitter-patter on the roof, but the gusts of wind caused it to hiss against the glass too. When King returned to the couch, he shifted her, opening her legs, and stretching out above her. Adelaide wrapped herself around him, holding him close. After kissing her softly, he asked, "Will you stay tonight? I don't want you driving home in this."

She smiled, sure she looked love-drunk, and hummed. "I'd love to." It really was the small things he did and said that mattered most.

Fingertips traced along her waist, tickling her with the gentle touch. She cupped King's face, deepening their kiss and slid her hands up the back of his shirt. Peeling each other's clothes off, they touched, rediscovering the way their bodies fit together. Their movements slow. Unhurried. He worshipped her, lighting her up like the lightning was doing to the night sky. They hadn't said the words yet, but Adelaide knew. He never left her in any doubt about the depth of his feelings. As much as she hoped King knew that she had fallen for him too, Adelaide wanted to tell him. She didn't want him to doubt what they had, not even for a moment. Those three little words were on the tip of Adelaide's tongue. She needed to say them, the urge getting stronger with each passing day to squash any question in King's mind about how much she adored him.

* * * * *

Adelaide opened the door, letting herself in after spending the night at King's. She'd intended staying while he was at work, having the house to herself all day, but their plans had been thwarted when the power went out and hadn't yet come back on. Instead, she came home but the noise that met her made her turn straight around.

Three weeks into class and Adelaide was loving it. She was powering through the materials, reading everything she could get her hands on. Every reference book, every article mentioned by her tutors or in any of the texts she read were added to the list. She watched every video and participated in the online forum, responding to most of the comments like they were encouraged to do. Learning about the body, how it interpreted signals, and dismantling many of the class's preconceived notions to help their clients build a new foundation was exhilarating.

She slipped through Liam's side gate, skipping along the flagstone pavers to the back door, her bag slung over her shoulder. Adelaide couldn't see his sporty black SUV when she looked through the windows of the garage. That meant she'd be alone for at least part of the morning—a much-needed quiet haven from the laughter and shouted smack talk at her house. It happened whenever Pop and Mum played Scrabble. As much as she loved the happiness her family exuded, she desperately needed peace and quiet for her project. She had a forum post to write on the topic they'd just covered in class—the impact of porn on partner connection and intimacy. It was only a short piece, but it needed to pack a punch, provoke discussion, and make her view clear at the same time.

That wasn't possible with yelling in the background.

Eternally grateful for the key Liam had given her, Adelaide crossed the patio and unlocked the back door, sliding the glass all the way open so she could capture the breeze blowing in off the ocean a twenty-minute drive away.

Adelaide had her head buried in her laptop, scrolling to find a reference she'd uncovered when the garage door began opening. "Honey, I'm home," Liam yelled as he rounded the corner a moment later.

"Doofus," Adelaide responded with a laugh, shoving down the longing for him to be serious. The guilt of even thinking like that while she was dating King sent her into a spiral of self-recrimination. It wasn't helping that they'd been spending so much time together either. Liam was enjoying his post-season holiday after the gruelling season he'd had. But taking a break just gave him extra time to study, so if they weren't gathered around his table working together, he was at their house with Lij.

He ruffled her hair, messing up the wave she'd managed to calm the frizz into given the humidity after the storm as he walked past. "Stop it," she grumbled, slapping his hand away.

"Sorry, babe." Liam didn't sound sorry at all. In fact, the glee in his voice was matched by the shameless toothy grin he shot her when Adelaide looked up and glared at him. "Whatcha working on?" He leaned over her shoulder at the handwritten notes on her page.

"Porn and the impact on intimacy in existing relationships."

"Yeah?" He cleared his throat and formed a fist, raising his hand like he held a microphone. With a serious expression, he asked, "Tell me, Ms McMahon, what do you think of… porn?" He wiggled his eyebrows and Adelaide snorted out a laugh.

He held out his fist to her. She spoke in her best professional voice, "Well, Mr Masters, it has its place. But there are problems with it too. Relying on pornography for arousal in place of focussing on the person or people you're with can be detrimental. It could create a block between partners, lessening the intimacy between them and reducing satisfaction with sexual encounters, especially if the impossibly high standards set in porn are to be believed."

Liam scrunched up his face in mock sympathy and Adelaide's gut sank. She'd left herself open for his next comment. "Aw, poor Addy. Can't King satisfy you like those girls get satisfied in porn?"

"Shut up," she warned, narrowing her eyes at him. Liam laughed and tugged on a half curl, watching it bounce as he grinned a devil-may-care smile. "Are you working today or are you just going to annoy me?"

"Eh." He shrugged and meandered into the kitchen. "I was going to have a shake then do a bit. Want one?"

"Steak in a glass? No thanks." The protein powders Liam added to his morning shakes kept him in shape—which Adelaide often appreciated as he sat at the table shirtless—but she wasn't one to drink them.

"Mhmm." He shrugged, and messed around in the kitchen, before placing a milkshake glass in front of her, complete with bamboo straw and a drizzle of what looked like caramel on top of the froth.

"Frozen mango, banana, a few macadamia nuts, low fat milk, and a dash of maple syrup—the real stuff. Nothing else added."

She smiled, sure that it was one of those swoony shy smiles complete with cartoon-character-esque long eye-lashed blinks.

Adelaide appreciated the kind gesture more than he would know. She'd skipped breakfast and was starving, her stomach rumbling louder with each passing minute. But she was on a roll and was loath to interrupt her progress by ducking home to grab something to eat. He'd made her favourite too—mango and banana smoothies were a staple for her in summer. Liam had obviously noticed too, although she had no idea he'd even seen her drink one. "Thank you."

"Anytime." He kissed her forehead, and went back into the kitchen repeating the process, and adding scoops of protein powder before he turned on the blender. With glass filled to the brim, he slid into his seat, and opened his books to get started. The sound of pages turning, the scratching of his pencil against paper, and the click of the eraser against his calculator were the only sounds in the room apart from the tapping of her fingers against the keyboard. Adelaide finished her shake and moved to the kitchen to rinse the glass. She glanced up at Liam and her gut sank. He was worried. Sad, maybe. She wanted to smooth out the furrow in his brow and laugh with him until those turned-down lips were smiling again. She wanted to reach out and hold his hand. Tell him he wasn't alone.

"Hey, you okay? Is everything all right?" she asked gently, giving him the opening to confide in her. He was a private person. He rarely shared things that were bothering him, but Adelaide suspected it was more a side effect of his parents' parenting than of Liam wanting to put up walls. He was like a puppy dog. He wanted love and affection, and he beat himself up harder than anyone she knew if he thought he'd let down the people close to him. The final game of the season was still weighing on him, but this was something different. This was almost fear in his drawn expression and pursed lips.

When he registered the question, Liam snapped his eyes up to hers and slowly placed his mobile face down on the table. He nodded, a short, sharp movement of his head. "Yeah, s'all good," he answered, a hitch in his voice.

She didn't believe him for a second, especially not when the speed at which he was tapping his eraser topped pencil against his notebook had increased. Adelaide flicked her eyes down to his hand and she raised an eyebrow. "Okay, 'cause I believe that." She sighed and went back to her seat, clasping her hands together on the table. "I understand if you don't want to tell me. I really do. But I'm here if you do want to talk."

"I'm just working out how many marks I need in the exam to pass my statistics class. But it's all good. It looks like I should be sweet." He flashed her the same fake-arse smile he gave to reporters when they asked him a ridiculous question, and Adelaide resisted the temptation to narrow her eyes at him. Liam may not have noticed her for the last decade or so, but she had memorized every expression and nuance. He was lying, but she wasn't prepared to call him out on it, not when they were slowly moving from her being Eli's little sister to Liam's friend.

He looked down and flipped the page of his textbook. The glimpse that Adelaide got, showed it filled with formulas and paragraphs of text. It could have been written in a foreign language; actually, most of it was probably in Greek, which explained why, when Adelaide looked closer, she didn't understand one iota of it.

Liam got to writing, the cute furrow between his brows deepening as his pencil scrawled across the page. Turning his phone over, he punched in something, wrote it down then flipped to the back of the book. Long, straight fingers scanned down the page until he found the answer he was looking for. He shifted back to his notebook and bit his lip as he dropped the pencil and rubbed his temples.

She asked, "Does it make sense? It looks complicated."

"Oh, sure." His voice came out at a higher pitch than normal again, and he cleared his throat before adding, "Yeah, I think I've got it. Statistics sucks, but it's all logic. As long as you can follow the basic rules, it makes perfect sense." He sounded too enthusiastic, too excited by it, but Adelaide had seen how hard Liam worked at his studies. She admired him. It was the off-season now, but he still worked out every day, he still had all the promotional obligations that went with keeping his sponsors happy, and, on top of all that, he managed a near full-time class load.

Adelaide rolled her eyes. "I'm just glad it's you and not me. This stuff" —she pointed to her laptop and head-phones—"is difficult, but to me it's interesting. Statistics just sounds hard." He made a rumbling noise of agreement as he closed the textbook in front of him, shunted every-thing to the side, and opened his laptop. Adelaide knew he had another assignment due soon, so even though she wasn't convinced everything was 100 percent, she was glad he could focus on it.

ELEVEN

Liam

THREE MONTHS LATER - SEPTEMBER

Final marks for the semester were being posted that day. Liam knew that out of the three subjects he'd taken, he'd already passed one before submitting the final assessment. The second shouldn't be a problem either. He'd contacted his professor and had a heart-to-heart with her, freaking out about the result. The prof had looked up his mark and assured him that while she couldn't give an exact grade, he had most definitely passed. He wasn't holding out hope for the third. Statistics had beaten him once again. For all the bullshit he'd told Adelaide a couple of months earlier about simply following the formula and reaching a logical conclusion, he neither knew how to follow the formula nor did any of the conclusions he came up with ever make any sense to him.

Results were always posted at 9:00 a.m. sharp. It was quarter past, and his phone had already vibrated with notifications. But Liam couldn't bring himself to look. As long as he didn't know the outcome, he still had some hope that he hadn't done too badly.

He took a swig of beer. It was too early to be drinking, but whatever. He'd done nothing but sit in his backyard moping since the epic disaster that his final exam was. Being unable to answer two out of the five questions wasn't a good start. It was a fit ending to a shit-tastic subject.

"Fuck it," he mumbled and brought up the app on his phone. His gut sank when he saw his marks, the credit and distinction for the two other subjects he was studying outweighed by the blunt Fail written next to statistics. He needed to start thinking backup plans. He clearly wasn't cut out for a business degree. Liam tossed his phone onto the table and chugged the rest of the bottle.

* * * * *

The pounding of his head roused Liam from near unconsciousness. A pickaxe was being punched into his skull, right behind his eyes. The pain made his ears ring. He winced, his eyes still closed, not daring to open them in case the room was too bright. The pain spiked anyway. He unstuck his lips and tore his tongue away from the roof of his mouth, the putrid taste making him want to gag.

He couldn't remember what he'd drunk the night before, but he did remember taking lick, sip, suck to a whole new level. As he peeked out from under his arm, testing the level of light in the room before he lifted it away from his eyes, he became aware of the heat surrounding him. Sweaty, stiff sheets were tangled under his sprawled-out body, and the skin on his abdomen stretched and pinched when he shifted his hips. It was about the only thing he could move. His legs were stretched wide, his sides pressed down.

Blinking his eyes open in a squint, Liam waited for the room to stop spinning and the near constant ringing in his ears to die down before he cast his gaze around the dimly lit interior. A head of blonde curls lay on his chest, her hand splayed on his stomach. Between his legs, using his thigh as a pillow, was a brunette. She had short hair, pouty lips, and breasts that he vaguely remembered sucking lemon juice off the night before. To his right, sharing his pillow, was a redhead—a natural one if the freckles across her shoulders were any indication. The remnants of her red lipstick matched the ring around the base of his cock.

Liam shifted again, trying to get comfortable on the too-hard bed. He'd fallen asleep somewhere unfamiliar again—the third night in a row—and now he had no clue where he was. He looked around the room, trying to place it. Had he been here before? There was no way to tell. Apart from the bed, with its grey sheets, heavy grey curtains drawn across the window, white walls, and furniture, there was little else in it.

The ringing in his ears started again and the woman be-tween his legs shifted, burrowing down as if she was trying to bury her head in her pillow. She shifted her hand, and Liam was suddenly very awake.

He reached for his junk just as the brunette punched her fist forward, lifting it to cover her head. Her hand connected with his balls as she moved, his sac recoiling into his body with the force. Liam cried out and curled in on himself, jos-tling all his bed mates. Blondie rolled away from him, taking the arm she had slung across him with her, and the ginger groaned, her face crumpling as if in pain. Liam blinked away the tears and breathed through the high-pitched squeal he wanted to let loose as he gripped his bruised balls in his free hand. With the other, he shoved at the brunette, knocking her head off his leg. With his legs spread and up in the air, cradling his emptied-out balls, Liam rolled toward red.

The peace as the ringing in his ears stopped was short-lived. Liam looked at the woman, trying to remember her name, but apart from snippets of drinking, flashing lights, and naked bodies, the last few days were a blur. It would be another awkward morning not having any clue what his hook-ups' names were.

Liam blinked. Ginger had turned green, her stomach tensing rhythmically as if she was readying to puke every-where.

Oh. Hell. No.

He sprang up, scrambling toward the edge of the bed. His head spun, his stomach lurched, and he half fell, half threw himself off the mattress. His knee connected with a body part—the brunette most likely—and an "Ow, fuck, watch it," sounded from behind him. He hit the polished timber, his shoulder and hip taking the brunt of the impact as he thudded to the floor.

"Sorry," he muttered, looking for his pants. The ringing sounded again, and now awake, Liam scrambled for his phone as heaving sounded behind him.

Screeching and cursing grew louder, and he gripped his head. The pickaxe had turned into a jackhammer and the smell of vomit had him dry-retching. He had to get out of there before he lost… the bottle or two of liquor he'd downed.

Why did he do this to himself?

Oh yeah, statistics.

He crawled out of the bedroom along the corridor where clothes were strewn. He spotted it. The ringing had stopped by the time he picked it up. Seven missed calls. All of them from Lij.

Shit.

He looked at the time and groaned. He was late. Really late.

He hit dial and stood, snatching up his jeans and slumping against the wall to step into them. "Lij, hi, I'm—"

Blondie stumbled out of the bedroom holding her hair off her back, the chunky carrots and pink foamy puke dripping from the ends and down her back between her arse. She kicked the door next to him closed behind her, and the bang ricocheted around his skull like a gunshot, exploding his brain. He dropped the jeans he had halfway up his leg and gripped his temple. Liam gagged at the stench that lingered, and he turned away needing to put more distance between himself and the others.

"—late," Lij muttered. Then he sighed. It was a put-out, frustrated sound that sent Liam straight back to his childhood. His mother used to make the same sound when she scolded him. "And I needed to get back home. I have a video meeting that I'll be late for if I kept waiting for you."

Liam was... struggling. With everything. Every insecurity, every one of his faults had seemingly magnified, concentrating with a laser focus on the detonator that would trigger an explosion. Once it happened, it would tear apart the fickle hold on his life that he was keeping together with a mix of that shitty packing tape with no glue and blind hope.

An hour before he'd received his marks, his sister had called. She was pregnant, and while that should have pleased Liam, the gloating made it hard to swallow. He wasn't welcome there; she'd made it abundantly clear when he'd asked for an invite to the baby shower. She laughed it off with a "oh no, that will only be for my close friends." His parents would be in seventh heaven, doting over Nessa as her belly grew and then over their newborn grandchild. The brush off had hurt almost as much as seeing the fail stamped across his transcript.

Liam rubbed his forehead, his shoulders slumping. "I'm sorry—"

"Yeah, I know." Lij sighed again. "Where are you?"

Liam hesitated, listening for any tell-tale signs of where he was. "I... I don't know."

"Liam—" Lij stretched out his name, pronouncing it in two syllables. There was so much disappointment in his voice that he hated himself even more for it.

"Lij, don't. Please. I know, okay. I'm a complete fuck-up."

"No, you're not. But you *are* going off the rails and I hate seeing you like this. Let's talk. I'm worried about you, but I've gotta stop and get some lunch, or I won't have time for anything until tonight."

"Leave it. I'm on my way home. I'll pick something up for you." Flashes of him driving the night before penetrated the fog of his memory and Liam swallowed. Had he really driven there? Had he been that stupid? He pulled on his clothes, patted the pockets of his jeans, finding his keys, and groaned. Shit, he hoped he was imagining things. But when he opened the front door and spied his black SUV parked on an angle in the driveway, the driver's front wheel halfway into a garden bed, he knew he hadn't been that lucky. Or maybe he had. By the looks of it, there was no damage to the car. He hoped that boded well for not having hit anything. Hopefully.

He unlocked the car and slid behind the wheel, backing out and leaving the unfamiliar house. He plugged his address into the nav and followed the directions onto the main road. But something made him hesitate. He was dizzy. Lightheaded from the booze, lack of food, or exhaustion after depleting every bodily fluid in him, Liam didn't know, but there was something off.

He pulled over, turned off the engine, and got out. The fresh air didn't help—summer was only a couple of weeks away and the heat and humidity combined were awful. He sighed and rubbed his forehead. If he got a rideshare, it'd get out. This shit always did. Same with a taxi. He bit the bullet and swiped at his phone.

Addy pulled up in her little hatch twenty minutes later. He opened the door and slid in, wincing at the dried cum on his belly pulling at his treasure trail. Her nose crinkled and she pursed her lips, a look of disgust passing over her features. "Jesus, you smell like you had an all-night orgy in a brewery." Her words hit too close to home. For the first time since he'd started this slide downhill in September, drinking and partying harder than he normally did, he was truly ashamed of himself.

He'd woken up with three drunk girls, whose names he had no recollection of, in a random bed after a night that was filled with enough liquor to last a lifetime. He'd probably just been driving drunk hours after he'd stopped drinking too. Add to that disappointing the woman he wanted with a fierceness that scared even him, and Liam knew he'd hit rock bottom.

Addy held her hand out, curling her fingers over in a "come here" motion. "Pass 'em over." He closed his eyes, wishing she meant something entirely different. But there was no arguing with her. She was absolutely right to demand his keys. It just rankled that she'd jumped straight to the correct conclusion.

"You don't know what happened." His voice was a mumble like that of a scolded child.

Her eyes flashed with something. But the emotion was gone in the blink of an eye, well before he could figure out what it was. She pursed her lips, disapproval radiating off her in the stiffening of her spine, and she looked him up and down, taking in the rumpled clothes. "Let me guess. You went out last night and got smashed, then hooked up with a vampire if the hickeys on your neck are anything to go by. And now, you're sitting on the side of the road with your car locked up, instead of driving home. How far over the limit were you when you got pulled over?"

"I didn't get picked up. But I think I'm way over," he mumbled, dropping the keys into her palm. "Thank you for coming."

She slid his keys into the cup holder and looked over her shoulder, checking her blind spot as she pulled out into traffic. "It's fine, but we're gonna talk about whatever the hell has happened to you. Your mood has been all over the shop these last few months, but this week has been on a whole other level." She sighed and carded her fingers through her hair, pushing it off her face. "I don't want to lecture you. I'm not your parents, but I do care about you. We all do. Let's just… get some lunch—your shout—then we'll head home."

"I don't really want to be seen like this in public."

"We won't be stopping. I'll take us through the drive-through." She paused and Liam could see the wheels turning in her brain. She wanted to say something else, but whatever it was, it went unsaid. Addy shook it off and concentrated on the road.

They were home in thirty minutes. Addy gave him his keys and motioned to his house. "Go home and eat, then have a shower. I'll give Eli his lunch and then, once I've eaten, I'll come over." Her tone was no nonsense, clipped and short. She was treating him like a child—clearly what he deserved—but something in him sat up and took notice. He wanted to please her again. He wanted to hear her eye-roll-laugh after he called out, "honey, I'm home," when he arrived to see her already studying. He wanted to see her get grumpy at him when he ruffled her hair, followed by the tiny secretive smile that tilted her lips up when she didn't think he was watching. He wanted her praise. Stupid considering who she was. Dangerous to his heart too. He hadn't been able to stop fantasizing about her, or her silver daddy in the making, and fucking her out of his system with other women wasn't working either.

It shouldn't surprise him. Addy had presence. She had a zest for life that was inspiring, and she lived every moment in the present. When she was with a person, she gave all her time to them, and Liam had grown to crave their moments together.

He knew when they were younger that Addy had held him up on a pedestal. Starting school and finding out that the kid who'd been nice to you was getting picked on wasn't something he could stand by silently and watch. He'd done the decent thing and stepped in to stop the fight. He'd never imagined it would change the direction of Lij's high school experience so dramatically. Nor did he think it would cement a friendship that Liam credited with saving him too. He'd gotten more out of their friendship than he could ever give back to Lij.

Liam's family had moved into their new house soon after. He'd had no idea he was going to be living next door to Lij and his family. But thank God they did. They'd opened their arms to him and shown him what being loved really was. He'd lost track of how many times he'd slept the night when home hadn't been inviting, or gotten help with his homework when his parents were too busy with his sister.

Lij's family actually made him feel wanted. He wasn't an obligation there.

But they'd gotten it wrong. He was a disgrace.

The side gate rattled and a few moments later, he heard the sliding back door shut. Addy called out, "I'm here."

"Coming," he yelled, towelling off his wet hair. He'd scrubbed away the disgusting mix of bodily fluids and lipstick all over his skin in the shower, but the underlying shame stayed firmly in place.

He slid on a pair of gym shorts and padded downstairs, the towel still around his shoulders hiding the worst of the hickeys along his throat and collarbone. "Coffee?" he asked as he passed her sitting in her usual spot at the kitchen table. He liked having her in his space. She was calming. Ironic considering the flaming pink of her hair this week. He wished he could reach out and finger the silken strands, but the closest thing he could ever come to it was ruffling her hair, and with his performance of late, there was no way she would tolerate it.

"Tea, thanks." He made their drinks, the silence between them brittle. "So, wanna tell me what happened?" Addy asked when he'd passed her the mug and sat opposite in his chair.

"Aside for not getting picked up for DUI, you guessed pretty accurately before."

"So why get drunk a few days in a row? It's not like you." She fiddled with the coaster that sat on the table, a habit she'd picked up from her mum.

"Yeah." He nodded and looked down to his mug, trying to figure out how to tell her without spilling his guts on just how completely fucked up his life had become. "I've had a few issues at uni."

"I can't help unless you tell me what they are."

Liam opened his mouth to protest. To tell her that she didn't need to solve his problems. He was an adult. He should be able to do this for himself. But apparently he was just as much of a fuck-up as his parents had thought.

She held up her hand and he snapped his mouth closed, desperately wanting her to be happy with him. "I know you and Eli are closer and I'm just the little sister who hangs around, but if I can help, I will."

He wanted to shout. To protest at how wrong she was. She was the woman who, with everything going to hell, had been there for him. He'd finally seen her, and it hadn't taken long for his heart to scurry across the table, putting itself in her hands for safekeeping. She was more than Eli's sister now. She had been for a while. She was Addy—bright, bubbly, dedicated Addy who went after what she wanted with a passion that left him wishing he was on the receiving end of the kind of love she shared with her boyfriend. It was completely fucked up that he wanted her boyfriend to want him too.

He sighed, his shoulders slumping, the weight of his dream future crushing him. "I failed statistics. For the second time. I worked really hard on it too. I thought I understood at least some of it, but I failed spectacularly."

Addy frowned, sympathy radiating from her as she tilted her head to the side and whispered, "Oh, hon." She tucked her hair behind her ear like she did when she was thinking, but her bright blue eyes never left his. "Can you do something that will give you extra credit to push you over the line?"

"I'm not even close to passing. When I asked them the first time, they told me it was only possible if I was borderline. I went even worse this time."

"Okay, so what are your options? Can you do another subject instead of statistics?"

"It's compulsory."

"Hmm. Quitting your degree is a bit dramatic. You don't want to do that—"

"I can't anyway. I'll lose my position on the team unless I do something else."

"Well that sucks." Addy was indignant, her watery eyes sparking with anger. For him. She was frustrated for him too, even though the mess he'd gotten himself into was entirely self-inflicted. The rock sitting on his chest crumbled just a little, his lungs expanding with air warmed by the sunshine she radiated. "Can you change degrees? Do something else that will get you a similar qualification?"

He shook his head, spinning his mug slowly. "I can't. My grade point average is too low. Failing the subject twice killed it. At this point I'd struggle to get into pretty much anything else."

She steepled her fingers and rested her chin on her thumbs, quiet for a moment. Her eyes snapped up, her spine straightened, and the smile that appeared on her face was excited. Over what though, he had no idea. But it didn't much matter. She was radiant, her eyes bright and her pretty bow lips totally kissable. His body reacted like a puppet on a string.

Addy rushed out, completely oblivious, "I don't know why I didn't think of it earlier." She bit her lip and Liam's cock bucked hard, the semi he was sporting hardening even further. God damn this longing thing he had going for her was set to kill him. He had no idea how his dick was even still attached after last night's session. But getting it up again was nothing short of a miracle.

He raised an eyebrow and adjusted himself under the table, shifting to loosen the pressure of his shorts on his cock.

"Okay, so you're stuck in your degree with a subject you can't get out of doing. I think your best bet is to re-enrol and get a private tutor. Some maths genius, perhaps?" She was looking at him expectantly, as if she knew a secret.

He huffed. At this point in time, anything was better than facing that stupid subject again. If he could get extra help, he might actually have a snowflake's chance in hell of passing it. But who? His tutors wouldn't spend any more time with him than they already had. The other students? Doubtful. "I'm shit outta luck with options and if I fail again, they'll kick me out of the uni."

"You do realize that my boyfriend is a maths teacher, don't you? He's brilliant at it." She frowned. "But I don't know if he knows statistics. You could ask him."

"He is? Huh. Makes sense." He had intentionally not asked any questions about the man, and the times they'd had dinner, he'd made sure to sit next to Lij so they could talk among themselves rather than being involved in the broader conversation. The less he knew about King, the better, because his dick was already obsessed. He didn't need his heart falling for the bloke too.

The news shocked him. But perhaps it shouldn't. King looked like a teacher—at least one of those model-esque teachers they pictured on social media memes that started with "what subject are you studying?" He had one of those kind voices too and was patient with everyone. Pop loved him and Addy's mum thought the world of him. Liam had wanted to hate him. He'd acted like a dick that first time they'd met, and hadn't been much better since, and yet the warmth that King radiated still drew him in.

"What's that supposed to mean?" She was defensive, but curious too.

Liam didn't hesitate. He couldn't blow his cover now. "He looked like he knew how to handle you, brat." He wiggled his eyebrows and flashed his teeth in a grin, laughter escaping him when Addy barked out a laugh, flushing a pretty pink across her cheeks. Her eyes lit up with humour. He loved seeing it, especially when he'd seen the disappointment in her gaze earlier.

"He's used to dealing with moody teenagers. When you start carrying on like you usually do, he's right at home. He says you're like his fourteen-year-olds."

"I don't act like a teenager," Liam protested a little too vigorously. She was right, but he couldn't help reverting to provoking a reaction out of both of them just to have a moment of their combined attention on him when they were together. An exaggerated eye roll was her only response.

"Call him. Maybe he can help." She stood and walked the phone around the eight-seater square table. King's number was already up on the screen.

He blew out a breath and looked up to her. Nerves assailed him, his belly flipping around as if he was doing cartwheels. On a roller coaster. Addy grasped his forearm reassuringly and Liam bit back a moan. His skin tingled where she gripped him and squeezed. His mind had conjured up infinite possibilities where she did exactly that to him, but never had those fantasies been so PG-rated.

King answered on the second ring. "Hey, beautiful." His tone was warm, and the deep baritone sent a ripple of awareness through Liam. Images of thrusting hips and breathy moans with deeper growls assailed him. Broad shoulders and blunt fingernails raking down sweat-slicked skin flashed in his mind's eye. The man had a voice made for sex. He could just imagine it being whispered in his ear. Growled as rough hands circled his hard cock.

Liam startled. *Fuck me.*

Blood rushed to his groin, his cock going from a semi to rock-hard, twitching and leaking pre-cum in a split second. Christ on a cracker. Even just hearing the man's voice in his ear sent Liam's thoughts spiralling. King was potent and Liam's body's instantaneous reaction had knocked his feet out from under him. He scrambled to regain his equilibrium. Choking out a self-conscious laugh, the quip flew off his tongue, his own inner brat making an appearance again. "I'm used to sexy and manly myself, but if you want to call me beautiful, go right ahead."

The rasp in his voice gave away just how turned on he was. Clearing his throat, and shifting in his seat, Liam hoped like hell that the wet patch he could feel on his shorts hadn't leaked all the way through.

"Who is this?" King demanded, the warmth in his voice replaced with a harsh bark. Anger and protectiveness, and a healthy dose of fear coated the words. Liam kicked himself, hating that he'd automatically reverted to an attention-seeking dickhead again.

Chastised, he put the phone on speaker. "Sorry, it's Liam. I'm here with Addy. She suggested I call you and…" This was stupid. He didn't deserve King's help, and even if he got it, he'd likely screw up over and over until King hated him.

There was silence on the other end for a moment. "And? What did you need, Liam?"

"Never mind—" Addy squeezed his arm again, grumbling about stupid men and tried to snatch the phone out of his hand. He held on tight, his lips turning up in a smile when she growled at him and smacked him gently across the back of the head.

"Ask him," she ordered impatiently.

"She suggested I ask you for help." He closed his eyes and pinched the bridge of his nose. "I've failed statistics twice and I was hoping you could tutor me when I retake it. It's running again over the summer. Do you know statistics? Is it something you could help me with? I'd pay you." He was rambling, his words tumbling out of him like an avalanche, nervous energy at having King on the line and Addy's hand still on him coalescing.

King's voice was relieved, a sigh and a smile both in his tone. "Statistics? Yeah, I've taught it before at high school level. Do you have the materials from this semester I can take a look at? Yours might be a whole lot more advanced than what I've done."

For the first time in a long time, hope flared in his chest. Even if King hadn't taught it at the same level, he knew some of it. He understood the basics, which was more than what Liam did.

He let out a relieved laugh and grinned happily at Addy. It was as if the sun had come out from behind a cloud. Warmth lit him up and Addy's responding smile had tingles racing through his body. "You'd be willing to look at it?"

"Of course. Even if I haven't taught it before, I'll be able to figure it out. When do classes start?"

"In a month."

He made a noise, a cross between a groan and a grumble. "Are you taking any other subjects?"

Liam shook his head. "No, it'd just be this one. I'll start pre-season training at the same time, so I can't do any more than that."

There was a pause and King answered again, concern lacing his voice. "I was going to head down to Sydney with Adds while she was studying—"

"King, baby, I'd rather that you stay and help Liam. I can look after myself. I know you want us to be together, but it's only three weeks. If you don't help him, he'll fail again and then he's out of the university."

Another grumble. "Yeah, okay. I can help you out. We can work around your training times—whatever suits. I won't have anything else to do, so I'm all yours." He sounded disappointed and Addy was staring at the phone like it held the secrets of the universe.

Wonder lit up her eyes and love poured from her. Something passed over him. It wasn't jealousy though. Sure, he envied their relationship, but he recognized the soul-deep longing to be part of them. Liam wanted. Desperately. The fantasy that he could tell Addy just how much he adored her, and hug King like he wanted to in that moment was overwhelming. As perfect as the fantasy was, it was just that.

He settled for asking, "Really?" His voice had pitched higher, equal parts shock and pure relief—hope—rooting him to the spot. Addy stood, moving behind him to wrap her arms around his shoulders. She pressed a kiss to his temple. Her warmth at his back, her solid presence, grounded him. He was spinning so fast that he thought he could lift off. "King, I'd really appreciate that," he choked out, his eyes burning with unshed tears. He took in a shuddery breath and Addy kissed him again, squeezing him tighter. He gripped her hand, threading their fingers together, and held on for dear life.

"No worries. Anytime, and please no paying me either. I'm happy to help you out." The warmth in King's voice slayed him, and he choked out a sob. He was being ridiculous, getting emotional over something probably trivial to anyone else, but to Liam it was a big deal. He'd hit rock bottom, been completely alone in the world, and then there was Addy and King who were helping him when he needed it most. He knew Lij was there for him too, but the look of disappointment on his face was too close to what his parents would say when they found out what was happening.

There was a dinging in the background and a rustling came over the phone, muting King's voice when he called out, "Wrap it up, kids. Off to class, please." The same rustling again and King added, "I've gotta run. Class is starting again. Can I say a quick hi to Adds?"

"Yeah. Yeah of course. Thank you. Here she is." He passed the phone to Addy so she could take it off speaker, but kept a hold of her hand, letting the warmth of her embrace seep through him.

"Hey, sexy," she greeted, her voice bright and bubbly to King's deeper tone that he could hear rumbling through the phone. Liam closed his eyes, picturing the two of them together. King all strait-laced with his tweed coats and button-down shirts—all lumberjack like with his beard and bulky clothes—and her all petite. He smiled, dangerously content. He couldn't believe this was happening. He was the luckiest bloke on the planet. Both King and Addy were prepared to sacrifice their time away—time that they could be curled up in bed together—for him. Who in the world did that? Who gave up their summer break, after teaching maths all year, to teach him? And not to want payment? It was too much. It was exactly the kind of thing a man Addy had fallen for would do.

TWELVE

Kingston

The last day of school was always filled with anticipation. Excitement buzzed in the air. The end was in sight and the kids, who were just as ready for some time off as he was, didn't sit still. He didn't have any work planned for his final maths class of the year. It was mostly spent with the kids on their computers or watching a movie, but this class was a little different. They were having a party of sorts. Hannah, the sweet thirteen-year-old who sat at the front of the class and listened to every word he said, was leaving. She was in the middle of a gaggle of teenagers, laughing and singing along to a song about Bruno. He looked out over the sea of familiar faces and smiled. They were a great bunch of kids. He'd enjoyed this class above all his others.

Arielle made her way over to him. "Sing with us, Mr V!"

"Yeah, no. I'm good." He laughed, rolling his eyes when she pouted.

"You're no fun."

It wasn't long after that the bell went. Music was shut off and the kids had their bags on their shoulders ready to file out the door. "So this was it. Last maths class for the year." A chorus of cheers went up and King grinned, happy that every one of his students had managed a pass. There was only an hour or so left of the school day before they'd all be free for the summer, and there wasn't a single sad face. Even Hannah, who was moving interstate, was grinning wildly. "It's been great having you all. Enjoy the summer. Best of luck for the move, Hannah."

"Thanks, Mr Vella. Bye." She waved as she walked out, trailing behind the others and looking around the room one last time.

In the last free period of the day, he cleaned up the classroom. He'd already emptied his desk in the maths office that he shared with four other teachers. The boxes of materials he'd built up over his career at the school had been taken home over the last few nights. He'd already said his goodbyes to his colleagues too. He was sad to be leaving, but excitement about his new position sizzled within too.

The school he was joining was considered a problem school. In a lower socio-economic area, many of the students struggled with affording resources. A new principal was shaking things up, implementing policies that ensured every student would get access to the minimum requirements, and she needed a team of people with the same passion for teaching as she had. He and Louise had clicked the moment they'd met. Instead of a one-hour interview, it had turned into two, the conversation flowing effortlessly be-tween them the whole time. He'd received the offer for head of the maths department the next day. The best thing about it was that they'd discussed his reasons for moving schools, and Louise had been horrified that he'd felt the need to keep his and Adds's relationship secret. She was also in complete support of establishing a LGBTIQA student association with him as staff liaison.

The final bell rang and King looked around the room one last time. It held fond memories. Tens of thousands of stu-dents had passed through there in his time at the school, and he'd taught his fair share. There had been ups and downs, difficult moments with students and their families, and ones filled with jubilation too. With a small smile, he shut off the lights and let the door click closed behind him. King took a deep breath of the heated air. Summer was here, and now, so was freedom for him and Adds.

Kids were running around everywhere, emptying from the rooms onto the concrete paths running between the buildings. They probably all looked like ants, madly follow-ing the leader to stream out the gates. He was subsumed in the mass quickly, getting jostled by heavy school bags and teenagers who were too excited to care. His phone vibrated and he saw the screen light up from its spot perched on top of the box of papers and books on statistics that he was tak-ing home. King was sure the grin that lit up his features was giddy. The butterflies in his belly took flight whenever he thought about his lady.

Congratulations, baby, you did it!

Happiness surged through him, making him fly. He was walking on air, the fool-for-love eye-crinkling smile he couldn't wipe from his face giving him away. "Hey, Mr V," Samuel yelled with a wave, he and his three mates jogging over to walk with him. They were the footy and swim team stars, all four of them competing at state level. They were the kings of the school. Good kids too. Hardworking and dedicated, but rowdier than anyone he'd ever taught.

"Mr V's gettin' laid tonight," Carter teased, stretching out the syllables of his last word and pointing to his smile. The boy's gangly arms and legs looked too big for his body, but it was what made him a superstar swimmer.

"That's entirely inappropriate to say to your teacher," he responded blandly, biting back a laugh.

"We're no longer your students," Max pointed out. "You don't teach here anymore and we've finished for the year." He high-fived Tristan then did their hand-slap-shake-elbow knock thing he and the other footballers did whenever they got a chance.

"You could be forty and you'd still be my students." King nudged Max's elbow with his own and smirked.

"Yeah, nah." Carter scoffed, rolling his eyes. "But seriously, that your girl?"

"It was. She was congratulating me on finishing school for the year."

They were joined by Jess and Izzy, twins who managed to look like real-life anime characters with their pigtails, long socks, and black chunky school shoes. "Mr V's got a girlfriend," Tristan explained, slipping his hand into Izzy's.

"Oooh, can we see pics?" Jess asked.

"Especially if they're X-rated," Carter added, wiggling his eyebrows. "Unless she's old like you, or ugly. Don't want to see her if she looks like a bloke."

"Carter," King warned, unimpressed with the cockiness. "Tone it down."

"There's no way," Jess added. "Mr V's got the hot-prof vibe happening. He'd totally be able to hook up with someone pretty."

"For the record, she is beautiful. But even if she wasn't, looks aren't everything." He paused for a moment, contemplating how to word his next comment, but blunt honesty seemed to be the best with this lot given the excitable mood they were in. "I also date men, so my girlfriend could just as easily have been my boyfriend."

"I didn't know you were gay," Tristan pointed out. "That why you run the queer kids club?"

"I'm bisexual, not gay, and yes, that's why I run it."

Carter's lips turned down in a frown and he asked, "Who's going to run it next year after you're gone?"

"Miss Stone is until another staff member volunteers." Another teacher had put her hand up. King appreciated the gesture—he didn't want the club to be shut down before he'd even finished. "Stay safe and check in sometime." He gave them details of his new school and nodded a goodbye to them.

He had his things loaded into his car and was on his way home to get changed within minutes. End of school year traffic was horrendous, and after an hour of battling it, he finally pulled into his drive. All he wanted to do was go for a surf to let off some steam, and then relax, cuddled up with Adds. But it wasn't happening—the surfing part at least. His parents insisted on having him over—an end-of-year dinner that they always invited Father Brendan to. His priest couldn't make it this year, much to his parents' disappointment, but King was relieved. As much as he wanted to introduce Adds to his friends and wider family, he didn't want Father Brendan to be the first.

He showered, changed, and headed on out the door to pick her up. Hopefully, he could convince her to stay the night. She was heading to Sydney on Sunday afternoon, ready to start her face-to-face classes, and he wanted to spend every possible moment with her. If it weren't for Liam, he would have made the trip with her. While he was bummed, he genuinely wanted to help Liam too. The man put up a cocky front, being a smart arse whenever given the chance, but King had seen him in a few quieter moments too—ones where he didn't know he was being watched— and had seen glimpses of a sensitive man beneath the bravado. King couldn't help wanting to get to know him. His attraction to Liam had been sizzling under the surface for months. It wasn't as if he would ever act on it, but he couldn't deny that he was intrigued.

But until then, he got to spend time with the love of his life.

Adds greeted him with outstretched arms and a kiss with smiling lips coated in strawberry-flavoured gloss. "Hey, handsome."

She took his breath away. Her hair was freshly dyed, the pink electric in its vibrancy. Styled in loose curls with a part pinned back she was stunning. Her black blouse was cute as a button, and paired with a flowy skirt and black ballet flats, she was sexy and adorable.

"Hi to you. You're gorgeous today and every day, of course." He kissed her again, slow and sweet, wrapping his arms around her and pulling her close. The subtle scent of vanilla filled his senses when he breathed her in, but there was something underlying too, something uniquely her that he couldn't get enough of.

The next three weeks without her was going to be hell.

"Hi, everyone, bye, everyone," he called out and whisked her out the door before they had a chance to answer. Carol came to the door, popping her head out as they stepped off the front stoop.

"Enjoy yourselves. See you sometime Sunday morning, Addy?"

As she answered, "Yep, I'll be back to pick up my things, then King is taking me to the airport," she ran her fingers down his face, staring into his eyes. They held a warmth that lit him up from the inside, an affection he was so privileged to be on the receiving end of.

"Okay, love. See you then."

"Bye," he answered absently as the door closed and he pressed his mouth to hers again. Sweeping his tongue along her lip, she opened immediately, and he licked in and tasted her. Sliding his hands down to her waist, he moaned as she pressed in closer. They were connected from top to toe. He would happily have stood there for hours taking his fill, but Adds's stomach rumbled.

"We should go. Sooner we eat, the sooner I can get you naked." Her grin turned wicked, and King reached between them to resituate himself. With his luck, he'd have a permanent zipper imprint on his semi.

With his parents' place around the corner from his school, it didn't take long to reach. He pulled into the drive of the modest single-storey brown-brick house and killed the engine. His mum was already waiting on the front step, her apron with images of her home city, Valetta, covering her generous bosom and waist. "*Aw sabiha*," she greeted, Maltese for hey, beautiful, rolling off his mother's tongue as sa-bih-ha. Cupping both of Adds's cheeks, she smiled and continued in English, "How are you, my girl?"

"I'm well, Mum." She beamed, his mother lighting up like a Christmas tree at the term of endearment.

"When are you marrying Adelaide?" she asked him, grinning when he rolled his eyes. He knew she was teasing him, but there was no exaggerating her desire for grandchildren. Marriage was the first step in her grand plan.

"Hi, Mum." He kissed her cheek as he held the door open for them to go in and took Adds's hand in his.

Dinner was already on the kitchen bench waiting for their arrival—a salad and baked pasta dish topped with flaky pastry. Timpana, baked macaroni with bolognese sauce, was his favourite as a kid, but the high carbs always sent his blood sugar levels haywire. He didn't indulge much anymore. It was easier to avoid it, rather than try to regulate it after the fact, so most of the time, he opted for julienned zucchini rather than actual pasta. But if his mum found out, he'd never hear the end of it.

"Hi, Dad," King called out as he walked through the doorway. "How are you?"

"Good, son." They hugged, and he turned his attention to Adds. With a cheeky grin, his father asked, "*Kif int*, Adelaide?"

The smile slid off her face when he asked how she was. She wiggled her hand as if to say fifty-fifty. "Eh, *insomma*." She turned to King and asked with a hopeful smile, "Did I say that right?"

He couldn't help his snort of laughter at his father's delighted clap and pointed to him.

"I'd say your so-so was perfect."

"Sit, sit," his mum directed and began plating up food.

"I can help, Mum." King pulled out a chair for Adds next to his dad where he could hold her hand while they talked, then went to his mum. "More salad for me than pasta, please."

"No, Kingston, you need to eat. You keep starving yourself and there won't be anything left of you. You're too skinny." She patted his flat belly and tutted. He resisted the urge to roll his eyes. There was no use arguing with her, but her fussing always screwed with his mood. His dad wasn't any help. His diabetes had progressed to Type 1, so he injected insulin. Dad took it as an opportunity to eat pretty much whatever he wanted—the opposite of the doctor's recommendations—but King wasn't going to let his condition progress that far if he had any say in it.

Mum pushed his plate toward him, readying to cut the next serving. "This is enough for four dinners for me, Ma. I can't eat that much. It's gonna go to waste." He trimmed his serve to a quarter of the size she'd dished up and slid the rest onto his dad's plate. "There, that's about right and Dad's got his serving too." He rolled his eyes at her grumble and took his and Adds's plates to the table before going back for his parents'.

Dinner was filled with his father lamenting King leaving his school. His mum had, surprisingly, changed her tune. When he'd explained to her what he hoped to do there, how much of a difference he could make, she became excited. She was still scandalized that they didn't teach religion at the school, but as King had reminded her, he never taught it anyway. His mum was still working on his dad's opinion, but Father Brendan had done a lot to reassure him that he wasn't upset King was moving on.

Conversation soon turned to excited chatter about Adelaide's upcoming trip. His parents were thrilled she'd found a path to follow that she was passionate about. Their love, encouragement, and acceptance were the greatest things about his parents

"Kingston, that's not enough," his mum bemoaned when he placed his cutlery on the plate with a chunk of pasta left. "You're losing too much weight. You're going to get sick."

"It is enough, Mum, and I'm not going to get sick. Please, let it go."

Adds cleared her throat, getting everyone's attention. "I meant to ask, did you see how much petrol prices have gone up? Hope you've filled up." She shook her head and grumbled, her exaggerated reaction and stolen piece of macaroni off his plate quickly redirecting his mother's attention. Mum wasn't an idiot—she gave him the "we'll talk about this later" look, but went with Adds's segue. He slid his palm onto her thigh and Adds shot him a lopsided grin as she threaded their fingers together. He squeezed, silently thanking her, then slipped his hand free to wrap his arm around her shoulders. King loved that she shamelessly redirected the heat off him. He leaned in, pressing a kiss to her temple, and smiled against her skin, imprinting the memory of its softness and her scent, hoping it would sustain him for the next few weeks.

"Yes," his mum answered, adding in a few more Maltese phrases about how much the oil companies ripped off the little guy and how the tax was ridiculous.

"English, Ma. Adds knows the basics but can't understand you when you rant."

"What about you, Adelaide? Did you fill up?" his dad asked.

"I won't be driving my car for a few weeks and I'm nearly full anyway."

* * * * *

"I'm so stuffed," Adds moaned as she rubbed her belly, still lying in the same position she'd fallen into after they'd arrived home. He slipped her shoes off and kicked away his own before crawling up and hovering over her.

"Too stuffed for me to make you feel good?"

"Mhmm." She nodded, her tongue poking out to moisten her lip. King wanted to chase it, to taste her. When what she said registered, he pulled back.

"You okay?" he asked, concern spiking in him. But instead of answering, Adds hitched up her skirt, wrapped her legs around his hips, and pushed his shoulder. She rolled him, straddling him as he landed on his back. Adds sat up, the heat of her pussy pressing against his groin. She drew the tip of her thumb over his bottom lip then ran her finger down, her soft touch burning a trail over his Adam's apple and over the hollow of his throat. She snagged the top button of his shirt and flicked it open, the second one following quickly.

He swallowed, humming at her teasing touch.

"I'm going to miss you," Adds murmured, cupping his face with both hands and leaning down to kiss him. It was slow and soft, and filled with so much emotion that King's heart was fit to burst. She nuzzled that spot under his ear which sent him wild. Adds knew him so well. Every sensitive part of his body had been thoroughly explored, the same way he'd done to her. "You're so damn sexy," she whispered, nipping his ear. Adds showered him with affection, her gentle touch a balm to his soul.

He steadied her hips and leaned up to kiss her. As their tongues tangled together, she smoothed her hand over the hair on his chest. It lit him on fire. Every nerve ending pulsing and sizzling with her soft touch. Pulling back, she hummed before trailing her lips down his throat and sucking a mark against his collarbone. King's cock flexed, blood rushing there until he was rolling his hips to keep up the friction.

She nibbled up and along his jaw to kiss him again. When she sucked on his tongue, King moaned, his balls drawing up high against his body. Adds rocked her hips, grinding on his semi as she palmed his pec and tweaked his nipple. Sensation rocketed through him, her touch as powerful as a lightning strike.

King gasped, his shaft throbbing as the beautiful woman above him worked her magic with her hips, even through their layers of clothes. He groaned on an exhale. "You feel so good."

"About to make you feel better."

THIRTEEN

Adelaide

She loved King's parents, but they had no idea how much damage they did trying to feed him so much. His blood sugar always varied wildly after he was there, and it tended to take days for him to get it back to normal. All the while King felt miserable. It wasn't only just exhaustion while his body processed the excess carbs turned sugar, but also the feeling that his body shape still wasn't ideal.

But no more. She was taking a stand.

He needed to be reminded of the man she knew. His personality was gorgeous—gentle and loving, loyal to a fault, and so willing to help everyone who needed it. But tonight was about the physical beauty she saw. This sexy, sensual man she wanted to devour.

His hand on her leg at dinner had electrified her. His simple touch making her want to get closer, to climb onto his lap and wrap herself around him. She wanted to kiss him until they were breathless and then do it all again.

She hadn't been able to do it then, but now she could.

King's bulky muscles were mouth-watering, his thick thighs and solid arse tempting her to grab hold. His stomach was flat but not ripped like Liam's. But who, other than a professional athlete's, was? She loved the layer of softness he had over those hardened muscles. And that cock? It was a thing of beauty. She wanted to ride it into the sunset every night of her life and see in the dawn with it too.

Undoing the remaining buttons on his shirt, Adelaide pulled it away from his body and kissed a trail down his chest, her tongue circling his nipples as the soft-as-silk hair tickled her chin and nose. She breathed him in, that blend of spicy and sweet so uniquely King driving her wild. Her pussy was already wet, her folds slippery as she rubbed herself on his jeans-covered length. Adelaide urged him to sit up, his stomach going taut while he held himself in a half crunch. She hummed, running her nails over the taut muscles before tearing off his shirt. The buttons at his wrists caught and Adelaide bit down on her lip. She loved him like that, tied up and powerless. He was all hers to admire.

Adelaide undid the buttons at the cuffs and slipped the shirt off, before wrapping the soft cotton around his wrists. She pushed them above his head. He could easily break free—hell, she hadn't even tied a knot—but that wasn't the point. She leaned down, laving his nipples on the deliciously broad chest under her until his breath was choppy and he squirmed. The deep moans and shudders erupting from King gave her a high. It was powerful having him at her mercy and making him see stars. She ran her hands down his thick arms, his biceps bulging as he strained. He would be exercising every ounce of self-control he had not to flip her over and ravage her, but there was no way she was rushing this particular little session.

She nuzzled the patch of dark hair between his pecs and followed the trail down his stomach to his belly button. His abs flexed in her hands. The way his lats narrowed to his waist was so damn sexy. Adelaide wished she had a photographic memory so she could burn King like this into it and never forget how debauched and needy he looked.

The bulge of his cock tented his jeans, and Adelaide cupped him, rubbing his thick shaft through the denim. A strangled gasp left his lips as she popped the button and licked and nipped his treasure trail. When she dipped her tongue in his navel, he arched up off the bed, moaning breathlessly. He planted his feet on the bed and thrust up, his eyes closed and mouth open as he silently begged her to keep touching him.

Tugging the zip through each of the teeth, she watched between kisses and licks of his belly as the head of his cock emerged, a wet patch on his black boxer briefs where pre-cum had pooled. She nuzzled him, before tugging his jeans down and whipping them off, tossing them aside. She didn't tease him, losing his underwear as soon as his jeans were out of her hands.

She licked his slit, tasting his salty essence and moaning as she brushed her fingertips over his sac. His balls were drawn up tight, close to his body. Primed already. Empowerment surged through her, the heady reality that her touch was doing this to King urging her on.

Wrapping her lips around his length, she sank down, taking as much as she could. He was thick, the biggest she'd ever had. She couldn't close her hand around his girth and couldn't get much past the head of his cock, but Adelaide worked him as best she could, jacking his iron-hard shaft as well as sucking and licking the most sensitive parts of him. King cried out as she brushed her fingertip over his crack and she pulled off his cock with a pop, her tongue following the path her hand had taken.

King shook off the shirt, freeing himself. He wrapped his hand around his cock and squeezed. "Fuck, I'm there," he rasped, his voice rough like he'd swallowed sandpaper.

Adelaide scooted off the bed and pointed to him working his dick. "Keep doing that. Just for a second." King nodded, cracking his eyes open and following her movements around the room. He licked his lips and groaned again as she pulled open the drawer and retrieved his lube and the slim vibrating plug she'd gifted him. Coating it in slick, she climbed on the bed and King spread his legs, opening himself up to her. She moaned, loving the vision before her. Thick, muscular thighs with a dusting of dark hair met, and at their juncture was his weeping cock. His fist shuttled slowly up and down his length and his balls twitched as she lowered her gaze to his tight pink pucker. She ran her lubed-up fingers over his cock, and King thrust into her grasp before she trailed her fingertips to his hole. Adelaide circled it until it was clenching and releasing, and she found herself desperately wanting a strap-on. She could just imagine what it would be like to sink into him. She shivered, her empty pussy clenching and her clit throbbing at the thought.

King was ready, desperate, and wanton for the plug to fill him. She pressed the tapered head to his pucker and watched enraptured as he bore down, his arse swallowing the black finger-like object. When it was seated to its flared base, she set it to a low vibrate.

"Shiiit," gasped King as he squeezed the base of his cock tight.

"You are so fucking sexy right now," Adelaide breathed. She wiped her hand on the sheets and reached into her bag for her phone. "I want you to see it." King eyed her warily and she asked, "Do you trust me?" He nodded, but the fear didn't leave his eyes. His erection flagged. "You can delete them once you've seen them. They'll be only for you. No one else will ever see them." King let out a breath and the tension left him. His nod this time came easier, and with a few pumps of his cock, he was back to steely.

Adelaide photographed him. He was a vision. One hand pressed against the padded headboard, the other wrapped around his cock. Feet planted on the mattress with his legs spread and his hips lifting off the bed, he worked himself. She changed angles, focussing on her favourite parts of him. Those lats, his hairy chest, the smooth patch of skin at his hips. She moved to the end of the bed and watched as a drop of pre-cum formed at his slit. He gathered it as his fist closed over the head of his cock and spread the clear liquid with his down stroke. She took another photo, zooming in on his sac and his hole clenching around the toy. His lube and pre-cum slicked fingers. She climbed up, standing and straddling his hips, her feet pressed against his sides. Adelaide focussed the camera down. She saw his jaw clench and his neck tense as he arched back, staving off his orgasm. Photo after photo was taken as he worked himself, until Adelaide couldn't wait any longer.

She passed the phone to him, got down on her knees between his legs, and opened her mouth. He directed the head of his cock to her tongue and jacked himself as she sucked on the tip, her tongue licking at his frenulum. The salty liquid was tangy and delicious. She wanted his load. Wanted it painted all over her naked body.

Adelaide unceremoniously stripped off her blouse and bra, getting naked with one hand as she stroked his balls. When she was nude before him, she batted his hand away, taking over stroking his cock. Adelaide flicked her eyes to the camera. "Photograph this and keep taking them until you come." He groaned and his cock flexed in her grip, clearly liking what she'd said. Fingers buried in her pussy, she rubbed her clit as she gripped the plug with the other, thrusting just enough that it hit his prostate with each pass. King jerked and cried out, his dick weeping. Adelaide eagerly lapped it up, her nipples pebbling as she imagined his seed coated all over her.

She shuttled her hand up and down his cock, twisting her wrist with each pass. Abandoning her pussy, she wanted to touch him everywhere, to feel his abs contracting as he neared the edge. She licked him, increasing the suction on his cockhead as she pressed down and hollowing out her cheeks on the way up.

King cried out, his cock pulsing on her tongue. She pulled off, pressing his cock between her breasts, and squeezed her elbows in until her breasts cupped his shaft. With her one hand rubbing his abs, and the other still stroking his prostate with the toy, King stiffened, and his salty essence shot out, coating her chest and throat. Cum ran between her breasts and she moaned, loving the warmth of his thick seed sliding along her skin. She kept working him until the aftershocks slowed and he was boneless. Clicking off the plug, Adelaide drew it out of him slowly, rubbing his cum into her skin. His eyes blazed, his cock twitching as she rubbed her legs together, needing friction there.

When Adelaide returned from the bathroom, King was standing in front of the hamper in the corner of his room, cleaning himself up with a shirt. "Lie down with me." She knelt on the bed and patted the soft sheet before picking up her phone. When King eyed it warily, Adelaide met his gaze, hers never wavering. She'd made him a promise and if he didn't want to look at the photos, she'd delete them. But she wanted to see the images and then have him fuck her into next week.

He propped himself up on his elbow, running his fingers down her back to her arse. "Behave," she ordered with narrowed eyes. "But only for a minute. Then you can get dirty." She opened her gallery, navigated to the first photo, and placed it on the bed between them. The image was one of

King's head tilted back, his strong neck arched as he cried out.

"I love your throat and the way your muscles tense."

His gaze snagged on hers, and she reached out to cup his face, her thumb skimming along his cheekbone. His stubble tickled her fingers. She swiped at the images, pausing each time until King tore his eyes away from her to look at them. When she reached the one of his chest, she added, "Your chest makes me want to snuggle into you and I want your arms around me all the time. You're the sexiest man I've laid eyes on, King."

He huffed. "I'm a work in progress."

"We all are, but I love this work in progress."

His eyes snapped to hers and he sucked in a sharp breath. "You love me?"

"Yes, I do. I've just been too chicken shit to say anything." She'd needed to get her head around how she'd managed to fall in love with two men. Every effort she'd made to scrub Liam from her heart had failed miserably, and their studying together had only made her feelings grow. But the way she felt for King was real. He wasn't a replacement or a consolation prize either. It was plain and simple when she boiled it down—she loved him. She pressed her lips together in a small smile, suddenly shy at the admission. "I love everything about you, King."

"I love you too." He reached for her, pulling her close. Every part of their bodies was aligned, pressed together from shoulder to toes. He leaned in to kiss her, slowly capturing her lips in a sensual glide. "Thank you," he whispered against her lips. "I'm not perfect, but you make me believe that one day I could be perfect for you."

"You already are."

King blushed at her words, the pink staining his cheeks creeping down his neck to his chest. Adelaide pressed a smiley kiss to his lips and laughed breathlessly when he flipped her onto her back, hitched her legs over his shoulders, and buried his face in her pussy.

FOURTEEN

Liam

Liam wandered outside and kicked a pebble across the drive with his toe, trying to act casual. He was anything but. His insides were jumping around like a jack rabbit. But it wasn't excitement. It was nerves. The need to say something before it was too late.

But he couldn't.

He could never say anything. Not out loud. Not to them.

Addy was walking her suitcase down the drive to King's Subaru wearing a flowy summer pale green dress and white slip-on sandals. She had her hair loose, the curls falling around her face and framing it. The freshly dyed pink gleamed brightly in the midday sun, highlighting the different shades in it. She was a vision. Absolutely gorgeous. His steps faltered as she looked over her shoulder, spotting him. The smile that lit up her face was radiant, like the sun breaking the horizon at dawn on a hot summer's day. It was as if the world was grey, and when she smiled it instantaneously transformed. Spectacular pastels grew in radiance with every second that passed.

A pretty pink flushed her cheeks and she looked away, and Liam's gaze clashed with King's. His eyes were dark when he raked his sight over Liam, King's lips twisting into a grimace. The man radiated a don't-fuck-with-me attitude and Liam swallowed, nerves surging within as he tried, and failed, to look away. Liam wiped his hands down his old training shorts—the tiny pair he was about to go swimming in—and regretted not putting on a shirt given the look of distaste King shot his way.

He wandered over to their front step, standing with Carol. "Hey," he greeted her quietly, oddly unsure of what to say to the woman who'd become like a mum to him. Her eyes were watery, her arms crossed over her chest, crinkling the green scrubs she wore. Addy handed her suitcase to King, who loaded it in the back of the car, and Carol bit back a sob.

It was three weeks, barely longer than a holiday. But Addy leaving was hard to watch. Hands shaking, he reached out to Carol and wrapped his arm around her shoulders.

"I'm sorry, I'm being silly," she mumbled, holding out a hand. "But look at her. She's all grown up."

He nodded, swallowing the lump in his throat. "She is, and she's going to make you so proud."

"She already has." Carol pulled back and looked up at him. "All of you make me proud every day. Even when my son laughs at me." She cast a glance back in the house and rolled her eyes.

"Don't worry about Lij. He's just being insensitive."

"He is, isn't he." She smiled a watery smile, wiped her tears away, and blew out a breath.

Then it was time. Addy walked back up the drive and held out her arms to Carol. "I'll text you when I land." They hugged tightly, the strength of their bond evident in their embrace.

"Call me when you get to the house. I want to know everything."

"I will. But you don't need to worry, Mum. I'm gonna be fine." Addy's smile was reassuring, excitement pouring off her.

"I know you will be. These are happy, proud tears, love. You're going to be amazing." They hugged again and a shuffling sounded behind him before the screen door banged closed. Lij and Pop walked past, making their way to their girl. Addy broke her hold on her mum to include Pop in the embrace, and Lij threw his arms around them too, hugging them tight. He may have teased Carol about crying, but he loved Addy just as fiercely.

It was a private moment between family members, and Liam felt like an intruder witnessing it. He looked away, only for his gaze to slam into King's again. They stared, Liam licking his lips as he preened under King's unwavering focus. King's nostrils flared, like a bull ready to charge, and Liam didn't know whether he wanted to provoke the man, just so he could feel a part of him against his body. Liam's breaths shallowed out, all the blood in his body rushing south. His cock thickened, and Liam clasped his hands in front of him, desperately trying to hide the obscene boner he'd be sporting any second now.

Movement next to him caught his attention—Addy and her family pulling apart. Liam wanted to say goodbye. Needed to. His body demanded that he get his fill of her gentle touch as if he was charging his battery. He stepped forward and brushed a curl away from her face before cupping her cheek and lifting her chin. He was standing far too close to her, half expecting King's fist to connect with his face at any moment. But getting to look into those beautiful blue eyes the colour of sapphires, was totally worth it.

Addy's breath caught and she planted her hands against his abs when he wrapped his other arm around her waist. Pulling her closer, he plastered their bodies together. He breathed her in, all warm vanilla and sunshine, and begged his already interested dick not to stand to attention.

Her hands scalded his stomach, making it spin and swoop as she brushed against his six-pack. He wanted to dip her and kiss her until she was breathless. But it was a fantasy. A dream that would never come true. Instead, he held her tightly and ruffled her hair—his way of saying I love you—and Addy responded, gripping his nipples and twisting. He sucked in a breath and squeezed his eyes closed, hissing as she twisted harder. His cock hardened and he pulled away, not willing to face her questioning gaze.

"That's for messing up my hair," she grumbled before adding in a murmur, "Look after King, yeah?"

Liam took another step back, his body screaming at him to do the opposite. "Don't worry about your man. I'll keep him busy." Liam winced, not intending the double en-tendre, and hoping Addy didn't call him out on it.

"Don't stress. King's got you. We'll both ace our sub-jects."

"I hope so." He smiled at her, forcing himself to be happy. He was genuinely excited for her. The passion she had for her course was unmistakeable, but he wished she didn't have to leave, albeit temporarily, to do it. He cleared his throat, dislodging the lump of emotion, and added, "Kick arse, Addy. See you soon. I'll miss you."

"I'll miss you too." She winked, then scampered off to the car, King already behind the wheel. He was white-knuckling it, his jaw tight as he looked straight ahead. When the door closed and Addy leaned into him, he softened, smiling at her and leaning over to press a kiss to her temple before flicking his eyes toward Liam. Their stare held for a moment too long, King's gaze riveting him to the spot. It stripped him bare. Left him naked. It was as if King could see every secret he'd been trying to hide.

"So, um… Yeah." He cleared his throat, motioned to his house with his thumb over his shoulder, and gave the oth-ers an awkward smile. He shuffled off and slipped through the back gate into the yard, diving into the pool for a few laps before King came back to start their tutoring.

Oh fuck. King was coming back.

* * * * *

"Before we get started, how do you learn?" King asked him. He was being... nice. The glaring, angry dude who looked ready to throttle Liam was nowhere to be found. It was as if they were different people.

Liam sat at his kitchen table, King resting his forearm on the surface so they were facing each other. King was giving him his full attention. When the man had walked in acting as if nothing had happened before, it had thrown Liam for a loop. Now all he could do was stare blankly at him. What sort of question was "how do you learn?" Wasn't that what a tutor was for? To teach him?

King chuckled, the sound a cross between exasperation and humour, but somehow Liam didn't think the man was poking fun at him. Maybe it was the buttoned-up look he sported in his long-sleeved white cotton shirt and jeans, or the kindness in his eyes that comforted Liam. Or it could have been the way he'd squeezed Liam's shoulder, reassuring him. King added, "You've never been asked that question before, have you?"

Liam shook his head and King's eyes flashed with something—excitement, maybe.

"Right, that's where we start then."

He explained that there were different methods of teaching, and teachers adapted their educational styles to the learning method of the people they were educating. When they only had one student, it was a matter of discovering which suited the learner best. When they were juggling a class, they taught different methods—some students picked up the first way, some the later options. "What are your strengths? Sport, obviously, but is there anything else? Art? Music? English? Science?"

"English. I'm good at writing."

King nodded, a smile forming. Liam sat back against the chair and blinked, his gut flip-flopping at the shape of his lips. Bringing out that smile was… heart stopping. Or maybe the opposite if the rapid flutter in his chest was anything to go by.

"Excellent. How do you study for the subjects that have a lot of written content?"

"I read anything and everything. I summarize the points in my own words—"

"How?" He paused for a moment, perhaps waiting for an answer, but Liam wasn't sure he understood. "As in, do you write it down? Speak it out loud?"

Oh. "I type it out. Is that… good?"

"Oh, yeah," King encouraged, nodding. "I'm trying to understand your process. The only right answer here is whatever works for you, so if you can narrow down how you learn, we can adapt the materials for this subject to your style. Then what? Do you do anything with those notes?"

"Yeah, I read and review them a few times. I look up practice questions and hand write mini essays using my notes. Typing them doesn't help me remember but, I don't know, maybe it's the process of writing it out that helps. First I refer to the notes and I keep going until I can write the essays from memory."

King grinned, his beaming smile lighting up his face. "Do you find you delve into the whys and the history and background information so you get a big picture of what you're doing, or do you focus on what's in front of you?"

He thought on that question for a moment, understanding finally dawning on why he found studying easier if he had extensive reading materials available. "I need to understand how it works and fits together to be able to put it in context."

King laughed. "I could hug you right about now. I wish my students were like you. Most of them ignore me when I try to tell them what the maths I'm teaching them is used for in the real world. But what you've said will help so much." He sobered. "When you're in tutorials or studying for your statistics exams do you do the same thing?"

"No, our tutor told us to memorize the formulas. The practice questions we do are set up in the same format as the exams, so they show us how to pull the information we need from the questions. We're then taught how to plug it into the formulas and get the answers. We have to write about the results we get, but I don't understand what the hell I'm doing."

"Because they're teaching you to rote learn everything. That's one of your roadblocks right there."

King's comment held a hell of a lot of truth. Every time Liam asked questions about why things were done the way they were, his tutors didn't seem to understand what he was getting at. They repeated the formulas and how to gather the information instead of explaining why the information the formulas gave him was important to know and in what contexts. He'd walked out of meeting after meeting still no clearer, and in the end he'd given up, struggling through the questions himself. Most of the time he could follow the steps the tutors gave him, but when it came time to get the information to stick, his brain was like Teflon.

"Your tutors are teaching you to approach the questions in the way that suits them as learners, and perhaps as teachers too. If everyone answers formulaically, it's easy to mark. But if the learning style doesn't suit you, you won't get any benefit from approaching questions that way. We need to find what works for you."

"Okay." It was logical. The real test would be whether he could actually make heads or tail of the information.

"Statistics is maths, right? It's a language. It has its own rules just like English has grammar and spelling rules. It has building blocks like words and sentences, and the data that we get as answers helps us build the paragraphs. Piece those things together and we can craft the story."

He huffed. "Makes sense in theory. It's the putting it together that I've failed dismally at."

King clapped him on the shoulder, squeezing him. His hand was cool, his grip strong. Comforting. "That's where I come in. I'm going to help you understand why you're doing these calculations, how to draw the conclusions from the data, and what the results mean. You are going to pass this course, Liam. I have no doubt that you can do it."

"You haven't seen how bad I am yet."

King laughed at Liam's quip, a rumbling chuckle from deep in his chest, and nudged him with his elbow. Liam liked the way he did that—touched him—and the faith King seemed to have in him was uplifting. It was as if he could do anything. But that was ridiculous. Liam looked away, heat flaring and crawling over his face. He realized he was smiling, a shy grin tilting his lips fractionally upward. He wanted King's confidence in him to be well founded, but his experience thus far with the evil that was statistics didn't reassure him.

"Are you doubting how good a teacher I am?" King raised an eyebrow, Liam's insides clenching at the sight.

"No," Liam hurried to reassure him, an irrational panic lashing out. "Just how good a learner I am."

"Don't stress. You've got this. Trust me." King pulled his chair closer until their shoulders were pressed together and knees knocking before he launched into a discussion on the basics of statistics, what they fundamentally were, their importance, and how they make data comparable. His passion shone through, just like Addy's did when she was talking, and Liam let himself get swept away in King's storytelling. He was patient and kind, going over things whenever Liam asked a question. King encouraged him to give his perspective too, something he hadn't really had much of outside of his relationship with Lij and Addy.

They spoke mostly about rugby statistics, King contextualising the concepts he was learning into something that made sense to Liam. King reached for his glass of water, finding it empty, and Liam jumped up, filling it from the dispenser on the fridge. He handed it over as King looked down at his watch, his eyes widening momentarily. "We've been going at it for hours. You must be exhausted."

It was only then that Liam looked outside to see darkened skies. He'd turned the lights over the table on what had felt like ten minutes earlier, but it must have been hours. The clock was ticking over to 8:00 p.m., the sun long having set outside.

"Yeah, starving too." Liam rubbed his belly, a louder growl letting loose. He'd been getting low-key protests for a few hours but had ignored them. It seemed that his stomach was done waiting.

King stood, pushed his chair in, and packed up his things. Liam knew what he was going to say before he'd opened his mouth, and he scrambled for excuses to get King to stay. He'd enjoyed his company. Talking came easily between them, and Liam wanted more of the warmth that spread through his veins when he was under King's spotlight. "You should stay. For dinner, I mean."

"I can't tonight. But thanks for the offer. Maybe we can do it next time. Let me know if you want me to come around tomorrow—"

"I do. I've understood more in these few hours we've been talking than I did in two semesters I've taken the subject. I definitely want to keep going."

King took his glass to the sink and held his hand out to Liam to shake. There was that cool, firm grip again. His hands were rough like Liam's. He didn't think a maths teacher would do anything physical for work, but he clearly lifted weights. Was that why he was built like a brick shithouse? Tall and broad, he took up a lot of space, but not in a bad way. His presence was calming in a make-you-feel-safe way. He was definitely a gentle giant, and after talking with him, he could see exactly why Addy had fallen head over heels for him.

He was kind, a good guy. It made his attraction to the man even harder to ignore.

King flashed him a beaming smile, one that lit up his whole face and made his eyes crinkle at the corners. It was heady knowing he'd done that. He'd worked hard to impress this man, one far smarter than him, and Liam's chest expanded in pride. He hadn't ever thought he would get such a kick out of pleasing his teacher, but that smile was worth the hours of battling a subject he despised. Except that he hadn't hated what he'd learned today. King had explained everything in a way that made sense. Liam had understood it too. Something inside him told Liam that the knowledge wouldn't slide right away either. It wasn't all jumbled up in his head, floating around and getting tangled up in each other like a knotted-up ball of twine. King had crafted a story and Liam followed it.

A weight lifted off his shoulders. Liam laughed, hope finally lighting the darkened tunnel he'd been stumbling through for far too long.

"Good work, man. Don't underestimate yourself. You keep working like you did today and you'll ace this subject."

"Thank you." His words were quiet but heartfelt, and King seemed to understand the weight of them, nodding and reaching out to squeeze his shoulder once more before letting go of his hand and saying goodbye.

Liam watched as his taillights disappeared around the corner. When he turned into his house, the silence that met him was deafening. He could go next door. He could spend some time with Lij, but in the lead up to the holidays, his friend was always busy with last-minute edits for Christmas releases. Maybe it was just an excuse though, because while he wanted company, Lij's wasn't it. He loved his best mate—they were brothers from another mother. He'd always be his closest friend, but Liam wanted Addy's easy comfort and King's warm reassurance. He loved their quiet study times together and wanted more of it. King too, if today was anything to go by.

Back in the kitchen, he collected the ingredients so he could grill steak on the barbie while he waited for the microwave to signal his baked potato was ready. When everything was done, he piled his plate high with meat, broccoli, and potato slathered in sour cream, chives, and grated cheese, and ate outdoors, the patio light creating a halo around the table. Beyond, the sky was dark. Muted noise from Pop's TV and the regular zaps from his neighbour's UV bug light were the only interruptions to the silence.

But it didn't distract him from turning King's parting words over and over in his mind. He couldn't get the other man's expressions out of his thoughts. Had he ever seen pride like that directed at him before? His teachers? Coaches? His agent? His parents? Liam's achievements might not have been as important to them as they were to him, but he'd done all right, hadn't he? Had anyone ever been proud of him like King had just been? Every time Liam answered a question correctly, he was met with King's smile. Even when they were talking and Liam was explaining his career stats—the number of penalties, assists, tries, and time on field—and King was writing notes, he'd been nodding, actively listening and encouraging him to keep going. King's attention, his constant praise, the easy way he spoke, and the effortless faith he had in Liam was motivation like nothing else. In the space of a couple of hours, King had bolstered Liam's confidence and had him riding a high. He could do this. He would do it. And it would be because Addy and King had been there to help him.

Liam hadn't wanted to face statistics again, but he'd never been more grateful to have support when he'd really needed it. Something told him that this go at the subject from hell would have a different outcome.

Maybe.

Hopefully.

King's words came back to him—*"Are you doubting how good a teacher I am?"*—and he smiled. No, after this afternoon's session, he had no doubt that King's students were the luckiest SOBs ever.

He yawned, exhausted after a day of both physical and mental workouts. It was early by most standards, but he'd been on the field at 5:00 a.m., starting their training before the heat and humidity hit. He'd gone for a swim that afternoon too, doing laps of the pool until he couldn't lift his arms just to shake off the disappointment of knowing he wouldn't see Addy for a few weeks. Liam was ready to crash. Dragging his feet up the stairs to his bedroom, stripping as he went, Liam face-planted his mattress naked as the day he was born. The chilled air from the air-conditioning vent above his bed washed over him, cooling his sweat-damp skin. His thoughts drifted back to King and their session. Why was he wearing jeans and a long-sleeved shirt during summer in sub-tropical weather? He didn't understand the man himself, but King was doing a hell of a good job helping him understand everything else.

* * * * *

His life consisted of the pre-season training Coach was putting them through and studying. Every year he questioned his career choice, the gruelling workouts taking their toll. Hour after hour of high-intensity exercise—workouts to build fitness, ball handling skills, tackling drills—you name it, they did it. Then he would drive home, listen to the recorded lecture, sit in on his online tutorial or read the chapter assigned to him, do any set problems, and work on his assessment, all before King arrived. They'd spent every afternoon together since Addy had left for Sydney a week earlier, and with the exception of their first tutoring session, King had stayed for dinner every night. They'd cooked together or ordered takeout, laughing and getting to know each other outside of the statistics umbrella they were under most of the time.

Lij had joined them after work last night, and they'd played poker into the early morning hours, only for his alarm to blare after three hours of sleep. He was paying for it that morning, Coach shouting at him more than once. This time, he'd fumbled the ball, dropping an easy pass when he couldn't hold back his yawn. Liam shook the weariness off and held up his hand in an apologetic wave.

Training wrapped up an hour later and Liam trudged into the change rooms following his teammates. Stripping off, he tossed his dirty uniform in his bag and reached for his towel, wrapping it around his waist. "Masters, my office when you're done showering," Coach ordered from the doorway. He would happily curl up on the floor of the shower and sleep, but he didn't dawdle, scrubbing himself down and washing his hair as the water sluiced over him. Sighing, he shut off the water, dried, and got dressed.

"What's going on, man?" Daz, his captain, asked. Liam shrugged. He had no idea why Coach wanted to see him other than his performance that day being lacklustre. Was that enough to warrant more than the dressing down he'd already received? Probably, but Liam hoped Coach would give him the benefit of the doubt.

Pulling on his shoes and socks, Liam answered, "No idea, mate. S'pose I'll find out." Leaving his gear in the locker room, Liam headed up the wide tiled hallway that smelled of old socks and humid air, toward Coach's office. He knocked on the closed door, his nerves playing havoc with him.

"Come."

Liam entered, closing the door with a quiet snick behind him. "Sorry about today, Coach—"

"As long as you being tired wasn't because you were out partying last night, I'll let it slide."

"No, just had some friends over after tutoring. It won't happen again." Liam hesitated and Coach tilted his head, silently encouraging him to explain. "I'm working with a tutor to pass the subject I failed last trimester. He's my neighbour's boyfriend."

"Well, keep doing what you're doing on field too and you'll have a good year. If you can pass that subject as well—"

"It'll be a stellar one." He grinned, confident that with King's help he could get there. "The sooner I kick statistics, the better." If he passed—no when he passed—he would move onto the advanced statistics class, and another fifteen odd weeks of spending time with King.

After the check-in, he walked back into the change rooms, intending to text Daz to update him. But when he picked up his phone, a notification was waiting for him. He eagerly opened it, thinking it was King planning dinner. He was bringing the ingredients over for a dish his mum cooked that Liam had salivated over when King described it. But the message wasn't from King. It was his mum.

Your sister needs furniture for the nursery. We've found some lovely pieces for it. Can you transfer $5,000? It would help her out a lot.

Liam sat down on the bench in the now empty change room, his gut bottoming out. He didn't know what to feel seeing those words printed on his phone. Anger? Frustration? Betrayal, perhaps? The request itself didn't bother him. He was used to giving them money. At least his mum had framed her demand in the form of a question this time. It let him pretend he could say no. But he never would. If his sister needed it, he would give it to her. That's what brothers did. He had money, she needed it.

That wasn't the problem.

What rankled him was... hell, he didn't even know anymore. He knew his mother would never reach out to his sister if he needed any kind of help. But then, he wouldn't go to his mum either. She'd tell him that he was an adult and part of being one was to take responsibility for his life, and fair enough. It wasn't that she'd asked for help when it wouldn't be reciprocated. It was more that the only time his mum reached out was when she wanted something, usually money. She never called or messaged him to say hi or ask how he was. She never sent him good luck messages before a game. They hadn't even remembered his birthday this year. It was Lij's family who'd brought him cake, complete with candles and silly presents.

It wasn't even that he already paid double the market rent for their property each week. For what he was paying, he could get a place on the waterfront, but he couldn't bring himself to do it. While the house he'd grown up in had some happy memories, most of them cantered around Lij, and now Addy. Moving meant leaving them—the family who'd stepped in as substitutes when his own were uninterested. Lij, Addy, Carol, and Pop were the closest thing to a family he had.

Of course, his father would disagree. It would be another thing he'd lecture Liam over if his dad ever heard his thoughts. But that was the way his father parented. He was completely hands off unless a punishment was warranted. Liam couldn't remember receiving a single hug from his dad, yet the man doted over his only daughter. He remembered back when he was little his dad saying that men didn't cry and hugging was for girls. It explained why his dad always had one ready for his sister, but never one for him.

Some things never changed, he supposed. Now he understood that she was their favourite. Back then, he thought there was something wrong with him. Still did sometimes, but he'd never done anything wrong. Never acted out. Never caused trouble. His only fault was that he'd simply been born a boy when his parents were desperate for another girl.

He was a terrible person to think like that, but at least now his sister had moved away and their parents had followed, their favouritism wasn't constantly being paraded in his face. Now it was just texts like these that did it. Was it too much to ask that he get a hello? A how are you? Liam knew better. He shook off the heaviness that had blanketed him and sent a text back, *Sure*.

Within moments another message appeared on his screen. *When are you transferring the money? I'm waiting at the store now. I'd prefer not to have to wait for long.*

Liam sighed, his shoulders slumping as the weight of his parents' expectations pressed down on him. He was kidding himself thinking even for a moment that he could say no to her. He opened his banking app, transferred the money, took a screenshot, and sent another text with the image included. His mother would keep hounding him until the money hit, and he didn't have the mental bandwidth to deal with her.

He had a mini test to study for, good company, and dinner with King to look forward to.

FIFTEEN

Kingston

"That's it, mate. Nearly there," Mike coached as King struggled under the weight he was bench-pressing. King grunted as he straightened his arms, and Mike guided the bar to the cradle.

"You really notice the difference even when it's only a couple of kilos heavier," King puffed, shaking out his arms. Every one of his muscles were screaming and at the same time were jelly-like. But he loved the burn from working out with Mike. The man was a machine, pushing him harder than any other trainer in the gym—except maybe Levi—and it was great to see him back at 100 percent. Heart problems had side-tracked him for a couple of months, turning him into a shell of the man King knew. But the surgery was successful, and Mike was back.

"Mhmm," Mike answered, leaning against the weight rack as he assessed him. "Have to say, King, I'm seeing the difference in your physique too. Your body fat is dropping and you're still bulking up. You should be really pleased with the changes."

King shrugged and nodded. "Yeah, so-so. Call me a work in progress." He smiled, thinking about his conversation with Adds all those months ago, and then the first time she'd told him she loved him. The butterflies in his belly took flight, and a sappy grin lifted his lips. Just thinking about her made him happy. He loved being in love with her, and that feeling permeated every part of him. He was more confident, happier, and was generally high on life. "But I'm liking where I'm at."

Mike nodded, a lazy smile spreading on his lips. "You look happy, man. Whatever you're doing, keep doing it."

King's grin widened and heat crawled over his cheeks. Mike was right. Adds had a profound effect on him. But it wasn't just her. It was Liam too. Their friendship was as easy as breathing, and the time they spent together had become his favourite part of the day. They'd fallen into this domestic bliss that King adored. It didn't matter whether they were working or cooking in the kitchen together, eating or watching a movie. Time with him was comfort and excitement at the same time. It was as if he was buzzing, an undercurrent of electricity flowing through him whenever he thought of Liam. Spending time with him amped it up to levels where he was sure Liam could see the incandescent glow radiating from King that seemed to grow every time Liam smiled.

He was itching to get over there already, and he still had a few hours before Liam would even be home. Taking care of Liam, teaching him, and encouraging him to shine, then watching his face morph from studious to surprised excitement when a concept sank in, fuelled him. King couldn't be prouder of how far Liam had come in such a short period of time. But it was more than that too. He loved seeing Liam happy. Liam was like a flower uncurling in the sun with even the smallest bit of attention, and King loved getting to see it.

He craved it.

They moved over to the mats ready to begin their cool-down routine, and Mike asked, "Any plans for today?" Mike stretched his arms above his head, before grasping his elbow and bending to the side, stretching his lat.

King copied the move. "I'm cooking dinner for a friend." It seemed like such a trivial word for his relationship with Liam. But at the same time, it wasn't. King loved hard and would do anything for the people he considered friends, but he didn't have many of them. So counting Liam among them was big for King.

"Nice. Any idea what you're making?"

He flushed again, embarrassed that he'd planned a full menu for what was supposed to be a simple Wednesday night dinner. He'd apparently inherited his parents' love of food—something he hadn't really indulged in except with Liam. It had become their thing, and King's heart tripped up in his chest, fluttering when he thought about Liam and being able to show him just how much he cared. He understood now why his mum got so much joy from cooking for her loved ones. He wanted to do it too, especially for Liam.

* * * * *

Liam rested his chin in the heel of his hand, watching enraptured as King used a fork to shred the beef. He'd had it slow-cooking all day, and the smell in his house was delicious. "So, once I've done this, we'll start on the ricotta."

"Do I get to help?" Liam asked, his eyes sparkling with excitement. They were mostly green tonight, and King couldn't tear his gaze away. He swallowed, cataloguing Liam's features, the curve of his jaw, the tilt of his kissable lips in a smile.

"Of course," King said, his voice rougher than he'd realized. He cleared his throat and added, "Once we've made the ricotta, we'll use it in the gnocchi."

Liam's groan was illicit. It painted pictures of writhing bodies and gasps of ecstasy. Of long lean muscles covered in a sheen of sweat. He could just imagine Liam slaking his lust with a beautiful woman. He was single, but whoever ended up in Liam's bed, whether it was for one night or many, was lucky. He was the sort of man who deserved to be loved and would give that love unconditionally back.

King unpacked the sous vide he'd borrowed from his mum, setting up the water to reach the required temperature, explaining it all to Liam as he went. Within thirty minutes he had it ready to start on the ricotta. "Hold this for me while I pour the milk in?" he asked Liam. They worked side by side, Liam reaching in front of King to keep the cooking bag steady as King slowly poured. "Once the milk has warmed, we pour in the vinegar and stir it until the curds form. Then we let it sit for twenty minutes."

"I had no idea you could make your own ricotta." Liam stuck out his neck to look inside the bag as the water settled around it, a smile filled with wonder, tilting his lips up and making his eyes sparkle. He loved seeing him filled with happiness.

Liam's gaze met his, and King's breath caught. His heart tripped over itself. Instinctively, King reached up, resting his hand on Liam's shoulder. Unable to tear his eyes away, he watched as Liam's pupils dilated, his emerald greens darkening. Those pouty lips parted and Liam's inhale was short and sharp. They were standing close, but having Liam in his personal space was as natural as breathing. Touching him was too. Liam had been starved of attention, and affection, somewhere. King hated that for him. The urge to comfort him and at the same time, show Liam that his friendship meant the world to King was strong. Like the advance and retreat of the tides, it also seemed inevitable. They gravitated toward each other. It was as if King and Liam were always meant to be something to each other.

Something important.

Something deep and irreplaceable.

Something to cherish and nurture, exactly like the man himself. King was so grateful that it got to be him.

SIXTEEN

Liam

The side gate closed, the chink of the metal catch clattering like it did whenever someone walked through. King called out, "Lee, I'm here," before sliding the back door open. He stood there in a long-sleeved black Henley and faded well-worn jeans that hugged his thick thighs. Liam wanted to touch the material just to see if it was as soft as butter, and the muscle underneath as firm as his legs looked. King shivered as the cool breeze of the air-conditioning washed over him. "Damn, it's freezing in here."

"It's really not." Liam had bumped up the thermostat by quite a few degrees since King had started tutoring him. He always ran cold and would sit in a tweed jacket shivering if Liam kept it at its usual temperature. "How are you always cold?"

King froze, looking at Liam like he was a deer in headlights, a weird vulnerability in his wide eyes. His sharp intake of breath surprised Liam. But then King blinked, seeming to shake out of it. "I... ah... lost some weight. It's a side effect."

Liam looked him up and down. He'd noticed his build before, jealous of the bulk he carried like he was a defensive footballer. He'd spied King's toned biceps and had his muscular thigh pressed against his own when they'd been working together, leaning over the textbook and puzzling out the questions. King had an almost barrel-like chest too, broad-shouldered and perfect for... well, Addy to cuddle into. He hadn't noticed it at all when King rested his arm across the back of Liam's chair as he leaned in close and explained correlations, dependent and independent variables. Liam hadn't noticed that their heads were close enough to feel the warmth radiating from King or how the world could fade away when they got lost in their bubble studying together.

Liam shook the thoughts away and refocussed on the other man. The layers made sense, and he turned off the air. King shot him a grateful smile and placed a few shopping bags on the kitchen bench. "Mind if I get dinner on so it has time to slow cook?" he asked.

Liam stood. "Yeah, absolutely. Want a drink?"

"Just water," King replied casually, and Liam's gut flip-flopped. He was looking away from Liam, his head in the fridge as he stacked a few packets of meat in it. He liked this, the companionship and comradery they shared. His attraction for King simmered under the surface, surprising him with its intensity, but these quiet moments when King showed him how comfortable he was in Liam's presence, were ones he collected and kept close to him like a dragon with its hoard.

Liam got him out a cutting board and followed King's directions, chopping bacon as King got the other ingredients ready—boiled eggs, breadcrumbs, fresh parsley, a ton of garlic, and salt and pepper. When everything was ready, King prepared the meat, laying the thin slices over strips of kitchen twine. "We basically spoon the filling onto the meat, wrap it, tie it up, and cook it on a simmer for a few hours. We'll do the vegetables after we finish studying if that's okay?"

"If it's simmering, there's a sauce, yeah?"

"Red wine, onion, carrots, and a few other herbs." He turned to Liam and smiled reassuringly when Liam's hesitance must have shown in his pinched lips. King knew he wasn't a fan of red wine. "It's good, you'll like it."

When they were done, the stuffed meat rolls immersed in a rich-smelling sauce, and their hands washed, Liam took their refilled drinks over to the table and sat down. King wiped the benches one more time and wandered over to him, leaning over Liam, one large hand closing over his shoulder and squeezing. King ran a finger over the open page of the textbook sitting on the table. "Are you good with this stuff? We looked at it yesterday."

Liam nodded, revelling in the warmth of the man at his back. He hadn't experienced this attraction to men before, but he couldn't bring himself to fret about it. He'd never been one of those men who were threatened by queer people. Maybe that was Lij's and his family's influence talking. If it was, he was proud to be open enough with himself to recognizing that his sexuality wasn't as straight as he'd imagined. Knowing that he could love more than one gender didn't frighten him. It reassured him. Made him certain that even though he'd never really been on the receiving end of the kind of unlimited love that poems were written about, he knew he could give it.

"Okay then, what are we working on today?" King asked.

"Dunno, teach. What should we work on?" he teased, looking up at the man who'd made him see.

"You've got your test coming up. Should we spend some time on that once we've gone through this week's class materials?" King slid onto the seat next to him, shifting closer so he could watch closely as Liam worked. He breathed King in, loving the scent of the spicy aftershave or deodorant that he wore. Maybe he should get some of it. But Liam had never worn those classic scents before. They seemed to be made for older guys. More sophisticated ones. Would something like that suit him? Probably not.

He shook out of the spell King's scent cast over him. Liam closed his eyes and imagined King kissing his neck. He was sexy as hell. Liam licked his lips, desire smouldering in his veins like embers about to ignite. "If I pass this subject, I'll have another statistics course to do. Can you help me with it?"

"Of course. I'd love to help."

"Good, good. I really want your help with it…" He sucked in a breath, tapped his pencil on the notepad, and swallowed down his nerves. "I'm really glad we're friends."

"So am I." King's words were quiet, and Liam shifted in his seat so he faced King, his legs bracketing King's. "Your company... it's kept me sane." King huffed. "I was worried I'd be lonely without Adds here. Eve, my friend, and I see each other a few times over the holidays, but I don't have too many other people I catch up with." He paused, chewing on his lip. "My parents try to feed me non-stop. They don't get that it's bad for my diabetes, even though my dad has it too."

Liam smiled sadly. He understood that King had once had an unhealthy relationship with food and that would have been made so much worse by parents who constantly encouraged him to eat. But all Liam could picture were the times when he'd arrived home after practice to dishes stacked by the dishwasher ready for him to load, with nothing left for him. He'd had more Vegemite sandwiches than was healthy, and if it wasn't for Carol noticing his weight loss and insisting that he go there for dinner after practice or evening games, he would have eaten countless more.

He cleared his throat, hating that his eyes burned with the memory. His voice hitched when he spoke. It was barely loud enough to carry between them. "When I was a kid, I used to have practice that went late a few times a week. Mum or Dad would pick me up, but they never saved me dinner if I wasn't there to eat with them. Our parents must have been at opposite ends of the bell curve."

King turned to face him, and the look in his eyes broke Liam. He didn't want his pity, but that wasn't what Liam saw. It was sadness and righteous anger. A tear slipped free and he laughed it off, wiping his cheek roughly with the heel of his palm. "Stupid emotions."

King didn't say a word, merely cupped his nape and pulled him close, wrapping his arms around Liam's shoulder and giving him a safe place to land. He held tight, sinking into King's embrace. He was bigger and broader than Liam, and all that muscle and warmth beckoned him to snuggle with the man. Liam never wanted to pull back. He wanted to memorize every sensation in case he never got to be close to King like this again.

"Your statistics joke was really bad," he whispered, and Liam laughed for real this time. "I want you to come with me next time I eat at my parents' house. They'd gladly add another place setting to their table any night of the week." He pulled back and Liam mourned the loss of King's big arms around him, until he rested both hands on his shoulders and squeezed gently. "I'm sorry you had such shitty parents. You deserved so much better."

The warmth that spread through his chest crawled up his cheeks, and Liam looked down, embarrassed by suddenly being shy after giving King a glimpse of his less than spectacular childhood. "Will your mum try to feed me?" Liam mumbled.

"Whenever you walk in the door."

"I'd like that." And he really would. Having dinner with King had become the highlight of his day. He hated being alone, and it was easy with King. It felt... right. He liked who he was with King. "Before Addy gets back?"

King nodded then admitted with a whisper, "I miss her."

He grasped King's forearms, squeezing just like King did to him. He missed Addy too, her smile and her easy presence. Her absence had struck him hard. King being there eased it, but he still found himself looking for her. Wanting her there. "I miss her too."

As if by unspoken agreement, they put aside their conversation and the heaviness that went with it and turned to Liam's study notes. He worked on problems while King coached him. It was as if the course materials were a picture that was slowly coming into focus. With every question he understood and answered, the image became clearer.

SEVENTEEN

Adelaide

Adelaide stretched her neck, releasing the tension there. She looked around the group of two instructors, and three other students. It was an intimate setting, but the lack of a crowd didn't make things easier. If anything, it amped up the buzzing under her skin. She'd prepared for this, rehearsed endless hours of her presentation and the session she was leading on consent. Each of the students had done their own seminar, including a group workshop on the topic, but from a different perspective.

Mallory's had been on consent under the influence. Jot had talked about new relationships and hook-ups, Alain had focussed on unprotected sex, STIs, and pregnancy. Hers was a different take again. Adelaide had planned an exercise on highlighting consent in existing relationships. Her question for the group was whether they were having sex because they wanted to, or because they subconsciously, or unconsciously, felt obliged to.

The room they were in was large and airy, three storeys up and overlooking a park. The half-height windows and gauzy curtains gave them privacy while letting in the light from the afternoon sun. Dust moats danced in the air as Adelaide stood and walked to the front of the room. The class was silent, waiting for her to begin. She smiled, a small tilt of her lips upward in acknowledgement for the encouragement the others had just given her.

She was the youngest in the class by far, and she had a lot to prove. Her instructors had already whispered between themselves questioning whether she had enough life experience to be a good coach. They were worried she wouldn't be taken seriously. She appreciated their concern, but it was misplaced. Their responsibility was to assess her performance in the course, not her capacity to run a business. Pointing that out to them had been an uncomfortable conversation, but she didn't appreciate being judged and found lacking before she'd even had a chance to present her assessment. They'd admitted her participation in the online forums had been exemplary, so erecting roadblocks now wasn't something she was going to put up with.

The knock at the door startled Adelaide. Two people slipped in. Why were they there? Surely they were in the wrong place. Adelaide swallowed and her eyes darted from the newcomers to her instructors who had stood and were murmuring hellos to them. They rolled out yoga mats and sat next to the other students.

If the instructors were inviting extra people in the room to throw her off, they were going to be sorely disappointed. Adelaide squared her shoulders, raised her chin, and pushed ahead with her workshop. She had structured hers differently to the others. They'd begun with a presentation. She was starting with a question and answer session. But first, the image. The projector beamed the black-and-white photo. A woman in the foreground, chin resting on her clasped hands. Reluctance radiated off her in her turned-down lips and the haunch of her shoulders. The background was blurred, but another person was clearly visible lying down, head resting on pillows.

"Good afternoon, everyone. Thank you for coming along. For this session I'm going to do something a little different. I'd like you all to spread out a little. Get comfortable. Feel free to sit or stand, lie down if that's best for you." The students shifted around, spreading out over the rubber mats. The latecomers moved too, both sitting away from the others. She smiled at them, nodded in acknowledgement.

She would get to introductions in a moment. Their entrance actually highlighted a point she wanted to make. But it would be better made if she waited. So, first, there was some introspection that she wanted her fellow students to focus on. "Look at this photograph. Study it. Without giving us your answers, think about whether you see yourself in either of the foreground or background positions."

She scanned the room, noting a nod and a tilted head. She saw one student look away, his Adam's apple dip as he swallowed. She kept her voice even, her tone and pace relaxing. Adelaide was aiming for her audience to almost go into a meditative state. "Close your eyes and catalogue your physical reactions to the image. What physical sensations are you experiencing? From the weight of your hair on your head, to the expressions on your face. Is your jaw, neck, shoulders, or back tense? Do you feel your core muscles or your intimate zones? What about your buttocks, legs, and feet? Your arms and your hands? What is your breathing like? Focus on that photograph in your mind's eye and feel the physical reaction your body is having."

While she spoke, she watched. Catalogued how the woman who'd entered the room late shifted, planting her feet on the floor a shoulder width apart while cowering at the same time. It was a classic fight-or-flight response. The man she was with turned away from her. But the shift wasn't a rejection. He sat up straighter, his elbows pushing out. It was as if he was making himself bigger, showboating as if to intimidate a threat. He was protecting her.

"Thank you. Open your eyes and relax." She smiled encouragingly at the room, nodding, and meeting every person's gaze. Reassuring them she was there. "Before we talk about it, let's discuss what happened at the beginning of the lesson. Two people who I'm presuming you're unfamiliar with entered the room after some of the presentations had already been completed. I don't know if you've been introduced to them, but I haven't."

She smiled at the latecomers, apologizing for calling them out with a tilt of her head. She moved over to them and held out her hand. "My name is Adelaide. Welcome to this afternoon's session." They shook and introduced themselves as Carl and Arwaa. She didn't push for any other information from them, but turned to the class and made her way back to the front of the room. "None of you objected to the interruption, and although there were a few looks between you when I began, you also didn't offer much resistance. Why was that do you think? Was it, perhaps, a feeling of obligation toward me or each other that you don't rock the boat?" She paused, aiming for dramatic effect but wasn't sure she'd pulled off until Jot spoke up.

"All of the above, I think."

"Thank you, Jot. That reaction, the desire to please and conform to what others expect, is a parallel to what we're discussing this afternoon. Are you being intimate with your partner, or partners, simply because it's easier not to object? On the flipside, is your partner having sex because they want to, or because they feel obliged to?" It took everything in her not to turn to her instructors to check their reactions, but Adelaide knew she needed to focus on the people before her above anything else.

So that's what she did. She led them on a guided discussion centred around first hearing, then listening to their inner self, the niggling whispered "no" in a person's subconscious. The gut feeling that something wasn't right. They raised expectations around consent and growing comfortable with each other, familiarity in a relationship breeding a reluctance to refuse intimacy for any one of countless reasons. Sometimes it was just easier to get the deed over and done with, than to say no and argue about it. But that meh reaction was very much settling. It was ignoring the boundaries a person should be able to set for their own body. It disrespected one's desires and own needs all in the name of a relationship, one that if not built upon an ability to communicate freely and openly, could breed resentment and numbness. Adelaide was a firm believer that sex shouldn't be endured. It should not leave its participants feeling numb or unsatisfied, especially if those participants didn't know what it would take to turn things around. Over and over she had to rein in the desire to turn the group discussion into a lecture—she was a passionate proponent of every sexual encounter being fulfilling for every participant every time.

Her time leading the class was coming to a close when Adelaide asked, "What are some ways we can communicate the need to slow down, to change the experience so that every person involved is engaging intimately, rather than carrying out a transaction?" The discussion picked up again and even though the chime sounded to mark the end of the forty-five-minute period, no one moved. The conversation continued, the instructors joining in and contributing their opinions.

Finally, when classes were wrapped up later that evening, and Adelaide stepped onto the footpath, the warm air settling over her like a blanket, she breathed. The assessment had been the most heavily weighted component of the module she'd been studying and she'd put her all into it. "Adelaide, can I walk with you?" Mallory asked.

"Sure. I was just heading to the train station. Are you going that way?" Before Mallory could answer, Carl and Arwaa stepped out of the building.

"Adelaide, well done on your session. It was impressive, both for someone your age to have that kind of insight, and to be able to run a seamless workshop when you are so early in the course," Carl said.

Arwaa held out a business card and added, "Carl and I run a club on the Gold Coast. We've been interested in getting someone on board who can help with coaching our clients. When you're back on the Coast, we'd love to speak with you about doing your placement with us."

"Did you know that I'm from the coast?" Adelaide asked. Their faces brightened and Carl and Arwaa looked to each other, a private smile passing between them.

"We had no idea when Charity invited us to come in. It was purely good timing that we were already in Sydney to be able to do so. They mentioned it after your presentation. It's serendipitous, don't you think?"

Adelaide's belly flip-flopped in excitement. Charity, one of the instructors, had been the hardest on her, their expectations the most difficult to satisfy. She must be doing something right for them to have invited a potential employer to her session. "I've had trouble finding a placement. Practitioners in Brisbane are concerned about losing clients if they train me up knowing that I'll base myself so close. The two that are there both wanted me to pay them an hourly rate to train me, and I just can't afford to do that."

Carl nodded and held out his hand, which Adelaide gratefully shook. "You'll get a call the day I step foot back on Queensland soil. Thank you for the opportunity."

Adelaide had a spring in her step, excitement bubbling in her veins as she and Mallory walked to the train station, and beyond. She couldn't wait to tell King.

"Hey, baby," she greeted excitedly as King answered his phone. There was noise in the background, like the television was on. It muted and there was a murmured voice, deep and familiar. "You at Liam's again?"

"Yeah. We've just finished eating. We were putting a movie on."

"What did you have?" Adelaide's stomach growled, her microwave meal still heating up.

"I taught him how to make *Braġioli*." King pronounced it braj-all-ee. She'd tasted the stuffed meat dish before—it was one of his mother's specialities—and Adelaide loved it. King showing Liam how to make it brought a wistful smile to her lips. Not for the first time that week she wished she was home and could join them. She could imagine the three of them pottering around in Liam's kitchen, laughing and teasing one another. "How was your presentation?" King asked, pulling her back into the present.

She fell into the little armchair beside her bed and sighed. She was tired, the long day taking its toll. The room she'd rented was a forty-minute train ride away from the college too, and while she was glad she was doing it on her own, her limited budget made it difficult. She wished she'd taken King up on the offer of paying extra so she could stay closer to the city. "The presentation went well." She could hear the excitement in her voice and her cheeks hurt from the smile splitting her face. "Really well." Adelaide launched into a description of what she'd covered and the news of the potential internship.

"I'm so proud of you, beautiful," King breathed, but there was a note of melancholy in his voice. She grinned. She'd left the best news until last.

"Oh, did I mention that the club is based in Surfers?"

"It is? Oh Adds, that's brilliant!" King laughed, his happiness shining through the phone. "Lee, Adds might have an internship at a club on the coast. She's coming home." Her chest tightened and longing shot through her. Who would have thought that being away for a week would have her pining for King and Liam? She missed her mum, brother, and Pop too, and she'd spoken or texted with each of them nearly every day, but she was desperate to see them. With another fortnight of classes to go, it was going to feel like forever. But at least her two favourite people were spending time together, bonding over statistics. She shuddered. She had no idea how King could enjoy it, but that didn't matter. He loved it, Liam was learning, and she was killing her course too. Two more weeks. She could handle it.

EIGHTEEN

Kingston

"You've been busy. I haven't seen you much," Eve commented, sipping her iced coffee. They were sitting on the deck chairs in his yard in the shade cast by the big poinciana. It was only 8:00 a.m., but the sun already had a bite to it that to even his perpetually cold body was like a warning to stay somewhere sheltered.

"I have. Been going to a friend's house every arvo to tutor him, then we've been doing dinner most nights too."

She tilted her head. "You're not seeing Adelaide?"

"She's in Sydney for school. She'll be home in a couple of weeks. Liam, the guy I'm tutoring, is her brother's best mate. Adds studies with him too."

"Cool." She took another sip and stretched her legs out, leaning her head back and closing her eyes.

"What's new with you?"

She shrugged. "Not much. Work, been out on a couple of dates but we agreed that we're not seeing each other again. Finished my Christmas shopping. I'm just happy to have a day off." Eve sighed and took another sip of her iced coffee. "How's Adelaide going in her course?"

King told her how Adelaide was killing it in Sydney, the potential placement she'd secured, and confessed that he couldn't wait to see her again. Eve sat up, turning on the chair and planting her feet on the grass. She rested her elbows on her bent knees and studied him with a furrowed brow and a small, secretive smile tilting her lips.

"What?" he asked, looking at her.

"You're different. When you talk about Adelaide, you get this spark in your eyes and a warmth in your voice that I've never heard before." Eve leaned forward and playfully punched his arm, laughing when King batted away her hand. "Aw, King's in love!"

He shifted mirroring her pose. Smiling, he thought back to when he'd first uttered the words to Adds. He'd known for much longer, but it had taken him a while to put his feelings out there. The realization had seeped into him, permeating until it settled into his very bones. The night of the power outage, he'd watched Adds sleep in the light of the flickering lantern after they'd made love. He'd brushed a piece of hair off her face and in that moment, he'd known. King finally had a name for the emotion that left him filled to bursting point with unicorns and rainbows, laughter, and a warmth in his chest that lit him up. But it still took him longer to tell her. It wasn't a fear of commitment that had stopped him—he could see himself marrying Adds one day—it was something else. Someone else.

Adds was the love of his life. She owned him heart, body, and soul. But he couldn't deny that his feelings for Liam were there. Their friendship was entirely platonic, even though it ran deeper than any he'd ever had before. He couldn't explain the intensity in his desire to bring a smile to Liam's lips. Knowing he was happy gave King a high that, if he allowed himself to admit it, he only ever got when Adds smiled.

Liam's friendship was a part of him, one that stood out, and he wouldn't ever pretend that he wasn't a priority for King. Their bond had only grown stronger since he'd said "I love you" to Adds too. He didn't know what kind of person that made him. A shitty one, probably. But even though Liam had snagged a part of his heart with the unshakeable friendship they'd formed, he didn't love Adds any less. If anything, it was as if he was feeling more, like his capacity for love was increasing to encompass the two of them.

It was that worry—the concern he was a shitty boyfriend for having a friend as important to him as his girlfriend—that had frozen the words inside him. But Adds always had been braver than him. She'd told King she loved him and in doing so, had freed him. Given him the strength to shake loose from the hesitation plaguing him. Her words had allayed his concerns that his attraction to Liam somehow detracted from how genuine his love for Adds was. Confessing his love had been easy after that. "I love her," he replied to Eve, smiling one of those love-heart-eye smiles. Heat suffused his cheeks as he rode the high that came with falling in love.

"You told her, didn't you? Oh my God, tell me every-thing."

He laughed, rolling his eyes at Eve's eagerness. That moment was private, one he didn't want to share. Eve was one of his oldest friends, but this was between him and Adds. "Well, we were in bed—"

"No!" she cried, scandalized. "You didn't tell her after you'd gotten off, did you? Or during? King, tell me you didn't do that," she groaned.

"Okay, I won't." He winked, grinning cheekily at her.

"Urgh. Tell me about her friends. Have you met them yet? Does she have any single guy friends she can introduce me to?"

He rolled his eyes, Liam immediately popping to mind. He should introduce them. Liam deserved happiness and someone to dote on him, but... no. Eve wasn't right for him. She was one of the best people he knew, but she wasn't for Liam. He couldn't put his finger on exactly why—or maybe he didn't want to—but he just knew.

But there was Eli.

"Her brother is single."

Eve raised an eyebrow. "Not Liam? The media has him on eligible bachelor lists."

"Liam's... Liam." King couldn't help the private smile when he thought of the other man. Their conversation the night before had broken his heart. He'd known from the way Liam responded to his touch that he was starved of affection but learning about the tough childhood he'd had, the coldness he'd lived with daily and seeing the scars it left, hurt King deeper than he cared to admit. He'd needed Liam in his arms as much as the other man did. That morning, he'd called his mum. He'd spoken to her honestly for the first time in a long time, explaining why he needed her to stop feeding him so much. He'd begged her to understand. Then he'd told her about Liam, and his mum had cried. She'd demanded that King bring him home.

"You like him."

"I do." He bit his lip, his chest warming again. After all he'd been through as a kid, King could understand why Liam's self-confidence had taken a battering after failing statistics twice and having an average year playing in France. The last season he'd played had been a massive improvement, and yet he was perhaps the most critical of that. He knew Liam blamed himself for the team's loss, which ended their chance to play for the premiership trophy, but that was ridiculous. There was an entire field of guys wearing the same jersey who should have been fighting for the win too. Liam couldn't carry the weight of their loss alone when the others were playing too. "He's a great guy. Smart and we have fun."

"Does Adelaide know you're falling for her study partner?"

King's gaze shot to Eve's. "What? That's ridiculous. I... I don't... No."

She hummed, the noise one of disbelief. "Me doth thinketh you protest too much."

He pulled out a blade of grass by his feet. His movements as he tore it up were short and sharp, anger and frustration at just how right Eve was bubbling in his veins. He took it out on the weed, intent on showing her no emotion. "*Me* doth thinketh you're so far off base you're on a different damn continent." His voice was a growl, lower than his usual timbre as he struggled to deny her comment.

"Am I?" She held up her hand when King opened his mouth to answer, silencing him. He grumbled instead, wishing she'd stop talking. "I think it's something you should talk to Adelaide about. It's something she deserves to know."

"Are you implying I'm lying to her, or that I'd cheat on her? I'd never do that. Never." He was adamant about it. He would never hurt her like that. He couldn't imagine ever hurting Adds. It'd break him knowing he caused her pain. That he'd destroyed her trust in him.

"I know you don't have a hurtful bone in your body." There was no challenge in her remark like her disagreement earlier. Eve's gaze met his and held. "I know that."

"Then why'd you say it?" He stood, walked over to the rubbish bin, and tossed the half full iced coffee he'd been drinking. There was no way he could stomach it now, not with his gut churning at even the thought of hurting Adds.

"Because I think if you really loved her, you wouldn't fall for someone else."

Her words struck King like a freight train slamming into him. It was the very reason that had made him hesitate to tell Adds that he loved her. He'd needed to be certain. And he was. But did he have it all wrong? Was his attraction, this desire to be around Liam and the importance of his friendship enough to be called cheating? What if it was more than attraction? Liam had captured a piece of King's heart. Was that cheating?

He wanted to puke, the fear that he'd done the very thing he found most abhorrent—hurt Adds—overwhelming him. If there was any question, any possibility, that she would think he'd cheated on her, he had no doubt he'd break her heart. He muttered, "I'll see you later," to Eve and walked away, his legs carrying him inside while his body went numb, dread settling over him.

"King," Eve called when he'd reached the top of the stairs. "I'm sorry."

"Yeah. I'll talk to you later." He nodded and went inside, letting the door click closed behind him. A moment later he heard the rubbish bin lid fall back into place and the gate rattle closed as his friend left.

He paced the small living room. His stomach churned, King trying his hardest not to bring up the milky coffee as he catalogued his feelings. He enjoyed spending time with Liam. They had fun together. They laughed, and they had serious moments too. He admired the man. Liam worked hard, always trying, always doing his best. He was persistent too, never giving up. Liam knew what he wanted, and he went for it, pushing himself until he got there. But he was quick to offer help too. He was there for his family and friends—he hadn't hesitated to offer up his house when Adds needed a place to study.

He was as beautiful on the inside as he was on the outside. The man was gorgeous. Brown hair that was just shaggy enough to look perpetually ruffled, hazel eyes that were more green than brown when he was happy and darkened when he was tired, frustrated, or angry. He had kissable lips and muscle tone that King could only dream of having. He liked touching him, liked feeling that restrained strength and coiled power under his hands. He loved the way Liam responded to his encouragement too—the shoulder squeezes and claps lit a fuse in him, giving him the nudge he needed to push through whatever roadblock he was stuck at. Liam did it back too, grasping his arms and meeting his gaze whenever they were having a serious moment.

It was platonic. It had to be.

King would never let the times they touched be anything but friendly, but did even thinking about how gorgeous Liam was count as cheating? Was it true that he was falling out of love with Adds to make room for Liam? It didn't resonate with him. Didn't ring true. King knew down to his very soul, without a sliver of a doubt, that he loved Adds. He couldn't reconcile Eve's reasoning in his mind—his heart wasn't a scale. He didn't take from one and give it to the other to balance the sides.

But was attraction plus feelings enough to be called cheating, even if he never acted on it? He hadn't thought so, but what if he was wrong? What if Adds thought it was cheating? Worry crept in. Concern that he was hurting Adds without even knowing it. He replayed every encounter, every moment he and Liam had shared, analyzing whether he'd overstepped. King looked to the bookshelf at his front door, his phone perched in the bowl. Adds might be in class, or she could be busy. Could it wait? Probably. But the thought of hiding anything from her was abhorrent.

King snatched his phone up and dialled. She picked up on the second ring, a smile in her voice as she answered, "Hey, baby. How are you?"

"I'm..." He hesitated, unsure of what to say. "I don't know."

"Talk to me. What's wrong?" He heard a voice in the background, an announcement of some sort.

"Are you in the middle of something?"

"I'm on the train, but there's only a few people in the carriage with me. I've got time. Talk to me." The concern in her voice broke him and he swallowed, trying to dislodge the lump in his throat.

"I was just speaking to Eve. She made me realize something... no that's not right. I knew it. But I didn't think it was a problem, until now. She does. She's convinced I'm lying to you. But I didn't think it affected you. Or maybe it does. But—"

"King, take a breath." Her voice was calm and collected, but firm. Instantaneously, he obeyed, sucking air into his lungs. After a moment she added, "Blow it out." Again, he followed her lead. "Right, now I want you to go slow. I want you to tell me first, what you knew. Then we can talk about whether it's an issue, okay?"

"Yeah," he rasped, grateful that she was so together about this. He closed his eyes and began talking, forcing his words out slowly. "I'm falling for Liam. But it doesn't change how I feel about you. I love you."

She was quiet for a moment, as if there was a delay in the line. It was only a second or two, but it could have been an eternity. King's heart slammed against his ribcage, nerves sending both his pulse and his blood pressure sky-rocketing. When she finally spoke, it was in a calm, soothing voice. One he could imagine her using on a cornered wild animal. "King, it's okay." She added quietly, "He's easy to love."

He blew out a breath. Adds understood. She knew Liam too. She'd grown up with him, probably knew him better than most with the amount of time they spent together. "He is. I like him, Adds. But, as I said, I love you. I didn't say anything because it doesn't change my feelings for you. You're it for me. I love you, without question, without limitation."

"I love you too," she murmured, the warmth in her voice wrapping him up like a blanket. "And I want to be with you too." She paused and King was about to interrupt, but she added, "Why did Eve say that it was a problem? Did she think you were lying to me by keeping it a secret?"

He cleared his throat. She never hesitated to ask the hard questions, and he owed it to her to give her a straight answer. It didn't make it any easier to tell her though. Fear, thick and heavy, coated him like an oil slick. What if his confession was the beginning of the end, just like Eve had suggested? He didn't agree with her. He couldn't. King knew his heart. He didn't have a single doubt in his mind that he loved Addy, just as much now as what he did before he'd gotten to know Liam. But it might account for nothing if

Adds disagreed. "She thought that if I really loved you, I couldn't fall for him." He hastened to add, "But I know how I feel about you."

She spoke slowly, as if she was picking her words carefully. "I think it's possible to love two people at the same time. I don't think love is mutually exclusive. I mean, it can be, like with cheating, but... I believe you, King. I know you love me."

"I wouldn't cheat on you, Adds. Never that. But was I cheating without realizing it? Is feeling something for another person cheating? Am I betraying you by being attracted to him? By enjoying the time we spend together?" He sucked in a breath, his chest heaving with the need for oxygen, and his heart shattered. Oh God, he really had been cheating on her. "I'm sorry. I'm so damn sorry."

He could hear her breathing on the other end of the line and King's heart shattered. He'd hurt her. It didn't matter how much he loved Adds, he'd done the one thing that as a man he swore he'd never do—he disrespected his partner by not being honest with them. He'd cheated on Adds, the love of his life. The silence stretched on interminably. "Adds, please say something."

"Is it shitty of me to say stop talking to Eve?"

He huffed. He wanted to think the same thing, but Eve was right. "No, it's not awful. I get why you might say that, but it's not really about Eve is it? It's about me. What I've done."

"What have you done, King? If you're concerned that you're cheating because you have feelings for Liam, then I have to say we're cheating on each other—like I said, he's easy to love. But if that's it, if you haven't taken it any further than acknowledging your feelings, then how could that possibly be cheating? I don't think it is."

He let her words sit, mulling on them for a moment. He thought he understood what Adds was saying. She continued before he could ask anything.

"I mean, some people might think it was cheating, but is it really up to them to decide? We're in this relationship, no one else. Isn't it up to us to choose what we feel comfortable with? Where the line is? And, for me, as long as we're together, happy, and love each other, then I don't think loving someone else too is cheating." She paused and when she spoke again, her words were quiet. "It's easy to fall for Liam."

Relief swamped him, but only momentarily. It wasn't just feelings. It wasn't just spending time with him. Where was the line? What if Adds thought those touches he'd believed were innocent, weren't? He needed to be straight with her. He needed to confess everything. "What about if I like encouraging him to work harder?" His belly clenched, knotting up and twisting itself into a ball.

"Unless you're blowing him, I can't—"

"Oh my God, no!" King cried out, his heart beating frenetically. "No, I was talking about squeezing his shoulder or telling him he's doing a good job."

Adds laughed, the sound musical and genuinely happy. "King, baby, that's you. You do the same thing to Pop and even Eli. When you talk to your mum, you have your arm around her more often than not. You're a touchy-feely guy, and I love that. I don't ever want you to change that. It's one of my favourite things about you."

"I am? It is?" He furrowed his brow, thinking back to how he was with his other students. He never touched any of them, at least nothing more than a high five. But his friends, the people he considered family? Absolutely.

"Yes! I love that you and Liam have clicked. He needs someone like you in his corner. Being attracted to someone else…. It's healthy to admire other people. I'd be more worried if you were completely blinded to everyone because we're together—that's a little creepy stalker behaviour. Acknowledging you're attracted to other people seems perfectly normal to me. You're not cheating, King."

He heard the determination in her voice, the warmth there and the affection. She loved him. He still couldn't believe his luck that they'd met and Adds had given him a second glance. She was incredible and she didn't think he was doing anything wrong.

"Okay," he replied, the tension in his body loosening. It was as if a weight was lifted off his shoulders. The knots in his muscles relaxed, and his jaw unclenched. The shroud of worry lifted and in its place was calm and peace. Gratefulness that Adds believed him and understood him too.

There was something more he wanted from her. Permission of sorts. "I want him to meet my parents."

"Oh, King." She sniffed. "Yeah. Yeah, I think that's perfect. He needs that. Your parents will love him."

"Is it okay? Is it crossing the line?"

"No, I want you to do it." Her voice was a whisper when she added, "King? Can you do something for me too?"

"Anything."

"Be upfront with me. If you want to act on your attraction, I just want to know. I don't want to give you up, but I don't want you to despise me if you feel like I'm holding you back." She cleared her throat, her voice wobbling. "I'm okay with the two of you together. As far as I know, Liam's straight but if there comes a time... then... it's okay. I won't say no, but I'd like the respect of you being upfront with me."

He swallowed, opened his mouth to reply, but no words came. "I know we haven't said we're exclusive, but I assumed we were—"

"We are," she hurried to reassure him. "I haven't been with anyone else, and I don't want to either. I'm just saying that I'd be okay with you seeing both of us. Liam's a good man."

"He is," King agreed. "And you're my world."

"Don't you forget it," she joked, laughing. "Love you, King. Now stop stressing. I'm not one of these insecure girls who thinks they can convert their queer boyfriend into a straight bloke who never craves dick again."

King barked out a laugh. Her comments shouldn't surprise him. After all, she was studying sex and intimacy; she had to have an open mind. But she still amazed him every day.

NINETEEN

Liam

Liam stared at the brown leather messenger bag with the rainbow ribbon tied to it. He couldn't believe he hadn't noticed it before. King brought his bag with him every time they studied together. But why the rainbow flag? And how was King gay? There was another ribbon too—pink, purple and blue. What did that one mean?

"I'm not gay," King answered with a smirk.

"I said that out loud?" Liam squeaked. "Shit, sorry."

"No, it's okay. It's why I have the ribbons there. People ask me what they represent, and I talk to them about it." He shrugged like it was no big deal, and even though King was clearly open about whatever his sexuality was, it was still personal to him. It was also a risk to be open with people; there were a lot of bigoted fucks out there. Was King putting himself at risk by advertising his sexuality, whatever that was? King added, "I identify as bisexual. I date both men and women. The same as Eli."

Liam looked up, meeting his gaze. His throat was tight and his words had fled. King was bi? It was as if a door leading to endless possibilities had opened in front of him. Symphonies played and choirs sang, celebrating this moment. Every fantasy Liam had hatched up with King and Addy, every inexperienced, fumbling kiss that his mind had conjured up with King suddenly seemed possible. Not probable, because he had to face reality—King and Addy were in an exclusive relationship. It wasn't as if he could realistically ever dream to catch the man's attention. But knowing King had been with men before... he internally groaned, wishing he could reach down and adjust his semi. Imagining that big broad man wrapped around another one, grappling each other for dominance. Damn.

Liam flicked his gaze up and met King's. His eyes were wary. Guarded. "Um," he started, not knowing what to say. He wanted to thank King for trusting Liam enough to tell him. For being open with him. King slid into the chair opposite Liam—the one next to Addy's—almost as far away from him as he could get and sighed. Liam started babbling, desperately trying to communicate what was going through his mind. "Your trust means a lot. I don't imagine that you share that kind of information a lot, but then again why would you have the ribbons on your bag if you didn't, right? Anyway, I appreciate you sharing it with me. It doesn't make a difference, just so you know. I've always had Lij's back and I'd do the same for you. I just want you safe. It's dangerous and people are shitty. But it's cool that you can be true to yourself. Yeah, cool. You're cool."

Liam stopped talking and looked up at King with wide eyes as the heat crawled up his throat along his cheeks. King bit his lip, trying to hide a smirk, but the snort that escaped him had Liam giggling. Within minutes, they were both laughing, King holding his stomach as Liam wiped tears from his face. The ridiculousness of his commentary hovered between them and set him off again every time he met King's gaze.

"You're cool too, you big dork," King rasped before launching into a fit of laughter again.

Liam was hyperaware of every touch, every look between them, during the tutoring session that followed. King was more reserved, encouraging him as he worked without his hands on Liam. He hated it. He wanted the casual brushes and the reassuring squeeze. He wanted to be held by him, to touch him back. But King pulled away every time they came into contact. Liam shifted in his seat, inhaling King's spicy scent, needing their connection.

He closed his eyes, letting his head fall forward. He sighed, desolation stealing through him. It was as if he was being punished—King withholding his affection because of Liam's stupid fumbling.

"What's wrong?" King asked softly. "We can wrap up if you'd rather finish early, and we don't have to do dinner if you don't want to, tonight or any other night." His words were quiet and resigned, as if it was a foregone conclusion that their friendship was coming to an end. Bugger that. Liam wouldn't let it happen. He couldn't.

"I'm sorry I didn't know what to say. I got flustered. I didn't know about your sexuality, but then when we were laughing, I thought you forgave me for screwing up." Liam swallowed around the lump in his throat, desperate for the return of his friend. "But you keep pulling away. It's as if you don't want to touch me anymore, like I disgust you."

"I…" King blew out a breath, his shoulders sagging. "I'm the one who needs to apologize. It's not you. It was me. I was worried about your reaction after you knew. It wasn't like I was trying to hide from you. I just never realized that I'm a hands-on person. It hadn't ever occurred to me that it's what I did with you, but then Adds mentioned it, and you noticed my ribbons and I freaked out."

"Why?" Liam implored, confused. Why would he freak out?

"I'm scared." King looked at him through lowered lashes. Curled in on himself, he was hiding. Making himself a smaller target. He'd seen Lij do the same. He'd done it too. Not to dodge punches like Lij, but to avoid the verbal barbs his parents had tossed his way his whole childhood. Liam reached out, curling his hand over King's forearm, and squeezed, trying to comfort and encourage him the way King always did. His friend's gaze dropped to where they were joined and he shuddered, the breath he sucked in choppy. King spoke again, his voice hesitant, "I got scared that you wouldn't appreciate me touching you, knowing that I'm attracted to men too."

Liam was struck dumb. He couldn't get thoughts of King and Addy out of his head. When he closed his eyes, the images he'd tried and failed miserably to repress popped up in his mind's eye. Every time it was an X-rated slideshow. Big hands digging into thick muscle—his muscle—before gliding up to hook under his shoulders. His mouth on smooth skin, dewy from the heat of their exchange. Masculine and feminine hands sliding down to tease the patch of soft skin at the juncture of his thigh. A hairy chest pressed against his back, a smooth one at his front, three sets of hips rocking and grinding together.

Above it all, the images that stuck with him the most were the kisses. Two sets of stubbled jaws brushing gently against each other as he tasted Addy's lips. Delicate fingers tangled in his hair and pouty lips nipped at his shoulder. Traded kisses. A soft exhale and slow touches, lips pressing together and tongues tenderly caressing.

Happiness. Love.

How could Liam not want it?

He swallowed down the question he was desperate to ask—was King attracted to Liam?—and slid his hand down to King's, grasping it. The invisible personal space barrier that normally operated with mates was nowhere to be seen between them, and that's exactly how Liam wanted it. It hadn't even disintegrated with Addy that quickly or so completely in the time they studied together.

With their gazes locked, Liam raised King's hand to his shoulder and held it there until King squeezed, before moving to Liam's nape and tugging him closer. Resting their foreheads together, Liam shivered, King's closeness triggering a need in him that was as unfamiliar as it was exciting and intimidating. "I've never not appreciated you, King," he admitted.

The night before when they'd made gnocchi, and Liam was full and replete, he'd fallen asleep on King's shoulder. King had shifted so Liam could stretch out, resting his head in King's lap as the other man ran his fingers through Liam's hair, massaging his scalp. It had been perfectly innocent, but Liam had wanted to curl into King. To hear Addy's sweet voice and to hold her like he had when she'd left. But King and Addy were together. They were an item. He was literally the third wheel. He had to stop reading something deeper in every touch. It was exactly why King had pulled back. Exactly what his concern was. He just didn't know that Liam was desperate for it to be true rather than the opposite. The stupid hope he held out was terrifying.

His heart wanted more of it.

So did his body.

If an innocent squeeze, or hug was all he could ever have, Liam would treasure it. He'd treasure every moment of praise. Liam wanted the impossible. His tutor, and the woman he couldn't get out of his head—his best mate's little sister. All he could do was dream.

* * * * *

He leaned into King's side, nuzzling their foreheads together. King squeezed his nape, before sliding his hand down Liam's back, tugging him closer. King manhandled him, pulling him one handed onto his lap. Liam straddled him, and King raised that strong arm of his, shifting so his fingers were buried in Liam's hair. The shiver that tore through him was embarrassing as fuck, but King's barely audible gasp had his dick standing to attention. King shifted, pulling their hips closer until their shafts were pressed together. They were both hard. Both wanting. Liam purred, King's hands on his bare skin magical. A brush of their lips and Liam closed his eyes, the ghost of that touch lingering. His cock tented his underwear, lifting the waistband and poking out above it.

Want flowed through his veins like a river. His cock throbbed and King hummed, pressing their lips together again. Their tongues tangled and King slipped his hand down Liam's underwear, fisting his dick. He moaned, reaching back to grasp the warm body behind him. Addy.

They shifted then and Addy wrapped herself around King. He thrust inside her and Liam watched enraptured where they connected. Hearing the soft moans and the deeper growls and the shlick, shlick, shlick of his hand working his cock pulled him closer to the edge. The two people he was falling for—or maybe already had—turned to him in sync and tugged him closer. Addy's lips closed around his shaft while King arched up, licking his balls.

Liam cried out, his eyes jolting open. It was dark, a sliver of moonlight peeking in between the blinds when the breeze blew them open. Alone, star-fished on the bed naked, his cock stood to attention, pre-cum leaking from his slit down onto his belly. He ached, his dick throbbing. It begged for attention. Liam grasped his length, his fingers spreading the pre-cum down, slicking his way and moaned.

He was harder than he'd been in months, already on the edge after his dream. Why did he have to wake? Why couldn't he have stayed there, pretending he had it all.

Closing his eyes, and breathing hard, he willed it to come back. His dream didn't, but his mind's eye conjured up a scene worthy of any porn movie. Liam sucked on his fingers, tasting himself, and wet them, letting spit drip from them as he dragged them down between his legs. What would it be like if King slid his thick digits between Liam's cheeks? His hole clenched and he circled it, wetting his pucker before pressing against his hole.

It wasn't enough. He needed the stretch. Would it burn? It didn't matter. Every nerve ending in him was alight. Lighting up like an Australia Day fireworks extravaganza. He pushed forward, breaching himself with his fingertip.

It was odd—the intrusion something he wasn't familiar with—but when he lifted his hips, rocking into his fist, his arse muscles tensed, and bliss shot through him. Liam moaned as his balls drew up tight. Fingering his arse with the tip of his finger, his other hand worked his shaft. Images flashed in his mind's eye of Addy and King kissing, the head of his cock in their mouths. The tingle at the base of his spine morphed into a rushing and Liam's balls drew tight. He slid his finger in deeper, grazing a spongey pad inside himself. A tidal wave of ecstasy washed over him, and his arse contracted, ropes of cum being sucked from his balls and shooting from his shaft. With each pulse his balls unloaded again, and Liam shouted. His heart hammered in his chest and his mind whited out, his breathing ragged.

With cum cooling on his belly, his finger still pressed in his arse, Liam let his legs fall open, shuddering at the pressure on his prostate. He brushed it again and his cock filled, the hardness from only a moment earlier returning. Liam sucked in a breath and pulled his fingers free, shocked at his body's reaction to the stimulation.

He didn't have the excuse of the cloud of sleep hanging over him anymore. No, he was well and truly awake now. He'd jacked off before, imagining King and Addy while he made himself come, but he shouldn't.

Not if he wanted to protect his heart.

There was one undeniable truth that Liam had to face up to in the dark of the night. He'd fallen for them. Together. The two of them. Addy was loving and uplifting. She brought out the best in everyone around her. She was fun-loving, but not shallow. She wasn't shy to tackle topics most people were embarrassed to and was passionate about the things she set her mind to. Since King had come into her life, she'd blossomed like a field of wildflowers, reaching for the skies and brightening the world with her beauty. Where Addy was bright sunshine, King was quiet and unassuming. He was a teacher and a nurturer, gentle and smarter than anyone Liam knew, and Liam was hooked. It was hot as hell to watch his brain in action. King made being smart and reliable, having loyalty to his friends, and loving with his whole heart sexy. There was no doubting the attraction he had to either of them.

To both.

In his dreams, Liam had imagined them naked. He wanted it for real. He wanted to see how far down the glimpse of chest hair went. Was it as soft as it looked? What was it like to kiss him? What about Addy? Would she welcome him being soft and gentle, or would she want it harder, deeper? What about them together like he'd fantasized so many times?

Alone they were amazing, but together they were everything.

Liam didn't know what it meant for his sexuality. King, Addy, and Lij would be the perfect people to speak to, but how when he couldn't admit who he was falling for? Curiosity had gotten the better of him before and Google had been his friend. The classification that seemed to fit him best was pansexual. He'd fallen for the person, or in his case people, not the body parts. He supposed that the multiple-person thing meant he was polyamorous too.

Going from identifying as straight to polyamorous pansexual in the space of a few months hadn't come as much of a surprise as he'd thought. He'd had threesomes and moresomes before, but none of them had ever involved feelings. None of them involved wanting to curl up in front of the TV and watch the footy together like he'd done with Addy countless times, or cook together like he and King had done almost every night since Addy left. If feeling something deeper for King and Addy than friendship meant his sexuality had changed—or he'd realized something that was always inside of him—so be it. Because this time, it wasn't just the sex he wanted, no matter how hot it would be seeing them both naked. No, for the first time in his life, Liam wanted to experience love. He wanted to give himself to them. He wanted to show them he could be all the things they needed too.

Talk about fantastical dreams.

Falling for them was easy. Surviving it with his heart intact was impossible.

* * * * *

The sun was cresting the horizon, the grey light of the predawn draining away the darkness of the night before. Liam hadn't slept after he'd let his imagination carry him away, tossing and turning for the rest of the night. Then Coach had slammed them again—like he had every day that week—stepping up their endurance training so they would all be at peak performance for the beginning of the season. A second night of no sleep and he was jittery with exhaustion. Liam had nothing on that day, no training and no tutoring, yet he was up at the arse crack of dawn.

But he did have a dinner, one he was nervous to attend. King was taking him home to meet his parents. Well, not quite. He'd invited him for a meal. Liam was the one who'd wished he could call it more.

The blurring of the lines between them was freaking Liam out. He wanted so hard and so much he ached. But it was impossible. King's news that he was bi had only inflamed his overactive imagination, opening up possibilities that weren't really there. Liam knew he was travelling down a one-way road to heartbreak, and yet he couldn't seem to stop. That was why he was loading his surfboard into the back of his SUV. It was why he needed to detach, to feel nothing but the power of the ocean under him. He needed to get out of his head and the only way he could do that—apart from playing football which hadn't worked so far—was to get back to nature. To worship its beauty and majesty.

He pressed the button on the tailgate and stepped back as it lowered, only to meet Lij's gaze as he did. "Glad to see you're still kickin'."

Liam crossed over the drive and propped his elbows against the fence, the scent of the night jasmine climbing on it still perfuming the air. "Sorry, been busy. Training, classes, and tutoring are kickin' my arse."

"King's there with you until quite late," he said, fishing for more information. Liam didn't know whether to be offended by whatever implication Lij was drawing, or to feel bad for rarely asking him to join them. He looked up at the sky, focusing on the grey of the dawn.

Deflection was easier than admitting to his oldest friend that he'd been ignoring him in favour of spending time with King. He knew his friendship with King had a use by date. Addy would be back soon, and King would have no reason to spend anywhere near as much time with him as he did now. Addy would have a break for the holiday period, then she'd go straight into her training. Understandably, they'd want to be together. Liam was trying to get his fill while he could, living in a dreamscape while he gorged himself, read-ying for the scarce times ahead. Every time he got a smile or a touch, Liam stored the feeling—the high—bottling it for the times when he was alone and needed sustenance. The affirmations, the encouragement that King gave him were like batteries, energizing Liam when he was low. He'd been texting Addy too, reading her words over and over, talking to her almost every day. It was stupid how much he missed her.

"Yeah, we've been spending a lot of time on my work and assessments, then eating tea together. How are your manuscripts going? Do you have many more you need to get through before Christmas?"

"I'm still snowed. I've had another three authors contact me wanting their stories edited urgently." He shook his head and rubbed his eyes, Liam noticing for the first time just how exhausted Lij looked. "I don't know why I do it to myself, but the money at this time of year is hard to walk away from."

Liam looked him over, noting the running shorts and beat-up sneakers he was wearing. "Go inside and chuck some swimmers on. Let's go for a surf together."

Lij's smile reached his eyes, an excited grin splitting his lips.

"Go," Liam encouraged. With Lij almost in the door, he added, "Sorry I've been a shitty mate. I should have made sure you were okay well before now."

Lij nodded and slipped through the door, returning a few minutes later in board shorts and thongs, with a towel slung over one shoulder and a surfboard tucked under the other. It was good to see him like that, and Liam realized how much he needed some time with his mate's grounding influence. He couldn't talk to Lij about what was going on, but at least he could reconnect with him.

TWENTY

Liam

Liam placed his cutlery side by side on the plate, the dish wiped completely clean. Mountains of grilled baby octopus served on pasta with roasted baby tomatoes, olives, and capers, fresh crusty bread, and a side salad had sat there. His belly was full to bursting point and as he raised his eyes, embarrassed that he'd eaten so much, his gaze found King's mum. Betty wore the proudest smile he'd ever seen, her eyes glassy with excitement. She held her napkin between her hands and laughed when he flushed.

"That was delicious. Thank you," he murmured, his cheeks on fire.

King reached out, grasping his nape, and squeezed. Liam closed his eyes, sinking into the warmth. He'd been with this family for a couple of hours, and in that time, he'd experienced more love being directed to him than he'd ever had from his own. King's mum had hugged him tight the moment they'd met, welcoming him to their family. Who did that? She was amazing. King's dad was quieter, but Liam instantly knew where King got his affectionate nature from. He'd patted the seat next to him, and as soon as Liam sat, Alfred had grasped his forearm and kept a hold of him the whole time. The man had ooohed and aaahed when Liam had explained what he did for a living and playfully smack-talked him when he realized it wasn't soccer but rugby that he played. The only time he moved his hand was when Liam had needed his arm to eat. He loved it. He loved them. The way that they interacted was so filled with love that Liam wanted to soak it in and never leave.

He understood what King meant now about his mother feeding him, but she'd seemed to respect his wishes, stopping when he'd told her he had enough. King had grinned like a loon when Betty asked him if it was too much. He'd hugged her when she offered to take some off his plate and had happily trotted over to the table to place it down. He'd rejoined Liam at the bench, bouncing on his toes, a giddy happiness flitting through him. Liam had nudged him with his elbow, grinning at King's happiness. Betty had noticed it too, and her corresponding laugh was hearty and happy.

Liam's plate hadn't resembled King's. It started off as a small meal, but his stomach had rumbled and Betty scooped up another serving, raising her eyebrow for confirmation. In the end, his serving rivalled Alfred's. He wasn't sure he'd get through it, but demolish it he did. Liam rubbed his belly and sighed happily.

"I hope you have room for dessert." She looked at him expectantly, eyebrow raised in challenge, and Liam laughed, joy suffusing him.

"Can I maybe have half an hour? Let dinner settle?"

"Be careful or she'll have you changing your surname to Vella," King warned with a grin, his hand still at Liam's nape. His thumb brushed his skin gently, a tease that sent electricity through Liam's body.

"Keep feeding me food half that good and I'll take your old bedroom." He winked at King, the grin he shot him cheesy. He was stuffed full, ready to be rolled into bed so he could sleep the food coma off, but at the same time he was light as air. Carol had welcomed him like this when he'd befriended Lij, opening her arms to him whenever he needed the love and affection only a parent could give. A decade later and he'd found another family. He pressed his lips together and blinked, his eyes stinging with unshed tears.

Lij hated Liam's parents. Addy went out of her way to show them that she was ignoring them. Carol kept a cool politeness about her. King was infuriated by them. King's parents didn't know the full extent of what he'd been through but, like Carol, they'd shown him what it was truly like being in a family. Why then hadn't his own parents? His sister? Was he that bad, that much of a disappointment that his own family hated him?

"Excuse me," he whispered, getting up from the table and rushing to the bathroom. His throat closed on a sob and he couldn't even get through the door before his legs gave out. He slumped against the frame, tears tracking down his cheeks as he bit his knuckle to stop his cries from being heard. What was wrong with him? He was a mess.

A hand landed on his shoulder. Strong and sure. King's. He turned, expecting to find his friend, but instead it was Alfred waiting with open arms. "Shh, my boy. It's okay." He drew him into a hug, and Liam wrapped himself around the older man. He buried his face in his shoulder and cried. "Kingston explained a little. You are always welcome here, okay. Our door is always open. With King or not, you can always come home. We wanted so many more children. They're a blessing. *You're* a blessing. We'd be so proud to call you another son of ours."

Liam didn't have words. He couldn't speak. The gaping void in his heart that his family had created was filled with a few sentences. With the affection of a man he'd just met. With the homecooked meal and pride in a mother's eyes, simply for finishing her food. He cried harder, squeezed tighter, and Alfred held him, rubbing his back and letting him get it out.

What felt like hours later, he pulled back, wiping his eyes with the back of his hand. Alfred reached into his pocket. "It's clean," he said as he handed a perfectly pressed hand-kerchief to Liam. He wrapped both hands around Liam's when he took it and added, "Take your time freshening up. We won't make a big deal of you coming back in when you're ready."

"I'm in love with your son," he blundered unthinkingly.

Alfred patted his shoulder and smiled genially. "I can see that. God works in mysterious ways."

He left Liam alone then. Leaning against the wall, he buried his face in his hands and shook his head. What the hell was he thinking? What had possessed him to open his mouth? How was he going to face any of them now? They were probably dissecting his confession while he was in the bathroom wallowing.

No, they weren't like that.

Alfred had promised, and King wouldn't use it against him. He was too caring, too sensitive to the needs of people around him to do that. They all were. They were a family who loved hard and with open arms. Who'd accepted him into their fold without question. Liam didn't need to know Alfred and Betty well to know he could trust them. That was all he'd needed apparently to give voice to his deepest most taboo secret.

* * * * *

"And time's up. Pen down." Liam dropped the pencil, his scratching on the notepad finally stopping after two hours of intense writing. It was the first time he'd completed a statistics exam, albeit a mock one. He'd walked out of every other exam without an answer for at least one question. But this time was different. King had challenged him, asking curly questions that required him to make multiple calculations before he could answer it. Liam's confidence was buoyed but nerves still jumped around in his belly.

King had established exam conditions the moment he'd walked in that afternoon. With a sheet of paper tacked to the wall, he'd written down the start and finish times and had allowed a calculator, fresh notepad, pens, and pencils. The only thing he hadn't insisted on was Liam wearing a shirt. When he'd placed the typed-out four-page exam before him, complete with a fake university crest in the header, Liam had swallowed hard. He'd looked up into those deep brown eyes searching for something—reassurance, encouragement, the unshakeable faith King seemed to place in him—and King hadn't disappointed. With hands on his shoulder, King had leaned in and said, "You can do this, Lee. I believe in you."

Liam hadn't ever worked harder at anything in his life. Rugby was physically exhausting and the strategy involved was far beyond what most people thought, but most of it came naturally to him. Sure, he had to keep his fitness up, and Coach's training regime killed him every pre-season, but it was muscle memory. It was reminding his body to do something that was as ingrained to him as the instinct to breathe. The strategy—reading other players and foretelling where the ball would be—was hours of practice watching the way other players moved and figuring out their tells. Statistics was like a foreign language, and every letter, every number he'd written on that page had represented days of work.

"Good job," King murmured, his hand on Liam's shoulder again. Liam closed his eyes and soaked up the encouragement, committed the memory of King's touch to his heart. He leaned over Liam and plucked the notepad from the table, the warmth of King's body a contrast to his always cool hands. "I'll have your marks back to you as soon as possible—"

"No, please," Liam cried, standing up and whirling around, ready to fall to his knees and beg if he had to. Instead, he found himself chest to chest, standing far closer than two friends would stand. But Liam didn't back down; he couldn't even if he wanted to. "Mark it now," he implored, his voice a low rasp. Liam reached for the notepad and brushed King's fingers, the simple contact sending a bolt of electricity through his veins. Their gazes clashed and King sucked in a breath, his nostrils flaring as his tongue darted out to wet his lower lip. He held his breath on the inhale, his chest expanding and brushing Liam's.

Liam didn't know who moved first. One moment they were both holding the notepad, and the next it was fluttering to the floor as Liam reached for King, dragging him closer. King's hands went to his chest, his fingers curling against his bare pecs as Liam wrapped his hand around King's nape and brought their faces together. His body demanded that Liam climb King like a koala. But his mind pushed him to savour the moment. Running his hand down King's back, Liam moaned and rubbed his cheek against King's stubble.

"We can't," King whispered, shoving him gently away. "I can't, I'm sorry." The other man moved quickly, sidestepping to pick up the notepad and shoving it into his messenger bag. "I'll text you your results later tonight, and maybe tomorrow we can meet at the library. Yeah, library might be an idea," he added as if it were an afterthought. Without a backward glance, King was out the back door, dashing away.

Liam was pinned. Unable to move. Shock ricocheted through his body like tremors after an earthquake. What had he done? He'd promised himself that his crush would always be unrequited. That King and Addy would never know about it—despite him telling King's dad—never mind ever having to shut him down. Looked like he'd failed spectacularly on both fronts.

The gate slammed and the sound of a rock hitting the fence reached his ears. When they'd moved in, his parents hated the grass up the side. They'd poisoned it and laid steppingstone pavers with palm-sized river rocks between them. It was murder on your feet if you missed the pavers, but the noise it generated was a great security measure to know when there was someone in the backyard. The noise meant one thing.

King hadn't left. He was still there.

TWENTY-ONE

Adelaide

Her phone rang, vibrating against her leg as she sipped her gin and blueberry cocktail with the other students at the bar they'd found hidden away in the alley. "Sorry, I need to take this," she said, lifting her phone and standing up. "Hey, baby, how are you?" she answered. King's breathing was ragged, as if he'd run a marathon. He didn't say anything, and a spike of fear crushed her chest. "Let me get somewhere quieter and we can talk."

She dashed up the alley away from the noise of the bar. It was just a hole in the wall with high-topped tables and chairs under a waterproof sail, but it was cute and hopping with people. They were out celebrating the completion of the second week of classes and their latest assignment. This time she'd facilitated a session where non-sexual touch was used to grow intimacy. But at that moment it was the last thing on her mind.

"Baby, what's wrong? Talk to me," she implored, ducking into a quiet doorway around the corner. She checked inside, making sure she wouldn't be moved on, but the café had closed hours earlier.

"I'm sorry," he sobbed. Adelaide's breath caught in her throat, that crushing fear decimating her ability to inhale. "Fuck, why now?" King muttered and there was a clatter as if he'd thrown something.

"What happened, King?" she choked out.

"He tried to kiss me—Liam—and I wanted him to. I wanted him so bad. But I pushed him away. I told him no, but Addy, I wanted him and I'm so sorry." His breath hitched on a sob and she could hear him sniffling.

It took a moment for his words to sink in. Liam had tried to kiss King. Shock stilled her movements, the nervous fiddling with the hemline of her singlet. Surely she hadn't heard right. But that was what King had just said; Liam had tried to kiss him.

She bit back a sob as her heart shattered into a million pieces. She'd loved Liam forever, and he'd never paid her much more than a cursory glance. She'd always been Lij's little sister. Now, she was his friend. At least she thought he was. Why would he do that? Why would he hurt her like that? Why now? Why, when she'd finally found someone who made her happy, did he decide he wanted to be with a man? Her man.

"Adds," King whispered, his voice broken. Rough and absolutely destroyed. "I'm sorry."

Oh, god, she was going to lose him.

Fuck. That. She was no victim. Adelaide lifted her chin, squared her shoulders, and stiffened her spine. She clenched her jaw. She wasn't giving King up. She wasn't stepping back. She wasn't letting King go. He was meant to be hers; Adelaide knew it to her very soul.

So what now? Blind panic lashed out. She wanted to tell King no. Irrationality made her want to pull the plug on their tutoring. To keep them apart. But she couldn't. It would destroy the very thing that she was trying to protect. King wasn't a piece of fine art to be locked in a gilded cage. He was a living, breathing man, with feelings that ran as deep as oceans. Feelings that Adelaide knew would be destroyed by her losing faith in him. She'd be asking him to choose. To sacrifice a part of him she had no right to ask he give up. Yes, she was his girlfriend and yes, they were exclusive, but she'd just promised him a week earlier that his attraction to Liam was okay. It was healthy. She'd promised him that she could handle it if he wanted to take things further as long as she knew about it.

King had done exactly what she'd asked. He'd pushed Liam away and called her to talk.

But damn, did it hurt. Knowing she would never be what Liam wanted was a tough pill to swallow. Liam making a move on King was like the universe was taunting her. It was as if the stars were saying a giant fuck you to her. Giving her a peek of what happiness with King was, and teasing her with close-ups of what a relationship with Liam was like. The very men she was in love with wanted each other, but she would only ever be on the edge.

Talk about un-fucking-fair.

Adelaide regretted ever telling King it was okay to want Liam. Once upon a time she didn't think either of them had a snowflake's chance in hell with the man. Turned out she was wrong. But the more important question was whether she'd encouraged King because it was a hopeless fantasy for him as much as it was for her? What kind of person did it make her to even think it? A shitty one. Adelaide needed to decide whether it was just platitudes or if she meant it.

No. Maybe?

Adelaide had no doubt that she loved King enough to give this to him. But could she do it knowing it was with Liam? Or would seeing them together destroy her? What was the saying? Set them free, and if they come back, they're yours? Who thought up something ridiculous like that? A maelstrom of confusion and hurt spun like a cat five hurricane inside her.

Adelaide trusted King. She loved him and had faith in him. So why was it so hard to summon that faith now? She closed her eyes, slumping against the wall. Tears wet her lashes, trailing down her cheeks until they dripped off her chin. Drip, drip, drip.

"King," she whispered, her voice breaking on that one word. Crying harder, she voiced her fears, "I can't lose you. I love you."

"Shh, my love. You aren't going to lose me. I love you." King's voice was rock steady. Strong despite the ragged sound of it.

"But you want Liam," she uttered, giving words to the unasked request.

"No. Yes, but not at your expense. I told him no. I told him I can't. I'm faithful to you, Adds. I love you and even though I've fallen for him too, I won't ever cheat on you. No matter what, you'll always be it for me. I love you, Adds." Something settled in her. Hearing those words, King's promise of fidelity, soothed her ragged heart. Her doubts, her insecurities were beaten back by the memory of those strong arms wrapping around her, and the rumble of his voice against her ear as she pressed her face to his chest. The strength of his beating heart.

The anvil sitting on her chest cracked, loosening its crushing weight on her. She could breathe again. Adelaide didn't know why, but the path before her cleared. King needed this. Maybe Liam did too. Whatever the reason, something inside Adelaide nudged her to encourage King. She'd needed to hear his words, needed to know he loved her. But something deep down also told her that King and Liam were meant to be together too. Before she could chicken out, let fear get in the way, she whispered, "Go for it."

"Go for what?" King asked, confusion lacing his tone.

"Liam. I want you to be with him—"

"Adds—"

"No, listen. I know we agreed to be exclusive, and I'm not changing my mind... well, not exactly. But something is telling me that you and Liam are supposed to be together too. I think you need to explore that. I don't want to break up; I'm not walking away. I'm... okay with you and Liam being together as well as the two of us still dating. I'm not

274 • ANN GRECH

saying we're over, go and be with him. I am saying that... I don't even know how to explain it." She dried her cheeks with the back of her hand and started again, trying to rear-range her jumbled thoughts into something coherent enough to make some kind of sense to King. "I'm in love with you, King. I'm not some martyr who'll walk away from you and say go and be happy with him. I'll fight for you, like some crazy stalker—"

A laugh burst out of King and the sound made Addy smile one of those tentative, unsure smiles. But the more she thought about it, the more the knowledge that this was what was meant to happen solidified within her. The more her muscles relaxed and the raging storm inside her settled.

"I'll share you with him. I can't ask you to give up who you are—"

"I'm in love with you too, Adds. Yes, I'm attracted to Liam, yes I want him, and I love him too, but the fact that I'm bisexual doesn't mean I can't be monogamous. I chose you because I love you—"

"I know that, and that's one of the reasons why I know I can tell you it's okay to do this. I trust you, King. I asked you to tell me if you wanted this friendship between you and Liam to progress, and you called me the moment it nearly went further. You pushed him away because you're faithful to me." She paused, knowing she needed to be frank with King, to lay it all out there for him in no uncertain terms, but she had no idea how.

She'd tried to tell him before. Hinted that her feelings ran deeper for the man than were obvious. But there were some things better off left unspoken. Was this one of those times? Confessing that she was in love with Liam too would only muddy the waters. It would complicate things even further, and King deserved better than that. It wasn't fair to lump that on him too. Adelaide was strong enough to deal with her feelings on her own—she'd had quite a few years' experience already.

"I didn't think anything between you two would ever be possible," she confessed past the lump in her throat. "Maybe that's why I said to talk to me in the first place. But now hearing you say how sorry you are, I understand the path we're supposed to take. I want you to have him, King."

"You want me to have him?" King repeated, disbelief colouring his tone. "Adds—"

"Liam's a good man. He deserves having someone like you love him. King, you're an incredible man. I want to give you the world, and if that means opening our relationship up to Liam so you can experience loving him, then that's what I want for you."

King was silent except for his heavy breathing. He sounded winded, his breaths choppy. When he spoke, he was unsure, his words slow and unsteady. "You want me to be with Liam too? As in a one-night stand?"

All the uncertainty plaguing her fled. As much as it hurt to want for herself what she was giving permission to King to do, Adelaide knew her actions were right. She loved King as completely as she was capable of. But she wanted more for him. Adelaide had no idea that Liam was attracted to him, but there was one thing she knew beyond the shadow of a doubt—Liam didn't play games. He was upfront with people. If he was only in it to get off, he put it out there before anything went down. He didn't fuck around with people's feelings. So, if he'd made a move on King, it meant something.

"If you both decide you only want to be together the one time, then yes. But if you want more, if you want to be together long term, like you and I are together, then that's okay too." Her voice wobbled on the last few words, and she cleared her throat, forcing herself to continue. She squeezed her eyes closed, shoving back the tears. She'd be fine. The pain was temporary, just until she adjusted to her new normal.

"King?" she heard Liam ask. "I'm sorry, I should never have put you in the position to make that call. Tell Addy I'm sorry for hurting her. I never meant to try to make you cheat. I reacted on instinct, and it was wrong."

"Lee, I..." King started, then paused. "Thank you."

"Yeah." There was silence and Adelaide held her breath, waiting to see what King would do. But she didn't hear a sound. Not even his breathing.

"King, go to him. Kiss him." *Like I would kiss you. Like I would kiss him.* "Make each other feel good. Open yourself up to the chance."

"I don't want to hurt you, Adds."

"You won't," she lied, bracing herself for when the eye of the storm passed.

She held onto the phone, listening to King as he sucked in a breath. She heard a door slam and the surprise in Liam's voice when he said, "King? I thought—" Their voices were farther away when she heard them speak next, but it was unmistakeably King. She couldn't make out what he said, but she knew. It was happening. They were together. She hung up, not needing to hear them get intimate. A prickling sensation like pins and needles set in, every pain receptor in her body on high alert, and Adelaide cried.

She didn't know how long she stood there, but it was long enough that her friend came looking. "Adelaide, oh my god, what's wrong?" Mallory asked, slipping into the doorway with her and grasping her arm.

Adelaide wiped her eyes and tried to smile. She was sure it looked fake—it was probably more of a grimace than a smile. "I'm fine, but I think I'm gonna go. I'm not really in the mood for company anymore tonight." With a nod, Mallory fetched Adelaide's bag while she ordered a rideshare.

She needed to be alone so she could process what was happening. The reality was that she could have triggered a rockslide. Something that would sweep the ground out from below her and leave her battered and bruised. King loved her; she knew that. But what if he loved Liam more? Adelaide wanted to be secure in herself. She wanted to be able to do the very things she'd told King she would do. But fear and insecurity were bitches.

An hour later she was in her rented bedroom, climbing the walls. She had a missed call from King. Was he calling to give her an update? To tell her what they'd done? Visions of Liam naked with King swirled around in her brain. Her insides were in a meat grinder, her breathing short and sharp. She couldn't suck in a full breath. Over and over she'd told herself that this was good. It was okay. Giving King more love was positive. Him being with Liam should make her happy. She knew that they were meant to be together. It was one thing she was certain of. But it didn't make it easier to swallow. The crush of pain on her chest was crippling, but the hollowness inside her—the emptiness expanding like a black hole—pushed back. The tears wouldn't come. Nothing would. She was numb.

She needed to... Adelaide didn't even know.

She paced. Counted the minutes that passed, unsure of what to do with herself. Should she call him back? Act like nothing was happening? She didn't know what else to do, but call the one person she knew would understand. Katy. If she wasn't around, maybe Robyn would be. Both of her friends had been in similar situations. Both had worried about losing their man to another person. In their cases, they'd fallen for the newcomer. Hers was decidedly different on that point.

"Adelaide!" Katy answered on the second ring. There were voices around her, laughter and talking. "You're missing girls' night."

"Oh, okay. I'll go," she mumbled, disappointment surging through her. She needed her friend.

"No, no, don't be silly. Adelaide's on the phone. Say hi." A chorus of hellos from Emma, Katy's cousin-in-law, Helena, Emma's daughter, and Robyn came through the phone. Robyn asked how she was.

"Yeah, fine," she choked out.

"No, don't do that. What's wrong?" Katy's tipsy giggles were gone in a flash and her serious side, the one filled with concern, shone. "We're here for you. I can take you off speaker if you need me to."

"No, it's okay unless Helena will understand."

"I've got it covered," Emma explained. "TV's a great babysitter."

Robyn sounded like she'd moved closer when she spoke again. "Adelaide, are you safe? Do you need us to call anyone for you?"

"No, it's nothing like that. I'm... Um, where do I start?" She huffed out a laugh that was more of a sigh and she grimaced as her voice wobbled. "I did something today that I know was the right thing to do, but goddamn it hurts, and I'm scared. I don't want to be because I know he loves me, but I can't help think that I might lose everything. But I could also lose everything anyway. I don't know if I'm making sense." Adelaide wiped away the tears that had started trickling down her cheeks again and closed her eyes.

"Who are you talking about, Addy?" Katy asked, her voice soft. Keeping her relationship with King a secret had once felt like the biggest hurdle they had to overcome. It paled in comparison. So much had happened in the last few weeks that she'd forgotten to fill her friends in on her beau. She'd been so wrapped up in studying and living in her little bubble that she'd pushed away her friends. How ironic that they were hearing about things when they got rocky.

"Remember the guy I met the night of the speed dating? We've been together since." She winced when Katy asked why she'd never brought him to their get togethers. "We didn't tell anyone because he taught at a Catholic school and what I do for a living might have threatened his job. I didn't want to risk his career taking a hit because of me. But that doesn't matter now. He starts teaching at a new school next year. He moved because of me, so we could be open."

"So what's happened, hon?" Emma asked.

"I can't give specifics because it's not just my story to tell." She sighed. "I'm sorry, the person who is affected has a lot to lose. I know I can trust you, all of you. I know you'd never say anything. You all know what happened to Levi when he was outed. It's like that."

"Okay." Katy's response was simple. Final. She wouldn't push. She didn't have to. Katy and Emma both knew she was talking about Liam. They knew he was the only famous person she knew. But neither would utter his name.

"King, that's my boyfriend's name, told me something. He loves me. He shows me all the time. We're exclusive and he'd never cheat, but he's fallen for someone else. I gave him my blessing to explore how things go with this person. It was the right decision. I know it was. But it didn't make it easy and I'm scared." She scrubbed her forehead and tucked her hair behind her ear. Pulling at a loose thread on the bed covers, she sighed and slumped, pulling the covers over her despite it being a warm night.

"I think I know how you feel," Robyn replied. She was opening the door for Adelaide to give her details without pushing or asking her directly. Robyn had gone through the same thing with Mike. The man he'd fallen in love with on a trip away had come back into his life, and Robyn was faced with an impossible choice—ask Mike to choose her or encourage him to have both of them.

"Yeah, you do. We were on the freeway, you know? The straight road. We could have gone down it and gotten to our destination like every other commuter—from A to B with a minimum of fuss." She shrugged. Doing things because they were easy had never been her style. She'd always needed to love her path and she wanted the people around her to love their lives too.

"But sometimes there's a fork in the road. A giant neon sign pointing at you to pull off," Katy murmured, her voice filled with understanding now. It was the same thing she and Levi had experienced with Connor. Adelaide had been there to witness Levi's dawning understanding. She was the one who'd encouraged him to talk to both of them.

"Yeah." She paused. Sighed. "The coast was clear and I thought we were cruising. We were on the straight road taking the easy way. It was the safe road to travel down." Adelaide blinked back the tears, imagining the beauty that King and Liam could create. The love they could find in each other. Liam had been starved of it all his life, and King had so much to give. He had more than enough to give to her and Liam. She believed it down to her bones. She drew on all her strength. All her confidence. She needed to go with her gut. They would get through this intact. They all would.

She hadn't known Liam identified as anything other than straight, but that didn't matter. She trusted him to treat King right whether it was one night or more. He would love King just as hard if given the chance. Liam hadn't had much of it in his life, and he knew how shitty it felt to be treated like an object. He treasured the people who showed him kindness, and King would be one of those people. She desperately wanted both of them to experience the kind of love they could give each other.

"But if we did stay on the freeway, we could have missed all the twists and turns. The adventures. The people and places you fall in love with. I wanted that for them, you know? Like that Disney movie with the race car."

"Were you suggesting something like public transport, or was it more like rideshare or carpooling?" Emma huffed out a laugh. "I'm sorry, that sounds so bad. My analogies are terrible." God, she loved her friends for running with her terrible riddles.

"I didn't want public transport, but yeah, maybe give him—or me—the chance to carpool? I think." Adelaide laughed too, confusion swirling around inside her. The tears came again, and her words were a whisper. "I just wish..." She shook her head, not wanting to finish the thought. She knew that what she wanted was important. She spent a lot of time talking in her videos about the importance of voicing your needs and desires, and she stood by that. Every person deserved love and sexual gratification if that's what they desired. The irony of keeping quiet here wasn't lost on her, but this time she couldn't. She wouldn't. This time she would be the one to show how much she loved both of them by giving King the chance to love Liam without her interference. She smiled, pushing herself to look like she meant it.

"I'm confused," Katy admitted. "So I'm just going to put it out there. Are you saying King and Liam are together?" Katy asked.

"I can't out him." Adelaide shook her head, her shoulders falling as she realized what she'd done. By saying she couldn't out him, she'd just done exactly that.

"Oh, honey. No," Katy murmured.

Her voice hitched. "It'll be okay, won't it? I just wanted him to take the long road and experience life to the full. That's all that's happening."

"Addy, you've been in love with Liam for years. It's going to destroy you watching them together." Katy voiced Adelaide's deepest fears, and she couldn't help the sniffle as the tears dripped down her cheeks.

"I'll be okay."

"Does King know how you feel about Liam?" Robyn asked.

"No. I couldn't bring myself to tell him. I didn't want to complicate their relationship."

"Good, at least I don't have to whip his arse," Katy mumbled, then added, "You need to tell him. You're sitting there hurting while he's with the man you've been in love with for years."

"Isn't that exactly how your relationship with Connor went down, and exactly how Levi and Connor got together?" Emma reminded her. "Adelaide needs our support just like you did."

Katy's only response was a grumbled acquiescence.

"I can't tell you what the right thing to do here is. But I can say that watching Mike leave for his first date with Ezio was the hardest thing I've ever done. I cried myself into a heap. I made Lexi and Jax watch *Bambi* with me for goodness' sake just so they'd cry with me." She huffed. "Not my finest step-parenting moment. But when Ezio and I were finally honest with each other, it changed things for the better."

"Same with me, Con, and Levi," Katy added.

"He's never noticed me before. Why would he start now?"

"Maybe all he needs is a sign to point him in the right direction," Emma added. Adelaide couldn't help but laugh at Katy's groan.

Twenty-Two

Kingston

"G o to him. Kiss him."

With her words playing on repeat, King acted on instinct. He let his legs carry him to the man he'd dreamed about. He was conflicted—how could he love Adds like he did, and want Liam so much? But it was a question he had to wait to answer, because rounding the side of the house, he spied Liam through the glass door. He was huddled over himself, sitting on his usual chair at the kitchen table. With Liam's elbows resting on his knees and his head bent low, King watched his chest expand and contract with each shuddery breath. When he lifted the heels of his hands to his eyes and rubbed, King couldn't wait any longer. His heart shattered knowing that Liam was hurting. There was no more hesitation, no more second-guessing. He needed to show Liam just how wanted he was.

King shoved open the door, the glass slider bouncing on the stopper in his rush to get to him. Liam startled, jumping up from the table as King strode through. "King? I thought—"

Sliding the phone gently on the table, he cupped the other man's face and drew him close. His stubble tickled King's fingertips, Liam's scent filling his senses. Liam's eyes slipped closed, and King eliminated the distance between them, pressing their foreheads together. Breathing the same air, King brushed his thumb over Liam's cheek. He couldn't describe the sensation except that it was right having this beautiful, complex man in his arms.

Liam's needy whimper echoed through him like a siren's call. He nuzzled their cheeks together and Liam melted into him. King sucked in a breath and slid his hand into the other man's hair while Liam gripped his hips. King groaned, his nerve endings sizzling as Liam's body connected with his from head to knees.

With shallow breaths, Liam whispered, "I'm so sorry." His voice was broken. Hoarse from the emotion riding him.

King pressed a kiss to his cheek. Soft and lingering. Liam slid his arms around King's waist and nuzzled into him again, rubbing against his face like a cat.

"Shh," King whispered. "I want this. I want you."

"But you've got Addy and I should never have crossed that line."

"She knows." King pressed his lips to the corner of Liam's, and Liam turned his face into it, bringing their lips together. He kissed him again, a soft, slow press of lips. It was chaste—not even a hint of tongue—but perfect in its simplicity. King knew just from that one touch that Liam wanted more than one-night with him. Feelings were involved, and as much as he loved it, it terrified him too.

Liam must have sensed the shift in him. The conflicting emotions. He wanted to dive in headfirst and show Liam just how good they could be together. But fear had him hesitating too. He couldn't lose Adelaide. He couldn't hurt her, and she was hurting. She'd put on a brave face, telling him to act on his attraction, but she'd readily confessed her fears too. Her broken-hearted sobs had shattered him. Destroyed a part of him that had promised not to hurt her.

He looked over to his phone and swallowed. His screen was dark. Adds had hung up. She was scared and insecure, and all alone. If he put himself in her shoes, he'd be a wreck. Every one of his fears would come to the fore, and he'd be convinced that their relationship would be on the downward slide to being over.

"Liam," he croaked, his voice cracking. He buried his face in Liam's neck and breathed the other man in. What should he do? Where did he go from there?

"Call her," Liam murmured, pressing a kiss to his temple and running his hands up and down his back. King exhaled on a shudder, Liam's touch and his words overwhelming him in the best of ways. It was too much, and not enough.

With his fingers tangled in Liam's hair, King nuzzled his throat. Pressing another soft kiss there, the warmth of his breath raised goosebumps. Having Liam in his arms was as natural as holding Addy, and that was a complete mind fuck. He loved Adds's curves and the beauty in her petite frame, and he'd well and truly fallen for Liam. But being selfish wasn't fair to either of them.

Liam picked up King's phone and handed it to him. "Go on." King took it from his fingers, Liam's touch lingering as he palmed the phone and brought up her contact. It went through to message bank. He hung up. What he needed to speak to Adds about wasn't something that could be said over the phone—not that he had any idea what to say.

King blew out a breath, his heart galloping in his chest. It wasn't as if Adds was there to answer his calls on a whim, but his gut churned. He needed to know if she was okay. "I hate this," he mumbled. "Not you. Not what's happening here, but not having her nearby. Not being able to make sure she's okay."

"What is happening here?" Liam asked, then shook his head. "Never mind. It's a shitty time for me to ask that question when you're worried about Adds."

King reached for him again, sliding his hand to his cheek. The uncertainty in Liam's gaze gutted him. He was doing a really shitty job of telling the people who were important to him how he felt. "I'm in love with Adds. I can see myself growing old with her, you know? But there's something about you too. There's something more between us that I can't ignore. I don't want to ignore it either. You're important to me."

Liam slid his hand to King's face, mirroring his pose, but there was wonder in his eyes. "I don't want to ignore it either." He pressed a kiss to King's cheek and ran his nose down the line of his trimmed stubble. "I've never done this before. Kissed a man. Never been attracted to one either. But you captured my attention straight away."

"I couldn't take my eyes off either one of you," King confessed in a whisper.

"Addy's beautiful. The two of you together..." He huffed out a laugh and shook his head, leaving the rest of his sentence unsaid. "See if she's available yet." There was no answer again, and King swallowed hard. "You know, I reckon we'd be able to get a flight. All up, we could make Sydney in a few hours." King snapped his eyes up to Liam. Was he serious? "You could surprise Addy and talk to her. She's important, King. If you're worried about her, we should go."

"You'd want that?"

He nodded. "Yeah, King. Making the trip isn't a big deal. If it means spending time with you, I'd go anywhere. I love you as much as I love Ad—" His eyes widened and he pressed his lips together, looking away. His cheeks flushed, the colour staining them a pretty pink.

King tilted his face up and smiled, biting back the jubilant grin. Liam was in love. With both of them.

"She's easy to lo— Fuck." King's gut bottomed out and the blood drained from his face. He clutched the chair for balance, dizziness descending over him. Damn it, how had he missed it? Adds had told him. Almost spelled it out for him. She'd agreed that Liam was easy to love. It was right in front of his face and he'd been blind to it. He'd put her concern for Liam passing statistics down to his friendship with Eli. He'd thought they had a sibling kind of relationship, but that was exactly what Adds had wanted him to think. His gut told him it was so much more than that. Her feelings went far deeper than the care she'd developed for her

290 • ANN GRECH

brother's best friend. She was in love with him too. That's why she'd been so upset. That's why Adds had confessed she would be cheating on him too if they accepted Eve's definition.

Why was he so blind? How had he missed it? It was right in front of him the whole time. He was a fucking idiot. King had done more than hurt her. He'd asked her to let him have the other man she loved—was Liam her first love? Had her teenage crush turned into puppy love and then morphed into something everlasting? Christ, he'd asked her to sit by and watch while he got to love on the man she'd wanted. Probably for years.

Flashes of memories hit him like a ten-tonne wrecking ball. The way Adds smiled at Liam. The affection in her eyes whenever she talked about him. The exaggerated brush offs and eye rolls when he did something to annoy her. That she knew everything about his playing career but didn't give a toss about any other players or teams. The way she cared for him, making sure he had company. That he wasn't lonely. King had mistaken her care as familiarity borne of a decade of friendship with her brother. But it was more than that. He was certain of it.

Adds had insisted that King stay behind and tutor Liam. She'd readily sacrificed time together that they'd been talking excitedly about for weeks. It had annoyed him. Frustrated King to no end. But Adds hadn't been fazed. She'd insisted on going alone as soon as she'd heard Liam was struggling. He'd wanted to complain, but seeing how much it meant to her had stopped him. He'd thought it was because of how close she, Lij, Carol, and Pop were to him. They were like his family. Now that King knew the truth of Liam's, he understood why she'd insisted. He would have wanted the same thing for Liam too. So he knew his gut feeling was correct, but now he was sure it had been motivated by a different kind of love for him.

She'd been prepared to sacrifice herself all so Liam wouldn't miss out on the chance to achieve his dream. Every little thing she did was choreographed so no one would realize how deeply she cared about him. She'd become an expert at hiding her feelings in plain sight. Disguising them.

He gripped Liam's arms, sure his eyes were wild with panic. "We need to go to her. Now." Liam nodded and looked down. But King wasn't done. He wasn't letting the people he cared about misinterpret his feelings. "Lee, look at me." He lifted his eyes. The usually green highlights in them had dulled to brown. The wariness in them screamed hesitation and fear.

"Yeah," he said, plastering on a small smile.

"Liam, I'm in love with you too. Whatever happens, we'll work it out, yeah?"

Liam bit down on his lip, his eyes instantly glassy. He blinked. Then blinked again. Liam nodded and with smiling lips, pressed them to King's. "You are?"

"I am."

"Good. Yeah, good." Liam laughed, joy radiating from him. King couldn't resist pressing his lips to the corner of his mouth again. He was right there. So tempting. He wanted nothing more than to taste him—every inch of him—but it didn't seem right without clearing the air with Adelaide first. "Should we, ah, pack a bag? Book some flights?"

"Yeah."

"We really gonna do this?"

King nodded his answer and Liam's shoulders relaxed.

"Good. I don't want Addy to think she's anything but the centre of us," King stated, determined to set things right. The weight lifted off his shoulders, making him lighter than he'd been in a long time. "And I want to kiss you properly. Both of you if I'm honest."

"Then let's go."

Fifteen minutes later, flights booked, they were on the road to King's house to grab an overnight bag. He had no idea what kind of reception they'd get from Adds, but holy hell, he hoped it all went well. There was no way this would end well if King was wrong.

* * * * *

It was late by the time they'd flown in, hired a car, and driven out to where Adds was staying. Neither of them spoke much during the trip, nerves getting the better of King. Liam had his head buried in his phone, tapping away on the screen until he handed it to King. In front of him was an apartment building in the city. "It's the only one I can find that's halfway decent," Liam explained. "We can get a late checkout on Sunday, which will be better with our flights on Sunday night too." Hopefully they'd have a night or two together that would be the beginning of something amazing.

If things didn't go well, they might be commiserating.

Once they were in the privacy of the SUV they'd hired, Liam twined their fingers together and held on, not letting go until they pulled up in the drive. King didn't know whether he had the right to hope for an outcome that saw the three of them together—he sure as heck hoped so—but he couldn't help it. So he'd spent the time trying to think through what he wanted to say.

It wasn't really a respectable hour, but Adds still wasn't answering her phone and he didn't want to wait. Worst case, they'd go to the apartment, check in, and return in the morning.

Liam had drifted off, the day's workout, test, and frantic race to get to the airport taking its toll. He was adorable. Like a kitten snuggling down into the seat, rubbing his face against the headrest he tried to find a comfortable spot. King wanted to wrap himself around the man and kiss him until they were both breathless. Or Liam was asleep. He'd be happy either way.

Instead, he ran his fingers through Liam's hair and pressed a kiss to his forehead, murmuring, "We're here." Liam snaked his arm out, hooking it around King's shoulder and pulled him closer. He was heavy and solid and so beautifully vulnerable in that moment. It meant the world that Liam trusted him enough to let go.

He should probably be worried about someone seeing them. Liam was a professional footballer. Former players had come out, but there was no one King knew of who was still playing. He didn't want to put that kind of pressure on Liam—his job was hard enough without needing to add coming out to the list of things the media could judge him for. Whatever their relationship would look like moving forward, it wouldn't be public. He'd changed jobs so that he and Adds could be open, but this was different. Liam was a celebrity in his own right, and being in the public eye was hard enough when the cameras weren't directed at him. King hated the idea that he could make things more difficult for Liam, so discretion would be essential.

TWENTY-THREE

Adelaide

Adelaide jolted, the knock at the door surprising her. The house was quiet. Marie and her daughter were already asleep. She looked at her phone. It was too late for visitors, but Adelaide didn't know her landlord that well. It could be anyone coming to see her. She tiptoed to the front door and peered through the peephole. She would know their outlines anywhere, even if the sensor light at the front door didn't light the area so well. Adelaide unlocked it, opening the door wide.

"Adelaide?" her landlord asked sharply. "What are you doing?" She turned to the other woman who looked at her with furrowed brows and pursed lips, rumpled from sleep and clearly annoyed at being woken. Adelaide cleared her throat. Her belly flip-flopped and excitement washed over her. She bit back the fizzy smile that wanted to break free.

"This is my boyfriend and brother's best friend. I've only just opened the door, so I don't know why they're here."

She didn't give Marie a chance to respond, instead slipping out of the front door and closing it behind her. They were both a sight for sore eyes. King was pensive, alert, and twitchy. Liam was his opposite, sleep-mussed and exhausted. But both were as beautiful as ever.

Adelaide looked between them, at the way Liam rested his head on King's shoulder and King's arm around his waist. It wasn't jealousy that hit her, but she did envy the hours they'd spent together over these last couple of weeks. She'd missed being in King's arms so badly. But now he was there. A giddy smile parted her lips. "What are you doing here?"

"We wanted to see you, Adds. Both of us." King let go of Liam and stepped forward, taking her hand and lifting it to his lips. He kissed her knuckles before threading their fingers together. "I'm sorry. I should have handled things differently. We needed to make sure you were okay."

"So you came all the way down here?" she asked, joy suffusing her at the gesture that meant more to her than she could express. She needed to be closer to him, to have his arms around her. She leaned in, and King obliged, wrapping her in his embrace. His scent enveloped her, the warmth and strength of his hug like a balm to her battered heart. He hugged her with his whole body, scooping her close and cradling her like she was precious. She was happy and scared at the same time, filled with a fizzing kind of excitement while fearful of getting hurt again. She wanted to kiss him—needed to—but didn't know where the dynamic between them stood. Would King and Liam being together change things between her and King? Could they show each other affection in front of one another? "Can I kiss you—"

King squashed her worries before she could explain. He pulled her closer, kissing her like he was a man drowning and she was oxygen. His touch was gentle and loving, and at the same time a little desperate. Ravenous and wholly consuming. She melted into him, touching her tongue to his when he explored her mouth, never wanting to leave the comfort of his broad shoulders and muscular arms again.

His hard cock was trapped in the confines of his jeans. It pressed against her belly and Adelaide shamelessly rubbed herself against him like a cat. She wasn't sure who whimpered—whether the sound came from King when she slipped her hands up under his shirt and raked her fingertips down his firm belly, herself when he cupped her arse, his huge hand covering one whole cheek in his firm grip, or Liam seeing it all go down from up close. The imagery her mind's eye painted of Liam getting involved too was far too tantalizing.

She forced herself to pull back and put a bit of distance between them. Panting, she pressed her cool hands to her flaming cheeks, pulling her elbows in front of her erect nipples. Adelaide was barely dressed, and while Liam had seen her in this outfit before, he'd never been there during a make-out session. She didn't know the ground rules between them yet, what they could and couldn't do, and she'd taken it too far. The brush of the soft cotton against her nipples, which sent zings of awareness down to her wet pussy, was too much for a first-time viewing.

Adelaide cleared her throat, but still sounded breathless when she asked, "So why are you both here?" then held up a hand to stop any protestations. "I'm not complaining. At all." She flicked her gaze between King and Liam and bit back a whimper when Liam stared back, his eyes dark and teeth biting down on those pillowy lips. He looked like a predator ready to pounce.

Damn did she want to be his prey.

His voice was gravel when he spoke, the rasp sexier than anything she'd ever heard before—except King's sex voice. "We—King and I—both wanted to talk to you. Can we?"

She hesitated. "Marie, the woman you saw, doesn't like strangers in her house. She's asked me not to bring any men here."

King ran his fingers through her hair and encouraged, "Pack an overnight bag. We've got an apartment near the city that we're all gonna stay at."

"We?" Adelaide asked, hesitating once more.

"Yes, we. But we need to have a conversation first." King lifted her knuckles back to his lips and kissed them, his eyes never leaving hers. "Go."

Adelaide nodded and dashed inside, her heart pounding erratically and heat crawling over her skin. She caught the door before it banged and whirled around, ready to duck into the guest bedroom where she was staying. "I made it clear that you were not to bring men around," Marie stated, the annoyance in her tone unmistakable.

"They surprised me. I didn't know they were on their way, and they aren't coming inside. I know your rules and I'm respecting them. I won't be back until Sunday some time. My boyfriend has a hotel room booked for the weekend." She didn't want to get on the wrong side of her, but Adelaide hadn't done anything wrong either. She just hoped that Marie didn't feel like her trust had been betrayed. But she didn't stick around to find out.

After throwing clothes and toiletries into her bag, Adelaide almost ran out again still wearing her PJs. "Shit," she mumbled under her breath, flustered by the surprise visit. Her thoughts were running around in circles, dreaming but not daring to hope what their joint visit might mean. She threw on the first outfit she found—a tank top, denim shorts, and a cardigan—slipped on a pair of thongs and called out in a whisper, "See you later," before locking the door on her exit.

King was there holding the front passenger door open for her, and he beamed as she slid onto the seat. He buckled her belt before pressing a lingering kiss to her forehead. He nuzzled her cheek with his short beard and whispered, "You have no idea how much I've missed you."

"I missed you too," she murmured back. "I'm sorry I turned my phone off. I know we're okay, and I want this for you, I really do—"

"Let's talk more when we get to the apartment." He kissed her again, a soft chaste brush of his lips against her temple, and stepped back, closing the door after him.

Twenty minutes later they were pulling into the visitor parking at a newer-looking building. Adelaide loved the atmosphere in the city. Even at night there were throngs of people moving about. She revelled in the vibrancy and speed of the city, the tall buildings and the energy that seemed to vibrate through the streets. But she already missed home, and seeing King and Liam only reinforced how happy she was living in her little suburb away from the hustle and bustle.

King slung Adelaide's backpack over his shoulder, carrying his duffel on the other as Liam picked up his own bag. Decked out in the team's colours, it was like a beacon to anyone who'd seen football teams travel before, but there was no one around to notice. Both the car park and lobby were empty except for the man sitting behind the desk.

The view from the apartment was spectacular—lights twinkled as far as the eye could see, and the moon reflecting off the water created an ethereal glow. Between the high rises she caught a glimpse of the Harbour Bridge lit up in Christmas colours. "Wow," she murmured as King wrapped his arm around her waist and looked over her shoulder. She revelled in his closeness, in the way he held her like she was his world.

"View's pretty good, isn't it?" King murmured.

"Certainly is," Liam added from behind them. She turned, looking around King's big body to see where he was. They were taking up most of the gap between the gauzy curtains that she'd pushed apart. He wouldn't be able to see much at all. But his expression told her it wasn't the view he was looking at, but King.

His eyes were dark. Jaw clenched, he radiated power. It was as if he was trying hard to hold himself back. Or coiling his body tighter ready to attack. She'd seen the look of intense concentration on him before during games.

Liam dropped his bag in the middle of the entry hallway and added, "I've been biting my tongue for what feels like a decade. Can we talk?"

"Yeah, let's sit." King motioned to the couch and Adelaide followed his cue, perching on the edge of the cushion. King slid in next to her, pulling Adelaide into his arms. Liam took a seat on the chunky timber coffee table so that he was directly in front of her, his spread knees bracketing hers.

"What's going on, guys? You're starting to freak me out."

Liam gave her a tentative smile. As far as smiles went, it didn't do much to ease the sudden nerves fluttering around. He reached for her hands, taking both in his. They were warm and rough, a contrast to King's perpetually cool ones. "King and I have had a bit of a heart-to-heart. I admitted a few things, and so did he. I know you know we're attracted to each other. I also know you told him to go for it. But we never intended to hurt you."

King ran his hand gently down her hair, adding, "When you'd hung up and I couldn't get in contact with you, we were both upset. I'll always regret letting you think that you're anything but the most important person in my world. Hearing you cry because of what I wanted broke my heart. I will always love you—"

"I know that, King. I knew it when we were talking too. I was hurting, because..." She stopped herself, not wanting to divulge that information. It was something that King and Liam didn't need to know. Not when they seemed to be working things out between them. It was enough that she'd always be friends with Liam. "Doesn't matter."

Liam squeezed her hands. His voice was low, and when she looked at him, she could see the concern mixed with something else. Fear, perhaps? "Can I tell you a secret?"

Adelaide untangled their fingers and cupped his face. He didn't need to worry. Despite the nerves battling for dominance in her belly, she smiled. Liam always managed to do that. As much as she had pined over him for years, he had always made her happy. "Sure."

He blew out a breath and looked to King. It was as if he needed the support. King leaned forward and dropped a hand on Liam's knee, squeezing it. Adelaide focussed on that, on the connection they had. Once again, she didn't experience any jealousy in seeing King's hand on Liam. It was a longing, but not just for her involvement. It was for Liam to experience King's entire focus on him. King had a way of making people the centre of his universe, and she wanted nothing more than Liam to experience it too. King would likely be swapping beds all weekend, but at least they could both be there with him.

Liam licked his lips and said, "I'm a blind bastard. I didn't see you until it was too late. You arrived home with King that first time and I woke up. I finally saw you."

She sucked in a breath, her heart slamming against her chest. Shock, and more than a little blind hope, held her captive, stilling her movements. She swallowed and spoke, her voice a squeak when she asked, "What are you saying, Liam?"

He looked down, focussing on their joined hands. He ran his rough thumbs over her knuckles and spoke in little more than a whisper. "You'd always been Lij's little sister to that point. But then it was as if the blindfold had been taken off." He glanced up and the truth in his eyes held her captivated. "I think I fell in love that day. Seeing you and King together made everything fall into place. I got confused. King was this beautiful muscly dude who made you smile and get all defensive over him. Then when you kissed, I couldn't take my eyes off the two of you."

She opened her mouth, but nothing came out. Closing it again, her gaze darted to King. He furrowed his brows, the encouraging smile he'd given to Liam falling from his face.

"Adds?"

"You love him?" Adelaide squeaked, ecstatic that he was in it for more than a one-night stand with King.

"And you." Liam let the words hang between them. The gears in Adelaide's brain ground to a halt and she blinked. Had she heard right? Was her brain playing some horrible trick on her, making her hear words that he hadn't really said? Liam held her gaze, his lips pressed together. It was as if time slowed down, then sped up again, the quiet of the night a buzz in her ears.

"You... you love me?" she stuttered, her brows pinching and her mouth hanging open. "For real?"

"Yeah." Liam nodded, his eyes searching hers for a reaction. Shock held her captive, but warmth unfurled in her chest like a cat stretching in the haze of the summer sun. Hope exploded inside her, effervescent bubbles rippling to the surface and making goosebumps break out on her skin. A hot flush whipped over her, electrifying her skin, and her core thrummed, want and need coalescing until she was practically vibrating out of her skin.

And still Liam kept talking.

"I want King, but I want you too. I know I'm being greedy, but—"

Restraint snapped, and Adelaide reacted on instinct, launching herself at him. Their bodies colliding, she wrapped her arms around his neck, crash-tackling him. Chest to chest, her knees on either side of his hips, Adelaide pressed her mouth to his, finally taking what she'd dreamed of for a decade.

One kiss, then two, and Liam's lips kept moving, garbled sounds coming out of his mouth as his brain took a moment to catch up to her whirlwind assault. Then the moan. The one she'd been waiting for an eternity to hear. The one that Liam made at her hands. He kissed her back, dipping his tongue into her mouth. She tasted him—that flavour that was uniquely him—and Adelaide moaned, desire swirling alongside the ecstasy.

He chased her lips as she broke for air. He slid his hand down her body, grasping her hip and holding her nape, tangling his fingers in her hair as he hauled her closer. Pressed against him, she could feel every ripple of his muscles as he moved. He was much leaner than King, his abs and pecs more defined. His training during the pre-season was gruelling. He was shredding fat, building muscle, and regaining his speed. Adelaide had catalogued all the differences between Liam and King before, but this was the first time she was close enough to him to feel it. The only thing she wanted now was King's touch too.

Liam lunged forward, joining their lips again, and she sank into the kiss, opening to him as Liam slid his tongue in alongside hers. They tasted each other for long moments, Adelaide not willing to let him up until she had her fill. Liam wanted her. He saw her as more than just Eli's little sister. And she was kissing him! The man she'd been in love with since she was practically a kid.

Another hand landed on her back, sliding down to cup her arse. King. He'd shifted so he was sitting next to Liam on the chunky timber table. She pulled back from Liam, still straddling his hips as he rested an arm behind his head and dropped the other to her thigh.

King hooked his finger under her chin, turning her face to his. "That's why you were crying when we spoke, isn't it? You're in love with him too, aren't you?" His questions were rhetorical. Certainty shone in his eyes, triumph sparkling in them. He'd done this—realized her secret and brought them together.

Adelaide nodded. Tears burned her eyes and she blinked them back, willing them not to fall.

King thumbed her cheek with infinite gentleness, wiping the stray drop and whispered, "I'm so sorry for hurting you." King pressed their lips together, kissing her slowly. His touch was gentle, savouring her. Worshipping her with his mouth. He licked at her bottom lip and Adelaide opened, wanting to fall into him. She reached for King, pulling him closer, needing to feel his body pressed against hers.

It was as if she was in freefall. Tumbling around in the sky and hurtling toward the earth all the while riding an adrenaline high that she never wanted to come down from. Liam's cock flexed against her pussy, long and hard between her denim-clad legs. She whimpered and rocked on him while King sucked on her tongue and cupped her breast, flicking her nipple with his thumb. Sensation rocketed through her, and she gasped, her empty channel clenching with the need to be filled by her men.

Her men.

She'd never get sick of that.

Liam sat up, his body pressing against hers. Their heat enveloped her, their hands trailing over her sensitive skin while King took her mouth and Liam kissed a line down her throat, scraping his teeth gently over her collarbone. Sucking his way back up, he licked her pulse point. The two of them had her pussy fluttering. She wanted to get closer to them. But all too soon, King pulled back.

"Can I kiss you?" Liam asked him. "I really want to taste you like that too."

King hummed and slid his free hand to Liam's nape, tugging him closer. The moment their lips met, Adelaide sucked in a breath. God, they were beautiful together. Their kiss was slow, their lips meeting and then separating after a moment. There was no tongue, no aggressive mauling of each other. It was sweet and gentle, and Adelaide's heart burst out of her chest.

Resting her head on King's shoulder, she pressed her lips to his throat. "Show me what you did after you kissed him for the first time, King," she encouraged.

Liam pulled back, blinking his eyes open. His cheeks were flushed, his lips wet. Shaking out of his stupor, he looked to Adelaide before pushing a lock of hair off her shoulder. "We came to you. We haven't even made out properly."

Adelaide sat up, her gaze bouncing between them seeing the truth of Liam's words in their expressions. "Right. Get up," she ordered, climbing off Liam's lap. Taking their hands in hers, she tugged them toward the bedroom. "Shoes and socks off."

She ripped the covers off the bed, tossing all the pillows to the floor in a messy pile. Her hands shook. Adelaide's heart gave an uneven stutter and her pulse skittered through her veins at the thought of being together. Of being with them. She wanted their first time—King and Liam's as well as her first time with both of them—to be more than just some fumbling, awkward experience. As a teenager with hormones flooding her, she'd imagined Liam picking her up and carrying her bridal-style into bed where he'd love on her for hours. Then when King came along, he showed her exactly what she'd dreamed of.

King was unexpected, but he was the best kind of surprise. Then when he'd admitted falling for Liam, she'd tried to be brave. She'd tried to hide her feelings and let King and Liam love each other without her interference. But this was how it was supposed to be.

Fear had turned into a sense of rightness, the hurt she'd experienced morphing into an overwhelming sense of awe. This was really, truly happening.

Adelaide was already loving every minute of it, but she wanted them to be right there with her. She knelt on the bed, holding her hands out, beckoning them closer. King moved first but Liam wasn't far behind, both climbing up and taking her hand in theirs. She squeezed them before taking their hands and joining them. Seeing their connection manifested filled her with joy. It wasn't longing anymore, not when she knew how Liam felt, and as much as she wanted to bask in the centre of their attention, she also wanted to solidify the bonds each of them had to one another.

This was it. This was her future right here in front of her, the two men she would love to her dying breath. With her heart overflowing, she said to King, "Touch him. Show him how you feel. I want to watch you."

King threaded their fingers together and brought Liam's hand to his lips, pressing a soft kiss there before grinning at Adelaide, happiness radiating off him in excited waves. Without breaking eye contact, King caressed Liam's hand, his wrist, then his forearm. The inside of his elbow had Liam squirming, his breathing turning choppy.

"Take your shirt off, Lee," King ordered quietly.

He did, and as soon as their hands were connected again, King went back to caressing him. Gentle swipes of his fingertips along Liam's bicep and triceps, his shoulder and along his collarbone. Liam tilted his head back, giving King more room and Adelaide watched enraptured. She couldn't wait to be the one touching him, caressing him as his eyes fluttered closed and his breath quickened. Anticipation and wonder arced between them, and her heart filled to bursting point as she gazed at the two men who'd captivated her. She loved them, and the certainty that they loved her back was uplifting. Empowering.

When King trailed his fingertips up Liam's throat, following with his lips, Liam's breath caught, and he sighed as King curled his fingers around Liam's nape bringing their foreheads close. He brushed their lips together ever so gently and Liam whimpered. Adelaide's heart broke for him, and the loneliness he must have experienced. But at the same time, it rejoiced knowing he would never be alone again. He opened to King and Adelaide watched as her men kissed each other the way they'd both wanted to. Liam pulled King closer, clutching at his shirt as they kissed. Adelaide smiled serenely, relief and love coursing through her veins.

She shifted, moving in behind King. "Lift up," she whispered, kissing his shoulder. Liam's hands went to the bottom of his shirt, helping her inch it up. He broke their kiss and watched as she lifted King's shirt to reveal a flat belly intersected with a line of hair from his chest disappearing down under his waistline. Adelaide had memorized her man's body, and Liam's hungry expression as he saw King for the first time mirrored what hers must have looked like.

"Fuck me, you're sexy," Liam breathed as King lifted his arms and Adelaide pulled his shirt away, tossing it to the floor. King snapped his gaze up and they stared at each other. "All your hair and your muscles. So different, but damn, I wanna lick you all over." Liam's voice was husky, raw with need, and his eyes were filled with heat.

Adelaide leaned in, pressing against King's back, and kissed his shoulder while Liam cupped his face and kissed him. When he broke away, King's chest heaved as Liam trailed his hands down King's sides.

"Teach me how to make you feel good, King."

"Making Adds feel good turns me on the most," he rasped. The smile that slowly spread over Liam's face was predatory.

"Oh yeah," he growled. "My fuckin' pleasure." He grasped her by the belt loop as King shifted so they formed a triangle. Her singlet was tugged off and she was eased onto her back, her shorts being dragged down her legs before she could squeak—not that she was protesting. It was surreal. She was living a dream. Adelaide pinched herself and blinked, still seeing both of them hovering over her.

"This is real, isn't it?" she asked, her voice hitching on a sob as reality crashed into her in a fireworks display of epic proportions.

"Yeah, Addy it is." Liam pressed his lips to her forehead, and she squeezed her eyes closed, blinking them open again to see their smiling faces above her.

"I love you. Both of you. I'm stupidly head over heels in love with both of you. I'm sorry I hid it, but I couldn't stop."

Saying the words to Liam was freeing. Like a weight lifting off her. The dam wall she'd erected around the part of her heart she reserved for Liam came crumbling down, the tide carrying her away. Their mouths were everywhere, their fingers trailing over her skin. Her nerve endings tingled as Adelaide's eyes rolled back in her head, and she arched into the two sets of lips that had closed over her nipples. King and Liam worked together without words, each one of them taking half her body to shower with their touch. She cried out as one of them brushed a hand over her pussy and shuddered as they pressed harder on her clit. Liam nuzzled her throat as King shifted, tugging off her panties before he climbed between her legs, pushed open her knees, and licked a line down her stomach.

"You never have to hide it again," King said, stopping to kiss her between each word. When his chin landed on her mound, he rubbed his beard against her skin, and Adelaide cried out, each hair acting like a tiny lightning rod.

"Oh, shit," she breathed, her hips lifting of their own accord to get closer to the sensation. He licked her, the hot swipes of his tongue sending sparks into her core. When King sucked on her clit, she saw stars, the dual sensation of Liam at her breasts and King at her pussy building her orgasm at a record pace. When King slid his fingers deep inside her soaking channel, finding her G-spot and lighting her up like a Christmas tree, Adelaide squeezed Liam's arm, her body shaking as the rushing in her core began.

King redoubled his efforts as Adelaide crested, teetering on the edge. Meanwhile, Liam bit gently down on her nipple, twisting the other one between his fingertips. The bite of pain mixed with the ecstasy King was unleashing on her shot her over. Adelaide cried out, her pussy clamping down as she fell into an abyss that felt a lot like heaven.

King pulled his lips away from her pussy but left his fingers buried deep inside her, slowly pumping in and out. Liam met him, hovering over her once more as they shared a messy kiss. Watching them together was incredible. The hottest thing she'd ever seen. Her pussy clamped down, spasming as Liam held King's face and licked her essence away.

"She loves that, Lee." He turned lust-darkened eyes to her and murmured, "Haven't had enough yet, have you?"

"Not nearly. Need you inside me. Want both of you at the same time." She bit her lip, excited to see how they'd interpret what she wanted. Adelaide didn't care. She just needed to explore this with them. She needed the connection. Needed to feel loved and the centre of their world like they'd promised she was.

King hummed and slid off the bed, bending to retrieve the box of rubbers and a bottle of lube from his bag. "Think you want to try DP?" He dropped his jeans and boxer briefs, and Adelaide licked her lips. The sight was familiar, but he never failed to thrill her when she saw King naked. Damn, he was a sight to behold. Thick and built from top to toe, and impressively well-proportioned too.

Liam let out a rumbling growl and her gaze snapped to him. His eyes were locked on King, staring at the gorgeous man naked before them. He had his hand down his pants, white-knuckling his dick. "Fuck me. Between the two of you,

I'm gonna blow my load before anyone even touches my cock."

King growled, stroking his thick length as he motioned to Liam with one finger. "Get those pants off. We have more orgasms to wring out of Adds before you're doing any coming." He flicked his gaze to Adelaide as Liam scrambled off the bed, shucking his shirt. "On your side facing Liam. I need to prep you. And you"—he pointed to Liam—"I'm waiting."

Adelaide rolled, laughing as Liam pushed his shorts and briefs down with absolutely no flare or hesitation, kicking them away as his hard cock slapped against his belly, before dramatically throwing himself back on the bed. With a grin like an excitable puppy dog, he hitched her leg over his hip and ran his fingertip down the centre of her chest to her belly button.

"Your boyfriend has a huge dick," he whispered, lifting his head up so he could perv on King, and biting his tongue as her man kneeled on the bed.

"I think he's your boyfriend too," Adelaide whispered, loud enough that King could hear as he settled behind her.

"Hmm, he is, isn't he? I like that—my boyfriend and girlfriend." He leaned forward and kissed her with smiling lips. Cool fingers nudged at her hole and the tip of Liam's cock poked her mound. Need flared within and her clit throbbed. Adelaide moaned and Liam dived in, kissing her harder, tangling his tongue with hers as King massaged her arse and slipped a finger in.

It was foreign, fullness where there usually wasn't any, but she loved it. It didn't take long for her guys to find a rhythm, and when they did, Adelaide alternated between pushing into each of them, back to riding King's finger, and forward to chase Liam's cockhead connecting with her clit on every teasing thrust. She was climbing again, their touch sending her soaring higher with every second they doted on her.

Liam slid his dick against her leg, leaving a trail of pre-cum along her thigh as he moved. Adelaide reached for him, closing her fist around his shaft, swiping up a drop of the clear liquid. She raised her thumb to her lips, but before she could suck on it, King grasped her wrist, licking her clean, then sucking her digit into the warm cavern of her mouth.

His moan rumbled through her body, and his cock flexed, growing harder against her arse.

Liam whimpered as King hollowed his cheeks and sucked on Adelaide's thumb like it was their man's cock.

"I haven't seen him blow a guy, but I bet King's really good at it," she drawled. King hummed, sending a jolt of lust through her at the picture in her mind's eye.

Liam clamped his hand around the base of his cock again, closed his eyes, and breathed out slowly. "Fuuuuck," he groaned.

King stopped teasing them, working on adding a second finger to stretch her. She gasped, the burn taking her breath away, but it quickly morphed into need. She was impossibly full, especially when he added a third finger inside her. Her begged pleas sounded garbled even to her own ears. With Liam's fingers thrusting into her pussy, and King's in her arse, Adelaide cried out, her orgasm slamming into her. She came on a silent scream, her core clamping down to hold her men where she needed them. But they didn't stop moving, didn't stop thrusting until she was spent. Like a rag doll, they manhandled her, rolling her to face King. Adelaide's eyes slipped closed as King pulled her on top of him so she straddled his wide hips. Adelaide cuddled into his big body, luxuriating in his thick arms wrapping around her.

King shifted, nudging his dick up until he notched it against her pussy. "She's tight, Lee. Go slow." The other man blanketed her back, resting his hands on her hips. A trail of kisses landed along her shoulders and down her spine, and Adelaide shivered, moaning.

"I've got you, Addy," Liam murmured, his heat disappearing. He pressed his cockhead against her pucker and growled. "God damn, your hole is practically begging me to come inside you. It's all open and stretched, trembling against my cock." He pushed forward, stretching her even more, and Adelaide arched up, instinctively pressing her arse into his slow thrust. She gasped as he pushed past her resistance and struggled to stay still as he waited for her to adjust.

"More," she begged when the burn turned to a throb, and Liam delivered, pushing forward in one long slow glide until his hips were pressed against her arse. "Oh God," she breathed. "More."

King moved then, thrusting into her pussy. Their moans echoed through the room as they thrust into her, short sharp punches of their hips and long, slow glides. The variation kept her on edge at the same time as racing toward an orgasm that she was convinced would knock her out cold.

Liam bent forward, his heat blanketing her back again, and she turned, needing to kiss both of them. King lifted his head in a crunch, his abs tensing even more as he shuttled his cock in and out of her, the hard muscle grinding against her clit, and Liam brought their mouths together. Their kiss was sloppy, more tongues than lips, but it was what she needed.

Grinding against her, their cocks deep inside her, her clit being stimulated to the point of overload and hands touching every part of her sent Adelaide into orbit.

The rushing began, radiating throughout her whole body in waves as she stiffened. Her shout rent the air and Liam and King stopped holding back, slamming into her as they used her to chase their own release. It renewed hers, her inner muscles clamping down and milking their seed from their dicks. She wanted to ditch the condoms, wanted to feel their release sliding down her legs after they'd filled her completely. The thought sent a pulse of lust through her, and Liam grunted, pressing his hips hard against her arse as he throbbed inside her. Adelaide cried out again and King moaned, cursing as his hips stuttered, pulling her hard onto his cock.

Her heart slammed against her chest, her hair matted and stuck to her skin in sweat-soaked pieces. King's chest hair was wet as was Liam's forehead when he rested it against her shoulder as he slumped forward. All three of them were breathing hard. Exhaustion washed over her—

Adelaide could sleep for a week just from their one session—but there was no way she was moving. She didn't want them to pull out, to leave her empty.

"I already want to do that again," Liam murmured breathlessly with a laugh.

Adelaide moaned at the sting as he slipped free and mourned the emptiness, crying out as King pulled out too.

"Shh, baby, we've got you."

TWENTY-FOUR

Liam

"Do you mind going over to the coffee shop across the road?" King asked him. He checked his man over and worry bristled in Liam. King clenched and unclenched his fists, shaking his hands out.

"You're trembling." Addy grasped his hands, squeezing them.

"Yeah. I'll be right if I can have something soon." King smiled, but it was strained. He must have gone too long without eating. Liam calculated it back. They'd skipped dinner, only having a snack on the plane, and King had downed a glass or two of water when they'd finally called it a night a few hours earlier, after hours of mapping one another's bodies.

He threw on some clothes and motioned to Addy. "Will you stay here with King while I run across?"

King shook his head. "Both of you go. Adds knows what I can eat."

Liam had noticed Grounds when they'd pulled in the night before, and he wasn't disappointed. The smell of perfect coffee permeated the air around them, reeling him in with the gravitational force of the sun. They ordered and joined the line of people waiting for their coffees.

The bell tinkled behind them, and Liam turned, doing a double take. "Mate!" He strode over and gave the big blond man a backslapping hug. "Addy, this is Bryce. He plays for Easts. I was a senior in the training camps when Bryce was coming into them. He was my little buddy."

Standing next to each other, the size difference between Bryce and Addy was comical. She looked up, her gaze keeping on going. He'd started off as the runt of the camp, but Liam had seen his brothers. None of them were small and now, years after they'd first met, Bryce was built like a brick shithouse—as tall and wide as a doorway. But his boyish smile was what stood out most. Addy shook his hand as he introduced them.

"Addy's a good friend of mine." The words left a bad taste in his mouth. He wanted to claim her, to advertise to the world that he was with the two most spectacular people he'd ever met. But he couldn't. Not really.

"Great to meet you," Bryce responded. "This is my girlfriend, Ava, and our roommate, Cole." Ava was gorgeous. Tall and slim with almost black hair that curled around her face. Cole was practically Bryce's opposite—dark and brooding where Bryce was sunshine and laughter. They all shook hands and Cole ordered while they caught up.

"How long are you here for?" Bryce asked.

"Just until tomorrow night. Addy's boyfriend and I fly back so I can train on Monday, but Addy has another week here after that."

"If you feel like catching up for dinner tonight, give me a yell. I don't think we have anything planned, do we?" Bryce asked, his gaze bouncing between Ava and Cole, who'd returned to them. It was clear he wanted both their opinions.

"No," Cole said with a small smile toward his friend.

"We're staying in the building across the road," Addy added. "We could order takeout and stay there if you'd prefer that to going out. Save you being plastered all over social media."

"Sounds good," Liam confirmed as he wrapped his free arm around her. She snuggled into his embrace, and Liam basked in it, soaking up her affection. "Will all of you come?"

"Yes," Bryce answered at the same time as Cole shook his head and said, "No." Liam snorted out a laugh at their contradiction, but Bryce's gaze never left Cole's. It was as if they were having a silent conversation, communicating something through their stare. When Bryce nodded and Cole inclined his head, Bryce's smile turned triumphant. "We'll all be there."

"Good. I'll message you to sort out the time."

Their order was called and Liam took the tray of paper cups, Addy gifting him with a sweet smile as she clutched the bag. He wanted to melt into a puddle of goo, his insides tingling with the way she looked at him. Waving their good-byes, they slipped out and jogged back across the street.

"They seem great," Adelaide remarked as they landed on the footpath in front of the apartment building. "King will pitch a fit if he doesn't get to meet Bryce—he's his favourite player."

Liam grinned, floating among the clouds. "Is that right?" He laughed. "Typical that he picks the nicest bloke in the league."

Addy cackled. "That's exactly what I said."

Liam stopped, feigning surprise. "You don't think I'm the nicest?"

"No." She shook her head and looked him down, her gaze incinerating him. He wished they were somewhere a whole lot more private than the lobby of an apartment building, wearing far fewer clothes. "No, you definitely take the trophy for the sexiest man in league."

King was upstairs, sitting on the couch with a glass of water at his feet, his fingers tapping out a staccato rhythm that stumbled when he got a whiff of the coffee. He was pale, paler than he'd been before, and shakier too. He took the unsweetened protein bar Adelaide handed to him and gave her a grateful smile, almost inhaling it.

"Better?" she asked.

"Yeah, I'll be right. I'll need to test soon, but I should be okay if—"

Adelaide held out the banana she'd added to their pastry order, and King's grateful smile floored Liam. He must have been starving.

"I could kiss you right now," King murmured to her, their lips only a hair's breadth apart.

"Eat first, then kiss me."

"Snack first, then kiss both of us. After that we're going out to breakfast," Liam added. They did exactly that, finding a café overlooking the harbour to eat at before walking along Circular Quay past the famous ferry terminal, the Opera House, and through the Botanic Gardens. Green and blue surrounded them, the grassy slopes and glossy plants hiding the fact that they were in the country's biggest city. The waters of the harbour lapped at the base of the path they were walking along, the heat of the summer sun loosening Liam's muscles.

They stopped at Mrs Macquarie's Chair, the famous stone bench cut from a giant boulder that had the best view in the city. Shaded by the giant fig trees, they relaxed on the grassy slope next to it until Liam's stomach rumbled again.

It was easy being with King and Addy. Their friendship made things familiar and comfortable, but the underlying current of attraction zinging between them had Liam buzzing. He wanted them back in bed, ready to touch and taste every part of them. But he held himself back. They had time, and he didn't want to rush things only to trip up when he had the two people of his dreams within his grasp.

After a lazy afternoon napping in one another's arms, watching bad daytime TV movies, and laughing more than he could ever remember, Liam's phone chimed. Bryce, Ava, and Cole were there and they had dinner with them. He scooted out from behind Addy on the couch and met them in the lobby. Inexplicably, nerves churned in his belly. Liam didn't know whether it was introducing King to his old friend or knowing that he needed to hold himself back from touching the two people he'd been all over a few minutes earlier. But as soon as the six of them were in the same space, his shoulders unknotted, and he breathed easy. Bryce had always been a great guy, and his friend and girlfriend seemed like good people too.

Except that Liam wasn't so sure Bryce and Cole were just friends. There was something about them, an easy friendship but also a familiarity that he sensed between them. Ava and Cole were the same, and the adoration in Cole's eyes when he looked at her was unmistakeable.

Unthinkingly, Liam rested his chin on King's shoulder while he snagged a spring roll off his plate. King laughed and swatted his hand away. Grinning, ridiculously happy to have this moment with his partners, Liam shifted closer, about to brush a kiss to his cheek when King stiffened. Wide-eyed, he cleared his throat and Liam's gut clenched, his world tilting. Logically, he knew King wasn't embarrassed by him. But the way he pulled away sliced him open. Liam swallowed. He was nothing if not a professional at hiding the hurt people inflicted on him.

"Liam," King whispered, before gripping his wrist. "Excuse us for a moment," he added, tugging Liam out of the room.

"It's okay," Liam assured him when they were in the privacy of the bedroom they'd shared.

"No, don't do that. You saw how much Adds was hurting because she didn't talk to us. I don't want any more misunderstandings. I moved not because I didn't want you to kiss me, but because I don't know if we can trust the others yet. I'm trying to protect you."

"You were?" Liam asked, the wound he'd been nursing getting stitched up. King gripped his nape and pressed their foreheads together.

"There won't ever be a day I don't want to kiss you." He pressed their lips together, his tongue licking along the seam of Liam's mouth. He opened to King, groaning as King pushed him against the door, aligned their bodies, and owned him in a fierce kiss.

Their return to the lounge heralded all eyes on them. His dopey grin slipped, and Liam stiffened, asking, "What?"

"Is it just the two of you who're together, or all three of you?" Bryce asked.

He swallowed, his gaze bouncing between the four people waiting for him. King's heat at his back lessened, his man stepping back and putting some distance between them. "What makes you ask that?" Liam hedged, his heart pounding in his chest. He thought he could trust Bryce, but the reality of doing so terrified him.

"The love-heart eyes you three have been making at one another all night has been a dead giveaway," Cole said blandly. "But the pash rash on your face makes it a no-brainer." Liam automatically raised his hands to his cheeks, and Bryce laughed, getting up from his spot on the couch.

"Like the ones you two were flashing each other in the coffee shop?" Addy asked, hand on her hip and her eyebrow raised.

"They were?" Liam snapped his gaze to his girl and then back to Cole and Bryce. He'd noticed something that evening, but not before. "You were?"

"Probably, but hiding sucks and I can't lie to save myself, so..." Bryce shrugged like it was no big deal and clapped Liam on the shoulder with a wide grin. The man truly did remind him of a bouncy puppy dog. "You look happy, man. Regardless of who you're with, we're happy for you."

"Hiding what?" Liam asked, before he blinked, Bryce's other words finally sinking in. Bryce laughed, his blue eyes sparkling in the dim light.

"The three of us are together," Bryce responded, slinging an arm around Liam's shoulders and nodding in the direction of his partners. "So, it's all good. If you and King are together, you won't get any judgement from us. We're stuck hiding too. We call Cole our flatmate, but he's not. I love him just as much as Ava."

"It's not just me and King," Liam rushed out, grateful he could share his sexuality with someone who would understand exactly what he was going through. He had Lij and King and although both identified as bi not pan, they understood same-sex relationship dynamics. But the added pressure of being a semi-public figure was something they couldn't understand. Bryce could. "Addy, King, and I are together. We're only new, but we're together."

"Just be careful who you're open with. Ava quit her job because of the rumours around our relationship, and Cole and I always have to be careful. We can't risk it getting out to the press, especially not in my rookie year. Can you imagine the media shitstorm?"

"How long?" Liam asked, sliding into the chair beside him. He'd been carrying around his secret for months, and although everything had finally come out in the open the night before, another person knowing was like a weight lifting off his shoulders. But Bryce, Cole, and Ava seemed to be pretty well practiced at maintaining a façade of friendship between them.

"A year in a few days time." Bryce returned to his spot on the couch and pressed a kiss to Cole's temple. The other man leaned in, wrapping his arm around his boyfriend while he reached for Ava's hand. It was a simple moment, one filled with intimacy, and Liam's heart ached for Cole. He'd first seen him as quiet and stoic, but Liam suspected that being kept a secret from the world weighed on him.

He would likely play the role of tag-along friend to King and Addy for the foreseeable future. Perpetually single to the outside world, he'd only ever be able to acknowledge his lovers in private. Liam looked between them, their eyes filling with concern. But they didn't need to be worried. As shitty as it would be for the world to never know how much they meant to him, he realized that it didn't matter.

Being with them was enough.

Addy reached for him, and he pulled her onto his lap, pressing a lingering kiss to her lips. She smiled against his mouth and he kissed her again, both of them leaning into their man when King slipped his arm around Liam's shoulders.

"But you've made it work. You're happy." Liam looked to Bryce for confirmation and grinned when Cole nodded, lacing his fingers with Bryce's.

"We've made it work. There have been a few rocky parts, but we've never doubted each other," Ava supplied.

* * * * *

Soft fingertips traced down his side and his cock flexed, thickening with the teasing touch. He hummed, and shifted, rolling his hips so those strong hands had room enough to continue their exploration. Addy shifted then, peeling herself away from him. He missed her warmth immediately, the cool air from the vent chilly on his skin.

"You cold?" he mumbled to King as the other man pressed himself against Liam's body. He moaned, needing to feel the man's weight. He hitched his leg up, wrapping it around King's hip, encouraging him to press him into the mattress. King obliged with a groan of satisfaction, and when their hard cocks lined up, sliding together, Liam almost rocketed to heaven. "Oh Jesus," he gasped as King ground down, bucking his hips forward and dragging his thick length against Liam's. "Fuck, do that again."

Spreading his knees, so Liam's legs were pressed open as wide as they'd go, he was entirely at King's mercy. His man took every advantage, licking his hand and closing his fist around both their shafts, using spit and pre-cum to lube his way. Liam arched up off the bed, digging his heels into King's arse as he bucked, chasing the high that he'd had no idea he would crave.

Having a bigger man pin him to the mattress had never been a fantasy of his, but now, he couldn't get the thought of it out of his head. King worked him up until he was on the edge, his body twitching and his cock throbbing and rock-solid. But then he pulled back and Liam cried out, grasping the tangled sheets and thrusting up, needing friction to grind against. King trailed his lips down his body and Liam moaned, anticipation bubbling in his veins. He loved getting his dick sucked. But somehow, he knew this moment would be life-altering. It wasn't because King—a man—was about to swallow him down. No, it had everything to do with the way he worshipped his lovers. He'd seen it on Friday night and again on Saturday when King had brought Addy to orgasm over and over before he let himself go. He'd never had that before, someone so attuned to his needs that he could trust them completely to take care of him.

King's lips closed over his shaft, the heated cavern of his mouth sucking him in, his tongue licking and stroking his cock, and Liam saw stars. Addy's mouth on his balls shot him to heaven. He was so close. But he needed more. He needed Addy.

Liam tapped her leg, closing his hand around her thigh and pulling her closer. Straddling him, she braced herself on either side of his head and leaned down to kiss him. Liam moaned, the dual sensation electrifying his nerve endings. "Sit on my face," he begged and cried out when she shivered, and King moaned, pulling off his cock.

"You like that, don't you, Adds," King taunted, shifting so he had his head buried between her legs. Addy gasped and rocked back, but Liam wasn't missing out this time. He tugged her up and shot King a faux annoyed glare. King grinned wickedly and licked a stripe up his cock.

"Please," he begged, his legs falling open and his hips coming up off the bed in search of King's mouth. His first taste of Addy's essence had him moaning. It set off a chain reaction, with Addy crying out and King rewarding him as he swallowed him to the base of his cock, his throat tightening around his shaft.

Addy braced herself on the headboard and rolled her hips, keeping Liam's mouth exactly where she needed him. With his tongue buried in her pussy, his hands filled with her breasts, and his dick down King's throat, Liam facefucked the man ruthlessly. He was out of control, need riding him hard, pushing him to the peak and beyond. The strength of his orgasm took him by surprise. Spurt after spurt emptied into King's throat, and his man lapped it up, the low moans spurring him on. His hips twitched, instinct to chase his orgasm for as long as possible driving him.

"Oh fuck, that was hot," Addy breathed, her fingers brushing his lips. She was working her own clit as Liam sucked in a much-needed lungful of air. But that wouldn't do. He speared his tongue inside her core and she tightened around him. He scraped his teeth gently over her clit, and she cried out, her channel rhythmically clenching as she came.

Only a moment later, the splash of hot cum—King's cum—landed on his belly. He rubbed it in, savouring the electric buzz still floating around his skin and the gorgeous view of Addy sated and exhausted above him.

King laid kisses up the inside of his leg and blew a cool breath over his hole. Liam clenched hard, shivering with the sensation. Every nerve ending lit up and his cock twitched, thickening at the thought. "Mmm, we'll come back to that," King murmured, flicking his tongue against Liam's sac.

"You're gonna make me hard again," he gasped as King did it again.

"Is there a problem with that?" he asked, his lips smiling against his skin. Addy slipped off him, lying down next to him. Liam locked his gaze with King, those dark eyes gleaming in challenge.

"Do you like to fuck, or get fucked?" Liam asked, the question popping out of his mouth before he could censor himself.

King choked out a groan and palmed himself. "With guys I tend to receive. My dick isn't exactly comfortable for most men to take, so..."

Liam laughed breathlessly. Oh fuck. "That feels like a challenge," he murmured, giving his semi a tug. "I can't wait to be inside you, but to take you? Oh, yeah."

TWENTY-FIVE

Liam

He pressed the garage remote strapped to his sun visor and eased into the drive. The usually empty garage had another car in it.

His parents.

Liam's gut clenched and nausea washed over him. Why now? Why when he was happy did they have to spring a visit on him? It was ten days until Christmas. Surely they were celebrating with his sister. They certainly weren't there for him.

"Who's that?" King asked. Liam shot him a look, one probably wide-eyed with panic, and swallowed. "Hey, what is it?" He threaded their fingers together and squeezed.

Liam shut off the engine and leaned back in his seat, absorbing the rock-steady support King was giving him. He was like a sponge, trying to soak up the strength to answer King's question.

"My parents." Liam's voice was quiet. Strained. He hated them, but at the same time he wanted their approval. He wanted their love. Desperate for it, he continually pushed harder. He'd tried to be a good boy, then a good man, just so that they'd notice him. But nothing he did was ever good enough. He'd tried and failed. Every day of his childhood was a battle, one he'd faced alone and lonely. He hated being back there again. Being so vulnerable. It was easier not to see them. Easier to pretend that they were more than a couple of hours up the road, because when he did, the nerves, the racing heart, and the constant nausea went away. But in their presence, they came back full force.

King stilled, his eyes narrowing slightly. He squeezed Liam's hand harder. "Did they tell you they were coming back?" King's tone was harsh, short with him. Liam's gut sank.

"No." His shoulders slumped. King was disappointed in him too. He'd already screwed things up. "I'm sorry."

"What for?" King asked, confusion written all over his face. He turned in his seat and added a second hand to their grasped ones. "You have nothing to apologize for. Them, on the other hand..."

"It's their house—"

"They treated you like shit your whole childhood. They still do. Why are they arriving unannounced?" It was a rhetorical question, one Liam didn't have the energy to answer. Instead, he held tight to King, getting his fix of confidence and love.

"Let's go see how long they're here for." He dragged himself out of the car, just wanting the whole episode over. Maybe he could crawl into bed and they wouldn't even notice he'd arrived. He was invisible to them most of the time anyway, so why not now? But King's hand at the small of his back reminded Liam that someone saw him. Two people, in fact. More if he counted the family next door who'd treated him like their own. King's parents too.

He slowed his step and basked in that. He pulled his shoulders back, letting the strength that the people who truly loved him infuse into his bones. "Mum, Dad," he called, his voice firm and vibrant.

"The kitchen." His dad's clipped voice carried over the short distance. There wasn't a hello. There certainly weren't warm embraces like Carol did or Alfred and Betty had. No, his father didn't even give him a full sentence. Liam's gut cramped. As much as he wanted to be strong, it was the little things—more so than the big things—that cut Liam deepest. He sucked in a breath, straightening his spine again, and took another step.

King rested his hand on Liam's shoulder, his touch like a silent sentinel. A brick wall of strength behind him. Liam leaned back, and King squeezed his shoulder gently. He'd never been more grateful for that touch.

"When did you get back?" he asked, his voice a higher pitch than normal. Liam cleared his throat, refusing the temptation of slinking back and hiding behind King.

Movement at the back door caught his attention. Lij. He hadn't heard the gate close or his friend trudging over the rocks. He flicked his gaze between his lover and his best friend, and their worried gazes slayed him. Liam crossed his arms over his chest, refusing to let his parents see the shake in them. All he had to do was figure out how long they were there for. He could make nice—he could even make himself scarce if he had to—and then they'd be gone and things would go back to normal.

"Saturday morning." His mum leaned against the kitchen bench and raised an eyebrow at him. "I've been cleaning since we arrived. You left the place in a horrible mess." That was bullshit. He had a cleaner come in weekly to make sure that the basics got done. He looked after his laundry and the dishes. The only thing that was a mess was the kitchen table, and that was because he was elbow deep in studying.

He flicked his eyes to the table and his gut clenched. It was completely cleaned off. Where were his things? King stiffened beside him, following his line of sight, and Liam shot him a small smile. He didn't know whether he was trying to reassure King or himself that everything was okay, but neither worked.

"Where are my things that you cleaned off the table?" he asked through clenched teeth.

This time his dad didn't even answer. He simply waved over his shoulder to the corner where there was a black rubbish bag by the door. They'd cleaned up all right. Liam pinched the bridge of his nose and sighed. At least they hadn't emptied it outside yet.

Lij took the opportunity to stride in and announce himself. "Mr and Mrs Masters, welcome home." He clapped his hands together, his voice overly bright. Lij was good at putting on an act, treating them as if they were his long-lost best friends. But Lij hated the sight of them.

When they were kids, the man he considered his brother from another mother had come up with an elaborate plot to rob a bank and pin it on his parents so they went to jail. Then they would use the money to pay for Liam's adoption into Lij's family, and a kick-arse rugby coach so Liam could turn pro. They were going to top off their criminal masterpiece with a bestselling novel and movie rights.

Lij didn't wait for a reply from his parents; they rarely acknowledged him either. Lij simply mouthed, "You okay?" to Liam, his gaze bouncing between him and King. Liam gave him a barely perceptible nod and moved to collect the rubbish bag again, but Lij was closer. He picked it up on his way past, crossing through the room and handing it to Liam.

"Hey, King." They gave each other a back slapping hug as Liam went down on one knee checking what was in the bag. Sure enough, his papers, textbook, and even his laptop were bagged up, tossed in there without any care.

"Good to see you, Eli," King greeted, hovering over Liam, touching his shoulder.

He sucked in a breath and retied the bag, placing it gently with his duffle by the garage door. King's piercing gaze followed him to the garage, and from the corner of his vision, he could see Lij shifting. He was watching them both, trying to figure out where their easy familiarity came from. A lot had happened in the weeks since Lij had seen them together. Since then, King had spent a lot of time touching him, and Liam spent even more leaning into that touch.

But as he returned to the main room, King moved closer to his father. He was brave and demanded respect. But this time, the respect wasn't for himself—at least not entirely. His father's habit of just ignoring the people he didn't deem worthy of his time wouldn't hold water with King. It didn't surprise him that he'd moved to stand directly in front of his father, close enough that he couldn't ignore King anymore.

"Mr Masters, I'm Kingston Vella." He held his hand out, and with his lips curled in disdain, his father shook it. When he quickly withdrew his hand, unconsciously rubbing his knuckles, Liam bit back a smirk. Score one to his man. King's grip strength was nothing to laugh about. He could be infinitely gentle, his whisper-soft caress one that could leave a person begging for more, but it didn't take a genius to work out that King had just squeezed the crap out of his father's hand.

"Kingston."

The awkward silence stretched on for a beat until Liam cleared his throat. "How long are you here for?"

"We're back permanently. Your sister and Michael will be here before Christmas. They closed on their new house last week and they're staying with us until it's renovated. It took longer than expected to find something they were both happy with close by, so it doesn't look like they'll be in when the baby's born. But that's good because we can help them out. It'll be so lovely to have them here."

"Oh. So you're all moving back?" Liam murmured.

"Yes, we'll need your room for the baby." His mum peered at him over her glasses, her face passively waiting for a reaction from him. But shock rendered him mute. Had he heard her correct? "In case you didn't understand, you'll need to find your own place. We've helped you out for long enough, and it's time you stop taking advantage. Nessa and Michael need our help now."

Liam opened his mouth to respond, but no words came. They'd helped him for long enough? Taking advantage? Of what? He paid them twice what the rent for an equivalent property was. He gave them money whenever they asked for it, and not small amounts either—close to a hundred thousand dollars over the last year. Was she serious?

His gaze bounced between his parents, but his father was scrolling on his tablet. Liam blinked. Turned his attention back to his mother.

"What?" King snapped at the same time as he questioned, "You said they settled on the house last week. How long have you known this was happening?"

His mum waved off his question as if he was being ridiculous. "Oh, Nessa always planned on having the baby here on the Coast. They've been looking for a house since she fell pregnant. Michael received the offer to transfer his job back to Brisbane at the same time, so we've all been looking forward to it. It's wonderful, yes?"

He ignored her question as his gut bottomed out. He was always the last person considered, but the first they went to when they wanted something. He was a pushover. *Liam's a pro-footballer. He has so much money; it's not like he'll miss it. And he's sponging off us anyway. He should help.* He could just imagine the conversation they'd have behind his back. They were delusional, the lot of them. He'd hoped, when his parents had excitedly bragged about his sister introducing them to Michael, that the man might round off some of their sharp edges. But he was worse than them. Self-absorbed and up himself. He fit right in.

"So, you've known for months? And you wait to tell me I need to move out the day you get here—"

"It's not our problem that you weren't here."

"What bloody difference will a day make?" he seethed. His voice wobbled, anger, frustration and betrayal bubbling under the surface. Why? What was so inherently unlovable about him that he was so easy to disregard? To toss aside? "I've got nowhere to go. It's less than two weeks until Christmas. I have pre-season training and assessments due soon. I can't just up and leave with no notice." His heart beat faster, his breathing rushing through his lungs. Panic clawed up his throat, overwhelming his ability to think straight. What the hell was he going to do?

Wide-eyed, he looked to Lij. The man's face was red and every muscle in his body taut. If looks could kill, the murderous glare he was shooting at Liam's mother would incinerate her on the spot. King shifted in front of him, his hands landing on his shoulders, thumbs at his neck. Standing close enough that he blocked his view of the two people who just didn't give a damn about him, Liam looked up into eyes the colour of dark chocolate and his breath hitched. He blinked back the tears that threatened to fall. Why were they intent on hurting him? He didn't want to let his parents see they effect they had on him, but his shaking was impossible to miss.

"Move in with me," King murmured barely loud enough for Liam to hear. Liam's eyes widened, a mix of excitement and fear of jumping in too quickly assailing him. King's smile was small, but reassuring, his eyes warm and affectionate. "You don't have to stay in my room—I have a spare—and my table is big enough for you to study on."

"Oh, and Liam, we'll need your rent payment for the week. Fix that up before you leave."

"Oh, hell no," King roared as Lij's patience snapped and he growled like a wild animal. "You do not get to hurt him like that then demand money from him. Not a chance. How dare you?"

His father's face went red and his mother's lips pressed together, her eyes narrowing into a glare. His father's voice boomed around the open plan room. "Who do you think you are speaking to us like that in our own home?"

King stepped up, his broad shoulders intimidating even from behind. His back was as straight as a rod, his fists clenched. King was perpetually unflappable, his waters running so deep that Liam had never even seen a ripple on the surface. But this was an entirely different King. He was spoiling for a fight, and Liam didn't have the energy to stop him. He was completely deflated.

Liam's heart shattered in his chest. He was going to lose his safe space. The home he'd called his own for nearly half his life. There weren't many happy memories there from when his parents were around, but even though he hadn't changed the décor, he'd made his own happiness there. He'd fallen in love with Addy and King right out front and sitting at the table in front of him. He'd kissed King for the first time there. He'd laughed with Addy and she'd given him hope when he'd needed it most. He was going to lose the very place where those memories had been made. He closed his eyes and let the tears roll down his cheeks.

King murmured, "No. No, no, no," and wrapped his arms around Liam. He held onto King like a life preserver, letting him prop Liam up. He borrowed his strength, needing it all just to stay upright. "I've got you. Come on, let's go home."

Liam nodded but he couldn't let go of King. Everything would crumble at his feet if he did. He clutched at his shirt, holding him close as he buried his face in King's chest. "I need you," he whispered, and King held him tighter.

Lij was standing close, whispering as he said, "How about you take Liam to your place. I'll get his things packed up and drive his car over." He felt King nod, but his guy didn't let him go. He held him tight until Liam could breathe again. When he pulled back, Liam wiped his eyes with the back of his hand and rested his hands on King's arms.

"You okay?" He nodded and King smiled, his expression filled with sorrow. He wrapped his arm around Liam's shoulder, and the three of them walked toward the garage.

He stopped at the foot of the stairs. "Lij, thank you."

"Anytime, bud." His friend walked up the stairs, stopping halfway up. "King?" His boyfriend paused and they looked over to Lij. "We need to talk."

"When Adds gets back, we will."

Lij nodded and turned again, heading the rest of the way up to his bedroom.

Liam really only had clothes and toiletries that needed to be moved. He kept his training gear in his SUV, and anything he didn't immediately need was in a separate storage shed so he didn't clutter the place up. Huh. Maybe Liam had been subconsciously planning for this day for a while. Either way, something shifted inside him. A weight lifted. For the first time, the steel cables of his parents' disapproval that had tied him down were falling away. They were loosening their grip.

Liam was free.

"Mum, Dad," he called. He didn't bother turning back to them. He didn't need to see their reactions. He was doing this for him. He'd gotten this far. Now it was time to completely sever the bond that had kept him going back for more punishment just so he could feel something with them. It was finally time to break free of their toxic clutches. "Consider this relationship over. It's not the Bank of Liam anymore. Don't ask me for anything again. It's not gonna happen. I refuse to be treated like shit again."

"Liam," his mum snapped. "You don't talk to us like that, or—"

"Or nothing. Lose my number." He took his key off the chain and dropped it on the table just inside the garage, picked up the garbage bag of his uni materials, and let King grab his duffel.

He walked out, letting the door catch on the wind and slam closed. His mother would hate it. He smiled.

Carol was there waiting for him. She held her arms out and he stepped into them, holding the mother he wished he'd been born to close. "You okay, love?"

"Yeah." He nodded. "I am now. Lij is inside packing for me. They told me to move out, but…" He sucked in a wobbly breath, hating that he'd let them see how much capacity to hurt him they had. "I couldn't hang around and pack. I needed to get out of there."

"I'll see if he needs any luggage. You want to put your things in Addy's room for the moment?"

"He's moving in with me," King replied with an affectionate smile. Liam nodded and after saying their goodbyes, King led him to the car.

"Could we maybe go see your parents on the way home?" he asked, his eyes filling with tears again.

"They'd love that." King slid his hand over the centre console and threaded their fingers together, holding on tight.

TWENTY-SIX

Adelaide

Adelaide unzipped her suitcase and dumped the last few days of worn clothes into the laundry hamper. She hated unpacking, but it was better than tripping over her own feet. King and Liam were downstairs with Eli, her mum, and Pop, waiting patiently for her to come down. She was scared. The tremble in her hands was more pronounced the longer she thought about what she had to say. It wasn't that she was worried her family would disapprove. Or maybe it was. She was going to tell them that she was dating two men. Pop liked to remind her that they weren't living in the 1920s, but even that might be too much for him. What would her brother think? She was dating his oldest and best friend. Her mother? She was the most open-minded of them all, but would this cross a line?

"Hey," Liam said from the gap in the screens that formed the wall to her bedroom. "You okay?"

She shook her head and bit her lip. Kneading her hands together, she responded, "Not really, no. I'm freaking out."

"C'mere." He held his arms out and she stepped into his hug. It was times like this that Adelaide was grateful they'd known each other for so long. He knew exactly what she needed. King would too—they were the same like that. "We're in it together. No matter what happens, we'll get through it."

"I don't want to fight with anyone," she mumbled against his chest.

Liam ran his fingers through her hair, tugging it gently until she tipped her head up. He pressed a lingering kiss to her lips. "It won't come to that. They'll probably be shocked—mostly at me—but they won't fight us." Adelaide hoped he was right. More than anything. Her family were everything to her. They'd been together through thick and thin, and Adelaide couldn't imagine fighting with them. "C'mon, let's go downstairs."

They walked hand in hand down the stairs, but she pulled away before they got to the kitchen where everyone was gathered around the table. Laughter floated in through the open windows—Liam's parents, sister, and her husband playing bocce and croquet in the front yard. Adelaide ground her teeth together, ready to go over there and give them a piece of her mind. She hated them. Despised them. They were shitty people who'd hurt a good man. Her man. Liam paused, his shoulders slumping when he heard the tinkling sound. She gripped his hand again, sliding her palm into his, and shot him a smile. "Fuck them. We've got each other."

Liam's responding grin was wide, happiness radiating from him. It was as if he was saying a giant fuck you to his parents. "We do, don't we."

She led him through the doorway and the voices stopped, silence immediately blanketing the room. "So, um, yeah." Adelaide huffed out a nervous laugh and looked to King for help. What did she say? She'd had a whole week to prepare how to tell them, and she still had nothing.

"What's going on?" Eli asked, his eyes narrowing on their joined hands. King stood, moving around the table to join them. He wrapped his arm around Adelaide's shoulder and his other around Liam's waist presenting a united front.

"Adds, Liam, and I are dating. We wanted you to know." Simple, direct, and leaving no room for dispute. King had nailed it. She threaded her fingers through his and smiled up at Liam. They'd done it.

The scrape of a chair.

Wordlessly Eli walked out.

Slammed his door.

The lump in Adelaide's throat was hard to swallow around. Her guys squeezed her hands, grounding her. Wide-eyed, she turned to her mum. Disappointment radiated from her in the shake of her head and her turned-down lips. Adelaide's breath caught and tears stung her eyes. No, they weren't fighting, but they weren't happy either. "Mum?" Adelaide whispered, her voice breaking.

"Adelaide, honey, did you not know, or didn't you care?"

"What?" she asked, horrified, reeling back like her mum had slapped her. "What are you talking about?"

"Liam was your brother's first love. It's taken him years to get over him."

"I... I had no idea." Anguish stole her breath, her knees buckling. King steadied her, taking her weight until she found her footing again. Her heart broke as she thought about Eli having to watch them together. She knew exactly what he was going through, except there was one difference. Adelaide had never gotten over Liam. "Go check on him. Please," she begged. Her mum nodded, giving her a tight smile, and followed Eli out.

Pop sat there, leaning back against the chair. His arms crossed, legs spread in a deceptively relaxed pose, he assessed them.

"Say something," Adelaide begged.

"Hmm." He lifted his chin and Adelaide turned into her guys, unable to stop the flow of tears. Her heart was being ripped in two. She'd broken her brother's heart, and her mum had actually thought her capable of not caring about her brother's feelings. "What do you want me to say, love?"

Adelaide shook her head. She didn't know what she needed to hear from him.

"The truth is that you don't need me to say anything. You want me to tell you I'm happy for you. That we can't wait to spend the holidays together and we're thrilled you've found love."

"But?" King asked as he ran his hand up and down her back.

"Eli loved Liam, but he never acted on it because he was too afraid to lose his friendship. What will it do to their relationship if you don't stay together? You're asking him to choose between his best friend and his sister."

Adelaide shook her head, her jaw clenching. Every muscle in her body was tense, trying desperately to stop her heart from shattering. "No, that's not fair," she whispered. "How about you ask how long I've loved Liam for? You're assuming this is new, and yes us being together is new, but I've loved him for as long as I've known him. And unlike Eli, I never fell out of love with him."

"And what if Eli was still in love with him? Would you walk away?"

"Pop," Liam and King warned simultaneously. King continued, "Adds hasn't done this out of spite. She was prepared to sacrifice her happiness for both Liam's and mine. That says more about her personality than you're giving her credit for."

Liam spoke, his words quiet, but their force packed a punch. "Lij is my brother. He's my person. He's the sibling I always dreamed of having. I'll never give him up. But in answer to your question, no, Addy wouldn't walk away, because I wouldn't let her. Neither would King. But the ball is in Lij's court here. The only way he'll lose my friendship is if he pushes me away. I don't want to hurt him, I never have, but I won't let him try to break us up either."

Adelaide lifted her chin and looked to her men, both of them meeting her gaze with steely determination in theirs. "The brother I know would never ask me to choose, because he'd know that I respected him far too much to risk their friendship unless I was serious. He'd trust me. He'd trust his best friend. He'd know that I'd never ask him to choose between us. I love him too much to do that."

She looked Pop in the eye. She needed him to understand. With every fibre in her being, she implored him to do just that. "You and everyone else needs to know that I'm not giving Liam up. Neither is King. Not for Eli. Not for anyone. This is real. We aren't playing games. I'm sorry I hurt him, but I didn't know." She sucked in a breath and held tightly to her men. Uttering her next sentence could change her family dynamic forever, even more so than her news only moments earlier. "I also wasn't asking for permission, so Eli is going to need to get used to our being together."

"Is that right?" Pop asked with a small but satisfied smile tilting his lips up. He stood and shuffled over to them. Cupping her face with withered hands, he kissed her forehead. "Good girl. You've got so much of your nan's fire in you. It makes me so proud. You love these boys and make sure they treat you and each other right." He peered up at King then Liam, his gaze never flinching. "Most importantly, be happy together."

"Thank you." She hugged him, the strength he wrapped her in disguised by a frail-looking body. "What about Eli?"

"He'll come around."

"And Mum?"

Pop shook his head. "I think once she stops to think about it, she'll be more disappointed in herself for believing, even for a split-second, that you'd hurt your brother.

She just wants you happy, all of you." His gaze wandered to the men by her side. "So seeing one of you happy when the other one thinks it's at his expense upsets her."

* * * * *

Two months later and things had somewhat settled down at home. Eli was just as angry and hurt that Liam hadn't confided in him as he was with her for dating his best friend and his first crush. That's all it had been for Eli too— a teenager's first love. But the shock of Liam's coming out had thrown him right back to where he was as a sixteen-year-old, his heart breaking over the boy he'd dreamed of and never had a chance with. Seeing his sister's hand in Liam's had gutted him all over again.

Adelaide understood why he was upset. She hated that she'd brought it all back up for him, but refused to let him hold it against her. They'd talked it out, looking back through school year books and laughing at themselves. Eli admitted to her how he'd idolised Liam, and with the free-dom that came from no longer being bullied, he'd explored his sexuality. At first he'd mistaken the combination of rag-ing hormones and Liam being front and centre as love, but realized after a while that it was an unshakeable friendship that drew them together.

Eli and Liam had spent a lot of time together too, talking and just hanging out. Reminding each other of the im-portance of their friendship. Living next door to each other had lulled them into a false sense of security. They'd become lazy in caring for their relationship. But Liam was taking the speed bump as an opportunity to rebuild it from the ground up stronger than ever.

They were still working through the fact that Liam hadn't gone to Eli with his questions about King. He was finally realizing that it wasn't because Liam didn't want his opinion. He hadn't been able to seek his advice. Liam didn't want Eli to think he wasn't important, and he was proving it. Slowly, they were reconnecting and mending their bond.

Adelaide was still upset with her mum. While she'd tried to put aside her hurt, it was hard. Her mother's reaction had shattered the faith she had in her, and the repairs to the cracks in the foundation of her relationship with her mum were going to take longer to fix.

King's parents had shocked the hell out of her. Betty had covered her mouth and burst into tears, scolding King for hurting Adelaide until she realized that she was holding Liam's hand. Hurt had turned to surprise, and when it dawned on her that the three of them were happy together, Betty had thrown her hands up in the air, praised Madonna—the religious kind, not the singer—and rushed into the kitchen to cook. Alfred had simply given his son a tight shoulder squeeze, had kissed her on the cheek, and had engulfed Liam in the longest, tightest hug she'd ever seen a parent give to their child. And that's what Liam was to Alfred, another son. They had a mutual adoration society happening, and it warmed Adelaide's heart seeing the beauty of the connection Liam had formed with the older man.

Everything seemed to be on easy street for the moment, those twists and turns, and highs and lows exciting. Adelaide knew that taking the road less travelled was worth it. Her relationships with her guys were blossoming. It was so much better than she'd even dreamed.

She was glad she'd waited to choose her career too. Content for her Patreon was flowing out of her like crazy, and the videos were blowing up, more and more people signing up every day. King's big reveal had them signing up in droves, and now that they had another partner too—albeit one who spoke off camera like King had done in the beginning—it was a hit.

Adelaide was loving her prac too. The Exchange was a member's only swingers club. When she'd heard about it, she'd imagined a seedy bar in an industrial estate with drugs, sex, and danger. It was the complete opposite of what she'd feared. The four-storey mansion built in the centre of Surfers Paradise was a wonderland of lust. A palace of pleasure. There was a hell of a lot of sex in the club—after all, that's what it was there for—but it was so much more than that too. It was a safe space for people to learn about themselves. A judgement free zone. Real relationships developed there, all the way from friendships to love, and they dissolved there too.

She loved observing and talking to the patrons. She'd helped one woman live out her fantasy. Five men, one for each hole and hand, took her in front of a crowd of people in the colosseum. The amphitheatre on the second floor was a haven for both exhibitionists and voyeurs. The woman's husband was one of those voyeurs, observing from his spot just off stage, living out his own fantasy. Adelaide's role had been to coach the men on what her clients wanted. It was their twentieth wedding anniversary present to each other—granting the other's fantasy. Adelaide had revelled in being able to help them.

She'd found her tribe. The people were fascinating, and she was learning so much. Adelaide was chomping at the bit to work there full-time after her second prac term; it was exactly what she wanted.

Her life had been hectic to say the least.

But she was taking a moment to unwind. It was her afternoon off and she was scheduled on again at midnight. She wanted to be at home with her guys—they craved every stolen moment together that they could grab—but all three of them had something on. She'd been invited to Robyn, Mike, and Ezio's housewarming. Liam had wanted it to be the day she introduced everyone to King, while he sat his final exam. But a night's sleep so broken that King had crawled into his bed and held him, and an email from Liam's parents with scans of the baby and "look it's a boy!" written in his father's perfect cursive, had turned her man into a freaked-out mess.

Adelaide was convinced his parents had timed the baby's gender reveal to coincide with his exams, but they were too negligent to have done that. It would have meant taking notice of what Liam was actually doing, and that was far beyond any level of care they showed him.

Liam's exam was on campus. She'd suggested that the three of them go, then head to the party afterward. Liam had acquiesced, wanting to please her, but Adelaide could see it was too much for him. She'd pulled the plug, suggesting just he and King go instead. Statistics was their thing, the mountain that they'd scaled together, and she wanted to give Liam the time together to fall into the headspace he was in when it was just him and King working together.

King was torn. He'd wanted to be with Adelaide so bad, but knew Liam needed him. It had been an easy decision for her—Liam's exam was more important. It was his last shot to get a pass, and King had a way with him that calmed Liam instantly and concentrated his focus. Knowing King was only a few metres outside the room cheering him on would make all the world of difference to Liam.

Adelaide smiled, one of those dreamy love-drunk smiles, as she thought about her guys and took a sip of her cider. The conversation around her buzzed, and Adelaide startled as Katy's cousin, Nick, asked her, "How do you guys know one another?" pointing between herself and the happy trio curled up together.

"Connor and I have been friends for years, and I met Katy and Levi through him." Connor snorted out a laugh, and Katy elbowed him while Levi blushed to the roots of his hair.

"Oh, now there's a story," Eddie teased in his beautiful British accent. Will, his partner, laughed and slipped a hand up Eddie's gauzy blouse. The man shivered, adjusting his spot on Will's lap as the other man pulled him closer.

"I helped Levi see what he was missing, that's all," Adelaide explained like it was no big deal. Truth be told, that conversation had been a pivot point for all their lives. "He just needed a nudge."

"In the form of a butt plug," Connor teased.

"You love it." Levi's voice was husky, and when he bit Connor playfully on his shoulder, the other man's breath audibly hitched.

She loved that Liam and King had that kind of relationship too. They were affectionate and loving, but playful and so so hot when they got riled up. Hiding was hard on both of them, and so was downplaying their relationship. At least her guys had Bryce and Cole. They'd been there for both Liam and King whenever they'd needed to vent. It was them who'd suggested that Liam have his own room in King's house, rather than sleeping in the same room. They'd suggested they do that when Adelaide officially moved in. She was ready and had stayed most nights with them since returning from Sydney, but officially moving out when she was still on rocky footing with her mum seemed like a recipe for disaster. An excuse to run away rather than work through her issues.

Adelaide thumbed her phone and sent King another message. Liam's exam was halfway done, and she was desperate for an update.

No sign of him yet. Some students have left, but he's still going. It's a good sign, baby. He's doing it.

It is. I'm so proud of him.

When she looked up again, there was a tense silence that seemed to be centred around Jake and Cassie. Cassie shook her head and cupped Jake's face, leaning her forehead against his cheek. Whatever she said was for his ears alone. Jake nodded and hugged her close, and after a moment, he smiled. "Might just have to get back into it though, if you guys are anything to go by." Adelaide had no idea what he was talking about, but it was probably a good thing. "Anyone know a good swingers' club?"

His comment surprised her, and Adelaide cleared her throat to stop from choking on the cider she'd just sipped. "Actually, I do." She reached into her purse by her feet and slipped Cassie a dark business card. The other woman looked at it with raised eyebrows and nodded before passing it to Jacob. He read it, slipped it into his shirt pocket, and gave her a small smile in thanks. It was a weird exchange, but Adelaide had learned not to judge a book by its cover. Her fantasy anniversary couple both walked in wearing buttoned-up suits looking straight-laced and uptight in every way. They were anything but.

She excused herself much earlier than the others, but she needed to get to King's house. Liam had finished his exam and wasn't up to going out afterward. They hadn't spoken much, Liam mumbling out that he was okay, but worry had spiked in her and Adelaide rushed out, needing to be there for him too. King was on the phone, pacing, when she walked up the stairs and spied him through the open front door. Liam was lying on the couch shirtless, his eyes closed, biting down on his lip with a beer in hand as he stretched out. He squirmed, but it looked like he was getting more comfortable, not freaking out about the exam. Relief swamped her. It was a good sign.

Adelaide pulled open the screen door and slipped through, dropping her purse on the sideboard as she made her way over to Liam. When she straddled him on the couch, he hummed and pulled her close, burying his face in the crook of her neck as he hugged her tight.

"How did you go?" she asked gently, a whisper against his temple.

His eyes were bright when he finally let her go enough that she could pull back to look at him. He puckered his lips and grinning, she obliged, taking his mouth in a long sultry kiss. Adelaide was never one to deny her men, or herself. Their tongues tangled and Liam slipped his hand up her skirt, cupping her arse as he moaned and thrust his hard cock against her. Sparks lit up behind her closed eyelids and Adelaide's breath caught.

"I did good, Addy," he whispered. "I know I passed. The questions were easy. I had to get a second booklet to write my answers on because I had so much to say."

"I'm so fucking proud of you, Liam." She kissed him harder, slipping her hand into his shorts and cupping his thick cock. Pre-cum wet her path, Liam arching into her touch as he slid his fingers up and down the lace covering her pussy.

They were writhing together, kissing frantically, but Adelaide couldn't get a decent grip with her dress bunched up between them and Liam's shorts in the way. She grumbled on a laugh, "Damn clothes," and King was behind her, easing Liam's basketball shorts down. The zipper on her dress followed, and Adelaide let go of her man while King slipped the dress off her, bra following a moment later.

Once she was down to only a pair of lacy panties, Liam looked her over and growled, but King's heat disappeared from her back. Adelaide cried out, and searched for him, twisting until she could see him. The smirk he wore was deviant. He brought his finger to his lips, quietening her as he held his phone in the other. His cock bulged in his jeans, his erection a rigid pole against his hip.

Whatever the call was about was important—but he covered the mouthpiece and whispered, "Put on a show for me."

Liam pulsed in her hand. "You like knowing that he's watching us, don't you?" she murmured against his throat.

He nodded and moaned louder when she closed her hand around his cock once more.

"I need inside you, Addy," he gasped. "King's torturing me." She ran her fingers lower, knowing just what King liked to do to him. It had started with the same finger-sized vibe she'd given King, a hint of what anal could be like for Liam if he wanted to try it. He'd been addicted since, desperate to take King's cock. They hadn't gone there yet, but he was nearly ready. He was taking a plug that wasn't far off King's girth. But King wouldn't rush things, no matter how much Liam begged. It made for fun nights teasing him as she and King edged him. More often than not, she was the beneficiary of his frustration. He ate her out like a man possessed when he was mindless with lust, and would usually fuck her and King senseless too. His refractory period was virtually non-existent when the thick plug was inside him, rubbing on his prostate, so they all took full advantage. They'd ditched the condoms soon after she'd returned from Sydney—their Christmas presents to one another were negative test results—and tonight was going to be another one of those nights where they let loose.

Her fingers circled around the base of the largest plug he'd worn yet. No wonder he was on edge. It was the width of a mini can of soda at its base stretching his hole tight. Her clit pulsed as she thought about how stuffed he would be feeling. Adelaide needed to see it. She clambered off and kneeled on the couch between his legs, lifting them so she could see his smoothed-out pucker. The sight took her breath away. Pink and slick with lube, Liam's rim was stretched tight around the plug. She leaned down, licking around it and nibbling his sac. Liam stiffened and crammed his fist into his mouth to stifle his shout. Pre-cum dripped from his slit, and Adelaide lapped it up, sucking down his cock.

He was hard as nails, his skin stretched tight over his thick rod. Desire pulsed through her at the sight of him wanton and needy. She wanted Liam as much as he needed her. Taking his cock in hand, she straddled his thighs, but she'd forgotten her panties.

"Shit," she grumbled, moving to slide off him. Liam growled, holding her hips in place before he grasped the thin lace and ripped it, yanking it free from her hips.

Adelaide's core clenched at the sight of his thick fingers piercing the thin material, it falling to pieces under his touch.

She sank onto him slowly, Liam filling her like the plug was filling him. She stretched around him, clasping onto his shaft as he bucked. It was like a whirlwind was set free. He moved at a frantic pace, hammering her G-spot with every thrust. He pinched her clit, lightning strikes of sensation morphing into a constant buzz that rocketed her to the edge of an orgasm far too quickly. He lashed her nipples with his tongue, sucking and biting on them. The warmth of his tongue and bite of pain from his teeth surged through her like a tsunami.

She bounced on him harder, her pussy clenching around him. He shifted, his fat cock deep inside her slid against her G-spot, lighting her up. The motion sent Adelaide past the point of no return. The quickening started, a rushing at her core as her nerve endings sizzled. She gasped as Liam shuddered, her pussy clutching him as the rhythmic clenching began. Euphoria washed over her as Liam pressed his finger to her arse, breaching her pucker as she trembled in his arms. He choked out a cry and thrust deeper, his body going rigid as he shot inside her. The heated splashes of cum hitting her already sensitive walls renewed her orgasm, and she clenched again, riding another wave of bliss.

Liam shouted, his hips lifting off the couch as King trailed his lips down her spine. There was a thud to the side and Liam pulled up his knees. The movement sent a shiver through her, his pulsating cock still lodged deep inside her, hitting her G-spot like a gold medal shooter at target prac-tice. The first splash of King's cum painted her arse, her hole clenching at the sensation. She wanted him inside her, to fill her up just like Liam was. She loved it. Was a complete slut for their cocks.

She didn't feel the second pump of cum, but from Liam's needy moan, he sure had. "Your hole is all open for me, Lee. It's begging me to come inside. You want me to fuck you so bad, don't you? To fill you up just like I'm doing, don't you?"

Liam cried out, his still hard cock throbbing as he pumped more cum inside her and King filled him.

"Want the whole fucking world to see you fuck me, King," Liam gasped, moaning as King leaned over her. She turned, needing his kiss. Their tongues tangled and King's wet fingers circled her nipples. He pinched them and Ade-laide's pussy tightened.

Liam bucked again, shuddering.

"Fuck," he moaned breathlessly, his softening cock go-ing steely again. "King," he gasped. "Again." King slipped his fingers between them, rubbing her clit as he pressed up against her back. Liam thrust messily, his rhythm off, but it was enough. Adelaide's body started climbing again, the dual sensation of Liam's desperate movements and King's measured touches sending Adelaide spiralling.

Her breasts bounced as she rode Liam, zings of sensa-tion shooting to her clit as King fingered her. Liam's cum dripped out of her pussy, King's other hand gathering the liquid and spreading it down. He was using their cum as lube, King stuffing Liam's arse with his fingers. She wanted to watch so badly. To see them together. She loved it. That first time when King had given Liam a blow job, she could have come just from watching them. Every time it only got better. She pictured King's fingers buried deep in Liam's arse, and her pussy clamped down, throbbing as she launched into orbit. Adelaide cried out, her vision whiting out as her orgasm hit, and Liam shouted, going rigid under her as his cock pulsed inside her again.

Breathless, she fell forward, but King was there to ease her back, lifting her off Liam until she had her head on the opposite armrest of the sofa. Liam's cock slipped free, but King's mouth replaced it, his tongue laving her. Licking her clean. She was well used, and had come harder than a freight train, but every swipe of his tongue sent licks of desire through her again. He did the same to Liam, licking up their combined essences from his cock.

"You're gonna kill me," Liam groaned, his body twitching.

"Best way to go," Adelaide responded, her voice hoarse from the shouts that had rent the air.

"Mmm," King finished, kissing a line from the base of Liam's cock to his navel. "I'm gonna make that wish come true, Lee. The whole world's gonna know when I finally get inside you properly."

Liam gripped King's shirt, holding him close. Their kiss was all tongues and heated moans. When Liam finally broke away, his chest was heaving. "No more of this 'just the tip' bullshit. I want you to split me in two."

"Soon," King murmured. "The night you get your results. You pass that subject and I'll give you my cock."

"And if I don't?"

"You'll get it anyway." King grasped Liam's soft cock, gave it a squeeze, and looked to Adelaide. She bit down on her lip, knowing King wanted to do something special for him. They'd talked about it at length—King wanted to celebrate the hard work he'd put in, but how? Liam had more money than King and Adelaide combined, and apart from his car, he wasn't one for material things. The things Liam wanted were personal. Intrinsic to human nature. He wanted to belong. To be loved. To be shown he was important. For someone to be proud of him. He wanted to be part of a family. To be cherished.

Finding the right gift to show him all that was harder than she'd ever imagined.

TWENTY-SEVEN

Kingston

The email was a good distraction from the never-ending pacing he'd done while Liam was in his exam. He'd worn a track in the concrete outside the lecture theatre. Waiting on tenterhooks, he snapped his gaze around whenever he heard the theatre doors whoosh closed. None of them had been Liam.

Louise, his new boss, had to sort some things out in preparation for the new school year, which meant King was going to finally see his new stomping ground. He was excited to get started, and with the summer holidays soon winding to a close, it wouldn't be long before he was back in the grind of things, except this time with a small group of staff to supervise and an opportunity to contribute to a new community.

Liam was one of the last to walk out, excited grin firmly in place. King hadn't had a doubt about his ability, but nerves could make even the best person choke. Liam had nailed it, and Louise had waited until they were home to call.

By the time his partners were making out on the couch, Liam buried deep inside Adds, all King could do was agree to a meeting with Louise rather than a discussion over the phone. It was worth prematurely cutting off the conversation. The fireworks they created were enough to set him off too. He desperately wanted to be buried inside his woman or man, but there was no way he was going to hurt either one of them. And without enough prep to take him, anal was off the cards for both of them. Addy didn't push him, content to wait for him to slide into her pussy. But Liam was insistent, and now he'd gone and built up the event in both their heads so much that he was freaking out. He wanted to go all out, show Liam how much he meant to him.

The thing was, King made it a point to show Liam every day how loved he was. How did he take it a step further?

A ring? It was too soon. While King was already all the way in, he didn't want to push Liam before he was ready. They were new, and he wanted to enjoy it without the pressures of a three-way wedding to think about.

It was why, hours later, when Adds and Liam were curled up together, fast asleep, and he'd been tossing and turning for what felt like an eternity, he slipped out of bed and made himself a cup of tea, trying to figure out what to do. Maybe he was overthinking things, but King wanted to go big. He wanted to scream it from the rooftops. Except he couldn't.

The creak in the floorboards alerted him to one of his partners waking. He looked across to see Adds wrapped up in the shirt he'd worn to Liam's exam, two buttons securing it in place and her shapely legs on display. King bit back the groan. It was the sexiest thing he'd ever seen.

"What's got you awake?"

"Keep thinking about how we can celebrate Liam passing statistics, but I'm coming up empty-handed."

Adds sidled up next to him at the kitchen bench and pulled out her own mug, making a cup with him. "What have you thought of?"

"A party, dinner. But it means he's back to being our friend, and I don't want that. I want it to be about him." Adds rested her head on his shoulder, and King pulled her into a hug.

"I keep thinking about how he wants the whole world to see you together."

King chuckled. "You caught that too, huh?"

"Yeah." Adds nodded. She tensed as if she wanted to add something, but thought better of it. When he encouraged her to speak, she pulled back, leaning her hip against the cupboards. Her brow was furrowed and she was biting down on her lip, her gaze searching the room as if to make sure there was no one listening. "I have an idea. But you might hate it."

He threaded their fingers together and raised her knuckles to his lips, kissing each one in encouragement.

"Okay, hear me out. What about porn?"

He choked out a cough and shook his head. "I'm not setting him up with someone so they can film porn."

"It's cute that you think I'd be okay with that," she quipped, her tone oozing sarcasm. "I was actually meaning that the two of you could film a session together. We can angle the camera so it doesn't catch your faces and I've got the software to edit it so it's more… professional."

"Hmm," he replied noncommittally. He didn't hate the idea, but it wasn't ideal either. No, he needed something else. King shook his head. "If we could do it before so it was ready to give to him that night, then it might work, but I don't feel right hiding the cameras so it's a surprise. And, anyway, I told him I wouldn't go that far until he got his marks back. I don't think he's ready yet."

"That plug…" Adds shivered and King hummed. "So hot."

"You should have seen him. He took it like a champion. So sexy."

Adds ran her fingers through her hair and pushed it off her shoulder, King repeating the move just so he could feel its silkiness. "I'm surprised you didn't say no to the video because of you being on camera."

"I don't have a morality clause in my contract anymore." King grinned, loving the thrill that shot through him when he thought about doing something so wicked. "It still can't get out—can you imagine what Mum would say if she saw my bare arse on TV?—but at least I'm not now looking over my shoulder."

Adds giggled, clamping her hand over her mouth to stop the sound from travelling. "Okay, so no broadcasting of your sex tape. We'll just have to do a live action spectacu-lar." She dragged out each syllable in the last word, her gaze locking on King's.

Adds had an idea, and he knew exactly what she was thinking. His gut clenched and cock hardened. King wasn't an exhibitionist—at least he didn't think he was—but he'd seen how much it riled Liam up when either he or Adds watched him. When King had laid him out on the deck chair in the garden and blown him, the thought of another person seeing them was what tipped Liam over the edge. He loved it. But they couldn't risk Liam's identity getting out. That was absolutely and utterly non-negotiable.

So whatever happened, they needed to protect that.

King couldn't believe he was even entertaining the thought. But the more he imagined it, the more he loved it. "We'd need a mask to cover his face."

"Can you imagine him? He'd be in his element." Adelaide hummed and closed her eyes, King picturing the sight right along with her. "He loves it when you unzip and he sucks you off."

King swallowed. He loved it too. "Would it be all three of us?"

"I can't participate, but I could guide you like during one of my sessions." King nodded, understanding her limitation. He loved the idea at the same time as he hated it. He wanted Adds involved, but if she could only do it in a limited way, then her suggestion was the best it was going to get.

"Are you even allowed to set something like that up? I mean, is it the done thing?"

Adds grinned and patted his chest. "Ah, my little padawan, you have a lot to learn about The Exchange.

There's a whole level dedicated to public sex. Not only is it the done thing, it's actually encouraged."

"Are we seriously contemplating this?" he asked, wide-eyed, the reality that he was talking about getting his cock out in front of a room full of strangers hitting him like a sledgehammer.

"Only if you're comfortable with it. And we'd have to give Liam the final say; he'd need to know about it before-hand so he can think through the implications. He might even need to get his agent on board."

"Yeah, that's not gonna happen." Liam's management had been entirely unhelpful when he'd confided in them that he was exploring his sexuality with two partners. They'd wanted him to immediately end their relationship, telling him that they would refuse to continue representing him if he came out. It had cut him deep—another example of someone not standing by him.

Adds had introduced him to her lawyer friends, Nick, Emma, and Robyn, for advice on getting out of the contract. But they'd all said the same thing—it was ironclad. He was stuck with them until they terminated. If Liam tried to get out of it early, he'd still be responsible to pay their manage-ment fees on top of those of a new manager. So they'd de-cided to sit tight and wait it out. If Liam was ever ready to come out, they'd deal with it then.

"No, I know. But, hey, it might piss them off enough."

They were quiet then, sipping their tea and standing arm in arm in the kitchen. It was a comfortable silence, the only noise coming from a storm bird outside, the familiar whoop, whoop, whoop noise comforting.

"I wanna do it," King murmured. No one could know it was Liam, but that didn't matter. It was King who needed to stand in front of the crowd and show Liam how loved he was. He bit back the nervous excitement flowing through him. "Yeah, let's do it. Can you set it up and we'll talk to Liam?"

"Will do. And I've got just the clients to step in as alternatives if either of you pull out. Worst case, you watch another couple get it on onstage."

* * * * *

Adds insisted he get a suit for their night together... performing? He didn't know what to call it. She'd described it as a demonstration. She'd even hinted to Liam what they were doing. His eyes had glazed over and he'd licked his lips, before sucking in a breath. The thought turned him on, and Liam turned on just did it for King.

The pants, shirt, tie, vest, and jacket were too buttoned up. He looked like a penguin. But when Adds suggested he try just the vest and pants, it had been like slipping into a second skin. The navy blue material was silky and showed off every one of his assets.

Liam's mask was ready too. They'd had to guess the fit, but the buttery soft leather would shape to the lines of his face. King sat on the bed, running his fingers over the supple material. It would cover half of his face, leaving only his lips and chin uncovered. Unless someone had studied every inch of his man's body, there was no way they would recognize him. He couldn't put it past rabid fans, but they had the protection of the non-disclosure agreements the club made every member sign. They themselves would have to sign one to walk past the front desk. And they defended the privacy of their members like bulldogs. It was the only reason why King was prepared to even present the idea to Liam.

All he had to do was wait for Liam to get home from training so they could check the results. He'd agreed not to look until they were together. There wasn't long left—he'd be there in a few minutes—but it was still enough time for King to freak out.

He paced, waiting for the door to close. Adds stood in the doorway, watching him with a small smile. "You're as nervous as Liam."

"I'm not nervous about his grade. I know he's passed. I am absolutely certain about that. But I'd be lying if I said I wasn't shitting myself about tomorrow night."

The gate rattled and pushed open. King watched as Liam hopped back in his SUV and parked behind his car. A minute later he was striding up the stairs, dumping his bag just inside the door. Liam was a stickler for keeping everything clean. He'd learned from an early age not to give his parents anything to complain about. Flying under the radar was easier than constantly getting in trouble.

Nervous energy radiated off him as he strode toward the bedroom and wrapped Adds in his arms. He buried his face in the crook of her neck and reached out for King at the same time. King blanketed his back, holding him tight.

"You've got this, hon. I have every faith in you."

Liam looked up at him and sucked in a deep breath. "My phone chimed but I couldn't bring myself to check it. My marks are in."

"Let's sit down and check them."

This was it. Months of gruelling work on Liam's behalf, and King wanted nothing more than for Liam to not only pass, but to get a good mark. He deserved it. King led them to the couch and Liam sat, pulling Adds into his lap. Sitting next to him, one foot under his leg, King sat sideways on the couch. They formed a triangle. Geometrically, they were strong, but it was nothing compared to the strength his boyfriend had displayed getting this far.

Liam pulled out his phone, navigated to the app, and opened the section with his marks. While it was loading, Liam squeezed his eyes closed. Waiting.

King ran his fingers through his hair, cupping Liam's nape and bringing their lips together. He kissed him, slow and sweet, distracting him from his nerves. They both needed the connection, and King loved the way Liam melted into him. The way he let King take charge and steer him. He trusted King, and that was a privilege that King would never abuse.

"You remember your promise?" Liam asked against King's lips.

King smile-kissed his lips. "Mmm, I do, and I intend to keep it." Nuzzling their noses together, he whispered, "Open your eyes, Liam. Look at your marks."

They did and King's eyes widened. The mark before him was a D. But not a D for fail. A D for distinction. Liam had achieved over 75 percent in the class. He'd not only passed, he'd aced it. King whooped and Adds threw her arms around Liam's neck, kissing him all over his face.

The whole time Liam sat there, his mouth open and his eyes wide. He blinked. Looked at each of them. Closed his mouth and re-opened it, trying to say something. But no words came.

King squeezed his nape and Liam melted into him, the familiar move warming King's heart.

"You did it," Adds squealed and Liam blinked again, nodding. His face brightened, his perfect lips breaking into a smile that was like the sun cresting the horizon, lighting the dawn sky up in a glow of warmth and promise.

"Third time's a charm," King murmured, pressing a kiss to his temple. Liam sucked in a shuddery breath and blinked back the tears on his eyelashes.

"We did it," he whispered.

"*You* did it." King squeezed his shoulder, rubbing the tension out of it.

"I couldn't have done it without you. Without both of you." Liam dropped his phone, forgotten on his lap as his arms came around them. He squeezed tightly, holding both King and Adds to him.

King admired the man in his arms more than any other. He'd overcome so much. Hit rock bottom and not only had he bounced back, but he was soaring. He was having a brilliant pre-season. He'd finally turned his back on the toxic relationship he had with his parents. He was blossoming in their relationship, was so very giving, and unfurling like a flower in the sunlight when he and Adds touched him, or murmured words of love to him.

Now, he was back on track with his long-term career too. He'd conquered Mt Statistics. Endured the depths of hell to fight through to the other end and come out victorious. He'd done it.

"I'm so proud of you. We both are." Adds kissed a line along his cheek to his lips and melded their mouths together. King watched in awe as their tongues tangled before they pulled apart and tugged him forward, their lips joining in a messy three-way kiss.

"Let's move this party to the bedroom. I have a cock to ride," Liam rumbled with a grin.

"About that—"

The pitiful whine Liam let loose, cutting off King's words, had him laughing.

"I told you that I was keeping my promise. But first, I have an option to give you." He slid the mask out of his jacket pocket and passed it to Liam. "Adds and I had a thought. It's totally up to you to say yes or no to, and it doesn't have to be for your first time—"

"Yes. Whatever it is, yes."

"That's not the way it works, Liam," Adds cautioned. "We need to explain it to you, then you can give your consent. Only then. There are things you need to think about before you make this decision. You can pull out anytime, even if you agree and then change your mind. It's not a problem. You won't be letting anyone down."

"So tell me then," he exclaimed, his earlier nerves replaced with excitement.

"I can do a demonstration at The Exchange. You and King could be my volunteers. You could be up on a stage, the whole club looking at you, or you could find a dark corner instead. It's completely up to you."

"What are you suggesting?" Liam looked to King, the green sparks in his man's eyes captivating King.

"I could top you."

"In front of an audience, or in a place where someone could see us?"

"If that's what you want," King hedged, ignoring the bend in his erection at the darkening of Liam's eyes as he answered.

"How will you be involved?" he asked Adds, his teeth biting down on his plump lip.

"I'd only lead you. No sexual touching between us. I'll be completely dressed, and if it's a demonstration, be mic'd up too."

"Will you be dressed too?" he asked King, his voice rough like gravel. Liam reached down and adjusted his hard cock.

"I will. I'll unzip and have you suck my cock. Then I'll slide into you, while you're on display for the club to see. The only thing you'll be wearing is this." King fingered the mask in Liam's lap, brushing against his straining shaft as he did. Liam sucked in a breath, his eyes going unfocussed.

"Fuck," he rasped. "When?"

"Tomorrow night if you want, or any other time."

"Tomorrow. I want tomorrow."

"You have to sign a confidentiality agreement. Whatever you see in the club can't leave its walls. Everyone else signs them too. You'll be protected. The mask is an extra level of security," Adds explained, her finger under Liam's chin, staring in his eyes as she spoke.

"I won't risk you," King murmured, kissing his shoulder. "If you have any doubts, then we won't do it. If you want to just hang around there to get a feel for the place, we can totally do that too. There's no pressure."

"Are you trying to talk me out of it or into it?" he groaned.

"Neither. This needs to be your decision."

Liam blinked his eyes open, bouncing his gaze between him and Adds. "And what about your decision?"

"We wouldn't have suggested it to you if we didn't want to."

Liam groaned, the sound pained. "Tell me again. Paint me the picture, and I'll give you my answer."

"I'll strip you naked. You'll walk out in front of everyone in nothing but your mask. I'll lie you down, strap you in, and worship every inch of your body. With my tongue, with my fingers, and then when I unzip and pull my cock out, I'll bend you over and take you so high when I sink into you that you'll see stars. Everyone will see you take my cock, Lee. Everyone."

Liam cried out, his hips lifting off the couch as a wet patch appeared on his uniform. His chest heaved and Liam sucked in long breaths as King kissed his throat. "Yes," he rasped. "Hell yes."

TWENTY-EIGHT

Liam

Dressed in a white fluffy robe, he was hot, but his feet were oddly cold. That never happened. Was that why King always had layers of clothing on? To stop his extremities from falling off? He looked over to his boyfriend. Dressed from head to toe in navy blue pinstripe, he was hot as hell. He shrugged out of the jacket, undid the vest, and peeled off the crisp white shirt he wore. Addy handed him the vest and he smiled gratefully before taking it and slipping it back on, doing the buttons up slowly.

They were sitting in a change room of sorts behind the bar at The Exchange, Liam's knees bouncing, just his toes touching the cold floor. Addy was with them too. In her little black jacket and blouse with pink three-quarter pants and the sexiest pink stilettos he'd ever seen. She looked like a pin-up girl. One of those gorgeous models from the 1940s and '50s.

"I've just got to go and check up on things," she murmured.

"Take your time, beautiful. I want a moment with Lee," King replied, kissing her cheek.

"What's up?" he asked, curious as to why King needed some alone time with him.

His man straddled the bench seat Liam was sitting on and ran his fingers down Liam's face. His eyes slipped closed at the gentle touch, Liam leaning into him until their lips brushed together. Warmth filled him, the familiar hit of do-pamine rushing through him and unfurling in his chest. Calm washed over Liam, his knees stopping their repetitive bounce as he tangled his fingers in King's hair and deepened the kiss.

"Are you sure about this?" King whispered against his lips. "You can walk away if you aren't. Adds has another couple on standby."

"I want this, King. I want *you*."

"You have me. You've always had me. We don't need to do this in front of an audience if you're worried, scared, em-barrassed, whatever."

Liam furrowed his brows, worried about King's insist-ence that he be okay with them going up on stage. Was it because King was uncomfortable? "Are you? Because if you don't want this, neither do I."

King took Liam's hand in his and pressed it to his groin. He was hard as a rock, throbbing under Liam's touch. "The only thing I'm worried about is not lasting when I finally get inside you."

"I'm serious, King—"

"I'm nervous." He smiled, but it was a little strained. "The idea of doing this in front of anyone but you and Adds is freaking me the fuck out. But getting to show you how much I want you in front of the whole building is hot as hell." King swore. It was the first time he'd heard his man swear except when he was about to come. He was worked up, scared but turned on too. "I want to show you that I love you. That even though I can't shout your name from the rooftops, I'll worship you in any way I can. This"—he picked up the leather mask sitting next to Liam—"is only to protect you. To hide your identity. It's not so that I can hide you away like a dirty secret. I'm so proud of you, Lee. To be with you, to love you. To be loved by you. It's a privilege that I get to do it. You and Adds are my soulmates. We belong together and will be in this life and the next. Heaven for me is right here, on earth with the two of you by my side."

"I love you," Liam whispered, leaning forward to connect their lips together again. Their kiss was languid. Slow and full of love.

"I love you too, and I want to cherish you. Can I make love to you up there?" King motioned to the stage. "Or at home in our bed?"

"Show me. Show them," Liam challenged, heat flaring in his belly at the look of pure adoration in King's dark gaze.

He stood, holding out his hand for Liam to pass him the mask. King secured it gently on his face, the elastic straps holding it fast. King's one requirement was for it not to fall off. He'd told the milliner what he needed, and even though the lady was an expert hat designer rather than mask maker, she'd readily agreed to try it. Of course, she had no idea it was for public sex, but she did know it was to keep his boyfriend's sexuality a secret. The rainbow flag she had flying in the window was what prompted King to walk in there in the first place, and as Liam floated in the knowledge he could be himself, he was grateful for his man's consideration.

King held his hand out, and Liam grasped it tight, laughing when King pulled him up, spun him, and dipped him low before kissing the V on his chest made by the robe.

The door opened and Addy smiled affectionately at them. "Do you want to do this?" she asked. At Liam and King's nods, she added, "Do you need to go through anything again?"

"No. I trust both of you."

King squeezed him, before taking his hand and leading Liam down the hallway. They exited out a door into the main bar area, and Liam instinctively grasped the tie on the robe. He would be naked in front of the patrons gathered there in just a moment, but he needed a second to get comfortable. Addy led them up the three steps, pausing at the top to pin the tiny mic to her jacket. Attaching the battery pack to the back of her pants, she tapped it, testing the volume.

She started speaking, but King had his attention, his finger hooked under Liam's chin and those chocolate eyes focussed solely on Liam. "I love you," he whispered before kissing him slowly. Liam wrapped his arms around King's neck and fell into his embrace, being carried away by his man's gentle ministrations. "Can I take this off you?" King asked against his lips, curling his fingers into the thick lapels of the robe. Liam slid his hands down King's front, curling his fingers into his man's belt loops and tugging him closer.

Liam nodded in answer to King's question and dived in again. He never wanted to stop kissing his man. Cool air hit his back a moment later, the warmth of the spotlights shining down on them in stark contrast to the air temperature. The robe pooled around his elbows as his lips connected to King's.

It was weird that Liam wasn't fretting about everything that had and was going to happen. He'd gone from being single to being in a relationship with the two people who meant the world to him. He loved them wholeheartedly. Touching Addy was like a wonderland—falling into the softest down pillows. She was curves and silk skin and tinkling laughs and sweet nothings. King was strength and kindness. Hard lines and planes of thick muscle. He enveloped Liam in his arms and the world outside—Liam's struggles and fears—fell away. He let go of King's belt loops and let the robe fall to his feet.

King nudged him, guiding him over to a white leather chair, except that where his arse would normally sit, there was an empty space, leg rests that would have his legs spread wide replacing it. "What the fuck is that?" he squeaked. His man stifled a laugh and squeezed his hand.

"Want to try it with me?" King asked him, lifting Liam's knuckles to his lips. When Liam nodded hesitantly, King beamed, the fear melting away as his man smiled at him. Addy moved around them, helping Liam into the seat.

"You okay," she asked, running her fingers through his hair.

"Yeah." She smiled at his answer and winked when King lifted his leg into the stirrups, spreading Liam wide open. The flush spread over his skin, heat crawling up his throat.

"You're beautiful, Lee," King murmured, his lips grazing Liam's skin. His man worshipped him. With every whisper-soft touch, every gentle graze of teeth and lips against his skin, Liam rose higher and higher, soaring among the clouds.

Addy's voice was soothing in the background, but all he could focus on was King's touch. King's kiss. King's hands roaming over him. Liam closed his eyes. The audience was hushed, their murmurs fading into the background like Addy's voice, his world narrowing down to the man in front of him. Warm breath coasted over his cock, standing rigidly at attention. A slow lick and a moan left Liam's lips. King sucked on his crown, his tongue trailing the length of his slit.

Liam gripped the headrest and arched into King's hold. A soft chuckle, barely a whisper of breath against him, before King leisurely travelled lower, nipping his sac and lashing his hole. Liam cried out, the sensations of King's warm, wet tongue on his pucker sending him skyward.

"Ready, baby?" King asked, nipping his inner thigh.

"Please," he begged.

King pulled back. Wetness circled his hole. Pressure. *Oh god, this was it. King was going to fuck him.* His pucker stretched, but not enough. Liam opened his eyes. King was squatting, his hand up at Liam's arse. He trailed his lips up Liam's leg. His eyes fell closed again, his cock flexing as King pumped in and out of him slowly.

Another pinch. Another finger. King was stretching him. Liam moaned. He loved it. Loved being King's. Loved it when King found that magical spot inside him that made him bow up and almost go off like a bottle rocket every time.

"We're going to work our way up from the smallest size plug to the largest." A thrill shot through him. This was it. He was finally going to experience King sliding inside him. He'd been stupid a moment earlier thinking King would breach him without any prep. His man was all about the build-up, and he made it so worthwhile. "King here is... well-endowed and his boyfriend is a little on the inexperienced side." King slipped his fingers out of Liam's hole, and he whimpered.

"Shh, it's okay." King hovered above him, leaning down to join their lips. The moment they touched everything fell away. Like a shield going around them, the audience faded, the lights dimmed, and Liam and his lovers were cocooned in bliss. "That's it, baby," King soothed against his lips. "Relax."

Liam's muscles unclenched and King pulled back. Still touching. Always touching. He adjusted Liam's position, spreading his legs wider. Addy ran her fingers through his hair. He loved it when she touched him like that. Soft and reassuring, she was checking in on him. He gasped when the cool wetness touched his hole, the pressure building again.

Addy was talking but all he could focus on was the stretch of his hole.

Things moved fast and slow at the same time after that. His muscles were weighed down, like he was wading through treacle, but time was speeding up around him. Sensation overwhelming him and sending him into a floaty, wonderful world of his cock getting sucked, his hole stretched, and his channel stuffed full of hardness and his nipples being pinched and nibbled on.

The chair moved again, Liam's legs lifting so he was bent in half, before the back lowered until he was lying flat.

"You okay?" Addy asked in a whisper against his ear. Liam nodded, moaning as King fucked him with the plug. "This is gonna get intense for a little bit. Not painful, but you're going to want to come. But King doesn't want that yet. So, use your hand to tap out when you're nearly there, okay?"

"Yeah," he rasped. His voice sounded like he'd swallowed a bucket of sand. Deep and raspy, he was so fucking turned on he was going cross-eyed.

Addy started talking again, explaining something about suction, and Liam's cock flexed. He was harder than he'd ever been before, desperate for King to suck him off. But it wasn't his cock that got a workout. Instead it was his hole, King pulling out the thick plug he'd been using. His hole clenched, empty and mourning the stretch. But King didn't leave him waiting.

Another cool touch against his pucker and Liam bore down, this time the stretch morphing into a burn that had a cry leaving Liam's lips. King's heat was against his side, as the sharp stretch stung him. He bent, bringing their bodies close. Liam reached up, clutching him and tugging King closer. With one hand on his shoulder, King squeezed and murmured against his lips, "You're doing so beautifully, baby. This is just as thick as my cock. You're nearly ready for me." It was what Liam needed to hear, the physical encouragement he needed.

"I need you," Liam moaned.

"Soon."

The chair moved again, Liam's knees lowering and his legs falling open. He was on display for the entire room to see. Hole stretched tight around a fist-sized plug, his cock slick with pre-cum leaking in a steady stream. He loved it. Loved being naughty and revelling in being the centre of attention even if for only a moment. But the part he loved the most was King's concentration on him and Addy's soft touches and reassuring presence. The way that even though, there he was—a minor celebrity—capable of being recognized and his secrets exposed, King and Addy were there. Protecting him. But also making his fantasies come true. They were showing the world around them exactly who they wanted. And it was him. He was being cherished. Cared for. They were standing up saying they were with him. Not turning away. Not discouraging him. Not judging him for things he had no control over.

No, these two incredible human beings were giving Liam more than just a bloody great orgasm. They were claiming him as theirs.

Liam's head spun and he sank further into the soupy float his body had drifted off into. Then it was there. Warm wetness like Addy's pussy rubbing over his cockhead. Instinctively he thrust up, trying to get closer. Ooohs sounded in the background, and the gravelly moan from King spurred him on. He clenched around the monster in his arse and scrambled to get purchase so he could sink into Addy's heat. His eyes sprung open, the spotlight almost blinding him, as heaven closed around his cock. But it wasn't Addy's pussy. She was right there, bending over him and whispering something in his ear. It was long and plastic, with nodules and ridges inside it. Warm and wet and tight. Liam shouted, his whole body shuddering as his hips punched forward, sinking deeper into the toy.

The vibrations started simultaneously. The ones in his arse hit his prostate and sent a lightning bolt through him straight to his balls. They drew up tight ready to fire off. The ones centred around his cock were different. It was more of a ripple like a wave. Suction and clenching at the same time as a milking sensation.

Oh fuck. Liam cried out, his body lighting up like he was made of neon.

His head fell back, his throat stretching. Liam gripped the chair, stopping him from slipping away, but Addy was right there. "It's okay. We're lowering the headrest. You're hungry, yes? Want to be fed?"

The words didn't make sense to Liam, but Addy's fingers in his hair settled him even as his head fell back. Then King was there, kissing him. Liam reached up, threading his fingers through King's hair, their tongues tangling as King's chin scraped against his nose. The zip undoing was like a thundercrack. Liam moaned into King's mouth, and King's lips turned up in a smile against his own. "Feed it to me," he begged.

King pulled away, and a moment later the soft skin of his sac was brushing up against his cheek. Liam breathed him in. King's scent was like a drug, one he'd gratefully gotten addicted to. Slightly musky, the smell of sex from the pre-cum dripping from his slit, Liam lapped at his balls, sucking one in, then the other. Laving King's sac with his tongue, Liam rode the high, loving the tensed muscles and moans he was ripping from King's chest. Gripping his solid arse, Liam manoeuvred King where he wanted him—straddling his face. Liam licked a stripe down King's cock and over his balls. He wanted to keep going. Wanted to taste King's hole like he'd done for the first time only a week earlier, but King's sexy-as-fuck pants were in the way, and Liam loved it.

He pushed King's hips back, positioning his cock at Liam's mouth. His man painted his lips with pre-cum, and Liam greedily lapped it up. He loved King's taste, salty and tangy; it was the evidence that he was pleasing King. Just like the crazy power that those shoulder squeezes had over him, King's pre-cum was an aphrodisiac.

He opened his mouth wide, and King pressed forward, his crown sliding along Liam's tongue. Grasping his hips, Liam pulled him closer, taking King as deep as he could. His throat opened up, and Liam instinctively sucked in a breath,

shuttling King's cock deeper. He swallowed, his throat closing around the cock it wanted to swallow, and King shouted
out.

It was too much far too quickly. King's cock stretching
his jaw, the vibrations in his arse, the suction on his dick. It
coalesced until Liam was about to tip over the edge, chasing
the high he was so close to. His body went rigid as the rushing in his balls catapulted him to the edge. Liam remembered King's instructions and tapped his meaty butt.
Instantly, the suction on his cock stopped, the toy getting
yanked off him. But then King's hand closed over him and
Liam shouted again, his orgasm rushing through him. Jets of
cum shot from his cock, coating his abs and chest. His chin.

King pulled back, his cock slipping from Liam's mouth on
a moan. King's tongue traced the length of his body, setting
every nerve ending alight even while the buzz from his orgasm sang through his veins. He leisurely stroked Liam's
cock, getting every last drop of cum out of him, stoking the
fire simmering in him at the same time. His fingers trailed
down his sac to the plug in his arse and slid it fractionally
out before pumping it in again. Over and over, he fucked
Liam's channel with the toy, Liam's cock going steely within
seconds. More moving his body around. This time, his head
came up and his body lifted until he was sitting once more,
his knees up around his shoulders and spread even wider.

King moved to his front, slowly pulling out the toy, but
before Liam could protest, he was there, the head of his
cock pressing against his hole. Liam opened his eyes, King's

face the only thing in his field of vision. Liam reached for him, cupping his face and bringing their lips together.

"Come inside me, King. Make me yours."

"You've always been mine and Adds's, baby. You always will be. We love you."

Addy's hand slid through his hair, but Liam needed more. He reached for her wrist, bringing her hand to his lips and threading their fingers together as King pressed forward. Even with the toys and the plugs, his hole stretched tight. Farther than it had ever stretched before. The pinch turned into a burn and King paused, reading the tight lines around Liam's eyes partially hidden by the mask. But Liam needed King inside him.

"More," he gasped.

King bucked his hips forward, his crown popping through Liam's resistance, and he paused. Liam hissed. Shuddered. Desire flowed through his veins like hot lava. If the storm in King's dark eyes was any indication, he was under the same influence. Reaching between them for Liam's cock, King stroked until he was hard again and ever so slowly pumped his hips forward until he was buried deep.

"You did it, baby. Took me all in. Fuck, you're so beautiful, and all ours," King uttered as he sucked a mark onto Liam's collarbone.

He pulled back, dragging his cockhead over Liam's prostate again and his body lit up. Over and over again, King's movements were slow and calculated. Long, deep thrusts. Unhurried lovemaking that set Liam's body on fire and sent his mind spinning. The whole time, Addy was connected to them too, holding his hand and brushing her fingers through his hair. King kissed him, languid strokes of his tongue against Liam's. His orgasm rushed at him, careening through his body at the speed of light. Liam gasped and pulsed in King's hand, the only warning before his consciousness whited out and star bursts exploded behind his eyelids. His body was picked up and carried. Higher and higher he rose until he was freefalling.

There was no hard landing, no bone-shattering crash. Instead, he slowly came back to himself in time for Liam to blink open his eyes and connect with King's. His man only broke his stare to turn his gaze to Addy, before he stiffened in Liam's arms and his cock throbbed. The heat of King's cum inside him filled him, painting a tattoo-like mark on Liam's body and his heart. King collapsed into his arms, and with his free hand, Liam cupped his face and brought King's lips to his. They shared a slow kiss. Lazy and satisfied, Liam didn't want to move. He never wanted King to pull out. To leave him empty again. But there had been a shift in him that night too. A moment when Liam had truly understood just what King and Addy would do to show him that he was theirs. To give him their hearts and tell the world he belonged.

Because it wasn't just public sex that they'd just had. It was so much more.

When King's softening cock slipped from his channel, Liam moaned, but King swallowed the sound. He flushed, heat crawling up his throat when King's essence started to slip out of him, thick drips landing on the stage. There were cheers and whistles and still the dripping didn't stop.

"You were so beautiful, baby," King whispered, his forehead pressed against Liam's pec. When he looked up, the emotion swirling in King's eyes floored him, stole his breath, and Addy's if her gasp was anything to go by. "Fuck, I love you more than I know how to say. Both of you."

A warm breeze swept him up, carrying him like a dandelion seed. Liam was lighter than he'd ever been. Happier with these two people than he'd ever experienced before too.

"Your cum dripping out of my arse is doing a pretty good job of it," Liam teased, taking King's lips in another kiss. Liam clenched his hole and another rush of King's cum seeped free, a laugh bursting out of King as it landed with a squelch.

"Seeing you trussed up like that? So fucking hot. You had me holding onto my sanity with a single thread. And the way you deep throated me? Absolute perfection."

The lights dimmed and Liam relaxed into the seat, ready to fall asleep. "Addy, can you get one of these chairs for home?" Liam asked in a mumble. "I wanna see you ride King's face while I fuck him."

She leaned in close, and whispered in his ear, "I want you and King to fuck me in it. Spit roast me."

Liam's cock flexed at the picture she painted and another dollop of cum leaked out of his hole.

"But first, we need to get you comfortable and warm before you fall asleep right here."

TWENTY-NINE

Adelaide

Adelaide stood in Cassie, Jake, and Phoenix's kitchen and dining room, empty glass in hand. She was speaking to Phoenix, the new guy at work. It was strange how fate intervened at the most serendipitous of times. Cassie and Jake had said they wanted to try swinging as a way to fill the gaping void in their relationship that Phoenix had left. They were in love with him, as he was with them. But something had happened. Something that rocked Phoenix to his core and had made him run, and they'd lost contact.

He'd only started at the club a couple of weeks before Cassie and Jake visited there. She'd talked them out of joining. It wasn't what they wanted or needed, and the impact that it would have had on their marriage would have been disastrous. But instead of leaving, they'd stopped to talk it out with her at the bar. Phoenix had been working, and the rest was history. She was now celebrating his moving in with them.

She smiled and nudged him with her elbow. "I'm really glad you didn't let fear win. Letting your heart decide was definitely the right way to go."

Phoenix's grin was firmly in place; he swooned when Cassie kissed him on the cheek and Jake joined them, wrapping an arm around Cassie's waist. Adelaide could see it as clear as day how the three of them slotted together.

"It was." He slipped an arm around Cassie and hugged her close to his side. Pausing, he looked unsure, biting his lip. "Can I ask a personal question?"

"Sure."

"The demonstrations you do with your volunteers... how does your partner handle that? Do they get jealous?"

Heat rose in her cheeks. King and Liam's first time together was "one for the ages." Apart from being hot as hell, it was beautiful watching their connection shift up a gear. Liam had let down his walls and King had wrapped him up safely, protecting his heart with everything in him. She wished she could have participated by doing more than she did, but when it counted, she was able to be there for him. He'd reached for her, holding her hand the whole time King made love to him. She was part of them when they came together. It was an incredible privilege. The final link in the iron-clad bond they had locking in place. Liam had been inside King before. They'd had fast and furious sex before. They'd all fallen in a heap, sweaty and exhausted together too. The guys had gone slow with her, making love to her, but it had never been like that between King and Liam before. Not to that extent.

394 • ANN GRECH

The love King had for Liam was obvious in every touch and every whispered encouragement. It was relatively vanilla and tame compared to some of the things she'd seen happen in the club, but it would always be her favourite.

King going hypoglycaemic after had rocked her to her core. He'd nearly passed out, but after a soda and snack, he was okay. He was too spent to move for a good hour, but Liam insisted he was starving. She'd offered to go out and get them food, but the glint in his eyes had made her pussy clench and a shiver pass through her. Within minutes, she was naked, splayed out on the table with her legs wrapped around his head until she was as exhausted as King.

Yeah, totally her favourite.

Adelaide cleared her throat and responded, "They're usually pretty different to the one you saw."

"Oh, okay." Phoenix seemed like he wanted to add something, but instead he kicked at an imaginary rock with his socked foot. Adelaide smirked, biting back a laugh at the way he was trying so hard to act casual.

Her phone vibrated in her hand. Lifting it, she read Liam's message and smiled. "Hopefully you'll get to ask them. They're on their way."

Phoenix's smile lit his face. "I'm glad. I'm dying to know who they are with you being so secretive about them all the time."

Her eyes widened before she blinked innocently. "I don't know what you're talking about."

"Sure you don't." He grinned, rolling his eyes.

"Yeah, I think we're ready to tell our closest friends. It'll be nice to be able to go some places together and act like it too." Adelaide smiled wistfully. It was the only thing she'd ever wanted, but circumstances had intervened. She and King had decided not to tell anyone they were together until the school year finished. When they were ready, they'd pulled Liam into their relationship and had to figure out how to handle it. Meeting Bryce, Cole, and Ava had been good for them. They'd seen how it could work.

Keeping their secret hadn't taken away from the love they shared. And now, they were finally ready to let in more of the people they trusted. "We've had enough of hiding, but it's been necessary. It still is."

Adelaide sensed their presence before she saw them. She turned, smiling one of those love-heart-eye smiles as they walked through the door with Levi and Connor already chatting like they were the best of friends. Mike got up to greet King, and Adelaide laughed at his surprised look. The Gold Coast may be a city, but at its heart, it really was a beach village where with six degrees of separation everyone knew everyone. King spotted her and his grin matched her own.

"No fucking way," Phoenix breathed as King walked across the room and wrapped her in his arms. She kissed him with smiling lips and laughed when Phoenix leaned against the wall, crossed his legs at the ankles, and drawled, "I can see why they wouldn't get jealous."

Adelaide introduced them and added, "Yeah, it doesn't normally get quite so physical in my sessions." Adelaide opened her arms to include Liam, leaning into him as he wrapped his arm around her shoulders.

"Wait, you saw us?" King squeaked, wide-eyed.

Phoenix nodded. "It was spectacular. Hot as hell, but beautiful too. I'm happy for you guys."

"How?"

"I'm the bartender who served you. But don't worry, no one will hear a word from me."

"You signed a non-disclosure agreement too," Liam concluded, his shoulders relaxing a fraction. But his eyes flitted to King then hers, looking for reassurance. Adelaide squeezed his waist, wanting him to know he was safe. No one in the room would betray their confidence.

"Yes, but even still, I know how important it is to protect the people important to you. You can lose everything when someone butts their nose in where it's not wanted." He looked to Cassie and Jake. "I lost the most important people in my life for years, but Adelaide helped me get them back. She also showed me that I have friends who'll help me, even if I hadn't met them yet. The non-disclosure agreement ties me legally, but I'll always protect my friends—Adelaide, and by extension the two of you, are among them."

Phoenix grinned, lifting the mood, and pointed toward his partners. "Now, if you'll excuse me." He strutted over to his lovers, joining them in their slow dance in the small space where Adelaide guessed the kitchen table normally stood.

Liam hugged her close. "I really like your friends."

"You heard Phoenix. They're yours too now, Lee. They're good people."

He smiled shyly at her words. "It feels good to open up our circle a little more. Bryce and now these guys. I just wish Lij had reacted the same way everyone here did."

"He's getting there," King reassured him. "He was scared of losing you."

A vibration had her pulling back. Liam's phone.

"Bryce, mate, how are you?" he greeted warmly. "Would you believe I'm at a party with your cousin Levi? I've just met him."

Liam snuggled close again, and Adelaide nuzzled his chest, loving that she could openly show them both affection. She heard Bryce respond from her spot against Liam's heart. "Yeah, cool." There was a pause, and Liam's brows dipped. He looked around, but Adelaide didn't know what he was searching for.

"You okay, mate?" he asked, concern lacing his voice.

Standing close, Adelaide heard Bryce say, "No. Um, I... I've lost my contract at Easts. They don't want me anymore. I'm a liability."

"What do you mean a liability?" Liam asked, his face scrunching up in confusion. He'd had a stellar year, and Bryce had always wanted to be a one-club player despite his family being on the Gold Coast.

King ushered them into the lounge room where it was quieter, and Liam put him on speaker. Bryce responded, saying, "The club sprang it on me today. Apparently, I don't have a playing position with them anymore. My management were furious, especially after the season going so well, but they've been on the phone to every club and I'm waiting for an offer to be put in writing." That was great news, but Bryce sounded miserable.

"So why aren't you happy?" Liam asked his brow furrowed and lips turned down, genuine concern marring his features.

"Because I either move to the Gold Coast, or I'm out of the NRL. I don't know whether to chuck it in and join Ava and Cole, or to move."

Adelaide shared a look with King, her gut sinking. Bryce was facing an impossible choice—move to the Gold Coast or give up his dream. Either way he'd miss out on something important to him. Leaving meant he'd be away from Ava and Cole. Their business tied them there. They couldn't just up and leave. They'd be separated, probably for the long term given the physical ties that would keep them in the city. But walking away meant giving up a dream he'd worked toward for half his life.

"I don't get it," Liam remarked. "You had the best rookie season I've seen in ages. You kicked arse."

"Apparently the team didn't want the bad publicity." Bryce sighed. "We're about to be outed. I had the editor of a column in one of the daily newspapers message me with photos. I either confirm our relationship and give them an exclusive piece, or they'll print an exposé."

"Levi," Adelaide called. "We need you in here. We've got an emergency." Her friend had been outed against his will too, and if Adelaide knew one thing these people did well, it was rally around their loved ones. Just like she, King, and Liam would always be together, her friends would always be there for one another.

The music was switched off and their friends gathered around in a circle. Adelaide took Liam's phone and held it out to the others. "Bryce, repeat what you've just told us. We've got a room full of friends who want to help."

Adelaide squeezed Liam's hand as Bryce spoke. Her friends were sharing glances, their unshakeable bonds extending to Liam's friend. Adelaide was proud to call them her friends, and she would do whatever it took to be there for them. When the room erupted in chatter, plans being made, she held tight to her guys.

Levi took the lead and was all business. "Okay, mate. Easts seem like a dead end, so we forget about them. Have you spoken with your agent and the Gold Coast team about this? What are they saying?"

Bryce's voice was resigned. He sounded defeated. "My agent wants me to deny we're a trio. They've suggested I come out as gay, tell everyone that Ava and I aren't really together and she's my closest friend. They want me to be the poster boy for gay athletes, and that'd be fine... except I'm not gay. I don't want to catfish anyone."

There were quite a few grumbled comments in response, a murmur of understanding rippling through the group. They'd seen bi and pan erasure before. Levi had gone through it, Mike's parents had struggled with it, and Jake's father hadn't even bothered to try to understand it.

Bryce continued, sounding a little more hopeful, but still down, "The Gold Coast team have already done up a welcome announcement. They've worded the press release as if they poached me. It talks about my stats and says how I'm an asset that they're grateful to have. They have a one liner in there at the end which says they're ecstatic I get to be my authentic self and the entire team are 100 percent behind me in every way. They haven't mentioned my sexuality at all, but the conversation I had with the coach was good."

"Coach is good people," Liam stated. "He'll support you. The players are good guys too. They'll probably be put out because of the media circus that's coming, but I don't think anyone will be overly shitty."

"What do you want to do?" Nick asked after introducing himself as Katy's cousin. "It's a big decision to move teams, especially with this hanging over your head."

Bryce groaned and she could hear Ava murmuring through the line. "I have no idea, but I need to have a game plan figured out so that I know how to respond. I'm floundering here."

"Let's put aside the contract and your agent for a moment and deal with the media," Nick advised. "You've got a few options on how to tackle them."

Levi added, "Agreed. If you'd like my help, I'm here for you."

"Yeah." Bryce cleared his throat and there was more talking in the background. Cole said something she couldn't make out, but it had Bryce's tone lightening and the smile returning to his voice. "I'm not really ready to come out, but

I'm also not going to lie about Cole and Ava to anyone either. You run a podcast, don't you?"

"I do. We can use it to take control of the narrative if that's what you're thinking," Levi responded, pride and a hint of determination to help his cousin shining in his eyes and in the set of his jaw. It wasn't going to be easy for Bryce, Cole, and Ava, but Adelaide knew with Levi's help they'd have a community behind them and friends to support them every step of the way.

She had history with so many people in this room. Connor, Levi, and Katy were the beginning. She'd been witness to Levi finally starting to see the light. Their relationship had inspired her to pursue her dreams. Katy, Robyn, and Emma had encouraged her to go on that date night where she'd met King. She and King had stopped for coffee at Mike's gym on their second date, and Mike and Levi both trained King. She'd inadvertently helped steer Phoenix back into Cassie and Jake's arms, helping him reconnect with the two people who'd loved him unconditionally for years, despite their separation. Phoenix had offered a friendship to Liam that she could tell meant the world to him. Now Bryce would become part of their group too, and by extension, Ava and Cole. The love in the room was palpable, as was the fierce protection of one another. Adelaide knew it was going to be exactly what Bryce and his partners would need.

After watching and waiting and finally trying to move on, she was going to take a page out of her friends' books. She was going to live and love her guys to the fullest, and she knew they'd do the same.

Their journey had meandered along winding roads, diverging and crossing, but never joining until recently. Now all their lanes had merged into one. It didn't matter whether the road ahead was bumpy because her guys were there with her. To hold her hand and love her as much as she loved them. They weren't on the freeway though. They weren't speeding toward some unknown destination, their eyes blinkered to the beauty of the landscape surrounding them. No, they were on the scenic route. The road less travelled. The one where they could stretch their legs and enjoy the sunshine together. The one that would take them their whole lives to travel. But it didn't matter when or where they stopped or what detours they took, because they'd already reached their destination. They'd already found the place they belonged. Their home. It was right there next to one another, the three of them together. Happy and in love.

Adelaide had loved King from early on. She'd fallen hard and fast for him. But although their relationship was rock-solid, they were incomplete without Liam. She'd come to realize she wasn't supposed to give up loving him. Instead, she and King needed to embrace him so that the three of them were whole. They'd needed to stop fighting the inevitable and let their journeys converge.

It had taken failing statistics twice for the roadblock to be broken. For them to face what was before them. But third time really was a charm, because now that they were together, Adelaide would never let go. She would never need to either, because the two men in her arms were a

part of her. Destined to live their happily ever after. Together as one.

And they lived happily ever after.

 Thank you for reading Third Time's A Charm. I hope you loved Adelaide, Liam and King's journey.

Want to read Ava, Bryce, and Cole's story? https://books2read.com/u/mBzpzk

She's picked her team. Now she just has to score.

When a summer storm sweeps in, Ava finds herself road tripping across the state with two sexy as sin strangers. A flat tyre delays their trip, and the only hotel in town with a vacancy has just one bed.

Even though the two men are complete opposites, both have her captivated. The only thing hotter than being with Bryce, the handsome footballer with a perpetual smile, and Cole, the dark and broody construction worker, is watching them together.

Their holiday fling soon turns into more, but the odds are stacked against them. Threats come in threes and Bryce has to face one that will change the path of both his life and career.

But Ava's playing for keeps. Can this trio emerge as the victors?

Triple Threat will be available on Amazon in 2023
https://books2read.com/u/mBzpzk

About Ann Grech

By day Ann Grech used to live in the corporate world and could be found sitting behind a desk typing away at reports and papers or lecturing to a room full of students. She graduated with a PhD in 2016 and is now an over-qualified nerd. But the grind got old, and the voices got louder. She still has the librarian look nailed, but she's a little freer to be herself now.

She's never entirely fit in and loves escaping into a book—whether it's reading or writing one. But she's found her tribe and loves her book world family. She dislikes cooking, but loves eating, can't figure out technology, but is addicted to it, and her guilty pleasure is Byron Bay Cookies. Oh and shoes. And lingerie. And maybe handbags too. Well, if we're being honest, we'd probably have to add her library too given the state of her credit card every month (what can she say, she's a bookworm at heart)!

In 2019 she was an Award-Winning Finalist in the Fiction: LGBTQ category of the 2019 Best Book Awards sponsored by American Book Fest for her story In Safe Arms.

She also publishes her raunchier short stories under her pen name, Olive Hiscock.

Ann loves chatting to people online, so if you'd like to keep up with what she's got going on:

Join her newsletter (you'll get two free books!):
https://landing.mailerlite.com/webforms/landing/d8m4r2
Follow her on TikTok or Instagram:
@anngrechauthor
Like her on Facebook:
https://www.facebook.com/pages/Ann-
Grech/458420227655212
Join her reader group:
https://www.facebook.com/groups/1871698189780535/
Follow her on Goodreads:
https://www.goodreads.com/author/show/7536397.Ann_
Grech
Follow her on BookBub:
https://www.bookbub.com/authors/ann-grech
Follow her on Amazon:
https://www.amazon.com/~/e/B00IJPO3EM
Visit her website for her current booklist:
http://www.anngrech.com/

She'd love to hear from you directly, too. Please feel
free to e-mail her at ann@anngrech.com or check out
her website for updates.

ANN GRECH'S BOOKS

RULE OF THREE

Three Hearts (MMF) (Also available in audio)
Yes, Captain (MM)
Triple Beat (MMF)
Threepeat (MMF)
Third Time's A Charm (MMF)
Triple Threat (MMF) coming 2023

PEARCE STATION DUET

Outback Treasure I (MM)
Outback Treasure II (MM)

SPINOFF FROM PEARCE STATION

Three of Us (MMF)

UNEXPECTED

Whiteout (MM)
White Noise (MM)
Whitewash (MM)

MY TRUTH

All He Needs (MMM)
In Safe Arms (MM)

STANDALONES

Home For Christmas (MM)
The Gift (FMMM - free for newsletter subscribers)
Take Two (MM – free for newsletter subscribers)

M/F TITLES

One night in Daytona
Ink'd